To the Solemn Graves

Kim Idynne

for Linda

Thanks for always letting me read your books.

Widow's Peak

Widow's Peak

"Death is a very dull, dreary affair, and my advice to you is to have nothing whatsoever to do with it."
-W. Somerset Maugham, recorded in Robin Maugham's *Conversations with Willie*

Milagros' fortunes changed when her husband decided that he didn't want to be dead anymore. It was a common problem at Widow's Peak, one that I discovered in a most gruesome way—and by then, it was too late to help her.

My family moved to Widow's Peak shortly after the millennium. My wife and I were doctors, she a gynecologist and I a psychiatrist; we had both drawn good salaries for some time, and we decided to start reaping the benefits of our hard work. My wife was the one who found the magnificent house off of Sutton Avenue.

From Sutton, a steep drive led up to a wooded cul-de-sac. Five homes stood at the top—grand houses on an immense stretch of land, with expansive lawns and expensive cars gleaming in the driveways. The houses below could be described as upper-middle class, but this was an elite and hidden neighborhood on the vast peak of a hill. The open house was the second on the right, an Italianate structure in varying shades of tan and chestnut, the picture of elegance. I saw the interior and felt that I was destined to live there. The rooms had the same clean and opulent look, with a profundity of windows that allowed the scent of pines to blow through the house. Outside was an abundance of nature, and I was heartened by the sight of gleeful children running through Sutton Avenue below— teens and preteens like my own children. It seemed such a happy place.

When the tour of the house was finished, we went outside and met some of the neighbors. They had noticed our arrival and come out to greet us—in their own way.

We met Emma Dalton first. She stood a few feet from the front step, waiting for us with a scowl. "You're here to see the house, are you?" she said, and without introducing herself she continued: "I hope you're not fool enough to buy this old place. Worst money pit I ever saw. Just wait until all those extra bills start piling up. If you're doing well now, you won't be after a few months of living in this shit hole."

Her language startled me. Emma was the oldest woman on the block, about sixty-five, elegantly dressed in a summer suit and matching hat. I suppose I expected her language to be just as mature and distinguished. Moreover, the house seemed completely updated and functional. I couldn't see it as a money pit, but her words made me wonder.

Then we met Victoria and Iris. Iris mostly stood by and sneered while Victoria listed off the evils of the neighborhood: children who delighted in pranks and harassment, astounding property taxes, a faulty sewer system, and much more. "We have a procedure in place to let new people into the neighborhood," she added. "Kind of an informal neighborhood association. People don't just move in. Usually, we find a candidate."

I thought I understood her implications perfectly. The neighbors' unwelcoming attitudes likely had everything to do with our skin color or our religion, and there were other ways in which we didn't fit in. These neighbors were white ladies who lived alone and drove fancy cars—BMW, Lexus, Mercedes—though one neighbor preferred the more practical Honda. My wife and I were born in India, and my well-used SUV bore a "Masha'Allah" sticker from the local mosque. I guessed most of the ladies to be Christian, though on closer acquaintance, most of them showed no religious inclination.

We moved in anyway. Truly, I loved that house. The first thing to delight me about it was the smile on my wife's face as we walked through its rooms and gardens. I couldn't have dreamt up a better home for us. I felt certain that our kids would love it, too, and that the neighbors would naturally come to respect us.

As I hoped, the children settled in nicely. They made friends in the neighborhood and spent the summer exploring the local hotspots: the northern woods, the southern woods that bordered our own property, the bike trails, the hidden river that ran through the forest, the furniture shop that housed a petting zoo. Every one of these places had a legend—including our own house. We had barely settled into the place when the kids came home and burst into the kitchen with exciting news.

"We live in a haunted cul-de-sac!" Yasmin blurted. "All the kids in the neighborhood have seen the ghosts of people who lived here before."

"This used to be a cult neighborhood," Aamir added. "That's why every house has a safe room. People built them to survive the end times."

"And then the end times didn't happen," Yasmin continued breathlessly, "so they killed themselves, and their spirits still haunt the woods. It's true, Dad—even the grown-ups said that this was a cult neighborhood! Sarah's mom told me about it. She said that all of these houses were owned by cult members."

"Hmm," I replied, trying to sound disinterested. Truly, though, their claims perturbed me. "Have you seen any ghosts?"

"Not yet," Aamir admitted grudgingly.

"You're not likely to. But fantasy is entertaining, so feel free to pretend."

Yasmin rolled her eyes as she walked away. "Dad, you make everything so boring."

"Tragedy shouldn't be exciting," I replied coolly.

My wife, Nadira, pointed out that we were living in one of these supposed cult houses "—and there's no end times room, or safe room, or whatever you called it."

Yasmin turned around with a gasp. "There is! You don't know about it yet, but we do."

"It's behind the cupboard," Aamir said. "Anna and Andrew have been inside of it. The whole cupboard pulls out, and there's a staircase behind it."

"Which one?" I asked, still trying to sound unruffled. The kids didn't know, so I made a casual inspection of the most likely cupboard, the tall one that stood against an inner wall. Nadira paced down the hall and back, and pointed out that there wasn't enough space for a hidden room behind any of the cupboards.

"There's one somewhere," Yasmin insisted. "Anna is going to come over and show us how to get inside."

I ceased to take the claim seriously. The next day, when the kids brought Anna and Andrew to seek the hidden room, I was preparing dinner alone; Nadira had stayed late at the clinic to help with a difficult birth. Anna was just a year younger than Yasmin, a pale, freckled girl. Her brother was twelve, like Aamir, and just as freckled. I greeted the kids and invited them to stay for dinner, and then I resumed chopping vegetables. Anna politely asked me to stop. When I put down the knife and stood back, she crouched down and reached under the island.

Beneath the island were two sliding latches. Anna released them and gave a slight push, and the entire island glided quietly toward the stove, revealing an opening in the floor and stairs leading below.

I was stunned. It wasn't until the kids began to descend the stairs that I acted. I ordered them to stay in the kitchen, and then I went down the staircase myself, testing each wooden plank before trusting it with my full weight. A bare bulb hung from the ceiling; the light flickered on when I pulled the cord.

The stairs led to a single concrete room, roughly thirty square feet, empty except for its artwork. I flipped a light switch, and the whole room became illuminated. Across its walls were scattered several crude images in the style of ancient Egypt. Most of the paintings were unfinished, but on the far wall was a completed mural. At its top, a large, featureless disc emitted rays toward two crowned human figures below. The figures were surrounded by smaller people with raised arms, rendered in yellow, red, and blue.

Yasmin had descended the stairs behind me. She peered over my shoulder and gasped. "It's a cult room! See, Dad, I told you!"

"Stay upstairs," I said, urging her away. "Now. Go back up."

I spent only a minute or two surveying the room, just enough to get a sense of what was there. I ventured to the mural and studied its details. In the center of the stream of rays was an ankh—from what I knew, a symbol of life.

Dinner was abandoned. I told the kids to order pizzas. While we waited for them to arrive, I sifted through the papers the realtor had given us. In the stack were several disclosures stating that there were no wells or separate structures on the property, but there was nothing about a basement or a hidden room.

By the time Nadira returned, Anna and Andrew had shared everything they knew about the house, devoured a whole pizza between the two of them, and returned home. I forgot all about Nadira's emergency birth and bombarded her with stories.

"They said that the man who used to live here before us—Ross Gates—supposedly died in a boating accident, but his relatives insisted that his wife had him murdered." I repeated the tale that the kids had shared: After Ross' funeral, his wife invited the guests to the house for a memorial. One of Ross' cousins took the opportunity to bring a psychic along. The psychic claimed that Ross had never left the house, and that his body was buried beneath the kitchen. This was how Anna had come to learn about the moving island: Ross' cousin, already aware of the secret passageway, had opened it and started to descend. Chaos ensued as the two families realized what was happening. The wife had the cousin and the psychic thrown out, and then she collapsed. She died soon afterward from heart failure.

"And before that, another guy killed himself in our basement—the guy who had this house built. That's what the kids said."

"I wonder if we should look up the house blueprint," Nadira replied, unfazed by my stories. "It's possible that the county has a record of the basement, but the realtor just didn't know about it."

"I hardly think it matters now. Even if it started out as a secret room, the neighbors seem to know about it. I'm going to see what I can find out from them."

A slight smile played on Nadira's face. "From which neighbors? The ones on our street? Good luck with that."

"I will get them to like me first," I said with confidence.

From then on, I buttered up the neighbors as best I could. We regularly held barbecues on the front lawn and invited the others to eat with us, and to come and go as they pleased. I made a habit of going to each door and politely inviting each lady, putting on my friendliest manner as I entreated them. In those short greetings, I also complimented their lovely homes and asked a casual question or two, hoping that conversations about the houses and neighborhood might become commonplace. My family cooked our most delicious recipes, though Nadira suggested that we avoid too much spice; the ladies didn't seem the type to tolerate it. The food didn't draw the neighbors in. We tried a variety of menus: Aamir thought the ladies would prefer "meat and potatoes drowned in gravy," Yasmin recommended "meat and vegetables drowned in butter," and Nadira suggested orange-glazed chicken with seasoned new potatoes. Still the neighbors stayed away, with the exception of Milagros—who, if not the most welcoming, was the least chilly of the neighbors. She was younger than the others, but had a guarded and tired face that made her look advanced in years. When she first showed up on our lawn, she refused to sit, and only stood and chatted with Nadira for a few minutes. When I mentioned the discovery of our hidden room, Milagros explained that the house had originally been built with a basement, but that it had been closed off and made accessible only through a secret entryway.

"Does your house also have a hidden room?" I asked.

She lowered her gaze and folded her arms over her chest. "Not that I know of."

Nadira excused herself, saying that she had to go inside for a while. The kids followed her, leaving me alone with the neighbor.

"They're going to pray," I explained. "They'll be back in a little while. You're welcome to stay and eat—or if you would like something to drink, I can get you something from the house."

Milagros gave me a questioning look. "Aren't you going to pray, too?"

I wasn't one to keep to a prayer schedule. I hadn't grown up performing salah, though my family kept to the other main pillars of the religion.

"I usually don't pray at all of the scheduled times," I said. "My parents always bundled their prayers into the evening prayer, and I got used to doing it that way."

"Oh," she said. "So, you're not a real Muslim."

I bristled at the remark. "I consider myself a real Muslim. It's like any other religion: people follow the core principles, but the ritual elements often depend on the culture."

She nodded absently. Then she gestured to the sticker on the back of our SUV. "What does 'Masha'Allah' mean?"

"Well, literally, it means 'What God has willed.'"

"What God has willed?" she repeated slowly. "Is it like . . . when something bad happens, like a death, and people say, 'It was God's will'?"

"No, it's generally meant as an auspicious term. It means that God has helped something good to happen."

"Oh." She frowned. A far-away look clouded her brown eyes.

"So, not something bad, like . . . a death."

"No, but people often say 'It was God's will' to help them cope with difficult events, like a death."

"But, don't your people believe that if something bad happens, it's because God has willed it?"

I hesitated. I suppose I was thrown off by the question. This wasn't the first time Milagros had questioned me about religious matters. She was a Catholic, and the portico of her house was decorated with numerous Catholic-themed reliefs: the Virgin Mary, Christ, and the saints. I had assumed that the topic came up simply because we were surrounded by its symbols.

"And even if someone does something wrong, it's all predestined?" she added. I saw something desperate, something urgent, in Milagros' face—some need for reassurance.

"I don't think that's for humans to know," I replied. "Our duty is to do our best, I think—our best to follow God's laws, and to treat one another as brothers and sisters. My wife put the sticker there to remind us that we've been blessed with fortune. We have two healthy children, our parents are—"

"But, let's say someone has done something," Milagros interrupted. I realized she hadn't been listening to me. Some other matter weighed heavily on her mind. "Something immoral. Is it really that person's fault? Or are we not at fault because God already planned it for us?"

I searched her troubled eyes, wondering what nagged at her. "Are you asking for yourself?" I asked. She didn't answer, so I added: "Since you're a Catholic, you could go to confession and talk to a priest—or a counselor."

Milagros chuckled nervously. She averted her gaze. "No, it's not for me. I just wonder what other people think about these things. Life is so complicated. Isn't it?" She turned and gazed at the houses at the end of the cul-de-sac. "I never imagined it could get this complicated."

She thanked me for my invitation, and then made a slow walk across the street and disappeared into her house.

The next evening, Nadira sent me to Anna and Andrew's house to round up the kids for dinner. I had some trouble finding the place, but after a couple of mistakes, I ended up at the right home. Anna and Andrew's father answered the door. "The kids went out to the hill," he told me. "They were here earlier, making pens. Do you want to come in? I can show you their work."

Steve led me to the wood shop at the far end of the laundry room. Among the tools and benches were elegant-looking wooden pens in various states of assembly, carved from exotic scrap wood. We spent several minutes there as I mused over the varying colors and patterns of the wood, and over the tools themselves.

He gave me a tour of the basement. In the center of the room was a pool table, and at the far end was a dartboard and a built-in bar with mostly empty shelves. Steve also had an exquisite coffee table made from scraps of oak and locust wood, cut and patterned to form a series of Celtic designs. He explained the nuances of the different types of wood and how they endured over time. I was fascinated; my father had been a skilled carpenter, and I had many fond memories of his shop.

"So," he said, "I heard that my daughter showed you the hidden room under your house. You didn't know about it?"

"We didn't. The realtor never mentioned it, and I looked through our contract papers again, but it isn't mentioned there either. The kids insisted that it used to be some sort of cult room."

"Well, I wouldn't go that far." Steve peered at me for a moment and asked: "Has anyone told you about Hank Dalton? He was the founder of your infamous neighborhood cult."

I said that I had never heard of him.

"Hank started a church that was all about surviving the end times," Steve explained. "His wealthiest members bought the property up there and had homes built with safe rooms where they could ride out the apocalypse. He lived in the house at the end of your cul-de-sac. To the members with less money, he started selling these ridiculous concrete domes that they could set up in their backyards."

"You mean . . . to take shelter from the apocalypse?"

"Exactly. Biggest con man I ever met. Before he disappeared, he made a lot of money by charging tickets for his conferences on extraterrestrials and eternal life. The couple that lived in your house were members, too. You'll want to hear the story, if you're living up there." Steve went to the bar and reached into the mini fridge. "Do you want a beer? I have Guinness and—oh. Do you drink?"

"Um, no. I don't."

"I have this carbonated water that my wife likes." He held up a green bottle. "I think it's horrible, but you can give it a try."

"Sure."

We sat, and he told me all about Hank Dalton and his Church of Eternal Life. "Right before he started his church, there was a news special about churches that offer eternal life on Earth to its members. Turns out there are plenty of those churches: The Church of Perpetual Life, People Unlimited, the Raelian cult . . . I don't know all the names, but the report mentioned that some of the founders had become enormously wealthy. Well, suddenly Hank was spewing all sorts of shit about how—pardon my language—about how God is an alien, and the second coming will be an alien encounter, and the aliens have advanced technology that allow their followers to live forever. Hank said that some of these other cult leaders had already met the aliens and had the technology. Oh, and he claimed that the ancient Egyptians knew all about it."

"That explains the hieroglyphs," I said. "They're all over our basement. Is it true that someone died down there?"

"Well . . . yeah. The guy who lived there was about to go to prison for fraud and sexual assault of a minor. Hank's right-hand man. Used his position to take advantage of people. He supposedly killed himself in that room. Another guy killed himself to join the aliens, and another vanished from his boat during a fishing trip. Everyone assumed he drowned, but there were die-hard members who thought he took off with the aliens. And there was one more who got a sentence for fraud. He died from a heart attack on his way to prison. That's how that hill got its nickname."

"What nickname?"

"People started calling it Widow's Peak. Those guys aren't the only ones who died. Most of the church members couldn't afford to live there anymore, and after they left, some other couples moved in. All of the men died in accidents within the first few years. Boating accidents, car accidents . . . ."

"You mean Milagros' husband, and Victoria's husband, and the others," I clarified, and Steve nodded. "You said *most* of the church members left. Did anyone stay?"

"Hank and Emma stayed."

"Hank, the founder? Emma was his wife?"

"*Is* his wife. I don't think Hank is dead."

I hesitated to ask the question that was forming in my mind. I had to reassure myself that Steve didn't believe Hank's claims. "What do you mean?"

"The neighborhood kids sometimes sneak around up there, and they started saying they'd seen his ghost. Anna saw him, too, but he ran off into the woods." He looked at me with a knowing smirk. "That was no ghost. Not aliens, either. It's life insurance fraud. That's why Emma could afford to stay: she got a multi-million-dollar payout after Hank supposedly died in a hiking accident in Venezuela. I think Hank was still living at Widow's Peak, happy and rich as can be. A house with a safe room—perfect place to hide if anyone comes looking."

The possibility began to sink in. The women living on that hill had some shared secret. Had they defrauded the insurance companies together? Is that why they hadn't wanted my family to move in—because we weren't in on the scam? Iris' words came back to me: *We have a procedure in place to let new people into the neighborhood. . . . Usually, we find a candidate.*

But the more I considered it, the more I doubted. "It doesn't seem worth any amount of money to spend your life in a hidden room."

"Well, you're right. Hank was adventurous. He was clever, too. I'm sure he found some way to escape whenever he felt like it. Knowing him, he probably took off and started a new life as soon as he could arrange it. If he ever got caught, he'd lose a five-million-dollar insurance payout."

I mulled over the possibility again. "But if he died in Venezuela . . . ."

"I'm sure he bought some phony documents and snuck back into the country. Before he left for Venezuela, he told me he'd found some other way to . . . how did he phrase it . . . 'live beyond death.' Another life of luxury and adventure. I didn't know what he meant, and I wasn't interested anyway. After he supposedly died, I got an anonymous letter—here, I'll show it to you."

He went to the hall closet and returned with a folded letter still in its envelope. The mystery was beginning to fascinate me, but I retained a morbid sense of dread, one that intensified as I examined the irregularly scrawled handwriting: *Truly I tell you that no man can escape his hell and experience the kingdom of God unless he is born again. Take it from a man who has been reborn and found paradise and the power of renewed life. Afraid you missed the boat? Don't worry—I will be in touch soon. Think it over. Heaven awaits.*

"I'm sure Hank sent it," Steve said. "This sounds just like his high-and-mighty BS. Look at the writing: it looks like someone was trying to disguise their normal handwriting style. The return address is the local library. I waited for a follow-up message, but I never got one. This letter came four years ago. It was four, maybe five months after his supposed boating accident."

"Were you a friend of his?" I asked.

Steve let out a sardonic laugh. "Hank didn't have friends," he replied flatly. "He was a sociopath. If he wanted me to join in, it was because he wanted to use me for something. He probably would have demanded part of my insurance payout."

My gaze fell on the clock above the bar. I suddenly remembered that my wife was waiting for me.

"I should go," I said, standing. "My wife will wonder why I haven't come back. I was supposed to get the kids and drag them home for dinner."

"They should be home soon."

"What's this hill they went out to?"

"It's over on the other side of the neighborhood. Have you been out there?"

"Not yet."

"It's a huge, treeless mound out in the woods," he said. "The kids go sledding there in winter, and in summer . . . well, I don't know what they do. I thought it might be a burial mound. I went out there with a ground-penetrating radar a few years ago to check it out, but I gave up pretty quickly."

I was intrigued, but I restrained myself from asking questions. As I started to leave, though, I noticed a crater in the wall next to the sofa, and I couldn't help commenting on it.

"Your neighbor's head made that dent," Steve said.

I probably looked confused. He clarified: "We used to have

neighborhood parties down here. Have you met Milagros?"

"I have."

"Her husband, Alejandro, threw a tantrum one night and smashed her head into the wall. We had to pull him off of her."

I was shocked, but only for a moment. On second thought, it wasn't very surprising. It seemed to explain Milagros' sad eyes and perpetual nervousness.

"He was going on about the Church of Eternal Life," Steven explained. "I can't remember what he was saying. Something about how the eternal life technology was real, and he was going to invest in a share. It sounded like he'd been in touch with some of the church members. Milagros . . . well, that was their first time at our house. She mostly sat there looking anxious, and when Alejandro started talking about the cult, she said something about how those men were committing a sin and they were going to drag Alejandro down with them. That's when he lost it. He pushed her so hard that her head went right through the plaster. We threw him out and my wife called the police, but . . . it sounded like Alejandro made up some excuse about falling over on her when he was drunk. He *was* drunk. The police found him passed out halfway up the road to Widow's Peak. They accepted his story, even though we all saw what happened."

"Well," I said, "perhaps it's a cold thing to say, but I'm glad he's not around anymore." I touched the broken plaster with my fingertips. "Do you want help patching this up? I have—"

"No, we're not going to patch it up. I promised Milagros I wouldn't."

I withdrew my fingers. "How come?"

"She wants me to leave it there as proof that her husband was abusive."

"Even though he's dead? What difference can it make now?"

Steven paused before answering; he seemed to choose his words carefully. "I just want her to feel reassured. Alejandro did die— supposedly. Milagros is convinced that he found a way to come back from the dead."

Those words stuck in my head. I remembered them as I mused over my conversations with Milagros, as I watched her movements from across the street. She looked like a woman who had once been beautiful, but whose slouched, slow figure and weary face gave an overpowering impression of pitiful defeat. I often saw her looking wistfully at our family gatherings. If she approached, she always did so with hesitance. Had Alejandro disapproved of her socializing with others? Did she fear the return of a controlling and abusive man? As the days wore on, I began to perceive Milagros more strongly as a woman who desired friendship but feared the consequences.

I had yet to win over the other neighbors. However, I had gotten as far as Emma's drawing room; she had invited me in on a particularly hot day. I was still wearing my formal work clothes and sweating in my long trousers, and Emma kindly offered me a glass of lemonade. An urn on the drawing-room mantle had her husband's remains inside of it, with a small plaque bearing his name.

"I hope you don't mind my asking," I said, "but my parents want me to help them with their end-of-life plans. They chose cremation, but I don't know the first thing about where to go. Can you recommend a place?"

Emma raised her eyebrows. Her expression turned cold. "That's what the internet is for."

"Of course." I bowed my head slightly, in apology. "I'm sorry. Death is a painful subject. I don't usually use the internet for something so personal. We try to go by word of mouth instead." I glanced briefly at the urn.

Grudgingly, Emma followed my gaze. "Well, there's the Cremation Society. I don't have much experience with those things, either. Hank was cremated, but he didn't die here. He had to be cremated overseas."

Later, I learned from Milagros that Victoria's husband had also died overseas. He'd once been stationed in the Philippines while he was in the Air Force, and had returned there to visit some friends.

Steve's claim that the neighborhood was the site of life insurance fraud was beginning to hold weight. I researched the history of the homes and found that at least one of the original families had been investigated for fraud. The husband had reportedly died in Yemen, and his body quickly cremated, with no proof of his demise except for two death certificates: one issued by a hospital, the other by the Civil Status and Registration Authority. The investigation had been a heated one, with the insurance company going to all lengths to avoid a payout. Their main claim was that black-market death certificates could be easily bought in some countries, Yemen being one of them.

"It's difficult when a family member dies overseas," I told Milagros, encouraging her to continue on the subject. "My grandfather died in India a few years ago, and he didn't have any close family left there. It took a while before we found out, and then we had to make travel arrangements. It's agonizing, having to wait, and having to deal with tedious things in the meantime." I gave a sympathetic glance toward Iris' house. "Iris' husband died overseas too, didn't he?"

"Yes. Somewhere in China." Milagros stared into her glass as she spoke. We were drinking together after another barbecue; she had brought a bottle of wine and downed more than half of it. I drank lemonade with her out of cordiality.

Nadira and the kids had taken the dishes into the house, leaving me to talk alone with Milagros. Even the kids had noticed that she opened up to me more than the rest of the family. I assumed, based on her comments, that this was because I was a psychiatrist: someone she could talk to about her troubles, and who could give sound advice. What her troubles were, though, remained a mystery.

I tried to think of a delicate way to approach the matter. A roundabout way seemed best, so I continued with the topic of spouses. "I nearly lost Nadira when she went back to India. She went on her own that time, and her taxi was in a traffic accident. She was okay, but . . . ." I hesitated, trying to work the subject in my desired direction. "I'm sorry if I'm bringing up a bad topic. I know you also lost your husband."

"My husband wasn't a good man," Milagros said softly. "And I didn't lose him." She turned to me, looking into my eyes with sudden intensity. "Listen: You're a religious man. You talk about morals and faith. And you're a psychiatrist; you talk to sick people. You know when people are delusional and when they're sane."

"Well," I began, but she interrupted.

"How much responsibility do you think we have to punish other people for their sins? If someone wronged me, *really* wronged me, it's okay to defend myself—isn't it? And if he puts my life in danger—if he threatens me—how much right do I have to self-defense? I was always told to 'put up with it,' that men are just that way, but it isn't true. You're not that way. You don't hit your wife and threaten her."

"Of course you have a right to self-defense," I assured her. "It's everyone's natural right."

"But how far can I go? If someone is really dangerous . . . ."

"Well, of course you should do what you can to defend your life. When it comes to punishment, though, we're not meant to handle these questions alone. That's why we have a justice system."

The intensity faded from her eyes. Milagros looked away with a short, guttural laugh. "The justice system," she repeated, her voice dripping with disdain. "The justice system helps those who have power. It stomps on the weak. It stomps harder when we try to survive."

She was looking at her house as she spoke. I pondered her words, in particular her identification with the weak: *when we try to survive*. Was she thinking of the days she had spent with Alejandro, alone in that house?

I decided to approach the subject more directly. "Listen, Milagros, I hope you don't mind my saying it, but I've been getting to know the neighbors, and . . . you are very well liked here, but no one misses Alejandro. He sounds like a brute. I'm sorry if I'm jumping to conclusions."

She continued to stare for some time, but finally she half-turned to me. Her gaze fell on the patio table. "I'm better off without him, aren't I? I could leave this place . . . sell the house, set up somewhere small and quiet . . . if he would let me."

"If Alejandro would let you? There's nothing he can do now."

She smiled wryly, still not looking me in the eye. "There's plenty he can do. These men don't stay dead. Alejandro is going to come back . . . soon. It will be any day now. I hate to think of what he'll do this time."

I chose my next question carefully. "Did Alejandro believe he could return from the dead? I know there was a group of occultists in this neighborhood, and that Emma's husband used to talk about eternal life."

Her face flushed. She laughed nervously. "Oh . . . I had too much to drink. I talk nonsense when I drink." Milagros got up from the table and stumbled.

I quickly stood and took her arm. She laughed again, saying she was fine, but allowed me to walk her to her front door.

"Thank you," she said. "It's good to know that I have a neighbor like you."

"Likewise. Come and see us any time, okay?"

Despite my intentions to make rounds with all the neighbors, I gave up on the other ladies and homed in on Milagros—and on Steve. My family began to comment on the amount of time I spent at his house. I was taken in by his hobbies and interests, many of which I happened to share. In mid-summer, he offered to take me fly fishing at a local trout stream, and I readily accepted.

When I came out of the bedroom in my wading gear, Nadira smiled slyly. "I see you dressed up for your date," she said. "Do you really want to wear that today? It's going to be hot."

"I'm more comfortable in these."

"Is this why you've been obsessing over your tackle box?" Yasmin asked. "You've been geeking out over it all week. I should've known it had something to do with Anna's dad."

"They're having a *bro*mance," Aamir said, and the kids laughed uproariously.

I didn't return home until late. Rain started to fall while I was still at Steve's house, and it made sense that I should wait until it stopped—so we tinkered in the wood shop for a while, and then we played pool. It was just after midnight when I scaled the steep drive to Widow's Peak, wearing my shorts and sandals and awkwardly lugging my rod, tackle box, and wading gear.

As I reached the end of my driveway, blowing uselessly at the mosquitoes that buzzed around my face, I stopped and listened. An unexpected sound had reached my ears: a faint sound of weeping. I stood quietly, peering into the dark. Perhaps I'd misheard; it might be a cat or some other animal.

Another noise, a slight creaking, drew my attention to the far end of the cul-de-sac. Emma stood on her front step. She had opened the door, momentarily illuminating herself in the entryway. She slipped inside and closed the door behind her.

The sound of weeping continued. The source came into view: a human shape, shadowy in the darkness, clumsily lumbering toward the side door that led into Milagros' garage. The house lamp illuminated the figure, revealing Milagros' slumped form. She carried a shovel, clutching it close to her body. I could see mud caked on the blade.

It was concern for my neighbor that made me investigate further. I worried about Milagros. She should have been free from abuse, yet she still feared her husband. I set my equipment on the lawn and quietly crossed to her garage door. Milagros had left muddy footprints in the grass. Using the light from my cell phone, I tracked them across the backyard and into the woods. The ground was still soft from the rain, and her steps were easy to trace. Some other pattern blended with the tracks: a deep, uninterrupted line, as though a stick had been dragged across the ground, or perhaps a thin wheel. It took only a minute of walking in the forest to see what Milagros had been up to.

Her tracks led to a fresh mound of dirt, long and rectangular, surrounded by footprints. The shovel's blade had left imprints where Milagros had tried to pack down the earth. And I wondered: *What did she bury here?*

Fresh in my mind were the strange images on my basement walls. I had painted over them, but in my memory they remained in vivid detail—and in the photos I had taken, which I frequently examined with a morbid fascination. The ankh, the mysterious rays, Hank's promise of eternal life, Milagros' certainty that her husband would return from the dead. These ideas tumbled around in my mind, and a new idea formed there: that Alejandro had, indeed, been coming back from the dead, and Milagros had to keep re-burying him.

I was still standing there, scoffing at my own paranoia, when a small figure poked through the mound of earth and disappeared again.

A cry escaped from my lips; I jumped back in surprise.

I watched for a few more seconds, and then laughed at myself. The figure had surely been an animal. A gopher, perhaps. Something small. To my anxious mind, it had looked like a human hand.

My phone light strayed from the mound as I doubled over in weak, whispered laughter—but my laughter died as the mound began to move. The hand-like figure poked through again, followed by an arm, and then another hand. And then the figure sat up in the dirt, a human figure that moaned and coughed and gasped for breath. It struggled to stand, its arms waving in a crazy dance as it tried to find its footing.

My mouth was open in a silent cry. I stepped back; a twig crunched under my foot. A garbled mumbling came from deep in the figure's throat as it turned to face me. It looked like a man. He stumbled forward and reached for me—and his words became clear.

"I don't want to be dead anymore!" he shrieked. "I'm not dead! I'm alive! *Estoy vivo!*"

Before I could move, his muddy hands grabbed my arms. I tried to twist out of his grasp, and as the phone light illuminated those hands, I realized with horror that the man's fingers were broken. The bone was exposed on one of his index fingers, poking through torn flesh. I was clutched in the grasp of a mangled corpse.

I screamed.

And then I shook him off and ran, making a mad dash for the safety of my home. Damaged as he was, the dead man followed me. As I staggered into my driveway, I heard him screaming in Spanish, and again came the defiant proclamation: "I'M NOT GOING TO BE DEAD ANYMORE!"

I burst into the house and locked the door behind me. My family was roused by the commotion. Nadira and Yasmin came and stood at the upper balcony, and **Aamir** gaped at me from the lower hall. "What's going on?" he asked.

"Nadira, call the police," I said.

"Okay." She started to head for the bedroom, but paused to ask: "What should I tell them?"

I yelled something like "There's a dead man outside!" Then I hurried past **Aamir** into the bathroom. Something about the man's filth on my arms and clothes was deeply disturbing—as though he might have some sort of zombie plague, some contagious condition that was seeping into my pores. I stripped off my shirt and scrubbed the filth from my skin.

When I came back into the hall, my family was gone. The front door stood ominously open.

"Nadira!" I shouted. I ran out onto the step, scanning the drive, and spotted the shadowy figures of my loved ones huddled on the road.

"Get back," I cried, rushing toward them. I saw the crumpled figure of the dead man, lying before them on the road. Nadira crouched with phone in hand, talking quietly with the police.

"Dad, look," Aamir said. He had fished the man's wallet from the filthy trousers, and now he held it open to me. "Isn't this Milagros' husband?"

Yasmin peered at the ID, visible through a plastic window. Then she studied the man's muddy face. "It *is* him," she said. "Alejandro Cruz."

As if in response to his name, Alejandro's eyes opened wide. With a groan of effort, he began to sit up. He moaned, mumbled, and then his garbled nonsense once again became a crystal-clear shriek: "I'M NOT GOING TO BE DEAD ANYMORE!"

Everyone screamed. Later, this made me feel better about my own reaction: I wasn't the only one who screamed in terror at the mere sight of a muddy, confused man.

In conversation with the police, I learned that Alejandro had indeed never died. Instead, he had secured a black-market death certificate in Mexico City. The plan was for Milagros to collect a life insurance payment and gradually transfer the funds to him. Eventually, though, Alejandro tired of the scheme. He wanted his life back, a life with his family and friends. Determined to never spend another moment in the safe room, he sealed it shut. That night, Alejandro argued with Milagros, became violent—and she fought back.

Milagros confessed to everything, with one exception. When asked whether she had struck her husband on the back of the head and knocked him unconscious, she refused to answer.

As the details continued to emerge, they only left me with more questions. Alejandro wasn't alone in his insurance scam. He had admittedly gotten the idea from other members of the Church of Eternal Life, now deceased and beyond the reach of the law, except perhaps for one. A man from the church was questioned and charged with conspiracy to commit fraud, but of those specifics I knew nothing. I began to brood over the possibility that a similar plan had been carried out in my own home. Had the previous owner killed her husband and collected an insurance payout? Was he a threat and a terror to her—or had she simply wanted the money for herself? Though the idea of psychic powers didn't hold much weight with me, murder no longer seemed implausible.

I wasn't alone in my suspicions. Soon after the incident with Alejandro, Steve invited me over for a few games of pool. "It didn't surprise me at all that Alejandro was still alive and taking the insurance money," he said gravely. "I suspected that was the case, but I didn't want to speak up because I assumed that Milagros was involved. I don't see how she couldn't have been. She would have had to collect the life insurance money. She had been through so much already, and I knew she was terrified of Alejandro. I hated the idea of her going to prison for fraud." He gave me an uneasy, perhaps guilty look. "It was wrong of me not to say anything. If there had been an investigation, Milagros could have been protected from him—and now she'll probably go to prison. I should have talked to the police about Hank. I should *still* talk to them."

"Milagros should have told them," I replied. "But I suspect she had been to the police before, and didn't get the help she needed."

Steve hesitated, pursing his lips. I saw that he was debating whether to speak his thoughts out loud. "It's not just his personality that makes me think he committed fraud," he continued. "Hank talked to me about life insurance fraud. He said that if there's no body, the beneficiaries have to wait several years to get a payout. He read an article about someone who bribed a boatman to claim that he had fallen into the ocean and drowned. Since there was no body, the wife had to wait seven years to get the money, just in case he showed up somewhere—and in the meantime, the guy got caught using someone else's identity. He got fourteen years, not just for fraud, but for identity theft and other crimes. Hank said that a fake cremation could be a workaround to get a faster payout." Again, Steve gave me that hesitant look. "The thing with Alejandro, though . . . it makes me wonder if there have been other murders."

"I've been thinking the same thing," I admitted. "I've wondered if Hank was murdered, and that's why you never heard from him again. Not that Emma seems the murderous type, but . . . she's certainly secretive. And the thing is, I saw Emma outside that night—the night I found Alejandro. She went into her house at the exact same time Milagros went in. Milagros confessed to everything except hitting Alejandro on the head, so it makes me wonder if someone else did it. And after hearing about the man who lived in my house, and how his relatives thought his body might be buried in the basement . . . ."

Steve nodded. "Wouldn't surprise me at all if there were more. As for your basement, how would you like to scope it out? The guy's relatives were never able to get access again, but it's your call now. I can bring my ground-penetrating radar. If there's a body buried beneath the floor, or behind the walls, it can tell us where to start digging."

I readily agreed, but said that I would choose a time when my family was out of the house. I didn't want to disturb them with my suspicions.

Milagros, meanwhile, was charged with first-degree attempted murder. Her sentencing took place some time later, but eventually she was convicted. Though there was evidence that Alejandro had assaulted her, and that she had acted in self-defense, the conviction rested on the fact that she decided to bury Alejandro alive instead of calling the police. Milagros was sentenced to twenty-two years in prison. Alejandro received a sentence of six years for bank fraud.

I grieved over Milagros' fate. True, she had committed an evil— yet I understood her terror, her feelings of helplessness and isolation, her certainty that the law would never protect her. Surely she deserved punishment—but twenty-two years! If she served the full sentence, she would be in her sixties by the time she was released, and have spent more than a third of her life behind bars. Details about Alejandro's abuse came out during the trial, details about years of "There's nothing we can do" from law enforcement and "Put up with it" from friends and family. It enraged me that Alejandro received no punishment for all the times he had attacked and beaten Milagros, for the ways he had terrorized her.

Steve came over on a Saturday when neither my kids nor Steve's were around. They had crept off to the local gravel pit, where some of the neighborhood kids went mud sliding in the rainy season. Though they hadn't told me where they were going, I heard their whispers and saw how they were trying to hide their towels and extra clothes—and though I knew they'd be trespassing, I didn't scold them. Instead, I called Steve and asked him to hurry over with his radar.

He showed up minutes later, with digging tools as well as the radar. Steve was a structural assessor by trade, but he was also a hobbyist who had helped the city locate a few long-buried artifacts. He started off by marking the basement floor with strips of tape. Then we carried the equipment down. The ground-penetrating radar looked somewhat like a push mower with a digital screen on the handle. When Steve turned it on, a series of black and white lines filled the screen. "It's kind of like doing an X-ray," he said. "You know what the image is supposed to look like, and you just keep an eye out for any abnormalities."

I nodded, though I didn't have the slightest idea how my basement was supposed to look on the screen. I watched closely, though, as Steve made a painstakingly slow trek back and forth across the concrete.

"Ross was really into these occult ideas," he said as he worked. "He insisted that eternal life was inevitable—through science, or through spirituality. He got into some trouble in our neighborhood for trying to lure people into his so-called church. He'd invite them to a Bible study, or to a peace activist group, or some other event that was actually a front for the church. It would seem legit for a few minutes, but by the end of the day, it was all about investing in the Church of Eternal Life. There was a big uproar at the Bible study. The organizers started talking about achieving eternal life through science, and the Christians were upset. Because, you know, they believe you can only achieve eternal life through Christ."

I listened with interest, but began to feel anxious that the kids would return soon—and then Steve stopped and said, "This looks like something."

In the center of the screen, the lines sloped up and then down again. "What is it?" I asked.

"No telling . . . unless you want to dig it up. Should I get the tools?"

Hesitantly, I nodded.

"All right. Let's gear up. You'll want a mask and goggles. And earplugs."

Steve used a rotary hammer to break up the concrete. Then we started digging. We hadn't gone five feet beneath the surface when I caught the first glimpse of pale bone peeking through the dirt.

We dug a little more with our hands—reluctantly, my own hands beginning to tremble with dread and revulsion—until the form of the human skeleton became unmistakable, with a jutting rib cage and lanky arm still swathed in bits of fabric, and a gaping, empty-eyed skull. Steve stepped back and spoke quietly. "Let's stop here. The police should do the rest."

I sat back, gazing at the bones that peeked through the dirt, and felt a deep sense of mourning. The skeleton was positioned on its side, and I could see that the back of the skull was caved in. A murder had surely been committed in my house. It had happened to this person, this man who was probably Ross Gates. The sight of his brutalized remains no longer evoked any abhorrence within me. It just made me feel incredibly sad.

The kids showed up before the police did, still damp from their excursion to the gravel pit. They had presumably hosed off at a neighbor's house and changed their clothes, but still bore numerous telltale traces of mud. The sight of them reminded me of Alejandro Cruz erupting from the earthen mound. I tried not to shudder as I took them into the backyard, where I quietly explained that a human skeleton had been found beneath our basement; the police would be in and out of the house, and would have to transport the remains, and we needed to let them have their space. The kids wanted to watch, but I refused to let them—so they ran off and told all of their neighborhood friends about the skeleton in our basement. Soon, we had gawkers lined up in the street.

Ross Gates was identified through his dental records. He had presumably died from being bludgeoned, a blow of such force that it had shattered his skull.

The sight of that broken skull, of the gaping skeletal mouth and empty eye sockets, haunted my dreams for some time—and that wasn't the end of it. Only days later, the scene repeated itself when police obtained search warrants for the remaining three homes. I watched from my driveway as Hank Dalton's skeleton was carried in pieces from Emma's house. After a long search, the investigators also found human bones in a walled-up closet in Iris' basement.

Nothing was found in Victoria's house. Not yet, anyway.

As the days went on, we picked up details from the news media. We learned that Emma had received nearly two million dollars from her husband's life insurance policy, and waited several months before beginning to make transfers to a bank account in Moldova. After only a few deposits, the transfers suddenly stopped. This, prosecutors presumed, was because she had murdered him, and thus no longer needed to move the money. The autopsy report matched the theory perfectly—but proving that Emma was the killer, that was a tricky matter. She vehemently denied any knowledge of his death.

Eventually, she went to prison.

Iris' husband had also been murdered. His death appeared to have followed Hank's by only a few weeks. Iris had made a significant mistake when concealing the body: she had enclosed with it the expensive Swiss sculpture she had used to bludgeon him, and the supplies she'd used to clean up his blood—all of which still bore her fingerprints and DNA. Iris insisted that she, too, had acted in self-defense, that her husband had blackmailed and threatened her, that he had assaulted her in a fit of rage.

Meanwhile, the Gates' insurance money had been inherited by relatives. The bank filed a civil lawsuit in an attempt to reclaim it.

I watched these reports with keen fascination—mostly, I told myself, because I had to be informed about what had happened in my home and community. I needed to know for my family's sake and my own—but knowing had drawbacks. At work, I found it difficult to focus on my patients. I was generally distracted and found myself having numerous small accidents: cutting my fingers while chopping vegetables, running a stop sign, missing my exits while trying to drive anywhere. I took a few days off from work and tried to settle down, but the reports continued to come, and they rattled me.

One night, after an evening news segment that replayed the footage of Hank's skeleton being removed from our cul-de-sac, I went to my wife and hugged her tightly. "I love you," I told her in a near whisper. "I love that you are good-hearted and reliable, and that you are kind, and that you are honest. Thank you for that."

Wordlessly, she returned my embrace. The sensation of her body settling into mine gave me a sense of comfort and stability.

"We've made this a happy place, haven't we?" I asked.

"We have."

"But this entire house is built on murder and deceit, and deprivation. Every embellishment was paid for with it. It doesn't look pretty to me anymore. It doesn't look like our home. And what kind of neighbors do you think we'll have now? What kind of people would want to live here?"

She tilted her head back and looked up at me. "Do you want to move? The kids love it here."

"I know." I kissed her forehead. "I suppose time and togetherness will take care of it. We will continue to make this a happy place."

And so I try. That is my job, after all: to create hope, joy, and everything that is sound and beautiful in life, even when the foundation of the past contains the ugliest of circumstances. But how can you repair the spirit of a home, a whole neighborhood, that was built entirely on depravity? Is it better to raze it to the ground and start over? Despite my family rituals and prayers, and despite all of my healing intentions, I remain haunted by the image of Alejandro Cruz clawing his way up from the earth in filth and agony. I am haunted, too, by his cruelty. I can't forget the corpse that rotted in the foundation of my own house, the grisly murders that financed these beautiful estates.

I have yet to find out if my vow to my wife has any merit—my assertion that time and effort will heal such ugliness. One part of me, the dutiful mental health professional, insists that it is more than possible. We need only to refrain from harping on what we cannot change, and to focus on what we can treat and create anew, in spite of what inevitably haunts us. Yet, the tragedy at Widow's Peak has perhaps given me better empathy for my patients, in that I now know what it is to meet real evil and violence, and to feel small and helpless in its stead.

I often visit Milagros. She, too, has faced evil, and through her I find a strange comfort. I know that she committed a crime; I know she chose wrongly, but when I see how much better she fares in prison, I find it easy to forgive what she did to escape her previous life. In prison, her eyes are no longer anxious, and there is genuine warmth in her smile when she greets me. She is creating joy on a foundation of wretchedness. My hope lives there in her smile.

II

A Foreign Bride

A Foreign Bride

"How will you differentiate between cold feet and actual fear? What if you misunderstood and then you can't take a step back?"
-Sarvesh Jain

Ivan spent an entire Saturday preparing the house for guests. He expected a long overdue visit from his old friend, Bill Johnston, and after that he would be welcoming his new wife. For her, Ivan planned to do much cleaning up of the expansive yard and a few repairs to the moisture-damaged house. His countryside home stood on a large plot, with a pond and a good swath of woods in the back. The front yard was also thick with trees, and through them, a long dirt path led out to the gravel road. Ivan spent a good two hours filling the holes in the driveway. He took a few minutes of rest; then he wiped the spills from the kitchen and the dust from the sitting room. It was a shame, he thought, that there was no woman around to perform such tasks—but that would be remedied soon enough.

More than a decade had passed since Ivan and Bill had last met. They had served in the air force together and kept in touch through phone calls and letters, encouraged each other through tough times, and lauded each other's successes. Ivan was excited to have a tell-all about his new fiancé, but his elation deflated when his friend arrived. Bill had brought his wife along. The presence of a woman always spoiled the conversation; it put Ivan on the defensive, meant that he would have to guard his words. Every exchange put forth one more thing he had to lie about—like the fact that he'd found his fiancé by perusing web sites with names like "Hot Russian Models" and "Mail Order Brides."

Hardly five minutes into their meeting, he found himself explaining it all away. "Some of the web sites have dumb names like 'Hot Russian Brides,'" he said with a chuckle, "but they're still a good way to meet people. They're really just dating services like Match.com. Members post an introductory video, and they make a list their hobbies and goals, and they try to find someone who shares their interests."

The trio lounged in the sitting room with drinks and a meager snack of crackers and cheese. Ivan took pains to limit his alcohol intake. He sipped his first beer at a snail's pace and restricted himself to one ridiculously small shot of vodka, afraid that his feelings of defensiveness might compel him to lash out.

"You were looking for a Russian woman?" Sharon asked.

Bill cut in, rather hastily: "Ivan's family is Russian."

"They are, but that's not the only reason," Ivan said. "I haven't had much luck with the women around here. I wanted to meet someone with more traditional values."

Sharon seemed to regard him with a sudden coolness. "What kind of traditional values?"

"I mean," Ivan replied, "women who still believe in being part of a team. A lot of people these days don't seem to believe in putting effort into a marriage. They treat it the same way they treat their clothes or their furniture. You find something you like, use it for a while, and pass it on to someone else."

The hardness in Sharon's eyes seemed to ease. She nodded.

"You have to be careful, though," Ivan continued, "because people lie on their profiles. Both sides have to be careful—the men and the women. There are probably a lot of creepy guys who go to these sites, but there are some pretty shady women, too. You have to consider why a Russian woman would want an American man—and we all know what foreigners assume about American men. They assume we have money. So, it follows that a lot of these women are more interested in money than marriage. Money and a green card— that's exactly what my first wife was interested in."

"He got taken in by a scammer," Bill explained. "She cleaned him out and took off as soon as she got her card."

"Well, I was a fool," Ivan said. "I paid for everything and didn't expect her to contribute. That should have been a red flag, but she was living in poverty, and I thought she would be grateful for a comfortable life—not that this is any kind of palace, but we lived well. I paid for our translation fees, and then I went to Russia to meet her. Then I paid for her visa, her plane ticket, her moving expenses, the marriage filing fee, her green card application . . . it cost over a thousand dollars just to apply for that damned green card."

"Did you have to pay the same fees this time?" Sharon asked.

"No. Yelena speaks English, so there were no translation fees.

We ended up ditching the service and making arrangements on our own."

"Is that wise?" Bill asked. "Don't they help screen people?"

"They already screened her. She is who she says she is." Ivan had spent countless hours each week ensuring that Yelena was genuine. She could back up every claim she had made, every interest she professed, with as much detail and engaging conversation as Ivan could have hoped for—and there didn't seem to be any need of his that would go unfulfilled. Yelena kept a good house, enjoyed intimacy, and was a skilled cook. She knew how to prepare all of Ivan's favorite dishes, including the sausage stew his first wife used to make. Moreover, she was frugal. It seemed unlikely that she would demand a shopping spree upon arriving, like so many "mail-order" brides supposedly did.

"We really hit it off," Ivan said. "We can talk for hours at a time. From the beginning, it was like she already knew me."

"So you think you'll get married?" Sharon asked.

"If she's up for it, and if she is who she says she is, then I can't see any reason why not. I'm not going to Russia again. She's going to come here instead, and she's doing it on her own dime. If we get along as well in person, we'll get hitched."

As Bill and Sharon readied to leave, Ivan felt a stab of disappointment. He had wanted to catch up with Bill, to confide in him alone, without having to pander to the interests of another guest. At the door, Sharon smiled at him and bid him farewell by saying "Good luck with your Russian bride."

Ivan smiled, chuckled, thanked her. After the door was closed behind her, he muttered: "Bitch."

When Yelena arrived, she took to the house with surprising ease. She found it charming and comfortable, and took great pleasure in roaming the back woods. Of course, Ivan had expected her to put on a show of acceptance and satisfaction, and he tried to keep his sense of awe in check. He watched Yelena intently, trying to catch any fleeting expressions of disappointment or disgust—but she seemed relaxed, always emanating a low-key but genuine delight. Gradually, Ivan began to shed the layers of stress that had built up over the past weeks. He'd had his own doubts, and his relatives and acquaintances had deepened them with the expected questions: *Won't she feel isolated? Won't she get bored? Do you really think she'll be happy living in that old house?* Ivan had comforted himself with the notion that the house was more than enough; it was simple, but wanted for nothing. Anyway, Yelena preferred quiet places out in nature, and had expressed a desire for a simple lifestyle. She had also grown up in the woods, near a marsh, and longed to live in a place that reminded her of home.

As for her looks, Ivan found her even more alluring in person. Yelena was young and slim with an impressive bust, and she carried herself in a way that was both elegant and confident. It was with some effort that Ivan forced his own restraint. He didn't want sex too quickly, as he had a distaste for easy women—but a frigid woman wouldn't satisfy him, either. Yelena, it seemed, was a perfect balance: she wanted to spend some time with Ivan first, to develop a physical connection before delving into intimacy—but once she delved, she delved deep.

Ivan's uneasiness and doubts evaporated, and for some time he allowed himself to revel in the thrill of his good fortune.

He'd been surprised by how quickly Yelena had chosen him from the crowd. Surely, with her looks, she'd had an abundance of offers, but she claimed that the others seemed "ingenuine." When Ivan asked her what stood out about him, she smiled and gave him a playful look. "Everything. As soon as I saw your profile, I knew you were the man I was looking for."

Ivan felt much the same way about Yelena. He had scrolled past the first few pages of trampy-looking women who reclined on beds and sofas in elaborate lingerie, their backs arched and breasts thrust forward, lips parted invitingly. Those images might have aroused most men, but to him they reeked of opportunism and dishonesty.

Like anyone, Ivan had his particular tastes. He'd skimmed past the fair-haired women and paused at the ones with dark hair and blue eyes. Most of those profiles were also quickly dismissed. Ivan wanted someone young and fresh, but mature—someone who had intelligence, but who knew her place. His first full stop was at Yelena's profile. Everything she'd written, every detail of her face and figure seemed to tell him: *This is the one.*

After a grocery trip, Yelena cooked the sausage stew he liked so much. Ivan watched as she flavored the recipe with bourbon and jalapeno peppers—the same way his first wife had done. Her hands moved deftly as she chopped vegetables and measured out spices. "Let me add just a touch of your beer," she said, and smiled alluringly. Ivan complied, sliding his bottle onto the counter. He inhaled the faint, pleasant scent of Yelena's shampoo as he stood beside her. A small wave of pleasure swelled in him—but now that he was looking closely at her, he noticed that her hair was lighter at the roots. "Do you dye your hair?" he asked.

"I do," she said. "I like this color. I've always kept it this way."

Ivan felt a familiar pang of disappointment, but he quickly brushed it off. So what if her hair was naturally a few shades lighter? At least she shared his taste, and made herself up accordingly.

She sat across from him as they ate. Ivan reveled in the flavors of the stew; it tasted just like his first wife's recipe. *Must be a Russian thing*, he mused, and looked admiringly at Yelena. She wore a light, form-fitting sweater that emphasized the curves of her breasts, a dark aqua shade that brought out the blue in her eyes. Such a beguiling addition to his kitchen.

The only thing Ivan really didn't like about her was her smile. It was her lips, he supposed. They were full, perhaps sexy to most men. Yelena's wide mouth and full lips gave her a striking grin, one that seemed to take up too much space; it dominated her face, exaggerated like the face of a clown. Perhaps that's all it was: Ivan found her smile somewhat clownish.

He tried not to think about it—but as Yelena met his gaze across the table, her lips spread wide, and Ivan shifted uneasily.

The day of the marriage, already scheduled, was fast approaching. Ivan no longer had any idea of canceling it. Yelena made his home complete. He drove to work in the morning and returned to clean, fresh rooms that still looked very much his own. Yelena's traces mostly showed up in the kitchen. Ivan often returned to find a strainer of chokecherries or cranberries sitting in a strainer, or some other native edibles washed and hung up to dry, and Yelena wandering somewhere in the woods. To Ivan's delight, she had a keen interest in cooking. She had been in touch with a cooking club at the local library, and soon had numerous sheets of information on native edibles. Soon, she was harvesting wild turnips and radishes, and preparing colorful salads with tiny purple and yellow blossoms and fragrant leaves. Ivan sat across from her at the table and gazed at her lovely form, her pretty face and dark blue eyes, and remembered how that face had secured his attention at first glance—as though he'd recognized Yelena as his own. Surely, fate had at last given him the relief he deserved.

Of course, there were little things that irked him. Yelena was a foreigner, and naturally, some of her customs were unlike his. A few days before the wedding, Ivan heard a rhythmic pounding in the back woods; he followed the sound and found Yelena sitting on a fallen elm tree close to the wetlands. The swamp had become a mere puddle after a spate of hot, dry weather. Perhaps she had forgotten Ivan's warning about it.

She sat profiled on the log, pounding away at a frame drum with her eyes closed, singing—or chanting, rather, in a strange monotone—in what Ivan presumed to be Russian. Wisps of smoke rose from a tiny bundle of sage that sat nearby on the fallen tree. Ivan stopped, taking in the sight: his soon-to-be wife, looking so pretty in her long green coat, her chin tilted up as she uttered that string of peculiar words.

Yelena paused with the stick still half-raised in her hand. She turned and looked at Ivan with placid blue eyes, and she smiled.

"You shouldn't be in this area," Ivan said. "Remember, that bog is dangerous."

"What bog?"

"This flatland right over here—it used to be part of the swamp. When it rains, the ground gets soft and acts like quicksand. I almost sank in it when I first moved out here. My boots stuck. I couldn't get them free for anything. I unlaced them and stepped back onto solid ground, and I stood there and watched the mud pull my boots into the earth." Ivan eyed the frame drum uneasily. "What's with the drum?"

She turned it in her hand, examining the mottled rawhide. "It's a hand-me-down from my grandmother."

"Uh-huh. And what's with the singing?"

"Did you like it?"

"Sounded more like droning to me. Not very musical."

"The forest seems to like it." Yelena gazed out at the trees. "It's important to spend time out in nature—especially the areas around your home, and the places where you gather food. We have to introduce ourselves and establish a relationship. Don't you agree?"

"Sounds very pagan. Anyway, I don't like you being out here."

"I will remember that. What about pagans—do you like them?" Yelena gave him a small, playful smile.

"I'm a Christian."

She laughed. "In what way?"

Ivan felt his expression growing cold. Yelena may have meant the comment as an innocent teasing, but that laughter mocked him.

"There are a lot of morels growing in these woods," she said, seeming not to notice his glowering. "They grow around the trees that are dying. The fruits take shelter in the decaying body and bloom there until the tree is completely dead. But you're a woodsman; you must know this already. I will make you a delicious morel stew."

"I'm not a fan of morels," he replied.

"You will be after you taste my stew. Try it once, okay? If you don't like it, I won't make it again. Tonight, though, we will have meat, and chickweed salad with wild radish." She stood and walked with him to the house, where she immediately began preparing dinner, humming as she worked. Yelena braised the meat and tossed the salad, and made a tangy tea of dandelion, honey, and spice. Ivan's hostility eased. Later, they made love, and Yelena's rude laughter was forgotten.

They married at the county courthouse. Ivan's cousin and an ex-neighbor served as witnesses. The ceremony was short, simple, nothing flashy. Yelena looked elegant in a slim blue dress; she had brought it from home, brought her own jewelry. Not like Sonia, his first wife. For her, Ivan had to buy the dress, the shoes, the hairpiece. Granted, Sonia had looked beautiful in her wedding attire, and Ivan thought it well worth the money at the time. But there were warning signs even then. Memories of that wedding day dominated his thoughts as he readied to take his vows.

"Do you take this woman, Yelena Rybakova, to be your lawfully wedded wife?" the officiant asked. "If so, answer 'I do.'"

Ivan blinked. The question seemed abrupt; he thought he remembered more lead-up to this part of the ritual, more specific promises around loyalty and sickness and tough times. Ivan looked into Yelena's dark blue eyes. She was calm, waiting. As Ivan opened his mouth to answer, she gave him an encouraging smile—and he caught a sudden stench of swamp, a pungent, decaying smell that nearly made him gag, a smell of death and memory and horror. He covered his mouth and coughed, trying to hide the gesture.

It's just anxiety, he told himself. *It won't happen that way again. Not with Yelena.*

"Sorry," he said, straightening up. He noted the officiant's startled look. "My throat's a bit dry today. Yes, I do."

A light rain began to fall as they finished the ritual. Yelena, to her credit, had anticipated rain and had the sense to bring an umbrella. Ivan sheltered both of them as they walked back to his car. Yelena looked up at him and asked gently: "Did you get cold feet?"

He put an arm around her, gave her a light squeeze. "No. I'm sure of things this time."

She prepared a special dinner that night. Yelena did, indeed, make a tasty stew of pureed morels. Ivan was impressed by its smoothness and robust flavor. Sonia's morel dishes had been inferior in comparison. Try as she might, she could never wash all the grit and sand from the deeply pitted caps.

Yelena paired the stew nicely with red wine and made a side dish of dock leaves cooked in olive oil and garlic. As Ivan sat down to eat, he noticed a dock root still sitting on the chopping board. He froze at the sight of it. On first glance, the root looked like a warped human figure with thin, hairy legs and stubby yellow arms. The dark purple head had a twisted streak of a mouth, a dark stub for a nose, and two yellow eyes—pale round orbs that stared in Ivan's direction.

"Can you get rid of that thing?" Ivan asked, gesturing. "Looks like a witch is staring at me."

Yelena laughed. Her clownish lips spread wide.

The following Monday, Ivan came home to find Yelena sitting near the bog with her drum and a smoking bundle of sage. She had twisted several dead-nettle plants into a skewed crown on her head. The green leaves and purple blossoms stood out against her dark hair, giving her the effect of an exotic forest nymph—but Ivan could feel his face settling into an expression of disapproval. Yelena's nature rituals got under his skin.

She turned to him and smiled disarmingly. "Hello, my dear. I collected a few more things for dinner."

"Yelena, I told you not to come out here. The ground is getting soft, and it looks like it rained again today."

Yelena glanced down at her muddy boots, at the tracks she'd made around the fallen tree. "I know, but I was very careful—see? I didn't go beyond this point. There are plants in this area that I needed. The morels grow best out here, for some reason." She gestured to the reed basket near her feet. "I know I made a special meal for our wedding night, but things will only get better from there—so I will make an even better meal." Yelena picked up the herb-filled basket and came to Ivan, taking his hand.

At home, she rinsed a bundle of dead-nettle and laid the plants on a dish towel to dry. "There are so many good things to eat in the woods," she said as she worked.

Ivan's gaze fell on the row of green stalks and purple blossoms. "What are those for?"

"These? They'll go into a salad. We'll have steak and a vinaigrette salad tonight."

"Sounds good." Ivan slid a hand around her waist. Her closeness aroused him; he pulled her to him, sliding his fingers beneath her cardigan, cupping her breast.

Yelena leaned into him, but focused on the herbs. "Steak with mushroom sauce. Mushrooms are my specialty. They're healthy, they're delicious, and they're fascinating. People say that morels seek the roots of dying trees because they prolong the tree's life, but they also help the tree learn how to die."

"Hmm. Sounds like a bunch of New Age bull."

"It's not all New Age. People have said for a long time that you can learn the purpose of a mushroom by looking at its form. Morel fruits have a labyrinth of doorways and portals, all compressed into one head—like a human brain that can both absorb and impart knowledge. What do you think? Does it look like a brain?"

"No." Ivan withdrew his hand. "Quit saying it looks like a brain. I won't eat it if that's what it reminds me of."

"Never mind. I prepared a different mushroom for tonight—my favorite." She took a small basket from the shelf below the cupboard and set it on the counter.

"Fly agaric," she said. "These are the most delicious."

Ivan peeked into the basket. The mushrooms had a milk-white stalk and red caps covered with pale, fluffy spots. Somewhere in Ivan's mind, there stirred a glimmer of warning—some cautionary memory about this brightly colored mushroom. "I thought these mushrooms were poisonous," he said.

"A little, yes, but not if you boil them for a few minutes and drain the water. It removes all of the toxins." Yelena grasped one of the dried caps and popped it into her mouth. She faced Ivan and smiled brightly as she chewed. "See? Harmless."

"You boiled them already?"

"Yes, they're boiled and dried. Tonight, I will use them to cook the best mushroom sauce. I'll soak them in vinegar first." She moved away, leaving Ivan standing before the spread of dead-nettle. He had never taken much notice of these plants before. Now, he thought they resembled a row of hulking green figures with lavender headdresses. Ivan was reminded of Yelena in the woods, with her long green coat and purple crown.

The dinner did, indeed, turn out to be Yelena's most flavorful recipe. She had chopped the mushrooms and cooked them with cream, white wine, and a few other ingredients from her growing collection of spices. Ivan wolfed down his steak and salad, and spooned the last dribbles of sauce from his plate.

"You liked it?" Yelena asked, gazing at the empty plate.

"It was amazing." From where he sat, Ivan once again admired Yelena's figure: the full breasts, the unusually dark blue shade of her eyes and the long black lashes that framed them, the dark hair that contrasted with her smooth, milky face. "I have to say, I feel like things are going really well for us. You know, this whole thing was really a nerve-wracking decision for me. Up until today, I think, I was still worried that you were just marrying me for a green card, and that you would end up leaving."

She nodded slowly, still not looking at him. "Is that your worst fear?" she asked quietly. "That someone might marry you and then leave you?"

Something about the question bothered him. Yelena's tone, for all its softness, lacked sympathy. She should have looked at him when she asked, at least.

With her fork, Yelena pushed a chunk of mushroom through the cream-colored sauce. While Ivan had gorged himself, she had eaten little. Most of the steak was growing cold on her plate. "That you would spend so much money to purchase a bride," she continued, "and the investment wouldn't pay off?"

Ivan stared at her. "*Purchase*? Are you really saying that? Didn't you also purchase your way here?"

"Russian brides have bigger fears, I think." Yelena was still sliding the bit of mushroom across her plate, watching it intently. "Most of us are poor, but we have family and friends. We leave everything we know, everything that might keep us safe, and we risk marrying an abuser—someone who wants us to serve and obey. How will he react if I don't obey? If I get on his nerves or make him suspicious? Those were my thoughts. I knew that when I came here, I might end up being murdered."

Ivan scoffed. "You thought I might kill you? Why? Were you planning to *do* something to make me suspicious?"

She smiled—a sad smile, at first, though it quickly became its usual clownish grin. "I'm not worried about that anymore." Yelena stood and took Ivan's plate. "I'm going to prepare dessert. This was my best dinner yet—don't you agree? But it's nothing compared to the dessert I will make."

Ivan looked at her in disgusted surprise.

"It won't take long." Yelena glanced into the living room, at the clock that hung on the far wall. "It's nearly done. I just need the trimmings."

She hummed in the kitchen as she stirred berries, honey, and granola on the stove. Ivan didn't stay to watch. He grabbed a beer from the fridge and sat in the living room, still scowling over Yelena's remarks—but the sweet and savory smells from the kitchen began to temper his mood. She was a good cook; he had to give her that. As in other things, she was much better than Sonia had been. Why had she said those things? Ivan had only meant to reflect on his own fears, but Yelena's words sounded like accusations.

After a while, Yelena left the dessert to cool on the counter. She disappeared into the bedroom and came back with a small stack of folded papers.

"What's that?" Ivan asked.

"Dessert," she replied. "Are you still hungry?"

He got up and followed her into the kitchen. She sat, placing the papers in front of her on the table. Ivan sat across from her uncertainly. Something didn't feel right. Even for a foreigner with a few odd customs, Yelena was being strange—and she still wouldn't look at him. Ivan had grown accustomed to seeing her gazing at him with a slight, playful smile; he had delighted in her attention. Tonight, she seemed cool and distant.

"It's warm in here," she said. She began to unbutton the cardigan from the top. A thin gold chain gleamed against her chest. Ivan had never seen her wearing it. Yelena didn't wear jewelry, aside from the plain gold ring he'd placed on her finger on their wedding day.

She unbuttoned down to her cleavage. A locket hung on the end of the chain, a golden oval with a flower etched on its surface. Ivan leaned forward to scrutinize it.

"What is it?" Yelena asked, finally looking at him. "Do you want to undress me?"

Her blue eyes were cool, seductive—but Ivan's focus was swallowed up by the locket.

"I don't think I've seen that before," he said.

"What? This?" She took the oval in her hand and pried it open with a fingernail. Yelena's gaze fell on the interior. "Maybe you have. My cousin has a matching locket." She nodded to the stack of papers. "These are her letters."

"Did she write to you? I didn't think anyone had written to you here."

"Oh, they haven't. These letters were sent *from* here." Yelena picked up one of the empty envelopes and placed it closer to Ivan. "These are letters from Sonia, my cousin and best friend. She sent them last year. She wanted me to come and visit her here, but I never got the chance. She disappeared before I could come."

Ivan studied the envelope, saw the incomprehensible writing in the center—but the return address, scrawled in English, was his own address. He looked again at the locket. It hung open on Yelena's chest, partially exposing the photo inside. Though he could see only half the portrait, he recognized the image instantly: the dark hair and pale face, an intense blue eye. Ivan's confusion became a pang of horrified realization. "You knew Sonia, my wife?"

Yelena smiled—that wide, unsettling grin—and at last Ivan realized why it perturbed him. Her eyes didn't smile along with her mouth. Yelena's gaze was often playful, often seductive, even cunning, but he had never seen a trace of warmth or affection there.

"What is this?" he demanded. "You knew Sonia, but you never mentioned it?" He waited for an answer, but Yelena's expression didn't change. In it he perceived spite and ridicule—a look he'd seen before and somehow mistaken for playful seduction. "What is this? I don't like being lied to."

"Who does? I'm here because of what Sonia wrote in her letters."

"What did she write?" Ivan stared coldly at Yelena. A vague smile still played on her clownish lips. He could have reached across the table and smashed that fat, ridiculous mouth. *Another liar. Another conniving phony.* Rage contorted his features, forming a mask of hate—but a growing fear crawled beneath it. "Did she accuse me of something? Sonia and I didn't get along in the end, but I never harmed her."

Yelena asked calmly: "Can you guess what she wrote?"

Ivan looked down at the letters. Yelena continued: "Of course you wouldn't know for certain. You never learned a word of Russian. Let me translate." She picked up the topmost letter and read in a steady voice. "'His paranoia keeps getting worse. I need to leave him soon. Today I think he threatened to kill me. He said that it would be easy to get away with murder here. Someone could throw a body in the soft ground near the swamp, and the mud would suck it down, and no one would ever find it. And even if someone found out, they would assume that someone strayed onto the soft ground by accident. Then he said that drowning in mud might seem like a horrible fate, but there are types of people who deserve it.'"

"I never harmed Sonia," Ivan insisted, his voice rising. "She harmed *me*. She used me, spent my money and wasted two years of my life, until she could get her green card—and then she was going to take off." Quickly, he corrected himself: "She *did* take off."

"She never left this place."

"Believe what you want. Maybe you don't know her as well as you think."

"I know Sonia. She wouldn't have cut off contact with her family and friends. Sonia wanted to come home to us, but you wouldn't let her."

"Is that what her letters say?"

"She wanted a plane ticket home, but it's not just the letters that say it. There are other things that speak. Other things that witnessed." Yelena's eyes seemed to grow darker as she gazed at him. "Things in the house, things in the forest . . . ."

Ivan opened his mouth to shout at her, but gagged on a sudden stench—the thick, putrid smell of a swamp, seeming to emerge through Yelena's lips. A smell of rot and terror. Memories flashed in Ivan's mind: Sonia's face, her wide-open mouth and frantic eyes. Her pleas and screams. "Bullshit!" he choked. "She was an opportunistic bitch!"

"Is it opportunism if we just want to live? If we just want to be with someone who will hold our hand instead of killing us? I suppose it might be."

Ivan felt sweat forming on his face and chest. The sudden heat and damp seemed to fill his lungs. He looked toward the front door, perhaps by some instinct for escape—but the doorway seemed a mile away, the wooden floor stretched to an impossible length. "What the hell did you do to me?"

Yelena began to re-stack the bundle of letters and envelopes. "Did you really think that you could just buy a human, and nitpick everything she did, and mold her exactly to your liking? I know a thousand little urges that you want fulfilled, because Sonia told me about them. I fulfilled them well, didn't I? Better than Sonia. She didn't cook well enough, didn't clean well enough, didn't look at you enough, didn't praise you enough, didn't stay home often enough, didn't report every minute of her movements while you were at work. How many of Sonia's urges did you know? She knew you well, but you didn't know her family, her friends, her interests? You didn't know that Yelena Rybakova was your wife's best friend?"

A slow cramp began to take hold of Ivan's stomach. He gripped the edge of the wooden table. "What the hell did you do?" he cried again.

"I cooked you a special dinner," Yelena replied evenly, "the way

Sonia always tried to. I cooked my best meal. I've had these mushrooms many times before. Eating a few bites will be okay for me, but will they be okay for you?" She spoke softly, expressionlessly, her dark eyes steady and unblinking. "These mushrooms live under the ground, and spread everywhere, even into the wetland. So does the morel—and that mushroom seeks death, sees it, remembers it, communicates it. I've seen it, too. On the days you're away, that's what I do: I go into the forest and eat, and look, and listen." She peered down at her own plate. Her brow furrowed. "Did I boil all of them? Maybe I forgot a few."

"Bitch," he hissed. "You poisoned me, you bitch!" Ivan jolted to his feet, supporting himself with his hands flat on the table. "You lying bitch. You're just like her—always blaming your dishonesty on someone else. If you were such a good friend, how come you never came to visit her?"

"I couldn't save the money. By the time I had enough, she wasn't here anymore—but you were here."

"You—" Ivan stumbled as his hands jerked from the table. The house seemed to sway gently around him; its features expanded, contracted, expanded again. He turned aside, trying to orient himself. Nothing seemed in its right place. The living room should have been to his left, not behind him—or had he moved? He couldn't remember which way he'd been facing.

"They especially like the wetlands," Yelena said in his ear. "They're drawn to it."

Ivan turned to her in a frenzy, but she wasn't there. Only the house was there, warped and wavering. "I didn't do anything," he moaned—and then he saw Yelena standing before him, the dead-nettle crown perched on her head. Her pupils had dilated into vast black pools. The wreath on her head was horned with dark purple leaves; her lips were painted lavender, and they, too, were dilated like the blossom of the nettle: a large, twisted, labia-like mouth. Ivan's voice rose to a panicked shriek. "She was a bitch! A lying, conniving bitch!"

"Did you know that sometimes, after a heavy rain, the bog becomes saturated and pushes up the objects that have fallen into it?" Yelena's voice seemed to come from everywhere. "The rainwater collects underneath the object and pushes it to the surface, where it can be seen by anyone. People have even found human bodies, preserved by the peat. They're called bog bodies. Sometimes they're so well preserved that you can look at a bog body and know right away who it is, because the face still looks the same."

"Where are you?"

"Oh—but that isn't a peat bog, is it? Sonia probably looks different by now."

Ivan grabbed the steak knife from the table. He lunged one way, and then another, swinging at the air. His hand struck the wall; the blade was flung from his grasp. "Where are you?" he demanded.

"Where I always am," Yelena's voice replied. "I practically live in those woods. I'm going there to pick morels. And you, you're a good husband—better than anyone knows. You'll help me gather them. It's something we do together as a happy couple."

He saw her then, hovering by the open doorway, the obscene purple crown still on her head. "Pagan witch," he hissed.

The hallway contracted, stabilizing enough to allow his passage. By the time Ivan reached the door, Yelena was gone. He stepped outside, still in his socks, mindless of the twigs and stones that jabbed at his feet. There—she was going around the house, into the woods! Her eyes were black as night, and the blossoms on her head were expanding, forming a pair of twisted violet horns. She grinned and fled.

Ivan followed the sound of rustling, of Yelena's heavy breathing and faint laughter. Rage drove him onward, though he scraped against trees and tripped over roots. A black spruce rose up suddenly, violently, before him. Ivan had fallen; the scaly gray bark cut into his forehead. He found himself faced with a smattering of milky white mushrooms, their crimson caps flecked with pale, fluffy blotches that looked like mold. Blood dripped from his head onto the brightly colored caps.

He tried to look around, saw a confused mass of twigs and pine needles. "Where are you?" he shouted.

"I'm here, dear," a distant voice replied.

He swore at her and grabbed the tree, hoisting himself to his feet. The fallen elm—surely that's where Yelena was headed, that place where she always pounded on that godforsaken drum and uttered those droning chants. Ivan listened, followed, stumbled his way forward through the woods, until at last he saw Yelena profiled against the clearing, facing him and smiling that wide, wretched smile. She didn't move as he approached.

With a grunt Ivan kicked her, shoving his foot hard into her stomach—but she didn't fall, or even stumble. Instead, Ivan's foot sank into her soft belly. He couldn't free himself. And it was cold; both of his feet seemed suddenly enveloped in cold. Yelena wrapped her hands around the mired foot and held it fast. She seemed unaffected, calm, as Ivan struggled and lost his balance. Yelena's smile didn't falter as she fell to the ground with him. He stopped fighting for a moment to see what had caught him so tightly—and then he screamed.

Yelena's belly was a dark, gummy pool of sludge. The whole of his foot had disappeared into it. Vermin crawled there, within the sludge and onto his ankle: leeches and woodlice and beetles. Above the tarry pit, Yelena's neck and face began to waste away—or was it Sonia's face? The skin rotted and separated, revealing bits of dirt underneath, finally giving way to bone. Ivan strained and screamed, but his movements only intensified his helplessness. He was stuck; he couldn't step back.

Frantically, Ivan looked around. He had wandered into the bog, onto the treeless flatland that became soft in the rains. *How did I get here?*

He had only a moment to ponder, and then he saw a rotting hand curling against his leg. Ivan shoved it away. His hands caught in the sludge that writhed within the decaying woman—and as he faced her, trying to free his hands, Ivan's gaze fell on the locket that hung around her neck. Its golden sheen peeked at him through weeds and mud.

And he realized why Yelena had seemed so familiar. Sonia had always carried a picture of Yelena in her locket. Ivan had only seen it once or twice.

He yanked an arm free of the corpse—but his elbow caught, and he realized that he had fallen. The cold earth had already swallowed his legs and sucked him in past his hips. He lay sprawled on his side, the bug-infested woman writhing close beside him. Ivan wailed and gagged.

"Help me!" he cried. "I didn't do anything! She fell in—I didn't push her!"

He froze then, seeing how his frantic movements were sinking him faster, how his hands had caught again in the mud. A thick branch had fallen nearby, only a yard from his head. If he moved carefully, he could reach it, could try to hoist himself up on it. Ivan wiggled his fingers, slowly releasing his hand. He stretched it toward the branch, saw thin weeds tangled in his fingers. No, not weeds, but a chain. A dirt-smeared oval hung there, bits of gold still gleaming through dark streaks.

The branch—he almost had it! It was just beyond his fingers. He stretched a little more, and a little more—and the branch receded farther, and farther, until Ivan felt the cold mud against his neck.

He stopped moving. The earth continued to swallow him up. It touched his chin, and in another minute it had touched his lips.

Some distance away, Yelena sat safely on the fallen elm. She watched as Ivan unwittingly kicked and stomped his way into the swampy earth. She saw his eyes bulge with sudden terror, listened to him scream at the ground as though it had thrown some unseen terror at him.

It took a long time for him to sink. Close to the end, Ivan managed to free one of his hands. It rose up into the air in a futile gesture, tangled with stringy weeds and something else. Yelena stood, moving closer to the tree line, and saw the muddy oval dangling from Ivan's fingers. As he disappeared beneath the surface of the bog, Yelena grasped the locket around her own neck—and she smiled.

III

Night Demon

Night Demon

"Those who dream by day are cognizant of many things which escape those who dream only by night." -Edgar Allan Poe, "Eleonora"

Jae rang his mother's doorbell with a new sense of trepidation. His mother and sister Mina had already met his fiancé, Isaiah, and welcomed him easily enough—but this would be the first introduction to Sora, who had made a rare trip from her home in New York. As Jae's oldest sister, Sora was the one with the most ammunition against him. She was a full eight years ahead, with a mischievous streak. She remembered everything since Jae's birth, including his difficulty with the move from Seoul to Minnesota (he had wet the bed for several months afterward) and all of his ridiculous childhood fears and clumsy accidents. Jae approached the family dinner with the usual anxieties of a youngest sibling: His sister would dredge up embarrassing stories from the past, or, because Sora loved weddings, she would nag them about getting married. At the moment, neither Jae nor Isaiah could even afford a ring. Moving in together was a way to start saving money— "foundation before fluff," as Isaiah liked to say. The two had just bought a condo in the suburbs and spent the last few weeks settling in. At age 24, it seemed to Jae like a good start. Most of his friends didn't have their own home, or a partner, or a savings account.

His anxiety about the family gathering proved mostly unwarranted. The five of them ate his mother's best side dishes and spicy noodles, played Catchphrase, and went back to the dining table for tea and tiramisu. Isaiah and Sora took a liking to each other and spent most of dessert in a passionate discussion about their favorite horror movies.

They had almost wrapped up the evening when it finally happened: Sora inquired about the new condo, and Isaiah responded with: "We love it. It's small, but it's cozy, and there haven't been any problems with it. The neighbors seem nice, too. Aside from Jae's nightmares, everything has been great."

Jae's mother and sisters looked at him questioningly.

Isaiah gave him a repentant look. "Oh. They don't know about it?"

"About what?" Jae's mother asked.

"It's no big deal," Jae said. "I've been having these weird experiences where . . . I'm waking up, and it feels like something is attacking me, and I can't move."

"It's a night demon!" Mina exclaimed.

"Well, it's not really at night. It happens in the morning."

"Right, when you're trying to wake up," Sora said with a knowing smirk. She sat at the head of the table, dressed in a "casual rebel" style that left Jae anticipating some impish prank or other embarrassment. Her T-shirt, visible under the leather jacket she'd worn all evening, even had the word "rebel" scrawled in black across the front—too young a style for a thirty-two-year-old, Jae thought, but that had always been Sora's way. "You know," she continued, "when you're asleep, your brain sends out neurotransmitters that paralyze your body so you don't act out your dreams. Sometimes it's still paralyzed while you're waking up."

"Maybe, but it's not just paralysis. It's a nightmare. Sometimes I can see the thing that's attacking me, and it has this giant, horrifying wasp head. And it feels like it's showering me with rage."

"That's not a nightmare," Mina said.

"It *is* just a nightmare," Jae countered, "obviously. But I'm not sure why I keep dreaming about a giant wasp thing that wants to obliterate me with hatred."

Sora laughed. "Sorry, but it's probably our fault. Remember when I made you watch that documentary about parasitic wasps?"

Jae tried to recall. He remembered a multitude of nature shows he'd watched with his sisters, but none that featured wasps. "What documentary?"

"It was about the different kinds of parasitic wasps. They lay their eggs inside other bugs, and the host slowly dies as the larva eats it from the inside. They showed a wasp injecting a spider with one of its eggs, and you were so horrified, you started to cry."

Jae's mother winced. "Please, not while we're eating."

"Fine. But you were afraid of wasps for a long time after that. And then there was the thing that we did to you—me and Mina, with the Halloween costumes."

"Yeah, let's not get into that," Jae said. "I've been portraying both of you as decent humans, so . . . ."

Isaiah raised an eyebrow at him. "What thing with the Halloween costumes?"

Jae shook his head. "Nothing. Just my sisters being evil."

"We put on our monster costumes and snuck up on Jae while he was sleeping," Mina said. "I was next to him, and Sora climbed on the bed and sat on him. He woke up and started screaming."

"We traumatized him," Sora added. "I'm sure that's what's causing your nightmares now."

"It's *gawi nulim*," Mina said. "A night demon. Even people who didn't watch movies about wasps, and people whose sisters didn't sit on them, have that experience. You see it when you're half-asleep because that's when you're the most vulnerable. It sits on your chest and tries to suck the energy out of you."

"It's just fear," Sora insisted. "It's called sleep paralysis. Jae, it only happens when you're lying on your back, right?"

He thought it over. "Yeah."

"Don't sleep on your back, then. Problem solved."

On the trip home, Isaiah drove his Subaru while Jae stole glances at him from the passenger seat. Jae preferred that arrangement. Isaiah always looked good behind the wheel of the car. Something about his posture, and the way he wore his hair swept back from his face, was reminiscent of James Dean. "Well, that was an interesting theory put forth by Sora," Isaiah said. "Don't you think that explains your nightmares? Or, your early-morning-mares, or whatever you would call them."

"I guess so. The costume thing was actually worse than she made it sound."

"How so?"

"She recorded it and posted the video on MySpace," Jae said. "A video of me waking up to monsters and having a meltdown."

"Ouch. How old were you?"

"Seven. They weren't always the best sisters."

"You don't say."

Isaiah went to bed early, having to wake at four-thirty for his morning commute. Jae's schedule was comparatively lax. He'd landed a position as an office coordinator at a local crisis center and arranged a six-day work week, ending his shifts at two o'clock. It gave him enough time to get home, exercise, shower, relax, and make dinner—a perfect setup for him. Isaiah had never learned to cook, but food was one of Jae's passions. As he lay in bed that night, snuggling under Isaiah's soft fleece bedspread, he thought of his good fortune with contentedness and gratitude. The queen-sized foam mattress felt like bliss. Jae had never had such a bed; he'd always slept on a cheap twin mattress, except in college, when he spent his nights on a foam ball-filled sack.

Just before he fell asleep, though, a feeling of unease nagged at him. Jae shifted quietly in the bed so that he was lying on his side.

When morning came, he woke before his alarm went off. Jae turned over to find Isaiah already gone. And then he realized: the night demon thing had not returned. Perhaps Sora was right, and he simply needed to try lying on his side for a while.

Jae's feeling of satisfaction lingered as he went through his morning routine. After he dressed, he went to the kitchen and pulled a pack of English muffins and a carton of eggs from the fridge.

As he turned around, something caught his eye across the room: a dark shadow where there shouldn't have been one. He looked up and froze; his breath came to a sudden stop.

In the entryway corner, hovering in mid-air, was a dark mist, a shadow formed in the shape of a woman—or at least, what *seemed* to be a woman, clad in a long black dress. Jae looked at her face and saw, instead of a human face, a terrifying yellow-and-black wasp head staring back at him.

A sudden crash made him jump. He looked down at his feet. The egg carton had fallen there, some of its contents now cracked and seeping onto the floor. Jae looked up again, but the specter had vanished.

He swore and stepped over the mess, peeking around the kitchen island at the empty entryway. "Okay . . . just my imagination. My nightmare still hanging around in . . . my . . . ." He fumbled for self-assurance. "Sleep paralysis, my ass," he muttered.

Jae decided to grab breakfast at the local coffee shop instead. As he hurried to get his jacket and shoes, he cast countless anxious glances at the corner, torn between convincing himself that he'd merely been hallucinating and that he was too mentally sound for hallucinations.

The rest of the day played out as usual: the crisis center was moving to another building, and Jae was responsible for managing much of the transition. His days of late had been consumed by inventories, work orders, and organizing teams to pack and move supplies, rather than the usual correspondences with clients, therapists, and social workers.

At home, he took time to decompress. He brought his oil paints to the kitchen and put some finishing touches on a canvas he'd been working on, a portrait of a friend's two-year-old son. As he worked, his gaze kept shifting to the entryway corner. Jae did the same during his half hour on the elliptical; he couldn't keep his eyes from the space where the specter had appeared. Even when he wasn't looking at it, his eyes darted around the room, just in case the thing showed up somewhere else.

After showering, he began to prepare dinner. Jae took out the gnocchi dumplings to thaw, and then dug through the cupboard with a frown. "I swear we had cashews," he muttered. "Wasp bitch, I hope you're not stealing our food, too."

He checked the clock: only four-forty. He had had just enough time to jog to the corner store. Jae stepped outside and locked the door, and stopped with his keys halfway into his pocket.

In the hall, just four doors down, stood a woman in a Victorian-style black and gold dress. Over her face she wore a likeness of the image that Jae had seen in his morning terror: a black visage with gold embellishments, with two long, thin horns protruding at the side like black antennae—and at the bottom, two jutting appendages that looked like the mandibles of a wasp.

"Hey," Jae called.

The woman didn't acknowledge him, but started away.

"Hey!" Jae hurried after her.

She paused, glancing back at him.

"Excuse me." Jae slowed as he caught up with the figure. "Do you live here?"

"Yes," she said.

"Were you in my apartment this morning?"

The woman stared at him. Jae could see her eyes through the mask holes, but her expression was unreadable. "What?" she asked.

Jae heard the sound of a door closing behind him, then the sliding sound of the lock. He turned to see a man, also masked and sporting a gaudy red tuxedo.

"No, I wasn't in your apartment," the woman said. "Why?"

The man sauntered towards them, stopping beside Jae. "Is there a problem?"

Although Jae was keenly aware that he was the normal-looking one in the group, he felt suddenly freakish. His sense of urgency gave way to embarrassment. "No. I'm sorry. It's just . . . ." He hesitated, trying to avoid some outrageous claim like *An insect-faced person has been sneaking into my room and sitting on me* or *A wasp-faced woman was levitating in my condo today.* "I saw someone with a creepy-looking mask hovering around my door this morning, and I can't figure out who it was," he finished.

The couple exchanged glances. "It wasn't us," the man said shortly, and took his companion's arm. "Let's go."

Jae felt his face flushing. "Yeah. I didn't think so. Sorry. It just kinda creeped me out." He was still making awkward apologies as the couple disappeared around the corner, into the elevator lobby.

"Jackass," he whispered, chastising himself.

A voice spoke up nearby: "You live at the end here, don't you?"

He turned. A man stood in the doorway just behind him—an older man of stocky build, with glossy black hair gathered into a thin ponytail. Jae recognized him from brief encounters in the hallway, but had never spoken to him aside from the passing courtesies of neighbors: *Hello, how're you doing, I'm good, thanks.*

The man stepped out into the hall, letting the door close behind him. He pointed toward Jae's place. "You live in the end unit?"

"Yeah."

"Well, that woman wasn't in your apartment. That's Lizzie and Alan. They're dressed up for the masquerade ball. It's a fundraiser they have every year at the government plaza."

"Oh," Jae said. "Yeah, I didn't figure they were snooping in my apartment. It's just . . . some weird things have been happening since I moved in."

The man laughed—a short, nervous laugh. He ducked his head and murmured, "Yeah. Your place is haunted."

Jae studied his face, trying to discern whether he was joking. An embarrassed smile lingered there, but as the man looked up sheepishly, Jae realized he was serious.

"Is that what people say?" Jae asked.

"Well . . . no. The people who lived there before said it. No one talks about it now, but something bad happened there."

"Like what?"

"A woman who lived there . . . she hanged herself. People treated her badly. Kids used to hang around here and call her a witch, and harass her, and do all sorts of things. A lot of these other neighbors are new, but I was living here back then. People used to smear feces on her doorknob, and write all over the door and windows, and put things on her car and in her mail slot—dead animals, garbage, things like that. They even threw things at her when she went out at night, so she was afraid to go outside. Once I found her crying because the kids threw a sack of feces at her, and it exploded all over her face and down the front of her shirt, and all over her car. She was crying so hard, she couldn't even walk inside to clean up. She was just sitting there in the parking lot."

Jae was stunned into silence.

"Afterwards, those families moved away," the man continued. "I think they didn't want people to know that their kids were the ones who did that."

"Wait . . . so, people knew who was doing it?"

"After she died, some talk went around about who did those things. People didn't care while she was alive, but after she died, I think some people felt bad. Well, not everyone. Some were just afraid that their kids would get in trouble. One of the local reporters published an article about it. The woman who lived here had been reporting those things to the police for almost three years. She called them more than two hundred times."

Jae felt another shock run through him, a jolt of astonished pain.

"The last couple who lived here didn't stay long," the man continued. "They mentioned that some weird stuff was happening in their place. I offered to call a shaman for them, but they don't believe in that kind of thing."

Jae stiffened, heard a warning echo somewhere in the back of his mind. "A shaman?"

"Yeah. A Native American shaman. They weren't interested."

"Native American, like, Dakota, or Ojibwe?"

"No, South American. The shaman I know is from Peru." He gave Jae a small, embarrassed smile. "Want me to call him? He'll come by free of charge. If you want him to do some work, though, there's a fee."

"Um . . . no thanks."

He nodded. "Most people say that. Let me know if you change your mind." The man began to turn away.

"Wait," Jae said. "Sorry, I didn't get your name."

"Walter. Walter Miller." He extended his hand; Jae shook it. "I'm Jae."

"Well, like I said, let me know if you need help. Good luck."

Jae returned home in time to finish dinner and set the table. Isaiah came home, kissed him, and chatted about his day—but Jae responded with distracted murmurs. Fixed in his mind was the image of a woman slumped in the parking lot, crying through a layer of shit. He stared at his plate during dinner, absentmindedly scooping up his food.

"What's on your mind?" Isaiah asked. "Did something happen?"

"Oh . . . ." Jae paused, debating whether to tell Isaiah about the tragedy that had occurred in their perfect little home. "I met one of the neighbors today. Walter. The guy who lives on our floor, the one with the ponytail."

"Finally. I feel like the neighbors haven't been very social."

"He told me our condo is haunted," Jae said. "He offered to bring a shaman by, to do an exorcism."

Isaiah scoffed and rolled his eyes. "Wow. Of course we meet the scammers first. Let's pass. I'd rather not host a heebie-jeebie show in our home."

Jae pondered those words. He had mixed feelings about the idea of shamanism. He had been raised to scorn such things, yet he retained memories from his youth that bore an intimate relationship with the supernatural. "My aunt Yeon-soo was a shaman," he told Isaiah. "She actually died because of it. Right before we moved here, she was beaten to death by someone who accused her of fraud. I don't know the details, but it had something to do with an inheritance. Some guy had a bunch of money, and he cut one of his relatives out of his will based on something my aunt said. I think she accused the guy of murder. Like . . . she claimed to have contacted the spirit of the murdered person, and it led to the will being changed. Anyway, the relative came around with his goons, and they told her to retract everything she'd said and admit she was a fraud. She wouldn't do it, so they beat her up. They might not have meant to kill her, but they beat her badly enough that she died."

Isaiah had stopped in mid-chew, and listened with wide eyes. He gulped his food down and choked: "Holy shit."

"I think that's part of the reason we left Korea. Like . . . my mom just wanted to get as far away from all of that as possible. She had my dad's life insurance money, and she got a little something from her sister, and she used it to move here."

"Wow. Sorry. Do you remember your aunt?"

Jae thought back, saw flashes of his aunt in his mind: her weathered face, warm smile, even the feel of her embrace. The bold splashes of color from her ceremonial dress. A concerned face leaning over him in the twilight. "Not really. I remember that I was really sick before she died, and she took care of me."

"Do you think she was a fraud?"

Jae reached into the past, seeking memories. Though he found nothing of substantial detail, he remembered the feeling of being protected and loved. "I honestly don't know," he said.

Jae woke to the sensation of extra weight in his body—not just a pressure in his chest, as people had described in the slew of online articles he'd read about "night demons," but a sluggish dead weight from head to toe. Even his brain felt as if it was suppressed by a heavy, wet blanket.

He realized with a twinge of dread that he was lying on his back. Jae struggled to open his eyes, and there it was: the gauzy shadow of an insect face, vague but distinguishable, only inches from his own face, looking back at him with dark eyes that gleamed anger and spite.

Jae could hear Isaiah making breakfast in the kitchen. He tried in vain to call out, but found his mouth and throat paralyzed—so he simply braced himself for the onslaught. The creature's rage coursed through his body in a wave, and then another. The entity sent its hatred again and again, all the while staring at him with those dark, featureless eyes.

Typically, Jae felt like the thing was trying its damnedest to destroy him. This morning, he noted, the effort seemed to have weakened. And he detected something new: along with the waves of anger lurked a potent strain of sadness.

He reacted in the usual way: *Hate all you want. I'm not going to let it affect me.*

Yet, it did affect him. Half a minute went by, maybe more, and the paralysis faded along with the sinister face. Jae heaved himself out of bed and went to the bathroom, pausing to place a hand over his heart. The last encounter had left him with worrisome heart palpitations; they had ceased after a few minutes, but today they lingered. Not until after Jae had showered and dressed, after breakfast with Isaiah, and long after Isaiah left to get a haircut and new tires for the Subaru, did the palpitations quit—but the fatigue remained. Jae muttered under his breath at the wasp-lady thing as he went about the task of arranging picture frames in the living room. He and Isaiah had mounted a large mirror behind the sofa, and Jae's final task was to hang the matching frames: dark gold with antiquing, two frames to border each side of the mirror.

He finished marking the wall in pencil and hammered in the first nail. As Jae stood on the sofa with frame in hand, trying to slide the mount over the head of the nail, an image in the mirror caught his eye: a figure dressed in black, almost human, but with large, dark eyes like those of an insect. It hovered just behind him, its thin-lipped mouth hanging slightly open.

He jumped; the frame slipped from his hand. Jae heard it crashing behind the sofa. By the time he had regained his balance and was back on the safe solidity of the floor, the image had vanished.

Jae swore again and pulled the couch away from the wall. The frame had broken in two.

"Bitch," he said out loud. "We can't order these frames anymore. These are, like, forty years old. They belonged to Isaiah's grandma." He looked up angrily, though he wasn't sure where to direct his anger. "That was really damn tropey, by the way— appearing in the mirror like that. Do you really have to do shit like that? What's the point? Messing up our picture frames, and scaring the crap out of me, isn't going to fix your problems."

Jae muttered as he went to the hall closet. He dug around for the super glue, found an unused tube, and retreated to the kitchen table to attempt the repair. "I don't know if I can get a glass pane in this size, either," he said as he lined up the pieces. "I might have to get it specially cut. Thanks, wasp bitch."

Jae set the frame section down to dry. Then he slipped on his shoes and went quietly into the hall. He went to Walter's place and knocked.

The door opened. Walter stood there with a bowl of cereal, his long, thin hair in disarray. "Morning," he said.

"Hi," Jae greeted him. "Walter, right?"

"Yeah." Walter leaned into the hallway, glancing down the hall toward Jae's condo. "How are things?"

Jae hesitated.

"She's still coming after you?" Walter asked.

"Yes," Jae admitted. "How can I get ahold of your shaman friend?"

Walter beckoned him inside. "Come in. I'll call him."

Jae took the following Monday off from work. The shaman had claimed that such a case would likely take several hours, perhaps even days of ritual. He would have to deal not only with the deceased woman's negative energy, but with other residue that surely lingered in such an old building. Jae had instant misgivings about the arrangement. *He's trying to wring a few days' pay out of me*, he thought. He decided to invite the man for just one day, to see how things panned out.

When the shaman asked for fifty dollars and lunch as payment, Jae was surprised. He'd expected a higher fee. He supposed the man wanted an extravagant lunch, but the man only said: "I'll eat whatever you have. I'm not picky."

The details were decided over the phone. When Sergio Mejia showed up at the door with a small leather suitcase, Jae resisted the urge to look at him with dismay. The man was small and skinny, so slight that he looked like he could be knocked over by the flick of a finger. And he was old—or what Jae considered old, with gray-peppered hair and a deeply lined face. Jae had already worried that

Sergio was little more than a showman. His father, according to Walter, was a lifelong shaman who had conducted healing ceremonies for tourists in Peru; he started traveling to the U.S. at the invitation of wealthy Americans who wanted ceremonies at home, and eventually settled in the southwest. Sergio became an apprentice at a young age, serving the same crowds of elite self-seekers.

Walter also showed up—more out of curiosity than anything, Jae assumed. He poked his head into all the rooms of the condo before settling down on the living room windowsill. The sill quickly became Walter's favorite spot. He spent most of the day sitting there, chewing on a toothpick from the box he'd brought with him.

As Sergio unpacked his case in the middle of the living room, Jae went to stand beside Walter. He felt safer there, he supposed, with someone who was doing something normal. "What's with the toothpick?" he asked.

Walter chuckled. He shifted the pick to the corner of his mouth. "Nervous habit. I used to smoke when I was nervous, but I had to quit." He tapped his chest. "Heart problems."

They watched as Sergio finished setting up the altar. The shaman laid out a patterned cloth, a pale beige sheet with repeating geometric designs. With slow delicacy he lifted the other items from the case: a few large seashells, wooden figurines, dried leaves and sticks, a small wooden cup, a plastic bottle half-filled with dark liquid. Jae felt a growing unease as he looked at the wooden figures, at the crudely carved faces and cryptic symbols. He wondered, then, if he had invited danger into his home.

The shaman seated himself on the floor. He placed a bundle of dried sage leaves into one of the large shells and poured some of the liquid into the wooden cup. Jae heard the flicking of a lighter. A thin stream of smoke rose from the shell.

Sergio turned to Walter. "What's the woman's name?"

"Klara. Klara Klauster."

The shaman nodded and stood up, cradling the shell in his hand. "Where is the toilet?"

Jae pointed the way to the bathroom. Sergio nodded, but didn't go inside. Instead he began to walk the perimeter of the living room, carrying the sage and a fistful of long-leafed plants that he thrashed rhythmically in the air. It produced a sound like wings beating—a soft, simple sound that calmed Jae's nerves. The shaman sang as he went, stopping every few feet, his voice rising and falling in a simple melody.

Sergio did the same in the bathroom. Jae peeked in to the strange sight of the shaman leaning over the toilet, pausing his song to blow sage smoke into the ceramic bowl.

Jae crept to Walter and whispered: "Is he blessing the toilet?"

Walter chuckled and didn't answer.

Sergio returned and sat on the floor. He picked up the wooden cup, slowly tipping it to his mouth.

Jae leaned close to Walter. "What's he drinking?" he whispered.

"Tea," Walter replied.

Every now and then, Sergio sang, sometimes shaking the dried leaves in accompaniment. Again, Jae felt a strange, deep sense of comfort as he listened. Though he couldn't understand a word that was said, and the tunes were simple, he found them inexplicably beautiful.

A sudden sweat broke out on Sergio's forehead. His face flushed. The shaman put the leaves down and stood up, walking quickly to the bathroom.

Through the closed door came the sound of violent gagging and vomiting, and after it subsided, the splash of diarrhea. Jae looked at Walter, wide-eyed, but Walter only shrugged. He sat in a chair near the windows, chewing on his toothpick—looking very chill, Jae thought, under the circumstances.

Sergio came out of the bathroom, pale and weary.

"Are you all right?" Jae asked.

The shaman nodded. He sat and closed his eyes again.

And so it began: the cycle of sitting, singing, and hurrying to the bathroom. After the third trip to the toilet, Sergio gave Walter a mildly incredulous look. "She's a tough one," he said. "She doesn't want to let go."

"Of what?" Jae asked.

"Her anger. What she went through." Sergio winced as he sat at the altar. He picked up the lighter and began to re-light the sage. "When someone lives for a long time with that kind of pain, they start to define themselves by it. If you interfere, they don't think you're trying to help them heal. They think you're trying to destroy them." He leaned forward, blowing gently as the sage leaves began to send up streams of smoke. "This woman went through a lot. There were too many people who were cruel to her, or who ignored the cruelty. She wants people to suffer the way she suffered, so they know what it's like."

"Great," Jae said.

Sergio gave him a cryptic look. "Don't forget, she can hear everything you say. I'm not just telling you what's happening. I'm trying to tell her, too."

The ritual went on. After a couple of hours, Jae became restless. He went to the bedroom and lay on the bed, listening to music on his mp3 player and trying to read *Shambala: The Sacred Path of the Warrior* to calm his nerves. The room seemed unusually humid, and the open windows hadn't prevented the place from filling with sage smoke. Isaiah wouldn't like that. He hated any kind of incense.

Two o'clock came and went. Jae was thinking up polite ways to get rid of the two men when he realized that Sergio had finished. The shaman knelt on the floor, looking ashen as he picked up the altar items. He folded the cloth and set it in the case on top of everything else.

"She's going to need some more help," he said, standing up to face Jae. "You can call me in a few days. Not before that. I need time to re-energize." He looked toward the kitchen and added: "What's for lunch?"

Jae hurried to set out the food he'd prepared. He hadn't put much thought or effort into it, but Sergio seemed pleased. He dined on chopped fruit while Jae spooned chicken salad onto a slice of bread. Jae set the sandwich in front of him, and Sergio nodded with a quiet "Thank you."

Jae served Walter, too, and then sat across from them and tried not to ask questions. Sergio was engrossed in eating, as if the task required all of his focus and effort. Walter kept his gaze on his food and ate silently.

When the meal was finished, Sergio picked up his case again. He gave Jae a weak wave and said, "Good luck."

Jae cleaned the toilet and tried in vain to air out the living room. When Isaiah arrived a couple hours later, he frowned and inhaled sharply. "Honey, why does our home smell like a hippie church?"

"Sorry," Jae said. "I forgot how much you hate incense. I didn't think of it until it was too late."

Isaiah sniffed again as he slipped his jacket off. "What is it?"

"Sage."

"Where did you get sage?"

Jae tried to think of an answer that wasn't a lie. "From Walter, our neighbor . . . and his shaman friend, Sergio. I invited them over, and Sergio lit some sage to scare away the bad energy, or something."

Isaiah raised an eyebrow. "Wow. You did the heebie-jeebie show after all." He leaned over, tucking his lunch box into the entryway closet. "So . . . you and Walter are getting to know each other?"

"He doesn't talk about himself much. All I got out of him is that he works the night shift as a 'maintenance technician,' whatever that is."

"We should invite him over for dinner. I miss socializing with my old neighbors; I feel like that part of my life is missing now. Do you think Walter would accept a dinner invitation?"

"Sure," Jae replied, trying to veil his unease. He wasn't sure he wanted Isaiah and Walter to sit down for a conversation.

"Is he weird?" Isaiah asked.

"Not really."

"What about his shaman friend? Did he seem like a flake?"

"No," Jae said—but although he said *no*, the question began to nag at him. Was Sergio a phony? Jae himself did not believe in magic and exorcisms. His mother had a special disdain for the paranormal, and had raised him to be an utmost skeptic—and yet, he had begun to believe that his home was inhabited by a spirit.

He began to doubt that, too. By the time he tucked himself beneath Isaiah's soft fleece bedspread, Jae had convinced himself that Sergio had, indeed, put on a farce. He had consumed some kind of mildly toxic tea with purgative qualities, and the rest was pure show.

And then morning came, and Jae's conviction vanished beneath the oppressive weight of an outraged, insect-faced demon. His lungs felt crushed, and throughout his body a wave of anger coursed. He blinked his eyes, and there was the flash of an angry face—a woman's face rather than an insect's, and not as vivid as before, but perceptible enough to terrify him. Jae closed his eyes to shut the image out. When he opened them again, the specter was gone. The rage also seemed to dwindle, and in its place he felt a surge of grief. It washed over him, seemingly from head to toe, and then up toward his head again. He found himself lamenting a tragedy that he had never witnessed. And he realized: it was *her* grief. The mystery woman had returned. Instead of unleashing her anger, she was showing him her sorrow.

Jae tried again to move. His arms jerked a little, and with some difficulty he pushed himself into a sitting position. "A few days," he whispered to himself. "A few days is only three days. I can make it until then."

Walter had told him the woman's name. Jae decided to look her up online. Even if he could find nothing else, he knew that someone had taken pains to report the details of the crimes against her. As he opened the web browser, Jae heeded Sergio's words: *Don't forget, she can hear everything you say.*

"All right, Klara Klauster," he said aloud, "Let's see who you are."

A search turned up a few news stories about Klara's abysmal fate. Jae switched to an image search and found a low-resolution photo of her, a traditional head-on portrait that looked like a driver's license photo.

As soon as he saw her, he wanted to paint her.

Klara had a severe but elegant face, with thick, dark eyebrows and startlingly large eyes, and highly defined cheekbones. Her nose was slightly hooked, and her hair was dark and short. "Wow," Jae murmured as he gazed at the photo. "You're unique-looking. I mean that as a compliment," he added quickly. "In fact, I would really like to paint you. I think you're stunning."

He hurried to find a blank canvas and chose one of several eleven-by-fourteens. On its surface he began to scrawl a light pencil sketch: the face first, and then a vague outline of the shoulders. He would have to paint her in different clothing. Her dark button-down shirt made her look pale and drab.

Jae initially thought that a Victorian dress would suit her for an oil portrait, and he began searching the internet for a model of Klara's body, but none of the dresses looked right. They were high-necked, stifling, and somehow didn't suit her black eyebrows and pale face. Jae tapped his fingers lightly on the keyboard as he considered other options.

"You look like an Adora Belle," he said at last. He did another search and found a red velvet dress that would suit Klara much better: a red dress with black trim.

As he worked, Jae quietly pondered his sisters' debate. Was the so-called "night demon" really some reflection of his own psyche? It didn't seem possible. Whenever Jae woke to the sight of the entity, its rage felt alien to him. It spoke clearly of a difficult existence, of hardships and unfairness and a gradually building anger against all that had happened in the course of its being. To believe that the entity was Klara Klauster—that was the most sensible explanation, though it remained both supernatural and unproven.

"I'm going to paint you looking radiant and happy," Jae said out loud, working over the details of her face. "Smiling mouth, radiant eyes, because that's what you should have had instead of shit and misery. Not a big, fake smile, but a genuine one." He commenced sketching, and continued to muse aloud. "People don't learn through revenge, so I'm not going to get revenge on you for scaring the living shit out of me every morning, or for giving me heart palpitations that I can't afford to see a doctor about. People learn through relationships. So, since we're both here, let's hang out together like this. And I will see your beauty, and I will showcase it." Jae paused, and added, "And if you insist on being a hateful hag, then, screw you."

The following day, he came home from work and had a snack of dinner leftovers. He placed a small dish across from him on the kitchen table, announcing out loud: "Klara, I know you can't eat, but I've heard that spirits are drawn to smells and food. Practically every religion says so. My Dakota friends do food offerings, and I really don't understand that much about it, but since I'm eating, you're welcome to have this food offering and eat with me." He leaned back and placed his feet on one of the empty chairs, adding: "It's yangnyeom cauliflower. I hope you like spicy food. If you don't, you can find a nice way of telling me, instead of crushing my chest and pummeling me with waves of hate."

Jae ate the snack without incident. No specter appeared, and the dish across from him simply went cold. After a while, he reached across the table and grabbed it. "I'm assuming you're either done or not interested. And since I don't know what to do with the leftovers, I'm just going to eat them."

Perhaps he offended Klara in some way. Maybe she didn't like spicy food, or was frustrated by her inability to eat, or was angry that Jae ate the food he had offered her—or maybe she was still just outraged at her own fate. Whatever the reason, the black-clad entity appeared on his chest the next morning, its dark eyes full of anger and despair, a silent blast of bitterness emanating from its mouth.

Jae closed his eyes and tried to will the ugly feelings away. After a minute, he sat up with an annoyed sigh. "Give it a rest already, Klara," he said, slowly swinging his feet over the side of the bed. "I know you went through something really awful, but you can't pull out your self-pity card and use it as an excuse to terrorize people. I'm sure the people who harassed you had their excuses, too. Other kids bullied them, their parents didn't care about them, and blah, blah, blah. The way you're acting, you're no different."

He stood up and went to the shower, eager to wash away the residue of her misery.

Sergio and Walter returned the next day. Jae had only been able to take a half-day off, so the shaman arrived at noon. He sat up his altar in the same spot on the living room floor and did his cleansing routine with the sage and leaves.

"It's a little bit lighter in here," Sergio said as he sat down at the altar. He reached for the bottle of dark gray-green liquid and tipped it, letting it trickle into the wooden cup.

"I've been trying to appease her," Jae said.

"Oh, yeah? How so?"

"Well . . . I talk to her, and I gave her some food offerings. Things like that."

Walter let out a short burst of laughter. The shaman gave Jae a perplexed look, and then he lowered his head and chuckled. "Well, we're laughing, but it's true that her anger isn't as strong. I can feel it already. There's some other feeling, like . . . curiosity, or like waiting. She wants to know what you'll do next."

Sergio faced the altar. He sang softly to himself while a thin stream of smoke rose from the slowly burning sage, and then he picked up the wooden cup and drank.

The room went silent. Jae waited until Sergio stood up, and then asked: "What's in the cup?"

"Cactus juice," Sergio replied. "Not a local type. They're from Peru. I grow them at home."

"What does it do? Does it give you visions?"

Sergio was quiet for a moment. "Not exactly. It opens you up. When you look around, you can see things more clearly. You can look at a person and see their thoughts and feelings. You can see what you're supposed to do next. You can see residue left behind from other people, and if it's strong enough, and if you're receptive, you can even feel it."

"Could I drink it, too?" Jae asked.

Sergio stared at him.

"Well, you said that when you have ceremonies with other people, everyone drinks," Jae reasoned.

The shaman lowered his head. He gazed for some time at the wooden cup. "Usually I would say no," he replied. "You're supposed to prepare beforehand. But it's telling me I should say yes." He lifted his head, looking intently into Jae's eyes. "What have you eaten today?"

He proceeded to ask a series of questions, mostly involving Jae's diet and overall health. Then he gestured for Jae to sit at the altar. "Don't drink until I tell you to. And try not to spit it up. It doesn't taste good."

Jae already suspected as much. He'd caught a whiff of the foul, pungent liquid as Sergio poured it into the cup.

Sergio knelt behind him. As the shaman sang, he whacked Jae's shoulders with the bundle of dried leaves and doused him with sage smoke. Then he quietly moved to sit beside him. "Drink," he said.

Only a small amount had been poured, so Jae knocked it back and swallowed. It left a gritty trace on his tongue and tasted mildly repellent—but then the aftertaste hit like the explosion of a foul cloud in his mouth, and he gagged.

"Rinse your mouth with water," Sergio suggested, "but don't swallow it."

Jae hurried to the kitchen. When he returned, he found Sergio still sitting at the altar, humming with his eyes closed. Jae sat on the floor nearby and waited.

Abruptly, Sergio opened his eyes. "You've been to this type of ceremony before?" he asked.

"No," Jae replied.

Sergio scrutinized him, and then gave a small shrug. "Well, like I said, this medicine doesn't necessarily create visions, but it shows you things. When we're awake, our senses limit themselves in order to deal with ordinary tasks. But this type of work is done in an altered state. It's like dreaming. Dreaming is the most basic altered state; it helps us deal with the world in ways that don't have to make sense. That's why you could see the specter when you were partially asleep, even though it didn't make sense for it to be there. Shamans train themselves to dream by day." He paused, peering again at Jae, and added: "You lean closer to a shamanic state than most people. You're . . . open, somehow. That's probably why Klara appeared to you, and not to your boyfriend."

Jae felt a pang of unease. He didn't want to be "open" in such a way—not to random ghouls and specters.

As if guessing his thoughts, Sergio added: "You will be able to feel the impressions that Klara left behind, and there's some other residue left here, too. I purged some of it, but there's a lot." He reached into his case and pulled out a smooth gray rock. "Shamans sometimes use stones to absorb the negative energy of a place. Then they bury the stone so that the earth can change the energy into something else. It's like using shit as fertilizer." Sergio grinned wryly. "But using yourself is more personal. Shamans have ways of protecting themselves from negative energy, but we can still absorb it. If there's a spirit still lingering around, it sometimes helps them when we're willing to see their pain and share it with them. We show them that it's possible to shed that pain, to process it and purge it."

"But . . . I'm not a shaman," Jae reminded him. "How am I supposed to protect myself?"

"At this point, I don't think you'll need to. Klara has already forced the worst of her energy on you. Now, you can show her that she can heal—and that you're going to help her."

Jae turned to look at Walter, who sat in his usual spot on the windowsill. Walter flashed a grin at him. "It can take a while to kick in," he said. "Takes a while to wear off, too."

"Like, how long?"

Sergio answered: "For the amount I gave you, not too long. Five hours, maybe."

"Five hours?"

Walter smiled again, guessing Jae's thoughts. "You might still be in it when your boyfriend gets home."

"Well, how exactly will I . . . ." Jae trailed off as a figure outside the window caught his attention: a distant cloud formed in the shape of a wasp head, sharply detailed, with two dark pockets for the eyes and trailing wisps for antennae. As the cloud began to drift out of sight, Jae stood and went to the window, watching as the form began to mutate. It joined with another cloud to form an elongated body, complete with a stinger at the end. No, not a stinger, Jae realized; it was an ovipositor, ready to parasitize and drain the life from whatever creature it chose as its prey.

"Doesn't that cloud look like a wasp?" Jae asked, as Walter turned to see what he was looking at.

"Which one?" Walter asked.

"That one. Look . . . it's attacking another cloud."

Sergio came to stand beside him. "Well," he said, "It's starting quickly for you."

"You see it, though, don't you?" Jae pointed at the drifting mass as it descended on another insect-shaped cloud—a beetle, perhaps, or a fly. The ovipositor penetrated the other cloud, and the fly shape began to contort; the wings separated and floated away, and the body swelled until the face caved in and the one dark eye burst into a fading wisp. The transformation struck Jae with a sudden, deep sadness, a sense of disillusionment and futility.

The event seemed proof of a harsh reality, of a world filled with self-serving violence, with creatures who energized themselves by attacking and destroying other lives. The emotional heaviness of that message crept into Jae's being, pressed on him until his shoulders drooped and his eyes ached—and he realized that he was starting to cry.

The harshness wasn't just outside. It was a reflection of things that had happened in this room: ugly, hurtful things. The residue of those events seeped into Jae like trails of smoke. He could see and hear them, somehow, manifesting in his mind as though they were his own memories: angry words, harsh blows, anguished sobs, petty and spiteful conniving.

The wasp cloud drifted out of view, but Jae could see others like it: a whole sky, an entire universe of parasites.

He turned away from the window, but there was no escaping it. The living room, despite being full of things that belonged to him and Isaiah, seemed coated with the grime of past tragedies. Jae became the magnet for its energy. It filled him up, whispered its despair and disillusionment until he felt sick to his stomach.

Jae headed for the bathroom.

Purging such energy wasn't as simple as Sergio made it seem. First, there was the battle. Jae stood in front of the mirror, staring at his own reflection, seeing the stark misery in his eyes and listening to the harsh voices in his head: *You are weak. You are stupid. You drank this medicine not knowing what it was, and now that you've seen what's behind it, you can't handle it. You want to get rid of it because you're afraid. Rather than act like a coward, you should just die.*

He closed his eyes for a moment, then opened them and faced himself again. Somewhere in all that negativity, there remained a strain of hope, a hope that lived in his own soul. Jae trained his inner voice on that note: *It's not just ugliness that transpired here. Beautiful things have happened, too. They are worth living for, worth working for. I don't have to hang onto this ugliness. I can wash it away, like Sergio said.*

With trembling arms, he vomited into the sink.

Jae felt the ugliness leaving him, just as though it had manifested into a tangible mass and collected in his stomach. Jae washed it down the sink. He grabbed a wad of toilet paper and scrubbed out the remaining traces, and flushed the wad down the toilet.

Then, he felt relief; he felt peace. The vanity mirror reflected weariness at him, but it was the weariness of exerted strength.

The afternoon continued in a similar cycle, with the impressions of misery becoming increasingly clear. Jae would feel himself absorbing despairing and hateful thoughts for twenty minutes or so, and then release them in another trip to the bathroom. Each time, he became more aware of the impermanence of those impressions. As he meditated on them, and countered them with his own thoughts, they lost their power. And with each round, the energy became more focused on one particular figure.

Klara Klauster had been a perfect target for bullies. Life had already made her quiet, sad, and alone, and she'd settled for survival rather than the pursuit of her dreams. She had stood in this same spot and looked into a mirror, had seen her own misery staring back at her and felt utterly defeated. *This world is horrible and cruel. People lift themselves up by stepping on me. I can't even make a haven from it in my own home; the world follows me and flings its hatred. I don't want to be a part of it anymore.*

Jae gripped the sides of the basin and shivered as Klara's grief welled up inside him. He listened to the sounds of his own ragged breath and saw the spattering of his tears against the white porcelain, and when he'd seen enough of that grief, when he felt that he had faced it and understood it, he lurched forward and purged it down the drain.

Walter was quiet throughout the afternoon and didn't stray far from the window, while Sergio kept busy with his rituals. The shaman occasionally washed Jae in sage smoke and beat his shoulders with the dried leaves, and traced lines across his neck and forehead with fragrant oil. After three hours of watching the cycle of purging, Sergio assured him: "You've done good work. This place feels cleaner now, doesn't it?"

"Yeah," Jae admitted, with a note of relief. "It's getting . . . less ugly. I don't know how else to describe it."

The shaman nodded. "Well, you don't need to explain. I know what you mean."

"I think I have a little more to do," Jae said, feeling an unsettling energy still churning in his gut. "It's not over yet."

Indeed, it wasn't over. Jae's stood again at the mirror, listening to the accusatory whispers that continued to trail into his ears like invisible smoke: *You phony. You pretend to care, but dealing with pain isn't this easy. You can't just throw up and make it go away.* Jae closed his eyes and countered silently: *I'm doing my best.*

He finished purging and gripped the rim of the sink, staring at his reflection. Jae saw exhaustion there, but it was a healthy exhaustion: flushed, damp, and clean, the weariness of a taxing but rewarding effort. He had a sudden wish that Klara could have stood here and seen herself the same way.

An idea struck him: It *was* possible for Klara's reflection to appear in this mirror with that same contented look. Jae went to the living room, where he had stashed the oil painting, and carried the portrait back to the bathroom. He held it aloft beside his own face, and he and Klara seemed to gaze into the mirror side by side. The brush strokes comprising her face had been blended so well that he could hardly see them. Jae had taken care with Klara's face, making it pale and true to her appearance, but with red and yellow undertones that made it slightly flushed like his own face, and with bright and shining eyes—as if Jae had anticipated standing like this beside Klara's image, as if this moment was his true purpose for painting her.

"Don't we look good?" he asked, matching her smile. "Even though I've been puking my guts out, and sweating, and I'm starting to stink like a sewer rat, I feel like things will be okay. I'm sure you looked like this at times in your life: happy, and full of plans and hope. I'm sorry that people stomped those things out of you."

The proclamation brought a sudden, unexpected wave of grief. It surged powerfully within Jae, and his smile trembled and vanished as tears began to flow down his cheeks. He set the painting gently against the wall and hunched over the sink, weeping into the basin.

The churning in his stomach dissipated as he sobbed over Klara's misery and loneliness. The last dredges of pain were released through his tears, and finally he sat exhausted against the bathroom wall, wiping his face and glancing at the painting beside him. "I'm beat," he said to the image of Klara. "I feel like that's enough for today. Don't you?"

Her smile said that she agreed.

Jae stood and brought the painting back to the living room. Sergio eyed it from his seat at the altar. "What's that?" he asked.

"It's Klara." Jae turned the portrait toward the two men. "I'm painting her. It's not finished, but this is what her face looks like. Don't you think she looks like a movie star?"

Perhaps Jae was mistaken, but the two men seemed to exchange uneasy looks.

"What's the matter?" Jae asked.

Sergio shook his head. "Nothing, yet. Just don't get too attached to her. Remember, she needs to cross over and move on, instead of being stuck here. Is that who you were talking to in the bathroom?"

"Yes," Jae replied uncertainly. "I think it's okay, though. I mean, she needs *someone* to talk to."

Sergio and Walter glanced at each other again, but this time, Sergio smiled. Then he asked Jae: "Are you hungry?"

Jae did, to his own surprise, have a bit of an appetite. He sated himself with a few fresh strawberries, but didn't dare eat anything else. Consuming the strawberries gave him relief; he had worried that when Isaiah came home, he would still be sweating and puking. Walter and Sergio did most of the talking during the light meal, while Jae was steeped in quiet self-reflection. He stared at the carton of strawberries with a keen sense of gratitude toward the people who had helped to grow and deliver this beautiful, life-sustaining food to his table. He felt the same toward the earth for providing it, and even for making it so pretty, vibrant, and complex.

"You did good," Sergio assured him again. "How do you feel?"

Jae hesitated, still fixated on a single, plump strawberry. "I feel like I know what people mean when they say that love is the strongest force in the universe."

The men laughed, jolting Jae out of his reverie. He looked at them in mild surprise, but then he smiled along with them. It was a corny thing to say, he supposed, but that didn't make it any less true.

After his guests left, Jae showered and put on fresh clothes. He was vaguely aware of a presence lingering in the bathroom with him, as palpable as a scent or a haze of smoke. Sergio's cactus juice liquid had other purgative qualities, it seemed, and Jae ended up making a few more trips to the toilet. As he sat emptying his bowels, he once again sensed some invisible entity hovering nearby.

"Could I have some privacy?" he inquired dryly. "There are some things a man has to do alone."

A voice responded: "Jae?"

Jae started. It was Isaiah's voice; he had arrived home earlier than usual.

"I'll be out in a minute," Jae said.

He hurried to finish. When he opened the door, Isaiah was on the other side. He peeked around Jae into the bathroom. "Who were you talking to?"

"Um . . . ." Jae wasn't a good liar. The best he could do was a partial truth. "I was talking to the ghost. As a joke," he added quickly. "I say stupid shit to myself all the time when you're gone."

Isaiah raised his eyebrows, then leaned forward and kissed him. "Right. What should we do for dinner?"

Jae was grateful for the change of subject, but as he headed toward the kitchen, Isaiah stopped and looked around the living room. "You must have cleaned," he said. "What'd you do?"

"What do you mean?"

Isaiah gave a little shrug. "I don't know. It just seems really fresh and clean in here today. Not as stuffy." His gaze drifted to the wall near the hallway, where Jae had mounted the unfinished portrait of Klara. "Your latest work is looking good. Are you thinking of keeping it?"

"Yeah, I wanted to ask your opinion," Jae replied. "When I'm finished, is it okay if we hang it there?"

"It looks great right there. Who's the model?"

Again, Jae was keenly aware of his lack of talent for lying. "That's . . . Klara, the woman who used to live here. She's stunning, isn't she?"

Isaiah's shoulders drooped. He looked at Jae in stunned dismay. "The woman who hanged herself in our home?"

"Please don't scold me," Jae said. "She didn't hang herself in *our* home. We made this place new. I just happened to see this woman's picture, and I had to paint her. When I'm done, let's leave it up for a week, okay? If a week goes by and it still bothers you, I'll take it down."

Isaiah sighed and folded his arms, giving the painting a critical once-over. "It is a great piece. I love the dress."

"It's one of the dresses Adora Belle wore in *Going Postal*."

To Jae's relief, Isaiah laughed. "You're such a nerd," he said, lightly slapping Jae's shoulder. "Good work, honey. We can leave it up. Just don't tell anyone the back story."

Jae spent the next morning at the new work site, checking inventories and making plans for the volunteers. He meandered toward the back corner of the building—a dark, vast storage room, with gray windowless walls and lights too weak and far away to provide much illumination. Volunteers had finished stacking diapers and toilet paper on the metal shelves, but most of the spaces remained unused, filled only by shadow. Jae gazed up at the rafters, making casual plans to improve the lighting, and caught sight of a flash somewhere off to his right—a wisp of luminescent blue.

He turned to look, saw nothing but gaping shelves. But after a moment, the wisp appeared again: an elongated streak that hovered in the darkness, near in height to him, seeming to emit from the concrete floor. As Jae stood and watched, the form became more defined, until he could see the hint of arms and a human face, and then two eyes looking directly at him. The figure's mouth moved, uttering silent and futile words.

Slowly, the figure began to drift forward. A jolt of fear coursed through Jae. He hurried out of the room, not slowing until he had reached the brightly lit grocery. He turned, shaken, and stared at the entryway until one of his co-workers jolted him out of his fixation.

"You okay?" Shelley, the junior manager, gave him a concerned once-over. "You look like you saw a ghost."

"Yeah," he replied, still breathless. "No, I'm fine."

The incident still disturbed him two days later, as he hung Klara's finished portrait. The paint that comprised the red dress was still shiny and wet, giving it a lustrous sheen below Klara's smiling and confident face. Jae stood back and admired his work. "There. It's good, isn't it?" he said. "Maybe you didn't have something like this before, but now you have someone who sees how beautiful you are." He looked around the living room, as if expecting a response— but there was no sudden image, no feeling of her presence. Jae assumed she was there anyway.

"Klara, I know you're not evil," he continued, reaching out to straighten the canvas. "I feel like you really wanted to love people, and you got hurt. But you know, not all people are bad. Kids are young and naive. They do stupid things like throwing dog shit, or terrorizing other kids for fun and posting pictures of it on MySpace, and they have no idea how much hurt they're causing. They're only thinking about themselves. If I end up having a kid with Isaiah, we'll raise our kid to be a better person than that. We'll teach our kid to stand up for the ones getting bullied. So, let us stay here and have a kid."

He took a few steps back, surveying the painting again. "Try to forgive those people, okay? I know the adults failed you, too, but in general, grown-ups aren't as cowardly as they used to be. We learn from situations like yours, and we try to improve ourselves so that it doesn't happen again." He glanced around the room. Isaiah was right: the space did seem suddenly fresh and bright, a clean slate for a new beginning. "Hang out here as long as you need to, but you should cross over, like Sergio said. Trust the force, or whatever. I'll keep your portrait here so you'll be remembered like this, but you should move on to whatever the universe has in store for you next. And I hope it's something really great."

A chiming sounded from his cell phone. Sora was waiting for him to buzz her into the building. Jae said a quick hello to her and dialed the front door code, and a minute later he was opening the door to her. His sister was dressed in a tight black T-shirt and leather jacket, with heavy eyeliner and a pair of silver chains around her neck. Jae stood looking at her a moment, suddenly dreading her impending departure. He found himself sentimentalizing her impish leanings, her too-young style of dressing, her eyes that always seemed to shine with life and spirit.

"How've you been?" she asked as she came inside. "Still having night terrors?"

"I don't think I'll have them anymore," he said.

"Oh yeah?" She paused in the entryway, slipping off her boots. "Why's that?"

Jae paused. "They . . . just haven't been happening."

She nodded and glanced around. "I really can only stay for a few minutes, but can you give me a tour?"

"Sure."

Sora strode to the middle of the living room, still looking around. "This seems like a nice place," she said. "Of course, you made it look good, but . . . it has a really nice vibe, somehow. Like, I walk in, and I immediately like being here." She looked at Jae and laughed. "Does that sound weird?"

"Not at all."

She pointed to the oil portrait. "Is this new? It's yours, right?"

"Yeah, I just finished it."

"Who is it?"

"It's . . . a woman who used to live here," Jae replied—and, despite Isaiah's request that the back story be kept secret, Jae found himself spilling all of it: the unsettling visions of the wasp-lady, the incidents with the masked neighbors and the broken picture frame, the shaman, and even the ghostly figure in the warehouse. He expected a mocking response from Sora, but she only listened quietly. "I know you don't believe in all of that," Jae said, "but that's how things played out. It could all just be a projection of my own mind, like you always say. But it doesn't feel that way."

"I know I say things like that," Sora replied, "but . . . that's more about what Mom wants me to say. It's not necessarily what I believe."

Jae gave her a puzzled look. "What do you mean?"

She hesitated. "You drank that tea with the shaman?"

"Yeah, I did. So what?"

"It's just . . . Mom doesn't want me to tell you about this."

"About what?"

Sora bit her lower lip, looking searchingly into Jae's eyes.

"What?" he asked. "Just tell me what you're thinking, okay? If it's something that involves me, I should know."

"Well . . . you know how I always said that I was a little bit jealous of you, because it seemed like you were aunt Yeon-soo's favorite?"

"Yeah."

"The reason she paid so much attention to you was because . . . you know how when you were little, right before she died, you got really sick?"

"Yeah," Jae said. "She was there, taking care of me. I remember that."

"Yeon-soo wasn't just taking care of you. She said you had some kind of shaman sickness, and the only way to cure it was to initiate you. She said that she always knew you would become a shaman, ever since you were born."

Jae processed the words with slow reluctance. "Shaman sickness?"

"I really don't know that much about it. It's a thing that happens to shamans before they get initiated. Supposedly."

"Okay . . . so . . . then what happened?"

"She was going to help with your initiation, and mom begged her not to. Yeon-soo didn't want you to become a shaman, either."

"Why?"

"She said it was a hard life. Even though she helped people, it was dangerous, and painful, and a lot of the people who came to her didn't really want to be helped; they always wanted to fix things in their own way, and if she didn't do what they wanted, they would lash out at her. You were supposed to go through some kind of ritual where you called a bunch of spirits and asked for their help. Yeon-soo started the ceremony, but she only let you call one spirit. She thought it might be enough to cure you, without letting you become a full-fledged shaman."

Jae stared at Sora with uneasy disbelief. He wanted to believe that his sister was remembering it wrong—but the explanation made too much sense. Though he tried to think of details that ran contrary to his sister's claim, everything seemed only to confirm it: His aunt's attentions, his awareness of spirits, his mother's insistence that he not believe in shamanism or anything supernatural. "And Mom didn't want me to know this?"

"No. Yeon-soo died a couple weeks after your ceremony. Mom was afraid that we were surrounded by spirits, and that you would get shaman sickness again, so she moved us to the U.S."

"Are you serious? Mom moved here because of me?"

Sora nodded. "Jae, you can't tell Mom that I told you. She'll be so pissed. She thinks that if you know about it, you'll start seeing spirits."

"Uh-huh. And what about this spirit that I supposedly connected with—back then, with Yeon-soo? Whose spirit was it?"

She shook her head. "I don't know. Those spirits aren't human. They're entities who help people. I think the one she connected you to was a spirit who helps you communicate with the dead. That way, you could still help people, but you wouldn't have all of the hardships of a shaman. Yeon-soo didn't really think it would work, though. She said that if you're destined to become a shaman, you can't escape it. Things will happen that pull you into it."

Jae thought over the recent ceremonies, and of what Sergio had told him: *You lean closer to a shamanic state than most people. You're . . . open, somehow. That's probably why Klara appeared to you, and not to your partner.*

"Shit," he said. "Well, that's a little too much for me to process right now, so I'm just going to blindly deny the possibility of whatever you just talked about." He started toward the hall. "Let's finish the tour."

"I should go. I want to get to Imade's house before rush hour. But it looks like you've got a good setup here: a nice home, and Isaiah seems great." Sora turned to Jae and surprised him with a hug. "Call me any time, for whatever reason," she said as she pulled away. "Okay? Whether it's something trivial, or something really serious, like you're being terrorized by a wasp ghost who broke your picture frame." She stepped back and ruffled his hair. "I miss you, little brother. Promise that you and Isaiah will come out to New York sometime."

"We will," Jae said.

Klara's portrait stayed on the wall, but Jae no longer felt her presence. The impression of heaviness and despair had vanished— yet he found that same aura in other places, in shadowy corners and in bright places where not all could be seen with the eye. In the warehouse he spotted again a strange wisp of light, a luminescent figure moving its mouth in some silent, grieving plea.

And Jae wanted to respond to it, but felt embarrassed. What if someone heard him talking to a ghost? And what exactly could he do? Calling a shaman into his private home was one thing, but to hold such a ceremony at work—that was out of the question. He would *have* to do something; it was simply his nature to help people who were suffering through tough times. But whatever he did in this case would have to be discreet.

Though Jae remembered little from his early childhood, he knew that his aunt Yeon-soo had been shunned. His mother claimed that Yeon-soo had forfeited having children, claiming that she didn't want them to suffer because of her, but added that "No one would have married her anyway." Plenty of people had sought Yeon-soo, but no one had ever sought her as a friend.

The knowledge of her loneliness sparked a certain fear in Jae.

He wasn't just afraid of risking his job, or even his reputation. There were other, more important things at risk. If he told Isaiah about his past, would Isaiah be okay with it? Isaiah, with his unfailing mockery for anything supernatural and his disdain for the spiritual? Would he accept what was happening? And if they had kids, what would they raise their kids to believe? Jae himself didn't want his child to grow up with superstitions, didn't want to have them himself—but exploring the reality was better than the night terrors, better than ignoring pain and letting it fester.

And Jae wasn't sure how to convince Isaiah, when he sometimes had trouble convincing himself. Isaiah would surely think he was delusional. He might even get angry, and Klara's portrait would likely end up in the trash.

But Jae tried anyway. He waited for a quiet moment after dinner, when Isaiah was on the couch with a glass of wine and the remote, ready for movie night. "Let's wait on the movie," Jae said, sitting beside him. "I didn't mention it, but Sora stopped by before she went back to New York, and . . . well, there have been some things happening, and . . . ." Jae trailed off.

Isaiah waited, looking at him questioningly. "What's going on? Is your family okay?"

"Yeah, they're fine, it's not that. I want to talk about us."

Isaiah paused, then set his glass down and turned back to Jae. He sat with his arm slung across the back of the couch, in that James Dean pose that Jae adored so much. "All right. What's on your mind?"

Jae hesitated, fighting a sudden urge to cry. It came on unbidden, and in that moment Jae realized that he was genuinely frightened—afraid that within the next few minutes, he might actually lose the love of his life. "Remember how you said that you're one hundred percent sure about us, even though we've never been through anything that really tested our love?" he asked.

Caution stirred in Isaiah's eyes. "Yeah."

"Do you still feel that way?"

Isaiah reached over and grasped Jae's hand. "Of course. Jae, you're the best. You're fun, and honest, even when you don't want to be—and you have the best heart of anyone I know."

Jae took a deep breath, letting it out in a long sigh. "Okay. I feel that way, too. You are the best thing that has ever happened to me, and I can't imagine ever needing anything more than you, or feeling like I can't come to you with whatever is on my mind." Jae squeezed Isaiah's hand. "And I have something I need to tell you."

The Likeness

The Likeness

On the slatted bridge, Naomi felt a chill emanating from the river. Winter hadn't yet arrived, but the cold had preceded it; it seemed to settle in along with tragedy, penetrating Naomi's clothes and clinging to her bones. She stood at the end of the pedestrian bridge and gazed into the churning waters. The heavy rains had raised the water level, breaching the banks and widening the once-small river, spilling it into a nearby playground. Two days had passed since Naomi's fifteen-year-old nephew, James, had disappeared from this spot. If he had been just a couple of steps back, the guard rail could have stopped his fall. If the water had been lower, he might have fallen onto the bank, and Naomi wouldn't be looking for him now.

She folded her arms over her wool coat, shuddering as she contemplated the many *if*s and *might*s of that day.

She left the bridge and trekked downstream, studying the ground for anything unusual. The police and a few dozen volunteers had combed over this area multiple times, but Naomi knew James; she was more familiar with his belongings. She meandered over the grass and into the woods near the river, hoping to find some trace of his survival, some evidence that he had made it out of the river: his phone, his keys, his shoe. Once again she found no sign of him—yet Naomi kept walking, driven onward by love, fear, and guilt.

A half mile down the river, she drifted in and out of a sparse and scrawny woods. Across the water, beside the main road, a row of tents popped up from an otherwise flat strip of land. Naomi crossed another bridge and approached the encampment, where a couple dozen of the city's homeless had taken shelter. At its edge she found a familiar face: Alice, who she'd met on the first day of the search—an old, gaunt-faced woman who shivered in a down parka with bits of white plumage poking through the material. She was crouched on the ground, trying with one trembling hand to turn the

"

knobs of a portable gas grill.

"Need any help?" Naomi greeted her.

"No, I got it. Finally. Damn thing's harder to turn off than it is to get started." Alice grabbed a kettle from the grill and poured the hot water into a plastic tub. Underwear and a few pairs of socks bobbed to the surface of the steamy water. "I guess you haven't heard anything about your nephew," Alice said, standing up to face Naomi. Her pale blue eyes bore a trace of sorrow—but perhaps they always did.

"Not yet," Naomi replied.

"Well, I'm real sorry. Hopefully this will put some sense into the other kids. When the water gets high, they like to come around here and jump off these bridges." Alice gestured to the white-slatted pedestrian bridge. "They don't care that it's dangerous, so I keep telling them this water is filthy. The meat processing plant dumps its waste in this river. Once I went for a swim, and suddenly I was surrounded by cow brains and other body parts."

Naomi grimaced as she looked at the gorged river. "I did not know that," she said. "My kids and their friends have gone swimming here."

"You best tell them to keep out," Alice said. "The water's polluted. That's why you never see any fish. The place upstream has a pretty lax permit, and still, they're repeat violators."

"Lovely," Naomi replied.

"Can I see the picture of your nephew again? I want to have a good idea of what he looks like. Just in case."

Naomi reached into her jacket pocket. She pulled out her phone and scrolled through the photo gallery, stopping at a recent photo, one with the clearest image of James' face.

"I just want to make sure." Alice peered at the phone, narrowing her eyes. "Yeah, I'm sure I saw this kid, or someone who looked just like him."

Naomi stared at her in surprise. "When? Today?"

"No. The day he disappeared."

"Oh." A sinking disappointment replaced Naomi's twinge of hope.

"I know I told you that already," Alice said, "but . . . I'm sure I saw him *after* he fell in—walking around in dripping wet clothes, on a cold day like this. I tried to talk to him, but he disappeared." She turned, pointing to the two-person tent just beyond hers. "These folks saw him, too, out by these tents. Just for a few seconds, and then he was just gone. It spooked them. Later on, when they found out what happened, they started saying maybe they saw a ghost. I told the cops about it—about seeing the kid in wet clothes, I mean. Not sure if they took me serious."

Naomi considered Alice's words. Hesitantly, she asked: "Did it look like he was injured?"

Alice shrugged. "Couldn't say. He was behind the tents down there, and he must've ducked down, or something. We looked around but didn't see him again. Haven't seen anything since."

"Well, thanks for keeping an eye out," Naomi replied. "I appreciate it. The police did mention that someone at the camp might've seen him, but . . . no one else said anything, and there was no sign of James here."

"Yeah . . . ." Naomi stepped closer, keeping her eye on the long row of tents. In a low voice, she said: "These two didn't want to tell the police that they might've seen him. They don't want trouble, you know? A lot of people already want to boot us out of here, and if it looks like a kid disappeared . . . ."

Naomi nodded. Quietly, she asked: "Do you think something might've happened to him here?"

"In this camp? No way." Alice shook her head vehemently. "Not in this row. These are decent people, trying to stay as far from trouble as they can get. Everyone's real tight, everyone knows everyone else and we help each other out—and if anyone approached your nephew, it would've been to give him some warm clothes. No, I can say for sure, nothing happened to your nephew at this camp."

Naomi lowered her eyes. Her gaze fell on the ratty-looking coat. She noticed that it was stained and discolored along the bottom. It was difficult, she supposed, for the campers to get decent clothes. There was a donation bin in the parking lot, and she had seen people picking through it before the donations got picked up, but it was mostly stuffed with kids' sizes. She had brought her own children's clothes to that bin as they outgrew them. "Listen . . . can I bring you a new coat?" she asked. "That one looks like it has seen better days."

"Well, it has. But those wool coats like you got aren't good for keeping the cold out." Alice crouched down beside the plastic tub. She added a few drops of powdered soap to the water and dipped her hands in, squeezing the laundry between her fingers and releasing it, swishing it in slow circles.

"Oh, I know," Naomi agreed. "What about a new down coat? And some gloves?"

Alice looked up and eyed her for a moment. "Well, if you want. We don't have much out here. It's been a cold year for everyone. We always appreciate a little more warmth."

As she headed back to the parking lot, Naomi kept thinking of Alice's bony, trembling hands dipping into the hot water. She knew that she hadn't offered the coat out of generosity, but out of helplessness: she couldn't make sure that James was warm and safe, but she could at least warm someone else. Seeing how the cold pained Alice made her think of James suffering that same cold.

Naomi's house was a short drive from the park. As she pulled into the back alley, Naomi scanned the garages and backyards for any glimpse of James—his face, his hair, his jacket—though she had no expectations. She simply looked because he was still missing.

A black Mazda was already in the back parking space. Judy's car. Naomi pulled into the one-stall garage and turned off the engine. She sat for a few minutes, thinking of what Alice had told her: *I'm sure I saw him* after *he fell in—walking around in dripping wet clothes, on a cold day like this. I tried to talk to him, but he disappeared.* Naomi's index finger tapped on the steering wheel as she ruminated on the words. *Maybe they saw a ghost.*

Alice wasn't the only one who had said such a thing. Naomi's sister, Leah, had called her that morning in hysterics, insisting that James had shown up in the living room.

"I need a place to stay," she'd said. Fear and frailty quivered in her voice. "Things aren't right in this house."

"Well . . . I would invite you here, Leah, but Judy's mom is staying with us." Naomi lowered her voice and checked over her shoulder, making sure the bedroom door was closed. The muted voices of Judy, Pam, and the kids sounded from the living room. "And I know you can't stand her," she added.

"It's just . . . I've been hearing things in the house," Leah said shakily. "Things getting moved around. Like . . . chairs moving, and doors closing. Last night I heard noises from the kitchen, and I went to the stairs—and I saw someone standing at the bottom."

"Someone was in your house?"

"Naomi, it was James!" Leah's voice was a near scream. Naomi winced, holding the phone away from her face. "It was James, and . . . and he had blood running down his face, and . . . he just stood there, looking at me. His clothes were soaking wet. I couldn't move. God, I just about fainted. When I went downstairs later, there was water all over the floor."

"You think he came home," Naomi repeated, trying to make sense of it. "But, what then?"

"I don't know. I screamed and closed my eyes, and then he was just gone. I opened my eyes and there was no James, but the floor was wet."

Naomi had mulled over the story, pondering all the ways it didn't make sense. She tried not to sound dismissive; Leah didn't have a reputation for honesty, or for sobriety, and Naomi was disinclined to believe her. "Maybe you weren't really awake," Naomi suggested. "I know you've had trouble sleeping. Do you think that James would come home for a few seconds, and then just leave? And why would he be soaking wet? It hasn't rained the past two days."

"Naomi, you don't get it. He's wet from the river."

"But . . . ."

"He's a *ghost*, Naomi!" Leah cried. Her breath came in agitated, tearful gasps. "He's dead, and he came back here to torment me, because—just because! Just like he was tormenting me all week, and accusing me!"

Naomi hesitated. She thought of the things Leah had told her about that day: *We were arguing. He lost his temper and tried to hit me, so I grabbed his arm. He jerked away and fell.* The story had bothered her. James wasn't one to hit. He would talk back, and make sarcastic comments, but Naomi couldn't imagine him trying to hit Leah. She couldn't even imagine him raising his voice. "Accusing you of what?" she asked.

The sound of ragged breathing stopped for several seconds; then it came again in whispery sobs.

"Why don't I come over later, and spend the night there?" Naomi asked. "If something happens, we'll both see it, and . . . we'll figure it out together."

"I don't know." Leah's voice fell to a barely audible murmur. "I don't know, I don't know . . . ."

"If you find another place to stay, you can do that—but I'll stay at your house tonight either way. Okay?"

The labored breathing continued.

"I'll be there after dinner," Naomi said.

Now, as Naomi remembered the conversation, she felt a vague sense of dread. Alice's story, though it could easily have been a mistake, made Leah's fears seem more substantial.

Naomi headed for the house and found Judy in the kitchen, stuffing a row of limp manicotti noodles. Naomi approached her from behind, sliding her arms around Judy's waist, pressing her cheek against the black hair that curled down to the nape of Judy's neck.

Judy turned around and broke into an affectionate smile, one now laced with sadness. She knew why Naomi was late. "Dinner's almost ready," she said, and gave Naomi a quick kiss on the lips.

"Sorry I wasn't here earlier," Naomi replied.

"Don't worry about it. I've got a handle on things here for now. Are you still planning to spend the night at Leah's?"

"She didn't really say yes, but I'll show up and see if she lets me stay. Is your mom here?"

"She went out with a friend for dinner."

"Where are the kids?"

"Probably in the fort."

"I didn't hear them."

"Well, they've been subdued lately," Judy said. "I hope they didn't run off. Will you call them? I'll have everything ready in a few minutes."

The kids were, indeed, quiet as they descended from the backyard fort. Naomi found them in the enclosure, at the top of a series of knotted ropes, climbing walls, and balconies. Eleven-year-old Avery wore an almost haunted look as she peeped through the canvas flap, as though expecting to find some disaster waiting outside. Her twin brother had a matching look of apprehension. They were quiet during dinner, too, except to ask a slew of questions about Leah: *Why are you staying there? Is it only for one night? Did she say anything about James?*

James, their only cousin, was a close friend to both Avery and Anton, and had been so since their birth. Only four years old when they were born, he had followed and looked after them tirelessly whenever he stayed at the house, which he did so frequently. Leah had been unemployed at the time, and was always off to one job interview or another, or starting and stopping random part-time gigs—or spending hours at the casino, drinking and playing away the few dollars she'd earned.

Naomi helped clean up after dinner and packed an overnight bag. From the bedroom, she could hear the kids playing one of the video games they'd gotten for their birthday. She finished packing and carried her bag into the hall, where Judy was poking around in the linen closet. "I'm heading out," she said.

Judy continued rummaging. "Do you know what happened to the extra pillow? I'm making up the futon for my mom. The sheets are here, but . . . ."

"Haven't seen it," Naomi replied. She called into the living room: "Kids! Have you seen the guest pillow? The one we keep in the linen closet?"

Silence. Naomi peeked around the corner, saw the twins sitting motionless while their virtual cars crashed onscreen. The two sat close together—closer than usual. Naomi had noticed that the twins clung together these past few days, and were quieter, often speaking to each other in whispers. She saw their anxiety and did what she could to comfort them.

Avery spoke up: "I threw it away. It was all stained. Jessie used it when she slept over, and she said it stunk and it made her throat itch."

"Well, that's gross. Next time you throw something out, tell us, so we can replace it. Okay?" Naomi turned back to Judy. "I'll buy another one on my way to Leah's. Your mom can use my pillow tonight." She kissed Judy's cheek and gave her a brief, one-armed hug. "Tell her I'm sorry I missed her."

Naomi went around to the back of the couch and leaned over,

hugging and kissing the kids, ruffling their blond hair. On screen, the cars crashed again. Normally, this would have roused some protests, albeit feeble ones—but the kids didn't complain.

Trepidation set in as Naomi backed the car into the alley. A visit to Leah's house always put her on edge, even when James had been there to ease the tension. And what was there now, in his place—a specter, a cruel prank by a neighbor, or just Leah's guilty imaginings? *He's dead, and he came back here to torment me. . . .*

Naomi glanced in the rear-view mirror. A moment later, she jerked forward as her foot stomped on the brake. She twisted in her seat, straining to see more clearly the road behind her: the garage, the neighbor's raspberry bushes, the chain-link fence beyond them. She thought she had seen someone there—a boy, someone about James' age, with the same build, the same light brown hair. The image had come and gone in a flash. Now, there was nothing.

She backed up slowly and peered into the bushes, just to make sure.

Her sister's house was only two miles down the road, but Naomi took a detour to a shopping center in the next town, where she stopped to buy a pillow, a down coat, and gloves. The sun was disappearing beneath the horizon by the time she pulled up to Leah's house, an old split-level from the 60s with warped siding and peeling paint. Leah took some time to answer the door. When she finally opened it, she gave Naomi a quick wave and beckoned her inside. Leah had her cell phone cradled against her ear; she listened to the person on the other end with quiet intensity, murmuring the occasional "Mm-hmm" and "Uh-huh."

Naomi glanced around the living room. She was always struck by how bare this room was. There were no decorations on the walls, no pictures, no shelves. A coffee table stood in front a faded blue couch, and was bordered by two mismatched armchairs—the same furniture that had always been there, but with a new addition. A handful of crystals lay on the table, mostly tapered, some cut into small spheres. Next to them was a snowflake-themed candle holder full of wood chips, and beside that, paper bags labeled "sage" and "frankincense."

Leah hung up and turned to face Naomi. "Hi. Uh, sorry, I forgot you were coming."

"No problem. What's all this?"

"Oh . . . um . . . I've been talking to some people . . . like, you know . . . well, you know that reiki place in town? There's a medium who works there . . . a woman who told me she's a medium. I went to see her, I went to the store, and, I asked for some advice . . . ."

Naomi watched as Leah began to pace a small length of floor. She was dressed in sweatpants and an over-sized T-shirt that made her look even thinner than she was. Her long hair was heavy with oil, as though she hadn't washed it in days, and the flesh beneath her eyes looked sunken and shadowed.

"You mean, because you think you saw a ghost," Naomi replied.

"Well, yes. I didn't *say* that, but . . . I said there was something in my house, like a spirit, and it just felt wrong. So, they made some recommendations." Leah looked down at the floor as she spoke. Her hands were raised to her mouth, one fingernail scratching absently at her lower lip.

Naomi nodded as she looked down at the collection. "And they sold you some crystals, and incense, and—what's this?" She gestured to the candle holder.

"Um, it's supposed to get rid of bad energy. I'm going to burn it tonight, before I go to bed. Oh—I should put these out now." Leah hurried to the table and began scooping up the crystals. "Tonight's the full moon. I'm supposed to leave these in the moonlight overnight, and then put them in the window and door frames."

Naomi picked up one of the smaller pieces, a black sphere, and rolled it gently in her palm. "Kind of cloudy tonight," she said.

"Well, I can't wait. I need to do something *now*." Leah grabbed the black ball from Naomi's hand. "And I already know you don't believe in this stuff," she added sharply, "but . . . just let me do what I'm doing. Something is really wrong in this house, and I need to do *some*thing."

Naomi watched Leah retreat through the kitchen and out the back door. She followed partway, but hung back at the kitchen counter, where Leah's laptop was open with the "sleep" screen on display. Naomi ran her index finger across the touch pad. A browser window appeared: an ad for a home exorcism.

"What the hell," she whispered.

Leah came back as Naomi scrolled through the rest of the ad.

"Oh," Leah said nervously, "I was just checking out some things."

"'Free house exorcism services for buyers and sellers,'" Naomi read aloud. "'Do you think your new house may be haunted? Are you selling a property that has been stigmatized by tragedy? Are strange phenomena scaring buyers away? Our real estate services include free exorcism rituals for homes that need energetic cleansing.'" She looked at Leah. "Who knew. Are you thinking of trying to sell this place?"

"No. I was just looking." Naomi switched to another browser tab. "I found this other guy who's highly recommended."

"By who?"

"One of my friends. And he has a lot of good reviews online."

Naomi frowned as she scrolled through the main page. She clicked on a link for "in-home services," and the frown deepened. "This guy charges six hundred dollars for two hours of sage, gongs, and bells."

"No, there's more to it than that. I called him, and he seems like he knows what he's doing. He gave me some tips, like . . . if there's a . . . spirit, or whatever, hanging around, and there's stuff in the house that belonged to that spirit, I should get rid of it, because spirits are attached to things."

"You're not getting rid of James' belongings," Naomi said. "We don't know that he died."

Leah closed the laptop with a loud *snap*. "He did die. I know it."

"There's . . . ." Naomi hesitated. "The police haven't found a body."

"But he's *dead*," Leah insisted, turning to look at her with fierce, red-rimmed eyes, "because his spirit is *here*. And I'm not imagining it, and I'm not mistaking some random intruder for my son, I know it's *him*, and he's coming for *me*, and he is *angry*."

Naomi didn't respond, but puzzled over Leah's behavior. Leah had never taken a special interest in the paranormal, or in spirituality—and she had never seemed afraid of her son.

"You don't know what he was like these past few weeks," Leah continued. "He's just angry. Talking back to me, trying to pick fights. Maybe it's a teenager thing, it's hormones and all that, but he's *mad*." She turned abruptly to Naomi, her eyes still weary with anxiety. "Sleep on the couch tonight," she said. "There's no way you won't see it."

"I'm not sleeping on that thing. My back can't take it. My butt can barely take sitting there."

"Sleep in James' room, then. And leave the door open. And get up right away if you hear *any*thing."

James' room was the first at the top of the stairs, on the left-hand side. While Leah performed her cleansing rituals and filled the house with fragrant smoke, Naomi took shelter in the bedroom, closing the door to keep the haze from entering. It seemed wrong to let those strange smells overpower whatever scent remained of her nephew.

Naomi wandered through the room, looking at the pencils and papers laid out on James' desk, at the manga sketches and comic book posters on the wall. She stood with her arms folded, resisting the urge to touch his belongings. The place seemed almost like a shrine, a room frozen in time, off limits to her intrusion—but she couldn't help reaching into the closet and touching some of his clothes.

The old house made its own noises: creaks, crumblings, groanings, even strange whistling and scratching sounds likely caused by wind and mice. Naomi lay awake that night and listened, trying to discern between the sounds. A couple of times she thought she heard floorboards creaking downstairs, but when she went out to look, there was nothing. Nothing except Leah creeping up behind her, full of fear, whispering: "Do you see anything?"

But Naomi didn't see anything. After a while she fell asleep. In the morning, remembering Leah's near-skeletal appearance, she decided to hunt around for some breakfast. Leah didn't keep a full kitchen, but she was likely to have eggs and bread.

Naomi was only a few feet from the refrigerator, already reaching for the handle, when she saw it: a word painted in red across the refrigerator door. *Confess.*

And in much larger letters, painted across the kitchen wall: *MURDER.*

She stood frozen for some time, and then chanced a quiet look behind her. Nothing else caught her eye; she heard no sounds of movement in the house. Naomi took a step closer to the lettering, peering around the fridge for a better look. Something wet soaked into her sock, and she pulled back quickly. A puddle of water had formed on the floor in front of the fridge.

"Leah?" she called.

She realized, when she looked again, that she hadn't seen the whole of the second word. It actually read: *MURDERER*. The sight of those accusatory words drained the color from Leah's face. She accosted Naomi with frantic "I told you so"s and "It's James, I know it's James!" Naomi sat her down in the living room and tried to calm her, but she was also deeply unsettled. The doors and windows were still locked from the inside; there were no footprints or other evidence of an intruder, and nothing looked out of place except for those ghastly words. The thought of vandals sneaking in and playing such a tasteless prank was disturbing enough, but the lack of such an explanation left Naomi with a deep foreboding.

"Let's report it," Naomi suggested, and started to stand.

"No!" Leah made a quick grab for her arm. "No, don't report it!"

"Why?"

"Because . . . it says *murderer*! He's trying to make me look bad! James keeps doing things like this, and I don't know how to *stop* it."

Naomi wondered what else had taken place here—what other events Leah hadn't told her about. "Have there been other messages?"

"He wrote 'murderer' and 'hell' last time."

"With what?"

"Paint," Leah said. "It was cheap acrylic paint and it came off, but—"

"Then it's not a ghost. Can a ghost manifest cheap acrylic paint? A person did this."

"James has paint! It's in his room."

Naomi paused, bracing herself before uttering the question that she didn't want to ask, but that wouldn't stop nagging at her. "Why do you think James would write 'murderer' on your walls?"

"I didn't kill him," Leah replied.

Despite Leah's intentions, the words sounded like an admission. Naomi's lingering sorrow and anger seemed to shift inside her, changing from a settled and muted thing into a slowly awakening beast. Quietly, she asked: "Did you shove him? Is that why he fell?"

"It didn't happen like that. We were . . . he was getting aggressive." Leah clutched at her knees, her fingernails digging into her skin. She was still dressed in her night clothes: socks and a long T-shirt that left her bare-kneed. "I was trying to get him out of my face. But I did not kill James. I *kind* of pushed him."

"But . . . you pushed him hard enough that he fell," Naomi said. "He stumbled backwards and couldn't catch himself, and he fell into the river. Is that what happened?"

"I was protecting myself."

"From James?"

Leah's eyes flashed with defensive anger. "You don't know what he's *like*. He's different now. Look what he's doing!" She thrust out an arm, pointing to the kitchen.

"James' ghost didn't write on your walls," Naomi replied.

"Well, *I* think that's what's happening. He's angry, and he's becoming . . . *evil*, and he wants revenge."

Naomi looked back at the kitchen, gazing thoughtfully at the graffiti. "Do you think one of his friends might have done it? James might've complained about your . . . aggressive episodes, and maybe his friends got suspicious. That doesn't look like revenge. It's an accusation."

"Driving me crazy is his revenge!" Leah half-rose from her seat, making another wild gesture toward the kitchen. "Scaring me is revenge, and not letting me sleep at night is revenge!"

Naomi closed her eyes, tried to direct her thoughts into a logical stream of focus—but her thoughts were dominated by bitterness, by grief. "And what about James?" she asked quietly. "Do you think he slept well at night, and that you didn't scare him?"

Leah settled back into the chair, shaking her head. "I am not listening to this now. I'm very aware of what you think of me as a mother, but I do not deserve this. Not right now."

"Leah, these things you're saying about James—that he's suddenly angry and aggressive—that doesn't sound like James. It sounds like you."

"Oh, right, you can't imagine your precious James being aggressive, but you can imagine *me* doing it."

"We've all heard you threaten him," Naomi said, and mimicked:

"'James, touch that remote again and I'll break your hand.' 'Talk back to me again and I'll bust those smart aleck—'"

"I was frustrated," Leah cut in. "Did I ever break his hand, or beat him?"

"I've seen you push him. I've seen you grab him, yank on him, smack his head—"

"Barely. All parents do that when their kids misbehave."

"All parents don't threaten to break their kids' bones, or to punch them in the face," Naomi said. "I would never dream of talking to my kids that way."

"I'm sick of being compared to you. You're not a single parent. You have money. You had money before you had kids. I had nothing—no money, no job, and no role model when it came to parenting, but I had James anyway, and I never get any credit for that. James had a great childhood compared to what I got."

"He didn't," Naomi replied dully. "You gave him the same childhood."

"I did not, don't you dare. You think Dad was hard on you, Naomi, but you were the little one. I was older, and I was responsible for anything that went wrong, and I always got the punishment. You were scared, but I got punished."

Naomi wasn't fazed. The question in her mind left no room for pity. "Let me ask you again. Did you push James into the river?"

"Quit changing the subject. You know I'm right."

"No, this is the subject," Naomi said, her voice calm, but with a noticeable edge. "You want to know why you have this accusatory shit all over your walls. If you pushed James into the river, you should confess it. That's what this so-called spirit wants. Right? Maybe instead of crystals and smoke, you can cleanse the house by admitting to some things, instead of making excuses."

Leah looked away again, shaking her head.

"Who knows—maybe you wrote those things yourself," Naomi suggested casually. "You feel guilty, and you're doing it in your sleep."

Leah faced her with a sardonic smile. "You should leave now."

"Right. I'll leave." Naomi stood up. She paused there, looking down at Leah as she spoke. "Forget the past and everything else. Maybe you didn't mean to kill anyone, but you pushed your son off a bridge."

"Get out," Leah said. "I'll handle this myself, like always."

Naomi thought: *And you'll call me for help in a few days, like always.*

The conversation re-played in Naomi's mind as she drove away. After a few minutes she pulled into the park where James had disappeared; she stopped in the main lot and sat for some time with her forehead against the steering wheel, her eyes burning with unshed tears.

Leah's claims weren't without merit. Their mother had died when Naomi was only six years old, and instead of grieving, their father became outraged at the burden of running a household on his own. Perhaps he had grieved inwardly. He had never shown it. Most of the housekeeping and childcare duties were shifted to Leah, who was thirteen at the time—and if anything was out of place, Leah was held responsible. True, if Naomi made a mess or misbehaved, she would be yelled at, spanked, and sent to her room, but Leah had been treated more cruelly. Leah had been slapped, derided, grounded for the most trivial reasons, deprived of pivotal events and opportunities that most teens looked forward to. As the older sister, she was supposed to take her mother's place; as a child, and as the target of an angry man, she naturally failed.

The public news station was playing on a low volume. Naomi had been too engrossed in her own musings to listen, but a stream of familiar phrases began to penetrate her thoughts: " . . . Litenfield Park. The homeless encampment has been the subject of public debate for several weeks, and those debates intensified after a teenage boy disappeared from the area. This morning, the Parks and Recreation Board announced that residents of the encampment will receive a 72-hour eviction notice. The board added that dignified alternative spaces will be offered . . . ."

"Shit," Naomi whispered.

She grabbed the new winter gear from the trunk and headed to the encampment. As she walked, she found herself once again scanning the area for a glimpse of James. Some other feeling, something besides the usual hope and desperation stirred in her— some new and unprecedented anxiety. Naomi realized that she was looking not just for James, but more particularly, for the specter of

James: a ghostly, wandering figure in dripping clothes, with deadened eyes and vague accusation in his death-pale face. She lowered her eyes and tried to focus on her memories of his warmth, his generous and loving nature.

At the tents Naomi found a few people milling around, but no Alice. She stopped at the first tent and called Alice's name, catching the attention of a middle-aged man a few spaces down. He looked the way Naomi expected a homeless man to look: scrawny and unkempt, with a haggard face and wispy, tangled beard.

"She's out somewhere, looking for a new place to stay," he said. "We're getting kicked out of here pretty soon. Lots of folks are trying to figure out what to do next."

"Yeah, I heard," Naomi replied. "I thought the city had some other shelter lined up."

"Well, they sort of do."

"Do you know where? I thought our shelters were pretty full up."

"They are," the man said, "but people don't stay, and most of those places are on a rotation." The man's voice was dry and scratchy, as if from overuse—or perhaps from illness. "They use a lottery system. If you win, you get a shelter bed for a month. Get to come in at ten o'clock at night, have a bed or a sleeping bag on the floor, have breakfast in the morning before they kick you out. No place to bathe or wash your clothes, or keep warm during the day. It's like that for a month, and then they put your bed or your spot on the floor back on the lottery."

Naomi nodded, trying to dredge up the kind of comment that people made when there was really nothing to say. "Well . . . good luck to you," she said at last.

"You too. Aren't you the lady whose nephew went missing?"

"Yeah." Naomi looked at the man's weary face. She watched him carefully as she asked her next question. "A few people said they saw him coming out of the river. Maybe I'm just hoping, but . . . I have good reason to believe that James might have run away."

"Hmm. Things aren't good at home?"

"No. They've rarely been good. Do you think you might've seen him?"

"Sorry, I haven't. I saw his picture, but I haven't seen the boy."

He seemed to be telling the truth. Naomi couldn't read any kind of anxiety in his response—and even if people had kept quiet before, for fear of getting kicked out of the encampment, that fear had already materialized.

The man was looking away, gazing at the row of tents, when he spoke again: "You know, I grew up rough. My folks were rough. They didn't know any other way to be. I ran away when I was fourteen, and I got sent home. I ran away a few more times, and I learned that most people will just send you home again. My parents always wanted me back, mostly to punish me, I think. I found a shelter for runaway youth, and I thought I had struck gold—I never knew there was such a thing! But they had to notify my parents, and I ended up at home again. See, my parents just weren't rough *enough*. So the next time I ran away, I didn't go to people who had authority. I didn't go to the cops, the shelters, my aunts and uncles, my friends' parents. I went to the homeless. And they helped me. Some of them, anyway. They helped me enough. So, if your nephew ran off and hasn't gotten caught yet, maybe he's with someone who can help. Not his aunties, not the police or child protective services or whatever, not the people who will say 'You belong at home' and send him back. Maybe he's with someone else who knows what it's like not to have any power, and who isn't afraid of getting in trouble with the law. You might try looking there."

Naomi stared at him. Then she glanced back the way she had come, toward the lot where her car was parked. She remembered, suddenly, that she had to get home. Her family was waiting for her.

"These are for Alice," she said, extending the bundle in her arms. "Do you think it's okay to leave them in the tent? I can just unzip it a little and stick them inside."

He shrugged. "I don't see why not."

She stuffed the coat and gloves into the tent, thanked him, and left. On the short drive home, Naomi kept the radio off. She had a sudden need for silence. In the back parking space she sat for a while and looked into the yard; she had a partial view of the fort that she and Judy had set up for the kids the previous year, when they had outgrown the swing set and sand pit. The yard had been set up for the kids ever since they were toddlers. Naomi had always wanted them to feel treasured, to enjoy home life in ways that she hadn't been allowed to. As children, she and Leah were expected to sit quietly. Sometimes, on summer days when they were stuck at home and their dad was at work, they would risk making small forts in the living room or setting up some other adventurous game. Everything had to be cleaned up and in its place before their father returned— but then he started arriving unexpectedly, at random times, and his outrage put a stop to those messes. Perhaps Leah still carried the same fear of punishment, or at least, the same expectation of what a home should look like. Her bare house, her empty yard, bore no traces of a child's life. It hardly looked like a grown-up lived there. When it came to looks, the house may as well have been inhabited by a ghost.

As she crossed the yard, Naomi heard a sound from above—a faint shuffling, and then a single knock, as though something had bumped against the wooden fort. She stopped and looked up at the enclosure, a tiny one-room cabin surrounded by a narrow veranda. Naomi moved closer and stood at the rope ladder. "Kids?" she called.

She watched the canvas door. It didn't move.

Naomi grasped the ladder and placed her foot on the bottom rung. She stood like that for some time, locked in a silent debate with herself. Then she stepped off and went into the house.

Judy and the twins were finishing breakfast. Naomi greeted them and hugged both of the children. She refrained from asking them the question that lingered in her mind.

Leah didn't call her the following day, or the next. Soon enough, though, Naomi received a phone message: Leah needed money. "It's not six hundred dollars," Leah said, "and it's not for a medium. It's just a couple hundred to pay the bills. Maybe you won't do it for my sake, but you could at least do it for James, if he's alive."

Naomi rolled her eyes, but she decided to ignore the accusation. Especially, she realized, because there was some truth to what Leah said. It was mostly for James' sake that Naomi wanted to know if Leah was still being "haunted," if James' likeness was still appearing in the night.

She arrived at Leah's house to find her occupied once again with a psychic—in person this time. The woman was standing in the middle of the living room, hands clasped. Leah quietly explained that the woman was trying to get a "feel" for the place.

The medium turned and greeted Naomi with a smile.

"This is Jacinta," Leah said, making a quick, nervous gesture. "She's the medium from the reiki place. She just came over for a consultation. A *free* consultation."

The woman bore none of the eccentricities that Naomi expected. Her manner seemed genuinely warm, and while Naomi would have imagined her in fancy scarves and gaudy jewelry, Jacinta was remarkably plain. She had short, dark hair and wore no make-up or jewels, and was dressed simply, in a white sweater and gray slacks.

They sat in the living room, Naomi and Leah beside each other on the couch, Jacinta in an armchair by the front windows. The medium leaned toward Naomi as she spoke. "I understand that you were close to James," she said. "When the people who know him are present, that can help draw forth his energy. It builds a sense of him, and that can help a medium get a better sense of his energy, too."

Naomi tuned out the rest of the words. She looked into Jacinta's eyes as if she was paying attention, but didn't nod or react in any way. She may as well have been staring at a wall.

Whether psychic or not, Jacinta sensed her disinterest. She shifted in her seat so that she was facing Leah. "Tell me what your son was like," she said. "What comes to mind when you remember him?"

"Um . . . well . . . ." Leah lowered her eyes. She sat with her chin resting on her hand—in the "thinker" position, Naomi noted— and raised her fingers to cover her mouth.

Naomi suppressed a scowl as her sister stammered and struggled to speak. It struck her, then: Leah had yet to express any grief over the fate of her son. Her worries had been self-focused: *It wasn't my fault. My house is haunted. I have to get rid of the spirit.*

Even if the spirit is her son, Naomi thought bitterly.

Provoked by Leah's lack of a tribute, Naomi spoke up: "James was always very mature for his age. When he was little, before he even started kindergarten, my partner and I adopted twins. We arranged the adoption a few months before the twins were born— and right from the start, before they were even born, James was ready to be their guardian. He told me and my wife that he was going to be their big brother. And then we brought them home, and even though James was just a little kid himself, he was always looking after them and protecting them. And he was so patient. He comforted them when they cried, and he even learned how to change diapers. He played with them and fed them and made them laugh. James has always been smart. And he's responsible. And he tends to be very serious, but he has a wicked sense of humor too."

Jacinta was nodding—a gesture of approval, Naomi supposed, because Naomi had stopped tuning her out. In a soft, unassuming voice, Jacinta asked: "What image comes to mind when you think of him?"

Naomi didn't want to humor the question, but the image of James' eyes came immediately to her: penetrating brown eyes set in a serious face. Not just serious, but sad—as though his eyes had seen into the future, and the burden of that future weighed on him. And something else, some other quality that always made Naomi feel a twinge of guilt. Not accusation, but something like it. Some quality in his gaze that was full of unspoken things.

Naomi stood up. "I'm going to get some water. Does anyone else want a drink?"

The other women declined. Naomi went to the kitchen and grabbed a glass from the cabinet. Leah's words reached her from the living room: "I haven't just seen James in the house. I've also seen him in the yard, out by the bushes—or I think I have, but then he's gone. And when I go out, anywhere—the store, when I'm driving down the road . . . ."

Leah's voice was drowned out by the rush of tap water. Naomi filled the glass, then closed her eyes and gulped it down.

"It's his hair, his stature," Leah was saying, "but when I get close, he's never there."

Naomi returned to find Jacinta still giving that approving, comforting nod. "That happens after a death," she explained. "It's not a supernatural phenomenon. Someone who has a daily presence in your life is suddenly gone, so your mind automatically searches for them. You see a likeness somewhere, and your brain turns it into the person you most desire to see."

"This isn't a likeness," Leah replied. "It's him. It's . . . the way he looks at me, and the way he carries himself. When I saw him standing there, at the bottom of the steps, it was *James*, glaring at me, and accusing me."

Jacinta regarded her silently. She watched as Leah fidgeted. Then she asked: "Were you and James struggling before he died?"

"Just a moment," Naomi cut in. "I just want to make it clear that James is *missing*. We don't know that he died. I mean . . . Leah, from the way you make it sound, he could be a runaway."

"He didn't run away," Leah insisted. "He's here. You saw it yourself."

The medium looked at Naomi. She raised her eyebrows questioningly. "Did you see something?"

"We had a problem with vandals," Naomi said.

"It wasn't a vandal, it was a ghost!" Leah cried. "What kind of vandal would leave a message like that?"

Again, Jacinta looked to Naomi. "What was the message?"

Leah stood up abruptly. Her arms gestured around the room in wild, meaningless spasms. "I'm sorry. I didn't mean for this to get so out of hand. Thanks for your time. You came over here, and I'm not even paying you, and it's getting late. You should go, really. I'll . . . think about what you said, and . . . I'll figure out what to do. Thanks for all your advice."

Naomi followed a few steps behind as Leah ushered the medium toward the front door. Leah was reaching for Jacinta; it looked like she was poised to push her, in case the medium didn't leave fast enough.

Jacinta paused at the doorway and turned to Leah—but when she spoke, she looked over Leah's shoulder, at Naomi. "I can feel his presence," the medium said. "He *was* here. I can feel that he lived here. But he's not here now. Not in physical form, or in spirit form." Jacinta smiled soberly at Naomi. "I hope you find him and bring him home."

The door closed. Without looking at Leah, Naomi asked: "Has anything happened since the last time I was here?"

"Of course it has." Leah went to the sofa and sat with a tired, heavy thud. "The same shit. Confess, killer, sin." Her voice trembled. "I'm going to use some of the money to put a camera in the living room. Then I can at least see if it's a ghost materializing, or if it's someone walking into the house. Except . . . they're not really coming into the house anymore. Last night, they wrote it on the front door."

"Wrote what?"

Leah paused. Her eyes became suddenly red; her face sagged with misery and exhaustion. "Child killer," she choked, wiping at the tears that spilled onto her cheeks. "I didn't kill James. It's true that I was mad. He was ragging on me all week. I pushed him. I thought I was pushing him against the rail. I really wasn't trying to kill him, I never would have done that. James is my son and I did love him, you know. Remember how dad used to push us? Against the wall, against the counter, whatever. It was like that. But dad would never have tried to kill us. It felt like he hated us, but he was mad at other things. Right?" She looked up at Naomi, her eyes suddenly bright with hope—or rather, with desperation.

"Leah . . . ."

"What?"

"Let me spend the night here again. I brought my overnight bag. We can sit here and talk, and you can tell me . . . whatever you want."

Leah let out a bitter laugh. "Why? So you can go home and tell Judy how screwed up I am? Or so you can call child protective services again?"

"Then, find someone who you can talk to. A therapist. Someone who's neutral."

Leah looked at the floor. She didn't respond, but seemed to be considering the idea.

"If there really is a ghost here, that's what it wants," Naomi said.

"I could go to jail," Leah blurted.

"For what?"

"I don't know. If I say I pushed him . . . and . . . considering . . . ." She looked up, her eyes suddenly hard with anger. "I know you and Judy called the county on me. More than once. I can't count the number of times you tried to take him away and act like the better parent. It's always, 'Leah, what did you do this time? Did you drink? Did you gamble?' I'm five months sober, and you will *never* know how hard that has been for me, but all you ever do is criticize. You act like I'm crazy while you're all cool and level-headed—even now, when *this* shit is happening! With that kind of past, and that kind of sister, the cops will write me off as a monster."

Naomi started to reply, but words felt useless. She had, in fact, praised Leah for her efforts at sobriety—but it had always felt like empty praise, because Naomi had lost faith in her, could never believe that she was telling the truth. She looked at Leah and thought of the past, of a multitude of memories of her sister: of love, of admiration, of feeling protected and nurtured. And who was Leah now? That dependable, strong, big-sister spirit didn't live in her anymore. If she had pushed James to his death, whether intentional or not, the event signified two deaths: his, and Leah's.

That night, Naomi didn't have to wait until morning to experience the specter. After a failed attempt at sleeping on the couch, she retreated to James' bed. In a half-sleep, she ruminated again on her nephew's penetrating eyes and serious face, and found with a shock that she couldn't remember him in detail. The boy she saw in her memories resembled James, but with vague and warped features—and though Naomi strained to remember, she saw instead only a likeness, a visage doused in water that ran into his eyes and down his cheeks, distorting them like melting wax. A cold conviction shuddered through her: James would not come back. Even if he returned, or was found, he would not, could not be the same James.

A crash sounded from the first floor. Naomi sat up. She'd been dreaming, she realized. Even as she hurried quietly to the stairs, listening for more commotion from below, Naomi's fears were fixed on the imagery of her nightmare.

Leah came into the hall behind her, hissing: "Turn on the light!"

Naomi flicked the switch. The stairway was illuminated along with part of the living room, and she noticed right away the crystalline sparkling on the floor, the gleaming spread of broken glass.

She crept down the first few steps and saw the curtains blowing through a jagged hole in the living room window.

"Okay, this is vandals," Naomi said. "They smashed the front window. We need to call the police this time. Go back to your room and call them now."

Slowly, Naomi made her way toward the mess. Her gaze stayed on the front window until she reached the ground floor. When she looked down, something caught her eye: a shard of curved glass, one that hadn't come from the window. She saw a few more misfit pieces, saw the gleam of water mixed in with the shards. Naomi made a careful effort to step around the spread of glass, and crouched to look at the largest fragment. It was the base of a water glass. She recognized the wave design along the bottom.

Naomi glanced up at Leah, who still stood motionless on the stairs. "Leah, call the police," she said again. She retreated to the kitchen and made a quick check of the cupboard, then the sink and the dishwasher; she poked around the rest of the kitchen, but didn't find what she was looking for.

When she returned to the living room, Leah had barely moved. She stood on the same step, both hands clutching her head. "Leah," Naomi called, "you had a set of eight glasses, right?"

"What?"

"In your kitchen. Your water glasses. You had eight of them, right?"

"Yeah. So?"

Naomi gestured to the mess on the floor. "Someone threw a water glass through your window. I think it's one of yours." Naomi started for the stairs, looking over her shoulder at the broken window and the darkness beyond. "It has the same design, and there's one missing from your kitchen."

"It's James!" Leah shrieked.

Naomi hesitated near the steps, looking at her sister's frantic face, trying to form words from the thoughts that churned in her head—practical words that would hide her growing suspicions. "Whoever it is," she said calmly, "we should be calling the police already. Let's go upstairs. I'll call."

The police cruiser didn't take long to arrive. Two cops searched the area, and though they didn't find a culprit, they did find something of interest. Across the peeling white paint of Leah's garage door, the word "confess" was written in red.

Leah wept when she saw it. "It's never going to stop," she cried. "He'll never let it go."

As the police tried to question her, she mumbled gibberish and shook her head. "No, I'm ready," she said. "Forget about the window. I need to talk to someone about my son."

Still, they didn't understand. Leah lifted her chin and tried to speak clearly. "I lied to the police about my son," she said. "James Buchanan. He fell into the river last week. I told the police that he just fell, and that it wasn't anyone's fault. But . . . we were arguing, and I got mad and pushed him. It wasn't even the first time I pushed him that day. I shoved him against the wall that morning, and he hit his head. And then he didn't come home, and he wouldn't answer my calls, and when I found him at the park, I just got mad. I didn't mean to, but I pushed him off the bridge, and . . . he drowned. That's the truth."

Except it wasn't the truth—not entirely.

James hadn't drowned. He turned up two days later at the police station in town, the same station where Leah sat down and gave her revised version of his disappearance.

Naomi got the call from the local police. They directed her to a hospital in a neighboring city, where the precinct's sole detective waited for her outside the room where James was recovering. "To be honest, his story doesn't really add up," the detective said. "He said he doesn't remember much since that day. Says he washed down the river and ended up with some homeless people—not the ones at the park, but some other group, except he's not sure where. He told me he started wandering and finally made it back here."

"Is he all right?" Naomi asked in a wavering voice, her gaze never moving from the door of the hospital room.

"He's fine. The exams didn't show any signs of injury. He doesn't have a scratch on him."

Naomi thanked the detective and hurried to the open doorway, and there he was: James, alive and unharmed, looking back at her with those serious, penetrating eyes. Skinny James, pale and lightly freckled, nearly as tall as her now. He sat on the hospital bed, dressed in jeans and a long-sleeved yellow shirt. The same clothes he'd been wearing when he disappeared, minus the jacket.

He didn't smile or greet her, but didn't resist when Naomi hugged him. He even hugged her back, though his embrace was limp and unenthusiastic. She clung to him as the tears began to pour down her face. Then she held him at an arm's length and said: "You're alive."

He looked back at her without emotion. "Sorry I scared you."

Naomi sat beside him. "Are you all right?"

He nodded.

"Your mom is here, too—at this same hospital, as an inpatient in the mental health unit. She'll be here for a week or so." Naomi paused, but James didn't respond. "She admitted to pushing you off the bridge that day," Naomi continued. "Among other things. She's been charged with child endangerment and reckless endangerment. I thought you would want to know that."

James' expression didn't change. "I already know," he replied.

"Whatever you want to tell me about her . . . ."

James' eyes seemed even more desolate. "There's nothing you don't already know." He averted his eyes and stood up. "Can we just get out of here?"

At home, Judy also greeted him with a tearful embrace. The twins, Naomi noted, didn't seem surprised or particularly relieved. They smiled and hugged him, but there was something calmly conspiratorial about those smiles, about their silence.

While the twins showed James their new games, Naomi slipped quietly into the backyard. This time, she climbed the rope ladder without hesitating. The sun had set, but enough light filtered in through the windows that she could see the rumpled sleeping bag and pillow, the portable space heater, and other confirmations of her suspicions. A trash bag full of paper plates, tissues, and red-stained paint brushes. Plastic containers smeared with food, a still-damp hand towel, a twenty-eight-ounce can of red acrylic paint, a plastic bin with water still in it. Naomi thought back to the image of Alice's hands: cold and trembling, dipping into the meager basin of water.

Naomi sat on the floor. She drew her knees up to her chest and contemplated what to do next. Reporting James' true whereabouts for the past week seemed like a self-defeating sin; it would throw everyone back into the same pattern of helpless pugnacity. Leah, having realized the truth—that James was not a malevolent spirit, but had systematically frightened her into confessing—would probably claim that she had confessed under duress. She was likely already saying it. She would go home, get a bit of counseling to show that she was trying to change, and go back to her old ways like usual—and Naomi would notice James being bullied and neglected, like usual, and nothing would be done about it, as usual. The child endangerment reports had never helped. Leah had always attributed them to "a personal grudge." It didn't matter what the details were; they were never severe enough. When Leah dropped off six-year-old James and hadn't fed or bathed him for days, and his hair was stiff with bar soap because his head itched and he'd tried to wash it himself, and he had eaten nothing except a pack of raw hot dogs he'd found in the fridge, it wasn't enough. When his head was sore because he'd bumped it when Leah pushed him, or when he assumed that a meal meant bread and butter that he prepared himself, because that's how he always got his meals at home—none of those little details were enough for the law to intervene.

James was quiet that evening. The family as a whole was hushed by thoughts that couldn't be spoken aloud. At night, Naomi pulled out the futon and fitted it with bedding while James washed up and brushed his teeth. He came out and climbed into the bed, mumbling a quiet "Thank you."

"Want to talk about your mom?" Naomi asked.

"Not really. Nothing to say."

"The cops must have talked to you about the vandalism at your house."

"Yep. They wanted to know if I did it, or if I knew who might have done it. I said maybe it was someone who saw her push me off the bridge. Or maybe they saw her hitting me some other time, or heard her screaming at me."

"She's going to get some more intensive counseling—"

"Yeah, that's always been a big help," James cut in.

"Well, she's never been committed before. Who knows." Naomi stood a few feet from the bed, watching James with her arms folded. She tried to choose her words carefully. "I don't think you'll be expected to live with her again—"

"She won't want me to," James said, staring up at the ceiling. "She's afraid of me now."

"And how does that make you feel?" Naomi asked.

"Safe."

"She'll probably want to talk to you at some point."

James didn't reply.

"And . . . that's something we can try to feel out," Naomi continued. "See if it seems healthy or not. It might be, and it might not. It's hard to tell with family. We tend to love family members even if they're cruel. My dad could be a nightmare, and I still loved him. Sometimes, anyway. When he died, it hurt, because I knew I would never be able to resolve things with him."

"I don't love her," James replied. "And I don't need to fix things with her. I fixed them myself."

Naomi nodded. "Yeah. I know you fixed them. I'm sorry you had to do that."

He looked at her with those stark, serious eyes. "Do what?"

"I'm sorry you had to hide, and lie, and that you couldn't ask me for help."

He rolled onto his side to face her. "Why, what do you think happened?" he asked. "The police didn't believe me either. Do you think that maybe I crawled out of the river and hid, because I was afraid of my mom? And that maybe I was so afraid that I threw my jacket away and grabbed a different one from the donation bin, and I pulled the hood up to hide my face, and I snuck around and hid until night . . . and then maybe I knocked on Anton's window and spent the night on his floor, and I hid in the fort after that. It could have happened that way. I'm not saying it did, but I can see why you might think that."

He looked so intently at Naomi that she was surprised at herself—surprised that she didn't feel consumed by guilt. That feeling was swallowed whole by her grief.

She went to the futon and sat beside him. She placed a hand on his arm. "I think," she said, "that maybe you were in our fort this whole time. And maybe I just want to say I'm sorry . . . that you couldn't come to me for help. That you had to walk all the way here, cold and wet, and that you were probably half frozen by the time you got here . . . and that you had to sleep on a hard wooden floor, in a sack, in my backyard."

Naomi didn't need to see any confirmation in James' eyes, but she looked for it anyway. He didn't give it to her. He looked at her blankly and spoke without feeling. "If it did happen that way," he said, "it wouldn't have been a big deal." James rolled onto his back again. He stared at the ceiling and asked: "You know what hurts worse than freezing half to death?"

Naomi's grief intensified, washing through her like a terrible wave.

"A lot of things hurt worse than that," he mumbled. Then he glanced at Naomi and added, "I'm not offended that you think I'm lying. I can understand why people think I was hiding from my mom. If I let there be a next time, I might die for real."

They sat in silence, Naomi watching James, James watching the ceiling. She wanted to say something comforting, but her thoughts were occupied with James' eyes. Something about them seemed different. They were still intense, still penetrating, but Naomi couldn't really *see* James in those eyes. And then she realized what was missing: there was no love there, no trust, no eagerness. The realization gave Naomi a sudden unsettling feeling that James had disappeared, that a hardened and apathetic likeness had taken his place.

She leaned over and squeezed his arm. It felt like a pathetic gesture. "We'll talk more tomorrow, okay? Let's get some sleep."

"Okay," he replied. "Goodnight."

Judy was already in bed, waiting for her with the bedside lamp on. "What do you think?" she asked. "Will he be okay?"

"I think he'll need some time," Naomi said as she pulled off her clothes, "but, yeah. As long as he stays with us, I think we'll all turn out okay. Things can start getting back to normal now. We can start laughing and joking around again, we can do fun things with the kids . . . you and I can make love . . . ."

Judy smiled.

"No more constant worrying and wandering around looking for him," Naomi continued. "No more arguing with Leah, no more child endangerment reports. James only has three years left until he's an adult. Now that his mom has admitted to some things, we might be able to keep him that long. Maybe." She slipped on a T-shirt and sat on the bed with a sigh. "That's kind of depressing, actually. He's almost an adult, and this is the first time we've been able to keep him away from her."

"Well, if it makes you feel any better, we know people who have survived worse childhoods and turned out okay," Judy said. "I think James will make it."

Naomi looked at her hesitantly, but spoke the thought in her mind: "He's been staying in our fort this whole time. The twins brought a sleeping bag and pillow up there, and a space heater, and there are paper plates and other dishes from food he's been eating. That's where all our leftovers went."

Judy looked troubled, but not particularly surprised. "I kind of suspected," she said. "Well, I didn't really suspect. It was more like a passing thought. But . . . ."

"Same here, except after a while I couldn't ignore it anymore. I think I just didn't look there because I didn't want to send him home again."

Judy, too, was reluctant to speak her thoughts. After a few moments she said: "The police are probably still investigating. They might ask if we found out anything about where he's been."

Naomi nodded absently. "And if we report it? Are we just letting him down again?"

"Maybe the state won't let them live together after this. Don't you think that after all this, Leah will let him stay here?"

Naomi thought of the fear in Leah's voice, the anxious fidgeting, the wild looks of terror when she talked about James. Would it be different now that she knew he was no vengeful ghost, but just the same old James? The James who never hit or even raised his voice? Naomi recalled farther back, to James' youth and Leah's angry defenses: *He's MY son. You don't think I can raise my own kid? I practically raised you, didn't I?*

"I honestly don't know." Naomi shrugged. "But I won't let him go this time. I love Leah, I always have, but there's no helping her, not unless she has some grand epiphany and decides to help herself first. I lost my sister a long time ago. I don't want to lose James, too. I just hope I'm not too late."

Judy nodded silently. Naomi sat admiring her face in the gentle lamplight: the thin nose and high cheekbones, the lively brown eyes always lit with warmth and kindness. Naomi felt an intense gratitude, then, knowing that the idea of James living with them wasn't a question; Judy loved him as much as she did, had always loved and welcomed him. "I'm going to sleep out there tonight, okay?" Naomi said. "If James will let me. I just want to be there in case he wants to talk, or . . . maybe in case he decides to run off again." She went to the dresser and slipped on a pair of pajama shorts; then she leaned over to kiss Judy. "Goodnight."

"Goodnight, love."

In the hall, Naomi stopped to pull a fleece blanket from the closet. The living room was silent, and for a moment she felt an irrational sense of dread—but she peeked around the corner and there was James, curled up beneath the bedspread, his hair peeking out at the top. Naomi suppressed a smile as she walked to the futon. "Can I sleep next to you?" she asked.

He pulled the bedspread below his chin, craning his neck to look at her. "What?"

Naomi tossed the pillow and blanket onto the mattress. "I'm sleeping next to you tonight."

"What for? That's weird."

"I know it's weird." She climbed onto the bed and leaned over him, trying to get a glimpse of his face—a lightly freckled face framed by pale brown hair, one that reminded her of the sister she had so loved. "You're almost grown up, and it's weird to sleep in the same bed as your aunt," she said. "We haven't done that since you were, I don't know, seven or eight. But I want to do this one last time. And it's a big mattress, and you have plenty of space. So, please humor me."

"Why?"

"I don't know. In case you want to talk all of a sudden. Or . . . maybe because I thought you were dead, and I want to bask in your presence for a while. Maybe I just want to let you know that I've decided to be there for you, even if I have to do something weird."

Naomi saw him scrutinizing her face, searching her eyes. "What are you going to tell the police?" he asked.

"You're staying here from now on. As long as you want, at least until you're an adult, and until you're all set to go out on your own, you're living with us." With emphasis, she added: "That's *all* I'm telling them."

James didn't reply, but Naomi finally saw a flash of feeling in his eyes. A sudden wetness, the beginnings of tears—but the flash disappeared, and he was hidden again behind a guise of dull indifference.

She leaned over and kissed his temple, and then snuggled under the fleece blanket. "Goodnight."

After a long pause, he replied: "Goodnight." Naomi rolled onto her side, facing away from him, and closed her eyes. Behind her, James added softly: "Thank you."

The words gave her a bit of hope, but didn't ease Naomi's anxiety. Leah had instilled in her the notion that a person's hope and self-worth, once dead, could not be resurrected through love. She feared the same for James. Memories of him rolled through her mind: his intense, sad eyes shining with sudden bursts of enthusiasm and love and hope, the sadness fading into the background while he basked in a temporary realm of safety, fun, and trust.

Long into the night, after James' breath took on the heavy, rhythmic patterns of sleep, Naomi lay awake, remembering, and wondering.

Lady in a Fur Wrap

Lady in a Fur Wrap

"It has been well said that mythology is the penultimate truth—penultimate because the ultimate cannot be put into words. It is beyond words, beyond images . . . . Mythology pitches the mind beyond that rim, to what can be known but not told."
-Joseph Campbell, *The Power of Myth*

Barron Coombs took yet another turn toward the gallery where his latest work was displayed. He'd spent most of the art fair hovering close to the gallery. Barron often overheard visitors discussing his paintings, and, always eager for an opportunity to self-promote, was happy to contribute to the conversations. The blue canvas was the first to catch the eye of anyone entering the room. It perched above several much smaller works, a stunning sea of ultramarine whose size surpassed all of the other paintings combined. As Barron entered this time, however, something else caught his eye: a young brunette who stood looking up at his painting. She had sandaled feet and wore a flowing white blouse over brown leggings, and her dark hair hung in waves just past her shoulders. Something about her figure captured his attention and made him pause in the entryway. She was alone in the gallery for the moment. The last day of the art district's spring show was coming to a close, and the crowds were at their thinnest: an ideal day for meeting people, especially for meeting the young women artists who were getting ready to collect their unsold works. Opening day was always too chaotic, the weekend choked with crowds and noise, and the days in between hosted no one of importance.

Barron took the opportunity to make an approach. As he sidled up beside the woman, he caught a glimpse of prominent cheekbones and long lashes framing large brown eyes. She was young, surely somewhere around Barron's age. His initial impression was that she could have posed for a goddess painting, if not for her big nose.

He stopped, stuffing his hands into his pants pockets and following her gaze. "That one's mine," he said. "The big one, titled 'Genesis.'" Barron half-turned to the woman, making sure his expression was one of innocent curiosity. "Are you also an artist, or are you a collector? I noticed you talking to the auction staff earlier."

"Artist," she replied. Her voice had a calm, soothing quality, with a subtle dryness. "New to this collective. New to the area, actually."

"Oh, you're in this neighborhood? I used to live in one of those tiny little apartments, too. Mine had a utility pole running right through the middle of the hallway. Everyone had to squeeze around it to get to the kitchen. A few years ago, those were all just a bunch of crappy, unwanted apartment buildings on a street full of boarded-up shops—but someone saw an opportunity, raised the prices and called them artists' lofts, and the place came to life again. All these little cafes and stores are new. They sprang up after young people moved into the neighborhood. Young people with money."

"Hm. Kind of contradicts my notion of the starving artist." She glanced at him briefly, but looked away before he could make eye contact. Barron regretted the missed chance. Women often told him that he had warm eyes and an alluring gaze.

"Oh, no one here is starving," he said. "Their parents sponsor them, or they find someone else to do the job." Barron watched her, waiting for her gaze to meet his, but there was no obligatory glance or nervous smile. She maintained an aura of perpetual coolness. "So, are you renting a gallery space here?" he asked.

"No, I just donated a couple of old pieces to the silent auction."

"Did they sell?"

"One sold, but not for much."

"Ah. How bad is it?"

"The minimum. Twenty dollars."

Barron let out a low whistle. "Well, that's typical. People don't shell out for donated art. If it ends up in the silent art auction, that usually means it's a throw-away that no one else wanted to buy. Which ones are yours?"

"I have two Greek goddess paintings. Daphne and Cornix."

He knew instantly which works she was referring to. He'd seen them several times as he passed through the front gallery. *Cornix* was a portrait of a raven-haired old woman with startling bird-like eyes. The other painting bore a hybrid figure: a tree in the shape of a woman. The figure was shown from a low perspective, as though the viewer crouched close to the ground; the result was a daunting, inhuman figure that towered over the viewer. The tree-woman's brown arms split into a profundity of branching twigs, her long green hair trailed purple blossoms—and above her, a thick forest canopy sprawled. Though Barron would never hang such artwork on his own walls, both pieces had demanded his scrutiny. His own canvas, in comparison, bore little life-like detail. Its surface was a solid, dark blue, with one lighter blue steak that flowed like a stream across its surface.

"Oh, you paint the goddess," he said casually. "Unfortunately, so do half the women in the cohort."

She nodded toward the large blue canvas. "I see that yours sold for two thousand dollars."

"Yes, it sold right away. I knew it would. People were already interested in it before the show. I've sold a few similar paintings, and they caught on."

"And what's the concept behind it?"

"Space. Creation. Color. Without the lighter shade streaking across, you have a vibrant but uneventful space. The streak transforms an eventless space into an arena of form and creation, of limitless potential. It *defines* this space—or interrupts it. You decide." Barron gave her a small smirk, adding: "Or it's just an over-priced splotch of paint. That's what sells these days. People are tired of looking at pretty pictures. They want *ideas*."

She shrugged. "Yes, or they want something that matches their living room set. How long did it take you to make this piece?"

"I covered the whole thing in one shade of blue and sponge-rolled it with a lighter shade. It took me about fifteen minutes. But hey, the canvas cost me fifty bucks, and I used two bottles of acrylic—not to mention the sponge and roller, the plastic sheet . . . ." Barron snuck another glance at the woman, studying her cool expression. "How long did it take to finish your Daphne painting?"

He knew it had taken a long time. The work was full of fine detail and layering that couldn't have been finished quickly. Most people in this situation would look embarrassed, but the young woman's face didn't change.

"I'm not a full-time artist," she replied. "I worked on it off and on for a couple of years."

"Well, you don't have to be a full-time artist. You just have to know how to market yourself. People complain that there aren't any art or literary movements anymore, and that it's all about marketing, but it's *always* been about marketing. A movement doesn't become prominent because of its originality or social importance, and artists don't become notable because of talent. They become notable because they get into bed with the influential, and that group defines the movement and markets it. Look back through history and you'll see it every time: artists become popular after they hook up with a notable person or group—or they die unnoticed, and some schmoozer decides to make a dollar off their work, and suddenly this unknown artist is touted as a genius."

"And who is your notable person?"

"I have more than one. Would you like to meet some of them? The guy who bought this painting is having a private event at Fuller Art Center this Thursday. They'll have food and drinks in one of the lounges, and access to some of the galleries. It's going to be a small event. They can only invite a hundred and twenty people, but they plan to keep it even tighter than that. I'm allowed to bring a date. You can persuade them of the high artistic merit of your goddess paintings. If you want to exchange numbers, I'll bring you along."

A vague frown touched the woman's lips. It was the first real reaction Barron had seen from her. "I don't know. That's not really my thing."

Barron shrugged. "Well, art as a profession isn't everyone's thing. You can certainly keep churning out work for ten dollars a year."

"Are you sure you want to bring a stranger to an exclusive event? You don't even know my name."

"What is it?"

"Voleta."

He extended his hand, and she accepted it. "Voleta? I'm Barron. Pleased to meet you. And yes, I would bring a stranger to an exclusive event. A fresh face is always a plus."

She pulled a cell phone from her purse and checked the display. "Do you have any other pieces here?"

"No. My other pieces are at galleries around the city."

"Well, the art fair is over. I should get my painting from the auction before the volunteers stash it somewhere."

Barron assumed she was making an excuse to ditch him, but she added: "Want to come with me? You might find a twenty-dollar throw-away that matches your living room."

They walked to the front gallery and spent a few minutes perusing tables loaded with sculptures and other 3D art, and walls cluttered with canvases. Barron didn't find anything worth his money—nor anything that matched his living room. He stood by as Voleta gingerly lifted the Daphne painting from the wall.

"So, what's the concept behind this one?" Barron asked. "It's Daphne turning into a tree, isn't it? To escape one horny god or another?"

"Yes, it is Daphne turning into a tree, supposedly to escape from Apollo. Maybe. I don't think Daphne or Cornix magically transformed into anything. I think it's more likely that they escaped, and the transformation was just some B.S. made up by a man unwilling to admit his defeat. Or maybe the women died and became something else . . . or they were never women to begin with. Cornix was always a crow, and Daphne was always a tree." Voleta finished lowering the canvas and stood looking at the image she'd created. "Tell me what you think is more likely: a man thinking he has got hold of someone, only to find himself clutching a laurel tree, or someone dying beside a laurel and becoming part of the root system?"

"Ah, interesting. The corpse *would* become part of that place, if left alone," Barron said. "It would become part of the food chain. That's likely, but I can't imagine someone mistaking a bushy tree for a woman. Anyway, those stories carry as much weight as the Easter Bunny or the Flying Spaghetti Monster. Less, actually, because those myths actually spawned real movements."

Voleta began to walk toward the front exit, with Barron following alongside. "And Daphne didn't?"

"No," Barron replied. "She's just a lasting symbol of a helpless woman. A sign of the times."

"Was she helpless? I think that's the question about these stories—stories about women shapeshifting, or putting on a glamour, to survive. In Greek mythology, the Cretan goddess Britomartis tried to escape by turning into a fish and got caught in a fishing net, and Ariadne used her threads to help a Greek hero—but if you look at older goddess symbology, the threads and nets are actually the goddess' own webs of creation."

"I don't follow mythology. I think artists have overworked that arena."

"We have, because whoever tells the story influences the interpretation. The Greek stories could be about men's fear of women who go outside the bounds of law . . . women who defy social conventions, because those conventions protect the corrupt."

Outside, they made their way past a smattering of tattooed youngsters who were heading into the arts building. Voleta abandoned her tiresome ponderings on mythology as they walked. She led Barron to the adjacent parking garage and stopped beside a battered Buick. "Hold this for a minute, would you?"

Barron took the canvas from her, tilting it back to get a better look. Something about Dahphe's posture disturbed him. The branches that made up her arms were stretched out at her sides, so long that they extended past the edge of the canvas. Beyond her featureless face, a profundity of branches crept across the backdrop like a dense capillary network, gave an impression of stifling vastness—an inescapable, smothering net. "She looks intimidating and creepy," Barron said.

"Is she intimidating? She's meant to be seen from Apollo's perspective. Of course, the viewer doesn't necessarily see what Apollo sees."

"Ah. You mean that his reaction, or his interpretation, is based on his character. Apollo was a powerful god. I don't think he would be cowed by a tree." Barron looked up from the painting as Voleta opened the trunk.

"I'm still moving the last of my stuff, so my trunk is full of crap," she said, rummaging through a heap of clothes. "Give me a second."

She took the canvas and set it down on an expanse of animal fur. Barron hadn't noticed it when she opened the trunk, but it was in full view now: a thick white coat accentuated with shades of gray. "I didn't take you for someone who does fur," he said. "What is that?"

"It's Yuka. My dog. She died a few years ago."

"What do you mean, it's your dog?"

"I had a Siberian husky since I was little. When she died, I found a taxidermist who preserved her coat for me."

Barron stared down at the gray-and-white spread. "Seriously? What is it, though? You made your dog into a rug?"

A tiny smile played on Voleta's face. "It's a wrap. Dog skin isn't thick enough to make a durable rug. I don't use this often, so it's holding up pretty well."

"A wrap? So, you wear it?"

"I've worn it a few times." She finished arranging the canvas and closed the trunk. "I keep it handy just in case. Last winter, I got a flat tire in five-degree weather, and Yuka's fur kept me warm while I changed the tire. The wheel and the lug nuts were frozen on, and I had to sit there and use a hand torch to melt the ice off. Every once in a while, I've found myself in a situation where I needed this wrap."

"You don't feel weird, wearing your dead dog's skin?"

"I do," she replied. "Every time."

"But you wear it anyway?"

Voleta smiled and turned to him. The movement startled him; it was the first time she had faced him full-on and looked him in the eye. Barron was not easily moved by women, but he found Voleta's eyes strangely fetching: deep brown pools full of warmth and amusement. "Are you having second thoughts about exchanging numbers?" she asked. "You can always find another date for your fancy art shindig."

"No, come along. You'll have fun. Anyway, all artists have eccentricities. Some cover themselves in piercings, some will only paint in the nude, some wear their dead dogs as coats . . . ."

Voleta pulled out her phone, still smiling. Barron heard the rapid clicking of her typing as she entered his name into her contacts list. "What's your number?"

He paused, enjoying her unruffled demeanor and this new insight into her mind. Voleta was perhaps slightly less ordinary than he'd supposed. He exchanged numbers with her, feeling confident that he had gained the acquaintance of someone who would keep him entertained for a little while.

He called her Thursday morning to make arrangements. Barron repeatedly offered to pick her up, but Voleta insisted on meeting him at the art center. "I'll be in the area anyway," she said. "I'll meet you in the free lot at seven-thirty."

The free lot was a parking space close to the grounds, tucked behind the sculpture gardens that sprawled in front of the galleries. Barron parked there shortly before seven-forty; he liked to be fashionably late. It gave the impression that he had more important matters to attend to. He had also taken extra time to groom himself beforehand, slicking his hair back and dressing in his trademark style: a thin gray suit with a white dress shirt.

He passed Voleta's old Buick in the lot. She wasn't there, so Barron kept walking, supposing she had wandered into the sculpture gardens. He had just left the lot when he spotted Voleta approaching him on the sidewalk, the fur wrap draped around her shoulders. Barron greeted her by asking: "You're wearing that hideous dog skin?"

"It's cold out. And this isn't hideous."

"Some of the people in there have an aversion to fur. They'll call you an egoistic animal killer."

"I didn't kill Yuka. She died."

"Fair enough. Have fun explaining that." As they started toward the art center, Barron's gaze dropped to Voleta's chest, where a strand of bright red beads hung, tinged here and there with lighter shades of orange. He leaned closer, trying to get a better look. "Are those seeds?"

She lifted a section of the necklace, fingering the beads. "Yeah. Mountain laurel."

"Cute. It suits you. It implies an affinity with nature, like your paintings. How far do you want to go with your artwork? Do you have a portfolio put together?"

"No."

"Have you ever tried to get a sponsor? You could apply for one, even with the two paintings you had on display."

"I haven't."

"You should try. It would help cover your living costs while you focus on your artwork. Don't bother going after sponsorships from art suppliers or magazines, though. Every other desperate artist is already going after them. You have to find a vacuum somewhere— someone with an unfulfilled need. Find out what's important to a potential sponsor and figure out how you can provide it. And don't waste your time babbling to them about your goals and dreams; they don't give a shit. It's a contract. They give you what you want, you give them what they want."

"Hm. And what are you giving?"

Barron cracked a grin. "A good protégé never tells. We sometimes reveal the terms of our contract for marketing purposes, but of course we leave certain things out."

"So it's all a sham."

"It always has been." Barron sighed as he looked up at Fuller Art Center. Rows of bright windows gleamed against the coming dark. He could see the party already started on the third floor, hints of elegance and conversation and newly forming connections. "My sponsor, Jared, is pretty loaded. He forked out nearly eight thousand dollars for this little get-together." He glanced at Voleta and gave her a quick, discreet once-over. "He'll like you. Just make sure you don't wear your dead dog into the party room. You can leave it at coat check."

They passed looming sculptures of a steampunk seahorse and a bisected stone woman, and ascended the wide front steps of the art center. Beyond the glass doors, the lobby was dimly lit. The gift shop was fully illuminated by contrast, the clerk ready and smiling at the counter.

"Exit through the gift shop, of course," Barron murmured. "I bet it will still be open when we leave."

"Let's go in," Voleta said. "It looks like they have a lot of prints. I just want to see what they've got."

The gift shop mostly contained T-shirts and poster-sized prints of Fuller's permanent installations. On the counter were file stacks of cardstock copies of paintings from the old masters, including several prints from Goya's *The Disasters of War* series. Voleta scrutinized the Goya prints, then passed them over and selected a postcard depicting *Lady in a Fur Wrap*.

"Does it look like me?" she asked.

The subject in the sixteenth-century oil painting, a young woman with flushed cheeks, was wearing a fur robe not dissimilar to Voleta's dead dog getup. Barron continued to study the image while Voleta paid the cashier. Most of the figure's body was obscured; one thin hand clutched the thick fur wrap that hung around the shoulders, and the face was tightly framed by a sheer veil. The woman, with her large brown eyes and dark, wavy hair, did look a bit like Voleta—except without the big nose.

"You know, no one really knows who painted *Lady in a Fur Wrap*," Barron said, "or who the subject is. It's usually attributed to Coello or El Greco, but some people think Sofonisba Anguissola painted it. What do you think?"

"Coello," Voleta replied without pause. "If you look at the way he paints eyes and mouths, and hands, and skin tone, you can see it." She grabbed a pen from the desk and wrote on the back of the postcard. "Today is the twenty-fifth, isn't it?"

Barron leaned closer. "Yeah. What are you writing?"

Voleta gave him a cryptic grin as she folded the postcard and stuffed it into her purse. "Private message."

"Ooh, a mystery. Will you say who it's for, though? Is it some artist lover hidden away in those little apartments?"

"Something like that."

"That's all right. I'm not the jealous type. I don't mind sharing you." He lowered his voice a notch and added: "I kind of like that idea, actually."

Barron viewed her out of the corner of his eye, trying to gauge her reaction, but she didn't give him one. The cashier, a college-age girl, blushed a slight crimson.

He turned and started toward the exit, but stopped when he found someone blocking his path. Louisa, another painter who lived in the artists' lofts, stood in the doorway and stared at him with a deer-in-headlights expression. Neither of them moved, and then Louisa's focus shifted from Barron to Voleta. Her lips parted, as though she was about to speak—but she lowered her eyes and hurried away.

"Someone you know?" Voleta asked.

"Ah, that's Louisa," Barron said. He resumed walking—slowly, though, to give Louisa a good head start. "She's probably jealous. We almost had a fling a little while ago. She turned out to be kind of a nut job."

"How so?"

"I'll tell you about it later. Let's get rid of your dead dog, and then I'll introduce you to some people." He glanced at Voleta's purse. "You're not going to tell me who the postcard is for?"

"Maybe it's for you. Wait and see."

"Ah, you're mysterious. I like that."

"I'm a bit like the painter of *Lady in a Fur Wrap*. I never sign my artworks, either."

"You don't? Are you serious? That's a mistake. You'll never get a following that way."

"Maybe it's my marketing gimmick," Voleta said. "I'm a nameless, ageless mystery artist. People will have to identify my works by a consistent pattern that shows up in each one."

"No one will bother if you don't get a following first." Barron gestured toward the staircase ahead of them. "Let's take the stairs. Elevators are for slugs."

They ascended to the Drummond Lounge, where guests were still just beginning to trail into the room. Voleta checked her dead dog skin near the entrance and shoved the ticket into her purse, and gave Barron a ready smile. "Shall we?"

The glass wall at the far end of the lounge allowed an expansive view of the city: a network of brilliant lights and countless pockets of shadow. Most of the guests lingered near that wall, chatting and drinking, posing in crisp dress shirts and skimpy dresses. Barron directed Voleta to the hors d'oeuvres table. "Don't act too eager to meet anyone," he advised. "Play it cool. Make them come to you instead. We'll make an exception for my sponsor, though, since he's the host. There's room at his table. We'll get some food and schmooze with him for a while."

Barron helped himself to a salmon tartine and a bowl of cold beet soup, and started his bar tab with a Dark 'n Stormy. His sponsor, Jared, sat at a low table surrounded by leather couches. He was a young man for someone in his field of work. He'd started a publishing company at the age of twenty-two, and in just a few years had made it a still-growing success. He was stylishly dressed in a black suit. Like Barron, he wore an open jacket with a white dress shirt underneath. Flanking him were a skinny blond and an older woman wearing what was obviously a wig. Barron perched on the loveseat nearest to Jared and set down his platter and drink.

"Jared," he greeted him. "You're looking sharp, as usual." He addressed Voleta: "This is my sponsor, Jared Tatum. He's the CEO of Tatum Publishing and Music Group. Jared, this is Voleta. She's a painter. She just moved here from . . . ." Barron gave Voleta a questioning look.

"I'm from here," she said. "I'm just new to the artists' collective."

Jared greeted her with an inoffensive coolness that matched her own, but Barron saw that he approved of her. He had a particular way of prolonging eye contact and giving a slight nod when he was interested in a woman. Initially, Barron thought it was an unconscious gesture, but now he interpreted it as a signal. Voleta was wearing another flowy white getup, a long dress that set off the bright red beads around her neck. Her hair was pulled into a messy bun at the back of her head, with a few loose locks curling against the nape of her neck. She looked a bit like a Greek goddess statue, Barron thought as he studied her figure.

They chatted for a while, and then Barron got up to introduce Voleta around the room. He enjoyed showing off his date, and was liberal with putting his arm around her, which she tolerated without any stiffness or protest. Barron admired her indifference. He liked the idea that he might be the one to stir her up.

Barron fetched another Dark 'n Stormy from the bar, though the few drinks he'd already had were beginning to affect him. When he turned to find Voleta, she was gone. He scanned the now-crowded room, until at last Voleta's white dress caught his attention. She stood near the glass wall with Louisa.

"What the hell," Barron muttered. He walked over to them, unaffected by the anxious look that came over Louisa's face when she noticed his approach. Barron had learned that it didn't pay to give any distance to those types of women. He had to show her that he could go wherever he wanted, do whatever he wanted, without any interference from her.

She took off as he drew near, leaving Voleta alone. Barron watched as Louisa scurried through the exit. He asked Voleta: "What did she say?"

He looked for signs of suspicion in Voleta's face, but there were none. "What do you think she said?" she replied calmly.

"We had a skirmish a while ago. She's been villainizing me since then. It's starting to get on my nerves."

"What kind of skirmish?"

"It was a misunderstanding. Look, I'm a guy. I like pretty girls, and I like to have fun. Who doesn't? Louisa is pretty. Not very smart, but she's pretty. I took her out and introduced her to Jared, and I tried to have some fun with her, and she flipped out."

"What did you do?"

"I invited her to hang out with us privately, and she freaked. Acted like we tried to attack her."

"Did you?"

"No. Not at all. She got scared because she was alone with us in the parking lot, and she just flipped out—but it looked bad because she got a couple of scratches on her arm. I just took her arm to walk with her, but she pulled away so hard that my fingernails scratched her. And then she filed a report about it to the art fair committee, since it happened at one of their events, and I almost got booted for the rest of the season. Fortunately, there are people on the committee who know my worth. They should be *begging* me to come back. I actually bring in people who spend money. Louisa doesn't do shit for their sales."

Voleta said nothing, had no reaction. She just looked at him.

"And Louisa didn't get reprimanded, even though she caused all this trouble," Barron continued. "I mean, where's the woman's responsibility in all this? Louisa acts all saintly when she's at an event, and people have this idea of her like she's . . . like she's a Sunday school teacher. But she isn't innocent at all. In private, she calls herself a 'rebel bitch' and talks about taking drugs. She sends out a totally different message, and then acts like it's my fault that I misunderstood her."

"I see," Voleta replied. "So it's okay to assault her, then—because you can nitpick some random thing she did, like calling herself a rebel or wearing a skirt, and then you can tell yourself 'She sent me a message.'"

Barron was acutely aware of the fact that he'd said something incriminating. He hadn't meant to say those particular words—not out loud, not to Voleta. "No, no. I just meant . . . she doesn't project an honest image of herself. She *acts* innocent, but she's not."

"What do you mean by innocent?"

Barron struggled for words. He'd had too much to drink; he

could feel it now.

"You mean, someone who doesn't deserve to be assaulted," Voleta suggested. "An innocent person is someone who doesn't deserve to be harassed, and women aren't innocent. Is that it?"

"What the hell. Fuck. That's not what I'm saying." Barron closed his eyes for a moment, rubbing his forehead. "Look, that's really not what I'm saying. Women get so defensive and judgmental over this shit. I didn't assault Louisa. I just made a pass at her. I read her the wrong way. She got scratched because she freaked out." He set his glass down on an empty high-top. "I don't feel that great. Let's walk around one of the galleries, okay? Or are you afraid to be alone with me now?"

"Not at all," she replied coolly.

They walked to the nearest gallery, a permanent installation mostly made up of oversized sculptures and some canvases on a central wall. The lights were dimmed. Barron expected them to switch on when he entered, but they didn't change, leaving the guests to peruse the gallery in shadow. "I don't know what was wrong in there," he said, meandering between the central wall and a sculpture made of busted toilets. "I started to feel really out of it."

"You're feeling better now?" Voleta asked.

"Yeah. Yeah, it's fine now. Seeing Louisa skulking around probably made me queasy. I shouldn't have to acquiesce to her stupid paranoia, but it gets on my nerves. Being attracted to a woman isn't a crime. People act like men are monsters just because they get turned on."

"Are you sure about that? All humans get turned on. Most aren't accused of crimes."

"Okay, let me ask you this: At the art fair, there was a painting of a female figure swimming in a pool. A bunch of male figures were standing around and staring at her, and they all had erections. Is that sexist?"

"I think the question should be 'Is the culture sexist.' In what—"

"That's not the question. My question is 'Is the message sexist.' No one wants to answer this because it's not PC, and that's part of what's ruining the dialogue about art, and that in turn is suppressing artistic expression."

"A message has context. Aren't you just arguing about it because you got in trouble?"

"I didn't get in trouble. I was innocent. The committee made a formal decision on it. They're artists; they get that this women-as-victims stuff is causing trouble. I see that theme in your artwork, too. Both of your paintings were of women who were assaulted by men. The theme is something like, 'Oh, women, look out, men are trying to harm you. You need to take back your power.' They're feminist fantasy portraits with no method behind them. You could paint twelve of them and make a Modern Feminist Mythology calendar."

To Barron's surprise, Voleta smiled. Her lips thinned as she pressed them together, and he realized she was suppressing a laugh.

"Is that funny?" he asked. "I think you know it's true. Really, what's the concept behind your work? You didn't come up with one. You borrowed one from pop culture." Barron stopped suddenly, realizing that he was getting angry. He had let Louisa's accusation get to him. He and Voleta had come to a stop beside the canvases, out of view of the entrance, with the exhibit wall between them and the doorway, and it occurred to him suddenly that he had walked behind it on purpose—that he was hiding in case Louisa walked by. He was sick of seeing those fearful, judgmental glances. Barron took a few quiet breaths, trying to ease his agitation. "Listen, I don't mean that as a criticism. I mean it as an encouragement. You have talent as a painter. I can see it in your work. You just need the right inspiration."

Voleta nodded subtly. "And you're going to inspire me?"

Barron clenched his teeth. Her coolness was starting to get on his nerves. Voleta leaned back against an empty space on the display wall and folded her arms.

"Is that an invitation?" he asked. "Yes, I will inspire you. Listen closely, okay? This is the most inspiring thing any artist will ever say to you. You know how there are all these paintings and sculptures with no obvious purpose or meaning, like mine. People always have to ask, 'What's the concept behind it?' And the artist gives an answer, and people buy it. You saw the piece I had at the art fair. Close your eyes and picture it."

She stared at him.

"Close your eyes," he repeated.

With a barely audible sigh, Voleta closed her eyes.

Barron moved his lips slightly nearer to her face. "Picture it. A deep blue background, like the sky at night, with a single streak of light trailing across. Ask yourself: What's the idea behind this piece?" He waited, but Voleta didn't make a sound. Softly, he continued: "It's ego. Desire. Complicity and pleasure. Can you see it?"

She opened her eyes. Her pupils reflected a low light somewhere behind him, and for a moment Barron was dazzled. Voleta had striking eyes, large and deep brown with thick lashes, complimented by black eyeliner that brought out the dark shades of her irises and her hair. Jared would like Voleta, too. He would forgive the too-large nose just because of those eyes and those full lips.

"I sold a slab of paint for thousands of dollars," Barron said quietly. "I will sell more slabs of paint, and people will mount them like trophies . . . like objects of worth and fascination. And I will go out and enjoy the money and the connections that I made. That's the concept. It may sound empty and narcissistic, but it's the nature of the art industry. Half of the artists in our community just duplicate the art they've seen, but they use different colors, or they draw a line or a spiral through it and say, 'Now it's original.'" He laughed, leaning forward slightly, and was hit with a sudden dizziness. Barron rubbed his forehead again, swearing under his breath.

"I shouldn't drink anymore," he said. "It's affecting me." He lowered his hand and tried to assess Voleta. She seemed unruffled as usual. "Did I scare you? Don't mind me, okay? Don't let me drink anymore. I'm supposed to hang out with Jared later tonight. You should come, too. He might even sponsor you. You're his type—and mine. We like brunettes, brown eyes."

"Hm. Yes, hair and eye color are such signifiers." Voleta gazed steadily at Barron. "You don't know me."

"I know enough. I've seen your artwork."

A faint smile touched her lips. "I actually don't paint much. I'm more of a performance artist."

"Oh yeah? How so?"

She didn't reply, just looked at him with those large eyes.

"Maybe you could perform a little something for me," Barron suggested. He stepped closer, placing a hand against the wall beside her neck. His other hand moved to her thigh, the fingers probing beneath the hem of her dress.

Voleta pushed his hand away. "Knock it off."

He glanced around the room. "Let me. No one's watching."

"I said no." She shoved him, sending him staggering back a couple of steps. "You're not my type at all. I don't like men who push themselves on women, just because they assume they can do it with impunity."

"What, are you saying that because of what I said? What did I even say?" Barron suddenly couldn't remember his own words— just that he'd uttered something he hadn't meant to. "Did I blame Louisa? You take me too seriously. I was joking about all that. I had to take a jab at her, after the trouble she caused." Barron recovered his balance with some difficulty. He felt suddenly, inexplicably weak, yet he managed to straighten up and face Voleta again. "I was buzzed. I'm really not some kind of predator, okay? My mother didn't raise me to be that kind of slime." He forced a smile, let his gaze rove over her. "You know, you're very alluring when you feel passionate about something. I really was joking, though."

Voleta folded her arms again. "There's a famous quote by C.S. Lewis that goes something like, 'Nothing helps towards a man's damnation so much as his discovery that almost anything he wants to do can be done, not only without the disapproval but with the admiration of his fellows, if only he can get it treated as a joke.'"

Barron rolled his eyes. "Oh, C.S. Lewis. There's a stick in the mud for you. Look, we're here to have fun. Maybe your idea of fun is different from mine. You lead the way, then. We can look at sculptures and have the same tired old conversations about concept and originality, or whatever."

Voleta didn't respond.

"Come on, are you like this every time you go out? You're *stiff.*" Barron grabbed her shoulder, gave her a light shake. "Really, you exude restraint. You're an artist. You need to experiment, play around. Do it for the sake of your art, at least. Your soul doesn't come out in your art. Your paintings are all replicas of what you think you *should* be: innocent, holy, a mass-marketed goddess. So many women artists are like that. Those are all reflections of your supposed obligations to everyone around you." Barron was aware that he was talking too much, that his criticisms wouldn't have the desired effect, but couldn't stop the flow of words. "Do something for *yourself* for a change."

"Is that what you said to Louisa?"

The question startled him. Voleta uttered it calmly, without emotion, yet those few words were confrontational. Barron felt flickers of anger in his core. The knowing, presumptuous look in Voleta's eyes transformed those flickers into creeping flames. He'd been looked at like that before. He resented being looked at like that.

"Your art," she continued dryly, "has no soul."

He was too surprised to reply—and then Voleta was gone. She disappeared behind the wall, into the shadows, without so much as a sound. Barron hadn't even seen her move. He took a few steps, peered around the installation wall, paused to listen. The gallery seemed empty.

"What the hell," he whispered. How had she vanished so quickly? He stepped into the hall, then returned to the lounge. Barron stopped near the doorway and scanned the room, saw a mass of smiling faces and swanky outfits—but no white dress.

At last he spotted her, seated on the loveseat where he'd first introduced her to Jared. Barron started forward, but halted again and leaned against one of the high-top tables. His legs felt suddenly, inexplicably weak. He felt his heartbeat accelerating, and for a moment his vision blurred. His arms, too, felt strange. Barron lifted his free hand, saw it trembling.

He sat on the stool, closing his eyes and focusing on his breath. Something didn't feel right. He wasn't just drunk. Perhaps he'd been dieting too much. Barron was strict about his weight, and had severely cut his calories to keep on track.

Jared noticed him and called his name. "What's the matter?" he asked, coming closer. "Too much to drink?"

"I'm fine," Barron said. "I just need to eat something."

"Are you dieting again? Don't overdo it, okay? Starving is for women. It doesn't look good on men. Stay here a second." He left, then came back a minute later with a small plate of arugula and fava bean crostini. "Eat this, at least. And no more alcohol. Are we meeting later?"

"I don't know," Barron replied. "I'll talk to Voleta. She doesn't seem to be up for it right now."

"Have you been able to get a drink into her? She seems sober."

"No."

"You're off your game. Convince her, okay? Tell her we're just going to hang out in the game room of a really cool house. I'll let her throw a few darts, or something." Jared patted him on the shoulder and walked away.

Barron ate the crostini, though it stuck in his throat. He went to the bar to get some water and pay his tab. Voleta was still sitting on the loveseat, chatting it up with Sera and Dale, two members of a local band, and Ben, a theater director. She seemed to be having a good time. Her eyes were lively, her expression one of ease and pleasure. Barron sat down heavily beside her, taking a moment to balance himself.

"Barron," Sera greeted him. "I was wondering if you were here. We just showed up."

Barron heard the delight in her tone. Sera liked him. She wasn't his type; she was a butch-looking blond with bad skin, but he suddenly appreciated her attentions. They might make Voleta re-think her stance.

"Yeah, I'm here. I see you've met Voleta."

Sera's smile faded. "Are you together?"

"I'm his guest," Voleta replied. "We just met."

They resumed their conversation—something about a community debate that took place at Ben's theater, some monthly event that Barron had never heard of and had no interest in, but that Voleta could talk about in eloquent detail. He listened as she offered her insights into the latest forum on the city's affordable housing crisis, and then he blurted: "You know, Voleta isn't as straight as she seems. Did she tell you that she had her dead dog skinned and made into a fur wrap? It's hanging in the coat check right now."

Sera gasped; her eyes widened. Ben peered at Voleta with mild curiosity and asked, "Is that true?"

Voleta smiled. "Yes, it's true. All artists have eccentricities though, don't they? Some cover themselves in piercings and tattoos, some will only paint in the nude, some wear their dead dogs as coats

. . . ."

A chuckle resounded through the group.

Voleta reached into her purse and checked her phone. "It's late. I should go." She stood up. "Have a good night, everyone." She gave Barron a friendly glance and added, "See you around. I'm going to head out with my dead dog."

Barron watched as she walked away. Sera began to speak to him, but he stood up, wavering for a moment as his legs nearly gave way. He walked after Voleta, assuring himself that he would feel steadier soon. He had eaten, and he hadn't consumed more alcohol than usual. Not really.

"Hey," he said as he reached the coat check. Voleta already had the wrap and was pulling it around her shoulders.

"Hey," she replied, but didn't wait for him. She headed for the stairs.

"Are you giving me the cold shoulder now?" Barron hurried after her, letting one hand trail along the wall in case he lost his balance. "Is that the thanks I get for bringing you to this kind of event?"

Without turning around, she asked: "Do I owe you something?"

"Were you offended that I hit on you?" he persisted. "It was a compliment. Or is it because of what I said about your painting? I just meant that you're talented, and you should use your talent for something more, instead of painting pictures of tired-out stories."

"It is a tired-out story," she replied. "*I'm* tired of it." Voleta stopped at the top of the staircase and smiled at him, her eyes once again full of amusement—yet he detected something else there, a flash of grief perhaps, or of mere disillusionment.

"You were offended," he said. "I know you were, because you made a petty jab at my painting."

"Oh, I was joking. Of course your paintings have soul. Even a simple shade of blue has soul. If I can't see it, isn't that a reflection of me, and not the artist?" Voleta reached out and lightly jostled Barron's shoulder. "You're too stiff. Loosen up a little. We're here to have fun." She began to descend the stairs, her shoes clattering loudly on the marble steps.

Barron started after her, clutching the railing for support—but his arms shook, and he felt a sudden sense of fear as he gazed down the long, hard stairway.

"Shit," he whispered. He turned around and went to the elevator.

Voleta had already gone through the doors when Barron reached the first floor. He swore again and stumbled through the exit, leaning against the metal railing as he made a painstaking trek down the wide front steps. He reached the sculpture garden and nearly gave up his pursuit, thinking Voleta must be far ahead of him, but then he caught sight of the white-and-gray wrap and the skirt of a white dress. Voleta had stopped on the sidewalk and was gazing up at the *Bisected Woman* sculpture. The sculpture towered over her, a double column of bronze, each an impression of half of a feminine figure— as though the figure had been split vertically down the middle. The halves were separated not only by distance, but by a thin, jagged slab full of sharp, angled edges, as though it had sliced down and cut the woman in two. The left-hand figure was positioned so that its single eye appeared to look down at Voleta.

"Hey," he said, stopping beside her. "Voleta. Listen, okay? I'm sorry if I offended you. Don't take off yet. I really want to hang out with you a little longer."

"Why? So you can take me to Jared Tatum's game room?"

Barron tried to scrutinize Voleta's face, but even under the bright lamplight, her features were blurry. His eyes couldn't quite focus. "Why? What did Louisa tell you?"

"Nothing I haven't already heard."

Barron's legs began to cramp. His lungs, too, felt strangely cramped. He was gasping for breath, as though he'd sprinted rather than staggered. The pavement scraped his palms as he fell to the sidewalk. Voleta looked down at him, her eyes still obscured—yet he saw the lamplight gleaming in those large eyes. She crouched beside him. He was vaguely aware of Voleta slipping something into his pocket.

"That's for you," she said.

Her face came into focus. As Barron looked at her unabashed smile, a sudden, suspicious horror rose in him. "Did you put something in my drink?"

"Of course not," she said calmly. "My mother didn't raise me to be that type of slime. But you wouldn't really know if I did or not, would you? I could be any kind of person. I could be a nut job, or a murderer, or a Sunday school teacher, or a rebel bitch. I could be someone who detests little shits like you. You think you can come after women who are nice, and who have no connections, and nothing will happen to you because of it. Well, I'm nice, and I have no connections—so come after me."

Barron heaved himself to his feet. Voleta was already far ahead of him on the sidewalk, going at an easy pace. He could see the pale fur wrap moving in the darkness.

"Hey!" he yelled.

Resentment drove him forward. Barron was starting to realize, now, how Voleta had led him on. Those incriminating words echoed in his mind: *Nothing I haven't already heard.* She had already heard rumors, already judged him, all the while playing cool. This whole time, she'd been toying with him. He could only imagine what had been said, and who had been saying it.

"Hey!" he said again, stumbling closer. He would make her stop—even if it meant another scratched arm and more accusations, or worse. Barron was not the type to be toyed with.

He grabbed at the wrap, but his fingertips slid uselessly against the slick fur. "I said stop," he muttered, and made a stumbling lunge. He grabbed at the fur with both hands, securing it tightly in his grip.

Voleta's head turned. Something about the movement of her head confused Barron—as though she had turned her head all the way around without turning her body. Her face shifted towards him, but her body didn't.

He released her, but only for a moment. Barron surged forward again and caught her in an even bolder grasp. His mouth opened to speak, but he found himself speechless, startled by the strangeness of Voleta's eyes. They were surely the same eyes, large and round, edged in black eyeliner—but the brown irises seemed to have expanded, so that even in that wide-open stare, not even a sliver was visible of the whites of Voleta's eyes. Barron saw anger there, a simultaneously threatened and threatening rage. And the nose—that too-big nose was a puzzling shade of brown, too, and then it escaped Barron's view as Voleta's mouth opened impossibly wide—a gaping, terrifying maw of sharp white teeth and long fangs, gleaming in the streetlight as the muscles beneath the fur tensed and made ready to lunge.

Barron screamed.

He came to in the hospital. Jared showed up as the last of Barron's wounds was getting stitched shut. He seated himself on the edge of the hospital bed and whistled as he surveyed the damage to Barron's arms. "Well, well. Who would've thought the night would get this kind of crazy? You were hoping to get worked over by a pretty girl, and instead you got mauled by a dog."

"It wasn't a dog," Barron rasped. "It was that girl."

"You sound like shit."

"I feel like shit."

"You didn't get mauled by a girl, dufus. You got clawed and bitten by a dog. People who were leaving the party saw you throw yourself at a stray. They said you screamed at it and lunged right on top of the damn thing. Look." Jared pointed to the wound on Jared's right forearm. "That's a dog bite. And those are claw marks. A girl didn't do that. Shit, look—you still have dog fur all over you." He reached out, pulling a tuft of white fur from Barron's matted hair.

"It was Voleta," Barron insisted.

"Yeah, or you mistook a dog for a fur coat. Your eyes doing their best work. You know you got poisoned, right?"

"What?"

"They haven't told you yet? I just talked to the hospital staff about it. The chefs at Fuller accidentally used leaves from a mountain laurel instead of a bay laurel when they made the soup. Mountain laurels are toxic. They can cause symptoms like the ones you had."

"I got poisoned? Did they admit that?" Barron thought back over the events of the night: his unsteadiness, his inexplicable sense of mortal panic. The impossible sight of a wolf's face, the gaping mouth ready to tear him to shreds. Had he really imagined it? "How the hell does something like that happen?"

"Not sure. I guess there are people who buy the seeds and leaves, even though they're poisonous. They must have ended up in the wrong shipment. The head chef that night was a sub, and no one in the kitchen noticed anything wrong until later. Hardly anyone else ate that soup. I tried a bite and thought it was disgusting; I hate cold soups. Seems like you were the only one affected. You can sue them, you know. They're probably already working out a settlement. They'll pay the hospital fee, at least."

"Damn right, they'll pay that and more." Barron tried to heave himself into a sitting position, but stopped and winced with pain. The back of his left hand, torn open by claws, couldn't withstand the pressure of his weight. He settled back onto the pillow. "Do you see my phone anywhere? It was in my pants pocket."

He'd had to remove his pants to get his leg treated—thirteen stitches and a few bandages. The dress pants were folded on one of the guest chairs. Jared fished around in them and held up a folded postcard. He peered at it, unfolded it, and gave Barron a puzzled look. "What's this?"

Barron recognized the image on the front: the Lady in a Fur Wrap. "Give it here." He took the card from Jared's hand and studied the words written in black ink on the back.

"What the hell," he whispered.

Barron spent most of the following day in bed. The doctors had warned him that it might take a couple of days for his symptoms to completely disappear, but in that time he made a few phone calls to acquaintances in the artists' collective. No one knew anything about Voleta. The organizers of the spring show didn't remember her. The *Cornix* painting, which one of the committee members had purchased for twenty dollars, was unsigned, and Voleta had asked that the work be paid for in cash. When Barron could once again walk without stumbling, he spent time near the artists' lofts, but he didn't find Voleta or anyone who knew her. He felt his legs becoming steady, saw his vision clearing up again—but the memory of that shocking moment, the moment that the wolfish face turned on him with slashing teeth and raging eyes, left him shaken and unfocused. He couldn't paint, or socialize, or think about much of anything aside from the strange, painful, and unexpected terror of that night.

Even after the pain subsided, other reminders haunted him: his damaged flesh, the postcard that Voleta had tucked into his pocket. With a scarred hand Barron reached for the crumpled card that sat on his bedside table, and he read once again the message scrawled on the back: *Lady in a Fur Wrap, March 25, 2019. What is the concept behind this work?*

Something Undone

Something Undone

"Those houses haunt in which we leave / Something undone."
-Elizabeth Jennings, "Ghosts"

I met Charlie Branford on my first day at Macalester College in St. Paul, Minnesota. We became good friends, and during our second year we were roommates, sharing an upper-floor townhouse a few blocks from the south side of campus. Charlie's girlfriend, Sofia, scored a more luxurious place on Summit. Most of the homes on historic Summit Avenue were built in the late nineteenth and early twentieth centuries. Several had been renovated and split into apartments, offering many a bachelor the chance to live in Victorian-style elegance in rooms once inhabited by the city's eminent financiers (or, more typically, by their servants). It was into one of these apartments that Sofia had moved, and when she expressed regret about the rental contract, I assumed she couldn't bear the expense—but her objection to the place was something unexpected.

"My dog won't go inside," she explained. "I had to take him back to my parents' house. He goes nuts whenever I try to bring him into the apartment. He barks and growls, and won't go more than two feet past the door. I thought he just needed to get used to it, but—" Here Sofia hesitated, biting her lip.

"Moving is stressful for pets," Charlie said. "He's never lived away from your parents."

"It's not that. I take him to other people's houses, and he's friendly and curious. There's just something about this place." Sofia paused again, and added with reluctance: "I've noticed it, too. Whenever I go inside, there's this . . . uneasiness. I don't know how to explain it. When I first saw the apartment, I thought I was just anxious about moving, but . . . I think it's something else."

"Like what?" Charlie asked.

"I don't know. I just feel like . . . there's someone else in there."

"What, like a peeping Tom?" Charlie asked. "Or . . . a ghost. You think it's haunted."

"I don't know. Whatever it is, Charlie won't live there." (I should explain here that Sofia's dog, in an unfortunate coincidence, was also named Charlie.) "Look." Sofia pulled up her sleeve, exposing a row of long red marks, some of which had broken the skin. "I tried to carry him inside, and he flipped out. Clawed his way out of my arms and ran back to the hall."

"Maybe he has taste," Charlie replied lightly. "I still don't understand why you'd want to live in one of those over-priced monstrosities."

She replied with a small gasp. "I love those houses! They're so pretty and elegant—not like those dull, mass-produced eyesores you find everywhere else." She glanced at me, knowing I was in agreement. "Robert, what do you think?"

"Beautiful. I always wanted to live in a Victorian-style home."

"You should pursue a different profession, then," Charlie said. "With teacher pay, you'll have to settle for a mass-produced eyesore."

Sofia continued: "I'm not sure how to talk the landlady into canceling my contract. I mean, what do I say? My dog doesn't like it? I can't live here because it's haunted?"

"You really think there's a ghost," Charlie said. "Of course, all the old houses on Summit are haunted. So people say."

"There's *something*. Tease all you want, but if you stayed there, you would notice it too. I spent one night, and that's when I felt it most—when I was in bed."

"Naturally, because you were dreaming."

"I did that, too. I had the strangest dreams. Don't laugh," she demanded as Charlie smirked at her. "Spend the night there yourself before you say anything."

"Can I sleep there?" I blurted suddenly. "If you're not staying there tonight . . . ."

Charlie pretended to give me a scathing look, but his eyes glinted with amusement. "Trying to put up with my woman, are you?"

"You could stay here, Sofia," I offered. "I can check out the apartment and tell you if I notice anything."

At the time, I had a strange sort of hunger for the idea of seeing a ghost. I was the only person among my relatives who had never encountered one. My mother, when she was a child, had moved with her family to an old house in Aberdeen, where everyone in her family observed the ghost of a young girl who seemed fixated on my mother's antique dolls. They moved out before the year was over. My father and his sister saw the ghost of their grandmother, who had lived with them for some time; she appeared as a specter of light, ascending the stairs night after night to the children's bedrooms. I'd heard other tales, many more, from grandparents, aunts, and uncles. It seemed that I alone had no affinity for the supernatural.

Charlie, who was well aware of all this, explained it to Sophia.

"I believe that," she said. "I've seen a ghost before, too, in the house where I grew up. I had the basement bedroom, and I hated it. I begged my parents to let me switch rooms with my brother. I said it was because the basement was cold and full of spiders, but really it was because I sometimes forgot to close the door when I went to bed—and every time I did that, I would see a human figure peeking through the doorway at me. It stood there all night long. I was afraid to get up and close the door, so I just covered my head until I fell asleep."

"Again with the bed," Charlie said. "And the darkness. You were dreaming, or imagining things."

"I wasn't. My brother ended up in that room, and when I talked to him about it years later, he told me he saw the same thing: a human figure peeking through the doorway at him. He always held a grudge against me because he ended up in that room. And it was just that room. Every other place in the house was fine. Smirk all you want, Charlie, but even you said that you've seen a ghost."

Charlie lowered his eyes, the smile fading from his face.

It was agreed that I would spend a single night in the apartment. Sofia had hardly moved anything into it, but there was furniture enough, including a bed and a battered two-seater sofa. I brought my own necessities and arrived at a late hour. The place was small, but its elegance surprised me. The main room featured a large fireplace with intricate brickwork and a marble mantel; it was separated from the kitchen by a grand arch with Roman-style columns, and the windows and walls bore similar decorative moldings. In the bathroom was a large clawfoot tub. I nearly filled it, but bathing at the apartment seemed inappropriate. I wasn't sure why. Minutes later, though, as I began to undress for bed, I hesitated again. It seemed indecent to strip front of—

And that is when I noticed it: the assumption that another

presence was in the room with me. Someone watching me.

I glanced around the rooms. Of course, I found myself alone, but I couldn't shake the sense that someone else was there—somewhere—perhaps around the corner, or just behind me.

I passed it off as mere suggestion, planted by Sofia's stories, yet I climbed into bed still clothed.

Scarcely two minutes had passed before I opened my eyes again. The curtains were thick enough to block any outside light, yet the room somehow remained illumed. Between my own jitters and the unreasonable amount of light filtering in, it was unlikely that I would sleep any time soon.

The glow, however, was not coming from the windows, but from the opposite side of the room. I lifted my head to look for the source, and that is when I first encountered the subject of my story.

A young girl stood in front of the fireplace. I thought for a moment that I must be imagining her, but after a few moments it was impossible to deny her presence. She had a slight luminescence that allowed me to see, even in the dark, the details of her Victorian-style blue-and-white dress and the stray hairs that had escaped from her neat blond ringlets. She was staring at me with a curious expression, and when our eyes met, she smiled and took a step toward me.

My reaction was one of mortal terror. I don't feel ashamed in confessing that I tried to scream in that moment. All that I could muster, though, was a small whimpering sound.

The girl's warm smile never faded as she approached the bed. As she drew near, she reached out and touched the corner of the bedspread—and then she vanished.

For a long time I lay awake, heart pounding, staring at the foot of the bed.

In the morning, as I was leaving, I paused to admire the entryway of the house. At one end was a grand staircase of highly polished wood, and the lobby walls were decorated with intricate paneling. A large fireplace was set beneath a row of arched moldings, and there were a few antique sitting pieces in the room: sofas with carved frames and deep green velvet cushions.

As I examined one of the wooden panels, it moved. I stepped back in surprise. A man in a felt hat stepped from behind it, looking just as astonished to see me. "Can I help you?" he asked.

I introduced myself and expressed curiosity about the history of the building. He said that he and his wife had purchased the place a few years prior and had it split into apartments, but tried to keep as close to the original style of the building as possible. "At least, we kept close to the renovated version," he added. "The house nearly burned down about fifty years ago, so they had to re-build." He gave me another uneasy glance and asked what business I had at the house. I explained the circumstances; he frowned and told me to stay where I was.

The man retreated behind the panel. A minute later, the landlady came down the grand staircase. I noted her brisk walk and stern face, already laden with suspicion at the sight of me. She was about forty, by appearances; she wore a business-style gray dress and had pulled her hair into a tight bun.

The lady abruptly demanded to know who I was. I introduced myself as "Sofia's friend," and her eyes narrowed. "Where is Sofia?"

"She . . . had a problem with her dog," I replied lamely. "Her dog wouldn't sleep here, so I let Sofia stay at my place, and I slept here."

Her expression became colder by the second. She held out a hand and demanded the keys. "We can't have random strangers coming in here. These keys are for tenants only. Tell Sofia that if she wants them back, she can come and talk to me."

As she huffed away up the stairs, I spotted a face peering at me through the second-floor railing: a boy of about five or six, probably alerted by the lady's loud admonitions.

Sofia was alone at the townhouse when I returned. Charlie had gone out to pick up breakfast. While we waited for him, I told Sofia about the encounter with the landlady.

"What about the apartment?" she asked. "Did it seem strange to you?"

I hesitated. I had planned to tell Sofia all about the ghost girl, but I suddenly felt too silly—or afraid, or uncertain about what I'd seen. I'm really not sure what prevented me from telling her. "Well," I said slowly, "I suppose I had jitters, after all that talk about ghosts. I did feel uneasy. And . . . I thought I saw . . . something. I don't know. Maybe I imagined it."

"By the fireplace?" she asked.

My face must have betrayed my amazement. "Did you see it too?" I asked excitedly.

"See what?" Sofia asked coolly. "What did *you* see?"

"I don't know. A movement, or something. I just assumed I imagined it."

"Well, I'm not living there. I'll tell the landlady I have to break my lease, even if she fines me."

"Don't give it up yet," I pleaded. "Even if you can get out of the contract, keep it for this month, at least. I can help you pay for it."

Sofia looked astonished. "Why?"

"I want to sleep there again."

"What for?"

"I . . . just want to know what it is that I saw."

She scrutinized me for a moment, and said: "The landlady won't let you stay there again."

"I'll go late at night and leave early in the morning. She won't see me."

Sofia didn't know much about the landlady's routine or movements, only that the lady lived on the second floor with her husband and son. When I asked if she knew anything about secret passageways in the house, and described how the landlord had appeared from behind a panel in the entryway, Sofia shook her head. "Those just lead to other parts of the house. There are smaller staircases back there that the servants used to take, so they wouldn't be seen by guests—but there's nothing secret about them."

Charlie returned then. He teased me about the haunted house while we fried the eggs and bacon, and continued to pester me while we ate. Sofia excused herself afterward and headed home. As soon as she was out the door, Charlie said: "So, you want to continue sleeping in my girlfriend's apartment. You're sure you haven't taken a liking to her?"

"To Sofia? No. To the apartment, yes."

"You sure? You're not perusing her underwear drawer, or—"

"No, Charlie, for God's sake. It's not that." I met his gaze as he sat down across from me.

"What is it, then?"

"It's just that . . . I didn't want to scare Sofia, but I saw something."

He raised an eyebrow. "On Summit Avenue? Such as what? The world's worst collection of Victorian houses? A great mausoleum of architectural monstrosities?"

I hesitated, anticipating Charlie's full-blown ridicule. "Such as . . . a little girl. Around six years old, maybe seven, with a blue dress and blond ringlets down to her shoulders."

He didn't reply, except to look mildly confused.

"A spirit," I added. "In the apartment. By the fireplace, a few feet from the bed."

Realization lit his eyes. "Ah," he said. "A ghost."

"Don't try to convince me I was dreaming. I had just gotten into bed."

"You sometimes sleep without realizing it. You know that. Whenever I tell you to lie on your side and quit your damned snoring, you always insist that you couldn't have snored because you were wide awake."

"That's different. I'm sure we have had those conversations about my snoring, but I don't remember those conversations because I really was talking in my sleep. This wasn't the middle of the night, and I remember it all too clearly. I swear, I had been in bed for maybe two minutes, and I saw . . . some sort of light by the fireplace. I glanced over, and just across from my bed was this girl."

"A glowing girl. Well, let's go with it. What was this six- or seven-year-old girl doing?"

I recalled the encounter in as much detail as I could remember. Charlie looked unimpressed. "And she didn't seem sinister, this girl?" he asked.

"Not in the least. I was terrified, though. I must have spent half the night staring at the foot of the bed, or peeking over the side to see if she was crouching down there. I half expected her to jump out at me."

Charlie chuckled.

"I felt like a child," I added.

"But you want to go back?"

"Yes. It was such a shock the first time. If she shows up again, and I'm expecting it, maybe I won't be paralyzed with terror."

"And what do you plan to do, if you're not paralyzed with terror?"

"I don't know. Maybe . . . communicate with her. Find out why she's there."

In honesty, I wasn't sure why I felt so compelled to return. I suppose a part of me enjoyed the idea of helping a lost spirit. It may have been vanity; I wanted to be part of something special. At the same time, though, I felt a deep fear at the idea of communing with ghosts. Throughout that first day, before I spent a second night at the apartment on Summit, I thought over my mother's stories of her home in Aberdeen. Having a well-tempered ghost for a playmate had always seemed exciting to me. Until then, I'd never understood the sense of dread and helplessness that came with meeting a ghost. My mother said that her father didn't want his kids in that house because "He was worried it would affect us." The haunting also seemed to confirm the possibility of other supernatural events: poltergeists, demons, possession.

When I returned home after that second night, I had another story to tell Charlie. "I saw her again," I said. "By the fireplace."

"When you were in bed?"

"Yes, but this time she stayed where she was. Her lips were moving, but I couldn't make out what she was saying. Then she gestured toward the fireplace, like she was trying to draw my attention to it."

"What time did this happen? Midnight? One o'clock?"

"A little after eleven-thirty. Around eleven, the first time. Why?"

"I was reading an article about the way brain activity changes at night. Most of these—"

"Of course you were. Always the cynic."

"It has something to do with the brain's efforts to cope with stress during sleep. It comes with feelings of uneasiness and dream-like visualizations."

"There was no uneasiness this time. At first, when I saw her, I felt afraid—but it didn't last long. She has such a happy smile on her face! After she disappeared, I felt a strange sense of peace. I felt . . . safe."

I began to make great efforts to discover the girl's identity.

Because notable people had lived in the homes on Summit, plenty of their stories and family photos had been archived. Sofia's place was no different. I found bits of information embedded in articles about the area in library records and history magazines. The next evening, Charlie found me sitting at the kitchen table, reading printouts from the Ramsey County Historical Society. His brow furrowed as he asked: "Aren't you supposed to be at work?"

"I have the day off," I replied. I neglected to mention that I'd asked a co-worker to cover my shift at the campus bookstore—I had wanted more time to pursue the ghost mystery—but Charlie guessed it anyway. He scolded my irresponsibility and took his usual jabs: "So, what did we learn today? Bankers and railroad tycoons lived in a mansion for a year or two, and left feeling even less fulfilled? Victorian-era wives have ugly, sullen faces?"

I didn't humor him with a response. He came and stood beside me, reading the photocopies over my shoulder. "Want to help?" I asked. "I'm trying to find a picture of the girl."

"No thanks. I've had my fill. My cousins talked me into doing a walking tour of Summit Avenue a few years ago, and I was bored out of my mind."

So he said, and yet he stood and gazed at the photos with interest. He pointed at the image of a young blond girl standing behind her grandmother and younger siblings. "Is that her?"

"No. That girl must be at least twelve. I'm looking for a seven-year-old."

Charlie sat down and flipped through an issue of *Minnesota History Magazine*. After several minutes, he beckoned me to sit beside him. "Look, here's a whole article about Sofia's place. Didn't you say there was a fire?"

"Yes, there was. It nearly destroyed the house."

Charlie pointed to a caption beneath an old photo of the house. "There are three architects listed here: the original architect, and two restoration architects. The house was built in 1898, and it was restored in 1910 and again in 1961. If it was so massively restored that they had to hire an architect, I'd say the house was in pretty rough shape. The fire probably happened in '10 or '61."

I examined the caption and corrected him: "The third architect was a renovation architect. The house was split into apartments in

'61."

"Then that puts the fire in 1910, doesn't it?"

The revelation narrowed my search to news stories from 1910. I had a college exam the next morning, so I skipped a night at the house on Summit—but I spent a good part of the next afternoon at the library, still pursuing the identity of the little girl.

After a futile search, I decided to inquire at the reference desk. The librarian, an older gentleman of perhaps seventy years, knew exactly where to direct me. The library had a few microfiche news articles about the 1910 fire, and those articles did mention the death of a seven-year-old Clara, who had become trapped in a second-floor bedroom. "You won't see it here," the librarian said, "but there was a famous picture taken of that fire. One of the neighbors was a professional photographer, and he had his camera out when the house was burning down. He got a shot of the bedroom window where the girl was standing."

My reaction to this bit of news was one of mixed repugnance and grief. I didn't particularly want to see an image of a child about to die—but I had to know if it was her.

We found the picture not in a news article, but in a collection of photos taken by the young photographer. "He did most of his work here in St. Paul," the librarian explained as we sifted through the images, "but these are from a gallery showing in New York. All the photos from the original collection are here, but the gallery didn't let him show the one of the burning house. Too morbid. And I'm sure the girl's family would have had a fit."

The collection consisted mostly of street-style photographs. The most striking prints were those of children: a young boy smoking a cigarette, the smoke pluming around his lean cheeks; child workers with dirty faces that bore all the seriousness and sadness of adults.

When he came to the photo of the burning house, I felt a painful stab of recognition. A child's head was framed in an upper window. She was visible only from the neck up, and though her features weren't perfectly clear, the shape of her head evidenced that her hair was done in the same style as the little ghost's hair. The edge of the fireplace was visible in the background, decorated with a highly embellished mantel that was now long gone.

"The nanny and the other house staff were yelling at her to open the window and jump, but she was such a little thing," the man told me. "Probably didn't know how to unlock it."

It took me some time to register his words. My attention was fixated on the heart-rending image of a child trapped in flame. The blaze washed the elegant background in an overabundance of light, giving an impression of an ethereal, half-destroyed temple, and leaving the girl's face somewhat in shadow.

I leaned forward to scrutinize the image and felt a small shock on closer observation. The child's gaze, though partly obscured, seemed to fall directly on the camera.

"She's looking at him," I said. "At the photographer."

"Haunting, isn't it? She disappeared a moment after this was taken. Probably looking for another way out, or maybe just trying to get away from the fire. They found her curled up in the corner of the room."

My own gaze didn't move from the girl's face. "A child was about to die," I said, "and he was just standing there and taking pictures of it?"

The old man looked surprised, likely due to the scathing judgment in my tone. "There was no helping her," he insisted. "The lower floor was impassible."

"Still . . . I would imagine I'd have done everything in my power to help her. Throw something to break the window, find something to climb . . . ."

"Easier said than done. You can't imagine how hot the fire was. No one could get close enough to help."

Nevertheless, the image put me in an angry state. To see a child looking back at you with such fear and despair in her eyes—and to exploit that fear in such a way! "Do you know how the fire started?" I asked, remembering the girl's gestures. "Did it have something to do with the fireplace?"

"Well, the story goes that the maid undid the curtains to shut them for the night, and one of them brushed against an open gas lamp. She left the room and didn't notice that the curtain had caught fire. By the time anyone realized, the west wing was going up in smoke. *Supposedly* that's what happened, but I wouldn't be surprised if something else is wrong with the house that makes it a fire hazard. That part of the house is always catching fire. Seems like people don't stay very long because of it."

That piqued my interest. I asked about the other fires, but he had no details to offer. I began to form my own conclusions. By the time I reached the apartment on Summit, I had a story all worked out: There was some flaw about the fireplace that made the room catch fire, and the girl was trying to draw my attention to it. By teaming up with the ghost girl and solving the mystery, I could save lives.

I checked the fireplace for anything unusual, but it was a fruitless endeavor. I didn't know what to look for, and couldn't be sure that the fires had originated from that point.

That night, I didn't see Clara right away. In my dreams, I heard her voice murmuring to me from across the room. I opened my eyes and tried with little success to rouse myself. A vague, fuzzy image hovered by the fireplace, and what I heard from it could easily be passed off as a dream: a little girl's voice saying *I was happy here. I felt safe.*

The rest of what she said was indecipherable, but I got the sense that she was talking about the fire. I felt her fear and anguish almost as if those feelings were my own.

It took some time for me to wake up. When I finally did wake, I was no longer in bed, but standing in front of the fireplace. It seemed that my own voice was murmuring, rather than the girl's— or perhaps I imagined it. My attention was quickly captured by a small, flat object in my hand. I felt my way toward the light switch and flicked it on.

Somehow, I'd gotten hold of a matchbook. I had never seen it before. I glanced around, made a quick search, and discovered what I assumed to be the source of the object: a small tin on the mantel, with a few old matchbooks still inside.

The incident disturbed me, yet I remained intent on pursuing the mystery. The next afternoon, unable to find any news accounts of the other fires, I decided to call on the records unit of the local police department. The young clerk informed me that unless I was directly involved in a reported incident, it could take the department up to a month to release the records to me.

"A month!" I exclaimed. "That's too late. Isn't there anything I can do to speed it up? Like . . . an extra fee, or something?"

"It might not take that long. Could be two, maybe three weeks."

I slumped with disappointment, leaning on the desk—both for support and for confidentiality. In a low voice, I pressed him. "Can't I just say I was involved?" I added with determination: "I was involved in one of these fires. I don't remember which year it happened, so I need reports from every year that there was a fire."

He looked at me stonily.

"Fine," I said. "I'll wait."

The reports didn't arrive for more than two weeks. In the meantime, I spent very few nights at the house on Summit, not wanting to get caught trespassing there—but those few nights that I did stay, I stayed with a ghost.

Those visits mostly took the forms of confused dreams. I didn't see the girl so clearly as I once had. Instead, I mumbled to her in my sleep. Once, while dreaming that I was looking for a candle to light, I woke to find myself rummaging through Sofia's dresser drawers. I pulled my hand back as though I'd been burned, remembering Charlie's accusation. The drawers were empty, but I still felt as though I had caught myself doing something mildly perverse.

When the incident reports finally arrived, I was shocked at the number of them, though they spanned a lengthy period of fifty years. The fires, none of which had caused fatalities, were attributed to various causes: hot ashes dumped in a waste bin, smoking in bed, a kerosene heater, a faulty oil lamp, a grease fire on an unattended stove top, a child who made sport of lighting his socks on fire, an evergreen Christmas tree placed too close to an open fireplace.

All of these fires were ignited in Sofia's apartment.

When I told Charlie about my findings, he said: "Looks like you might have yourself a ghost after all—a pyromaniac ghost."

"I can't believe it. She doesn't seem the malicious type. I swear, whenever I've seen her, I've felt a strange sort of comfort and peace."

"That's how she lulls you," Charlie suggested. "She makes you feel safe so she can put you off your guard. You told me that after she talked to you, you nearly lit a fire yourself."

"Yes, but she can't be trying to do any harm. I've never seen anything angry or calculating in her eyes."

"In the—what—one minute you've spent looking into her

ghost-eyes? Two minutes, maybe?"

I considered his theories mutely.

"Fifty years is a long time to haunt a place," Charlie said. "To stick around that long, I'd think you would have to hold quite a grudge."

He made a good point, but I found an explanation. "I don't think it's her soul that's hovering there. It does seem like she's talking to me personally, but I think what I'm seeing and hearing is more like . . . an imprint. A strong impression she left behind."

"An impression of desperation and terror, I would imagine."

"It isn't like that. Most of the time she spent there, she must have been happy. That's what she left behind."

"That doesn't explain the haunting or the fires. Contentedness doesn't make a haunted house. It doesn't create phantoms and poltergeists, and it doesn't burn houses."

I returned to the apartment that night with Charlie's claims still vivid in my mind. I didn't go to bed. I sat upright on the sofa, watching the fireplace and waiting for Clara to appear.

Nevertheless, I began to drift. A dream-like state washed over me, and a now-familiar feeling crept in: wistful happiness marred by pangs of grief and hurt. This sensation always led to a fixation on the fatal fire. Even as I reveled in happiness, the thought of that terrible event consumed me—and then my hands were fumbling, looking for something to light. I didn't understand my own desire to re-create the fire. I wasn't angry; revenge had no place in my mind. This house had been a happy one. I was as certain of this as I was of my own happy childhood.

As if to confirm my feelings, a girl's voice spoke the words out loud: *I was happy here. I felt safe.*

With horror, I realized that my own voice had spoken the words along with her. The two voices blended perfectly, matching syllable for syllable. I sat up straight, fighting off slumber. The manipulation of my voice and hands felt like a violation, an intrusion—as though I'd been possessed.

I didn't see or hear Clara again that night.

"You're not looking well these days," Charlie said when I returned home. "You can't be getting much sleep, with all your late-night sneaking into that ugly house and your early-morning creeping out again. Sofia's going to get the rest of her things on Saturday, and then she's returning the keys—and that will be the end of it." Without looking at me, he added: "You sure you don't just have some sort of obsession with Sofia? Some fetish?"

"No, Charlie. She's nice, but I'm not the least bit interested in her." (This wasn't quite true. I found Sofia extremely attractive—but then, I found many women extremely attractive, so it wasn't of much consequence.)

"Look, I'm just going to say it: I'm concerned about the amount of time you're spending on this ghost girl," he said. "It was interesting for a while, but it's . . . not healthy. I feel like I shouldn't have humored it, and I'm glad it's almost over. I just hope you don't find some way to keep it up."

"Thanks for your concern, but I'm fine."

"What kind of outcome do you expect from all this?"

"I'm not sure."

"You must have some idea. Knowing you, you probably believe you're going to help this poor little soul find closure and move on to the afterlife—even if you have to compromise your education, or your job, to do it."

I looked at him without answering.

"I'm just saying, don't invest so much in a ghost that you give up what's important. People believe whatever they want to believe. That doesn't make it real, or valuable."

"I don't," I replied. "I want to believe that my loved ones are at peace, not that they're stuck in an eternity of restless wandering."

"You say that now, but you're infatuated with your family's stories: the ghost girl who played with dolls, the floating nun at St. Joseph's—"

"I'm *interested* in those stories, but what does that have to do with anything? Sofia saw something by the fireplace too, but she won't admit she saw a ghost."

"Ah," he said. "So, Sofia started this whole fireplace obsession."

"She only mentioned it after I did. And it didn't start with Sofia. The dog, remember? This all started because the dog wouldn't go into that apartment. But I suppose you can explain that, too, by saying that there's some sort of electromagnetic field that upset the dog, or maybe a high-frequency sound that we can't hear."

"Does that make less sense than the ghost of a dead girl?"

"None of it makes more or less sense."

"What *doesn't* make sense, though, is how you're diverting all of your energy into this ghost mystery, which is wholly unrelated to you, and ignoring your own obligations. You were late to exams, you haven't been studying—"

"I did fine on my exams. Yes, I was late to one, but I finished it and did well. All of that is my own choice, and it's kind of you to intervene, but I have my reasons for what I'm doing. It may seem like nonsense to you, but to me it's a child who needs help, and it's *important*. Anyway, you can't entirely dismiss it. Even you have seen a ghost."

He averted his gaze, and I asked again: "Haven't you? Sofia said you have."

Charlie grabbed his jacket and headed for the door. "I'm going to work. Don't start any fires tonight, okay?"

I didn't start a fire that night, though I easily could have. I showed up at the apartment with a lighter and two candles. This would be my last night, and I wanted it to culminate in something— even if it meant acting on my compulsion to light a fire.

I absolutely meant to resist such an urge. I simply wanted to understand Clara's intentions. Was it really her desire to have me burn the place down all over again?

With a candle in hand, rhythmically tapping it against the base of the sofa, I stared at the fireplace and waited—half an hour, an hour. At length, even though I saw no hint of the ghost, I began to speak to her.

"Are you setting these fires?" I asked out loud. Receiving no response, I added: "You said you felt safe here. You must know that other people can't feel that same safety because of the fires. Do you realize that? Someone else could get hurt. Someone could die." My voice was low and soft. Perhaps I was afraid of being caught by the landlords, but I believe I spoke softly because I was anxious that someone in a neighboring room might realize I was trying to talk to a phantom. "It isn't right," I added. "It shouldn't have happened to you. It shouldn't happen to anyone. To think that you might be doing it on purpose . . . ."

I trailed off as some movement caught my eye—a shimmering in the air, like a heat wave. It vanished after only a moment, but I continued speaking, just as if I could see Clara standing before me. "I can't imagine how awful it must have been, watching everyone down below and realizing they weren't going to rescue you. They tried, you know, but there was no way to get in. By the time someone got a ladder, it was too late. Maybe you didn't know how hard they tried. People got burned trying to get into the house to save you. It just wasn't possible."

Again, the air shimmered. Clara's form began to take shape beside the fireplace and fizzled out again, but I felt her presence acutely. She waited, listened intently to my words. Perhaps that, too, was a notion of my own vanity, but I couldn't let doubt rob me of my chance.

"It might have looked like people just stood there and watched," I continued, "but people were calling out to you, telling you to unlock the window and jump. I think they did everything in their power to try to help—but humans have limited power, don't we? If I had been there, I would have done everything in my power, too. I swear it."

After that, I sat in silence. Clara's presence lingered for a few minutes, and then it seemed to quit the room. I put the candles away and went to bed.

The night passed without incident. On Saturday, Charlie and I took his truck to the house on Summit. The landlords were out, but Sofia had made arrangements to leave the keys with a trusted tenant. The tenant was a young woman, probably a student. She had a room on the first floor, but we found her at the landlord's place, where she was playing babysitter for the evening. She chatted with us for a while, and then helped us prop the doors open so we could move the furniture out. She even helped us heave the bed frame and mattresses down the stairs and into the truck. When we went back for the rest, we got an unexpected shock: The house was filling with black smoke. It rolled down the grand staircase and seeped from between the wooden panels, thick and silent.

"What the hell," Charlie exclaimed. "Something's on fire!"

The young woman swore under her breath. Then she gasped. "Franklin!" she cried, staring up at the black cloud. "Frankie is up there!"

"Who's Frankie?" Sofia asked.

"The landlords' son. He's little—he's only six! I left him up there by himself." She ran to the side of the room and tugged at one of the wooden panels. It unleashed another cloud of smoke, and she jerked away, her hands shielding her eyes.

I rushed up the grand stairs, trying to stay beneath the smoke as it stung my eyes and invaded my lungs. Even when I scurried up the stairs on my belly, I was gagged and blinded. I reached the landlords' second-floor apartment nevertheless. The boy was already in the doorway, coughing and choking and crying. I grabbed him and rushed back to the stairs.

Crouching low again, trying to blink away the searing smoke, I saw another child standing across the hall. It occurred to me then that other people must be in the house; I didn't know how many tenants lived there. I was about to call out when I recognized the blue Victorian dress and blond ringlets.

Clara stood there, clearer than I had ever seen her. In that moment I expected to see a look of terror on her face, but it wasn't so. She looked at the boy in my arms, and then she looked into my eyes and smiled—a wide, trembling smile, and her eyes shone with utmost gratitude and relief.

And then, slowly, she vanished. The last I ever saw of her was her happy smile. Her expression said everything: *Thank you for saving him.*

It was an easy rescue, but that was the lesson I took from it: that Clara found relief in seeing a child saved from the smoke and flames, that the sight of it brought her some long-sought peace.

Or maybe I just believe what I want to believe.

The fire was blamed on overheated wiring. The blaze had started between the first-floor ceiling and the second floor. Neither the chimney nor the ghost had anything to do with it.

Although the ordeal with the apartment was finished, Charlie continued to make jabs at my newfound superstitions. Once when I was alone with Sofia, I inquired about his attitude, thinking he was merely trying to avoid being ridiculed for his own experiences. "Don't you think it's telling that he's so smug and cynical about it?" I asked Sofia. "And in spite of his own experiences, I think. Didn't you say that Charlie has also seen a ghost?"

She hesitated. "Yes, but . . . he would get mad if I told you about it." Sofia paused again, pursing her lips, and finally added: "I'm sure you know how close he was to his sister. Do you know how she died?"

I did: a car accident on the freeway, in winter, while driving home from a relative's house in the south.

"The day it happened, Charlie heard her calling his name from the back yard. She had a rabbit hutch out there, and when Charlie looked out the window, he saw her standing behind the hutch and looking up at him. No coat, no hat, in the middle of winter—and she looked upset. He thought she must have gotten home early, and he was worried that something was wrong with the rabbit. He was supposed to be taking care of it. So he ran down and went out to the hutch, and his sister was gone. The rabbit was huddled in a corner with its eyes wide open, and it was stomping its foot. I guess rabbits do that when they're scared. Charlie was sure he saw her, but there were no footprints in the snow except his. A couple hours later, his family got the call. She had died around the time Charlie saw her in the yard." Sofia looked at me with a grave expression. "I really shouldn't have told you, but . . . I don't want you to keep pressing Charlie about it. He doesn't want to talk about it."

I nodded, feeling suddenly regretful. "I understand."

Years passed; the fires at the Summit house seemed to have ceased. Occasionally, I visited the neighborhood and even made inquiries to the tenants of the house, but no one seemed uneasy about the residence or mentioned anything unusual. By all accounts, the ghost girl hadn't re-appeared. I like to believe that she no longer needed to.

I remember Clara with a sad affection, but I'm no longer interested in ghosts. I find that as people age, as death becomes commonplace and we're left alone with our memories, people themselves become haunted—and my own experience made me more cynical about tales of the paranormal, rather than less. After a while, I tired of hearing about such special encounters. I tired of hearing about the excitement and mystery of it. Perhaps the sense of intrigue is what makes those stories so dubious. I tend to put more faith in people like Charlie, who keep the details to themselves with a grave mourning, and who respect the dead in silence.

The Hidden Narcissus

The Hidden Narcissus

"I wonder if the course of narcissism through the ages would have been any different had Narcissus first peered into a cesspool. He probably did."
—Frank O'Hara, *Early Writing*

"Hi! Welcome! It's so nice to finally meet you!"

Lily greeted the guests with the expected smiles and forced delight. She maintained a grin as Shaniya led a mini-tour of the new house, and responded to the guests' expressions of approval and awe with "Yes, Shaniya's uncle put a lot of work into it" and "Yes, it's much nicer than our old place" and "Yes, we've been enjoying it." The house was a Cape Cod style with wide windows and front-facing dormers, and a few unique touches: a columned gazebo adjacent to the kitchen, and a rosebush-lined walkway to the arched front door. It boasted a charming enough appearance on the outside, but the inside bore startling elegance: built-in libraries and cabinets of dark cherry wood, polished hardwood floors, a grand fireplace with gold trim and an intricately carved arch, and carefully chosen antique furniture.

"They're not mine," Shaniya explained as her guests gaped at the Baroque lounge chairs. She was dressed in a casual contrast to the décor, in beige corduroy pants and a green shirt that matched her eyes, with her hair hanging loose down her back. Lily, too, had gone casual for the evening; she supposed the guests would have something to say about it later, when she and Shaniya were out of earshot. "Well, now they are, but this was all my uncle's furniture. Ours didn't really match, so we gave it away."

"We put it out for curbside pickup," Lily corrected her.

Vera smiled. "That bad, huh?"

"Yeah." Shaniya gestured around the room. "All these cabinets with glass doors are empty except for some books. We don't really have anything to fill them with."

"Nothing a few bottles of wine and a few more books can't fix," Gary said. "I'm probably the odd man out when I say this, but I'm not a fan of clutter, even if the clutter is so-called priceless artwork."

"That's why our house doesn't reflect my job," Vera said. "We have a few paintings on the walls, but Gary loathes sculpture and anything else that might be mistaken for knick-knacks."

Vera was Shaniya's co-worker at a local art gallery, but with her art history degree she'd nabbed a finer position than Shaniya could hope for. While Shaniya smiled at customers and rang up orders, Vera, the "fine art consultant," was traveling and selecting new pieces for the gallery, and arranging them into carefully thought-out displays. She dressed the high-brow part, in a silk wrap dress with a cleavage-flaunting cut and flared sleeves that she managed to keep from swishing onto her plate as the foursome settled into their meal. Her husband was more conventionally attired, in dress pants and a pressed button-down shirt.

Vera led much of the conversation with anecdotes about art, art history, and art sales. While the other three plates were cleared bite by bite, Vera's food mostly remained untouched. Finally she laughed and said, "I should shut up and eat. This food is great, and it's probably cold by now."

"Yes, the food is wonderful," Gary agreed, and Shaniya smiled and said "Lily made everything," and then Gary commenced with the typical questions of a stranger: "How long have you two been together" and "Are you married" and "Lily, what do you do for a living?"

As the questions wore on, Lily felt a familiar disappointment settling like a stone in her belly. *Shaniya hasn't told these people anything about me*, she thought. *They have no idea what I do or how long I've been around.*

Gary switched his focus to Shaniya, with "How do you like working at the gallery" and "Do you think you'll stay there" and "I hear one of the managers is leaving; maybe you'll get a promotion!"

Vera took tiny bites of her food, cutting into the chatter every now and then. Lily supposed she took small bites so it was easier to talk while chewing. Vera admired the antiques again and commented on the dining table. The piece was an antique hand-carved oak with an embellished apron, its surface set with less impressive instruments: a chipped ceramic platter full of Parmesan-crusted fish, a frayed breadbasket, and discount plate and flatware sets.

Vera eyed the damaged platter as she asked: "And you just inherited the house and all the furniture? You didn't have to share it with anyone? That's a pretty good start for a twenty-four-year-old."

"There aren't a lot of people left in my family," Shaniya explained. "I don't have siblings, my mom's brothers didn't have kids . . . and of the people who are still living, I was the only one who didn't have a house, so he gave it to me. He left a few things to some other people, but I got the basics."

"He must've had a pretty lucrative job," Gary said. "What did he do?"

Lily spoke up: "Nothing this lucrative. He was a journalism professor. Shaniya's family has some pretty dark suspicions about how he got this house."

"Like what? Crime on the side?"

"As far as we know, he wasn't wealthy," Shaniya replied, "but he had some high-society connections—and he suddenly came into money and built this house. We don't know where he got the money, but we know that he set up a secret surveillance system here, and then a bunch of his friends ended up being branded as communists. This was around 1950, during the Red Scare. I think this place was built in '51. My mom thinks he got paid to spy on his friends. Well, we all think that."

Vera's eyes were round with intrigue. "What kind of surveillance system? You mean, like, hidden microphones and cameras?"

"Microphones everywhere, and . . . ." Shaniya hesitated. Lily saw a hint of reluctance in her green eyes. "I'm not sure what else. He took it all out before he died."

"Well, that's not creepy at all."

"I know. Sometimes I'm not sure I should tell people about it. I don't want people feeling paranoid every time they come over."

"We think it's pretty likely that he got some money to set up surveillance operations here," Lily said. "I mean, he was hanging out with novelists, screenwriters, college professors, poets . . .

people who were prime targets during the Red Scare. And a bunch of them ended up getting arrested, dragged into hearings, losing their jobs, losing their homes, basically just having their lives ruined."

She continued the narrative with anecdotes she'd heard from Shaniya's family: writers who never published again or surreptitiously tried to publish under other names, teachers forbidden to teach, divorces and break-ups and failed custody battles, depression-induced deaths and bitter flights to other countries.

"And your uncle lived here until he died?" Gary asked. "I would have thought he'd get run out of town at some point."

Shaniya shook her head. "Nope. I don't think people knew what he did. It was more of a deathbed confession."

"I wouldn't call it a confession," Lily disagreed. "It was more of a, 'I should probably have all of this creepy shit pulled from my walls before you move in.'"

Vera nodded absently as she looked around the room. "It's a beautiful house, though. I especially love this mirror. It looks like it belongs in a palace. Do you know anything about its history?"

Lily lifted her gaze to the antique mirror. It was a large piece; the height of the glass measured 5 feet, not including the frame and the intricate arch on top. Below it, set onto the floor, was a small glass-door cabinet—empty, like most of the others, with a cornice that served as a mantel at the base of the mirror. Unlike the rest of the decor, it seemed to contrast with the piece above it. The mirror was far more exquisite. Its silver frame was intricately inlaid with tortoiseshell and stained ivory; each corner bore a silver medallion bordered with delicate gold vines, and each medallion was engraved with the image of a woman in one of four actions: in one she held a pair of scales, in another she petted the head of a lion; in the third she poured liquid from one cup into another, and in the fourth she calmly held the neck of a snake. Lily explained that the grand mirror had been imported from Augsburg sometime in the late 18th century, and belonged to a New York family until the owner's death in 1951. Despite its remarkably high value, Shaniya's great-uncle insisted that it had been given to him "as a gift."

"We couldn't find out anything else about the history," Lily continued, "but I think we figured out its symbolism. See these little silver plates on the corners? We think they represent the four cardinal virtues."

Vera stood up to get a closer look, and Lily followed. She heard the clatter of dishes behind her as Shaniya began to clear the table. "We did some research, and we matched the one with the snake to prudence," Lily said. "The scales are justice, the lion is fortitude, and the cups are temperance. Kind of ironic, that the guy was using a virtue-themed mirror to ruin the lives of his friends."

Vera raised her eyebrows. "He used the mirror for surveillance?"

Lily glanced at Shaniya, who had paused with the stack of plates in her hands, and saw a vague tension in her face. Lily had slipped up, mentioned something she'd promised she wouldn't—but there was no use apologizing now.

Shaniya's lips pressed together. When she spoke, she spoke with reluctance. "It's a one-way mirror," she admitted. "My uncle replaced the glass."

Gary twisted in his seat, straining to look behind him. Lily noticed his slow, careful movements. With his stiff physique and near-bald head fringed with gray hair, he looked old—perhaps much older than Vera. While he wasn't quite dressed to match his wife, he didn't look shabby either. Surely he had money. "You mean, a two-way mirror?" Gary asked. "One that you can see through on the other side? Did he have a camera behind it?"

"He . . . didn't say much about what he did."

Lily continued: "It's pretty obvious that he screwed over his friends, but he never admitted to it. The only reason we know about the surveillance stuff is because he needed help taking it out of the walls. He had terminal cancer, and he wanted all of that stuff gone before he passed the house to Shaniya."

"If you ever want that mirror off your hands," Vera said, "the gallery could arrange an auction. You could bring in your retirement savings with that piece."

"It wouldn't be easy to remove it," Lily said. "You can't really tell from here, but that whole unit is built into the wall."

"I guess that's a good strategy," Gary said. "If you've got a secret camera back there, you don't want anyone to be able to peek behind it."

Again, Lily and Shaniya exchanged silent glances. From where she stood, Lily could see that the mirror was so close to the wall as to be slightly embedded in it. Behind the glass, she knew, there was no wall—only another sheet of specially engineered sound-canceling glass, designed to protect the viewer from being discovered. Lily had stood behind it, in the little secret room, and looked out into the dining and living rooms, at the stairs that led up to the bedroom she shared with Shaniya. Something about that experience was deeply unsettling. It made her feel detached from her own life, and from everyone outside that room—like a cockroach waiting for a chance to creep out into the open.

Lily didn't speak any of these thoughts out loud. Nor did she have any desire to. This time, she kept her mouth shut.

"I knew Vera would land on that mirror," Shaniya said. She set the empty platter beside the sink, where Lily was scrubbing the plates; she leaned back against the counter, folding her arms across her chest. "She must have known right away where it was from and how much it might be worth. She doesn't do antiques, but she knows enough about art history to recognize German Baroque."

"Oh, yes, she's super impressive." Lily set a plate on the dish rack and slid the platter into the soapy water. "Has nice tits, too. I get why you have so many compliments in the bag for Vera. I was kind of surprised that she's doing the vapid sugar daddy thing, but, whatever suits her."

Shaniya didn't reply. She didn't move. Lily looked up and saw disbelief, disappointment, even a trace of disgust in Shaniya's face. "What's that supposed to mean?" Shaniya finally asked.

Lily shrugged off the implied accusation. "What? You like to compliment her. And I did catch you checking out her cleavage."

"Yeah, and I 'caught' you doing the same thing, because yes, she was wearing a low-cut dress. It's impossible not to notice."

"Uh-huh, I know. Impossible not to ogle the amazing Vera."

"Lily, please don't start doing this again," Shaniya said. "You do it nearly every time I invite someone over. 'You compliment everyone else more than you compliment me,' 'You—'"

"That is not what I said."

"It's insinuated, Lily, and it's part of your 'You're a crappy partner' routine. I can't compliment anyone, or spend time with anyone, or talk about anyone, without you making it into an accusation. And Gary is a 'vapid sugar daddy'? How the hell do you know what kind of person he is?"

"Fine," Lily replied, "I'm basing it on one dinner, but I think it's a fair description. Or maybe you found his conversation to be—"

"His conversation was fine," Shaniya snapped. "He was friendly. He was—"

"Yeah, and he knew absolutely nothing about me. He didn't know if we were married, he doesn't know what I do, there were times that he couldn't remember my name. You come home and talk about Vera this, Vera that; I have to listen to you ramble on about her—"

"I do not."

"—and you have clearly never said a word about me to Vera, like I'm not even worth mentioning."

"Lily, Gary was asking those questions, not Vera. I don't know Gary. I've never even met him before, so—"

"It's not just that," Lily insisted. "This whole dinner was like a love fest between you and Vera, with Vera like 'Oh, I'm so amazing! Listen to me talk about all the amazing things I know!' and you like, 'Oh, yes, Vera—'"

"Bullshit, Lily, that's not what happened."

"Let me finish."

"No, you let me finish this time. I'm not listening to this shit again."

Lily felt herself wincing. "Gee, thanks. Way to shut me down."

"I'm not listening to it because I'm fed up with being accused. I'm sick of always having to defend myself. I didn't do anything wrong." Shaniya's voice rose; Lily heard an uncharacteristic anger stewing there. Maybe, too, a vein of sadness. "I did not flirt with Vera, and I did not ignore you," Shaniya continued sharply. "I didn't talk down to you. I didn't ridicule you. I wasn't rude to you. I didn't exclude you. Name one thing I said to you, or about you, that was rude."

"It's not what you say." Lily heard a vague tremor in her own voice. Grief, perhaps—or maybe fear. "It's what you don't care to say."

"Like what? Lily is a great cook? Lily is really good at carpentry, Lily can fix anything around the house, Lily is great at sports, Lily is a genius at puzzles, we're saving up for a piano because Lily is a great pianist? I say those things. They're never enough for you. You bitch and complain that I don't compliment you enough, but whenever I do, you shit on it and say, 'Okay, well, you said that, but you didn't say this other thing. You said something nice about me, but you smiled at this other person more than you smiled at me.' And it's always a double standard. Can you name one nice thing you said about me tonight?"

Lily balked. The new stream of accusatory words sank in her throat.

"This is *your* problem," Shaniya said. "And you need to figure it out. Every time we talk about it, I think we've come to an understanding, and it just starts all over again—the petty little jabs, the hypocritical accusations."

"Fine, Shaniya." Again, Lily heard the faint trembling in her own voice. Definitely fear. "I'm a piece of shit. I'm petty, I'm selfish, I'm jealous, I'm unpleasant to live with. Thanks."

Shaniya pushed herself away from the counter. Her voice softened, sounded suddenly weary. "Think about what I said."

"I am."

Lily kept her gaze fixed on the dishes as Shaniya walked away. She listened as the soft footsteps retreated across the living room and stopped at the front closet. She heard the rustle of clothes as Shaniya pulled out her jacket and slipped her shoes on, the creak of the front door opening.

Again with a note of fear, Lily asked: "Where are you going?"

"I'm going for a walk."

The door closed, and Lily was alone.

Later, as she lay in bed, Lily heard Shaniya's return: the light creaking and groaning of the staircase under Shaniya's feet, the rush of water in the bathroom faucet. And then Shaniya was beside her, quietly slipping under the sheets. For just a moment, Lily felt a familiar twinge of relief—a sensation that always filled her when Shaniya was suddenly beside her, and the other half of the bed was no longer empty and cold. Relief now mixed with the pain of loss, though Lily hadn't actually lost her. Not yet.

After that small moment, Lily resumed the train of thought that had run through her mind since Shaniya walked out the door. *She left like that to make me feel guilty. She left to scare me—to remind me that she can ditch me at any time. Why does she even need me now? She has this fancy house that's all paid off; she doesn't need me to help with the rent. That's why she's so confrontational all of a sudden. She can bitch at me, and shake me off, because now she can get by on her own. She's picking a fight so she can take off and make me look like the bad guy.*

The inner monologue continued late into the night. As the hours passed, a new anger sparked in Lily's mind. *She knows I have to work in the morning, and yet she comes off with all this 'You're a nagging, hypocritical, petty little bitch' speech. She knew I would be up all night thinking about it. I can't even take the day off, because I need my measly eleven hours of sick time for when I actually get sick. . . .*

Lily rolled onto her side, then onto her stomach, trying for a more comfortable position. Nothing was quite right. No matter how she lay, her body felt bony and awkward, the pillows too flat, her neck too stiff.

Beside her, Shaniya also shifted, and sniffled, and sighed.

At work the next morning, the silent narrative continued: *Shaniya got this chunk of money from her dead uncle and hasn't shared the account with me. Makes it easier to split up. She called me names and swore at me, but somehow I'm the villain.*

Lily sat at her computer, trying to edit the latest batch of drivel that had shown up in her inbox. She had worked at this third-floor office for a few years, settling into it after her pursuit of a journalism career didn't pan out. The office specialized in editing conventional romantic fiction—not her favorite genre by any means, but it paid the bills. And "copywriter" was a bit of a misnomer; she considered herself, as she loved to tell her co-workers, a "ghost writer for imaginative perverts who failed grammar school." Today's project was yet another tale of an ostensibly independent, but ultimately addle-brained woman falling for an aggressive and muscular bonehead. Lily felt especially aggravated about the task today. Whenever someone stopped by her cubicle to ask what she was working on, she replied with comments like "Misogynist self-hatred disguised as piety" and "The worst story of the decade. I feel like I always get the shaft."

The task dragged on. Lily tried to focus so she could get it over with, but Shaniya's words echoed in her mind throughout the day, dominating her thoughts. Petty. Hypocritical. Bullshit. Bitch.

In the break room, she leaned back in one of the chairs and closed her eyes. She hadn't packed a lunch, and was too tired to eat anyway. Better to rest when she had a chance. This room was usually quiet; the furniture was shabby and stained, and the table full of food smears and crumbs, though Lily's co-workers rarely ate here. Typically they stopped in to microwave their lunches; then they fled outside or to other parts of the building, as though they couldn't wait to get free of the bland, labyrinthine system of cubicles.

"How're you doing, Lily?" Mark, one of the other editors, came in to fill his water bottle at the cooler. Lily waited for the *glug, glug, glug* to stop before she murmured: "I'm beat."

"Busy weekend?"

"Not really. I just didn't sleep last night."

"Is it because of that creepy old house?"

"It's not that old," Shaniya said.

"Creepy, though."

Lily had told everyone at the office about the house and its history. It was her bit of intrigue to add to the office chatter. She'd said the house was creepy, that she felt watched—though she hadn't actually felt that way at all.

"I'm getting used to it," she said. "Don't know if I'll stay, though."

"Really? You're thinking of selling it?"

"It's not mine to sell. I'm just not sure how things will be with me and Shaniya. She's got this house, she inherited some money— not much, but still, she's financially well-off now. And if she did want to sell the house, she would make a shit ton off of it."

"So . . . ."

"So, she doesn't need me to split the rent anymore."

"Aw, is it that bad? I thought you two were doing all right."

"Sometimes. Not so much lately."

"Well, I hope things turn around. Good luck."

Lily watched as he left the room. She waited a few seconds to make sure he was gone. Then she stood up with a grimace, mimicked, "Good luck," and headed back to her cubicle.

As the end of the workday approached, Lily became aware of a growing sense of unease. She realized she was nervous about facing Shaniya, who was usually mellow and predictable, but who now seemed to be showing a new, more volatile face.

By the time she returned home, Lily had come to a decision. She packed a weekend bag—quickly, because she only had about half an hour before Shaniya came home—and made a phone call as she checked to make sure she had everything she needed. Clothes. Toothbrush. Face soap. Shampoo. Credit card. Phone charger. I can survive on those.

"Hello?" a woman's voice answered her call.

"Hi, Mom. I was wondering if I can come and stay with you this weekend."

"We're not home this weekend. We went to Leesburg with Jamir and Andrea."

"Oh . . . is there maybe someone who can give me a key?"

"No, no one has a key. No reason to have a house sitter

anymore, since the cats died."

"All right. I'll talk to you later, okay? I'm going to see if Violet will let me stay at her place."

"Why? Is something the matter?"

"No. Not really. I just want to go out of town for a while

"Well, your cousin already has a full house. Bill's brother is there with his family."

Lily's shoulders sagged. "All right. I'm going to call her anyway. Bye, Mom."

Violet, too, turned her down, and so Lily stood there with phone in hand, looking down at her bag—packed, but with nowhere to go.

And then she thought of it.

In the kitchen, she grabbed a pen and notepad. In a hurried scrawl, she wrote: *Shaniya, I decided to go out of town for a little while. We can talk when I get back, but right now I think it would be good for both of us to have some space.*

She read the note a couple of times and felt a small sense of triumph. Now, she thought, it was Shaniya's turn to worry about being abandoned.

Lily checked her bag again, and then added a few items to it: granola bars and other snacks, napkins, a trash bag, a pair of hand towels. She grabbed a few other things she would need, starting with a large plastic bowl and a gallon jug of water. Lily arranged the items beside the grand mirror in the dining room.

She stood and gazed at the antique monstrosity. Lily had always thought the mirror gaudy from a distance, but up close she could see some of its charm. Miniature figures of animals, foxes and deer and birds, were hidden in the silver borders, woven into a network of flowering vines and decorative knots—a metal-bound imitation of life.

The mirror was bolted in place with a double lock, one on each side of the mirror: a silver, square-edged bolt just behind the justice medallion, the other behind temperance. Lily triggered the first bolt by pushing it in. It popped out slightly, enough for her to grasp it and slide it from its place. Then she unlocked the second.

With a gentle tug, the mirror pulled out about an inch from the wall. It stopped with a soft click, and then swiveled on one set of hinges, and the doorway was open. Lily knew that she could easily maneuver the locks from inside the room, but she checked them anyway, pushing them into place and sliding them out again, just to make sure.

In the small room, set against the back wall, was an old sofa. Lily was about to set her bag in front of it when she noticed a small puddle of water on the floor. It seemed to have welled up from a four-inch-long crack in the concrete.

"Shit," she whispered.

She looked around the room. To the left was a toilet and sink. Whether the toilet was usable, she wasn't sure; she and Shaniya had never tried it. Maybe the plumbing had burst, and that's where the water was coming from. But the puddle didn't seem to be getting bigger, and though the room maintained a musty scent, it didn't reek of sewer. Not yet, anyway.

Lily crossed to the right side of the room and set her bag on an empty plywood bookcase. She moved the rest of her provisions inside. After another test of the bolts, Lily pulled the door shut and locked it.

Silence seemed to press in on her. It amplified the sound of her breathing—or perhaps she breathed heavily because she was anxious. As she gazed through the mirror into the rooms outside, the densely insulated walls around her also seemed to close in. She had never been in the room with the door closed and locked; she supposed it made the room that much more confining. Behind the mirror glass was another window, a sheet of sound-canceling glass, bordered by soundproof walls: barriers inside of barriers, surrounding and enclosing her.

Lily began to pace the length of the small room. Her thoughts homed in once again on Shaniya's sudden bout of assertiveness. It was unlike her to be so direct, so harshly accusatory. It was unlike her to give ultimatums. Something must have triggered it. Was it an affair? It must be, Lily supposed—or if not an affair, the desire for an affair. First a better house, a better bank account and a better lifestyle, and now a better partner. Spying on Shaniya was Lily's way of pursuing her suspicions. It was unlikely that Shaniya would discover her, or that the idea of Lily being in the hidden room would even enter her mind. Shaniya never opened the room and didn't want anyone to know about it. This hidden space made her uneasy, and she didn't want anyone else getting creeped out or messing around in it.

Lily was still pacing when the front door opened. She stood attentively at the glass, watching as Shaniya passed through the living room. Shaniya went to the kitchen, as usual, to clean out her lunchbox and fill her water bottle. *She's probably reading the note*, Lily thought, and watched with keen eyes, wanting to see the expression on Shaniya's face when she came out.

To the left of the door were the wall contact microphones and amplifiers, carrying the sounds of activity in the kitchen: drawers and cabinet doors opening and closing, the faucet starting and stopping. Shaniya liked to assure people that the house's spy gear had been completely pulled out, but the reality was that her uncle had died in the process of removing it. In this room, certainly, the basics remained.

Shaniya stayed in the kitchen so long that Lily gave up and sat down. The reaction was long past; there would be no seeing it. And when Shaniya finally did come out, Lily couldn't see her expression anyway. She was too far away, and her face was veiled behind her long hair.

She stopped in the living room. Lily watched intently, overcome by a sudden desire to see that face. Shaniya plugged her phone in, set it on the end table, and straightened up, brushing her long hair back behind her shoulder. The gesture eased some of the anger in Lily's heart. It brought with it a stream of pleasant memories: the silky feeling of that hair, the sensation of the strands brushing against her. Lily could almost feel the welcome tickle of it on her skin. Soft, light brown hair with red undertones, trailing over the cute spray of little freckles across Shaniya's shoulders—freckled just there, and nowhere else. The memory of Lily's lips brushing against the length of that dappled flesh.

Shaniya had turned away; her face remained hidden. It was

fascinating, Lily realized, to watch her like this: at a distance, unaware of Lily's gaze. It was a chance to observe without arguing, without acting, without pressure—and thus, to admire.

The doorbell rang. When Lily heard Vera's voice at the front door, she scowled to herself. A knowing scowl, full of smug disgust. *Well, well. I guess you had to get into her pants as soon as possible, before I come home.*

Vera's voice carried through the amplifiers: "I come bearing gifts. We wanted to say thank you for the dinner and drinks."

"Oh, flowers! Oh, these are so pretty."

"These are the ones you like, right?"

"Yes, they are."

"Anyway, we both had a great time last night."

"Well, so did we."

"You'll have to come to our place some time."

The banal chatter continued as they crossed into the kitchen. Vera was wearing another fancy get-up, a knee-length bodycon skirt with a matching blazer—a blazer that any modest woman would have worn a shirt beneath. The conversation became muted for a while, and picked up again as they returned to the dining area.

Shaniya carried a crystal vase full of flowers. She headed straight toward the mirror, slowly, steadily—and as she looked up from the vase, her gaze seemed to fall directly on Lily.

She set the vase on the mantel. Her fingers gingerly probed the flowers, arranging them in a neat display. "Lily will love these," she said.

Lily looked down at the bouquet, the pinwheel-like flowers with chiffon-like petals, the golden cups protecting delicate stamens and pistils. They were narcissus minnows—not Shaniya's favorite flowers, but Lily's. Her beloved grandparents, now deceased, had planted those same flowers in front of their house. Lily always associated them with the happier memories of her childhood.

"Do you know why they're called 'minnows'?" Vera asked.

"Because they're small," Shaniya replied. "Miniature flower breeds are sometimes called minnows."

"Oh. I thought maybe it had something to do with the pool in the Narcissus myth. I assumed he died and got eaten up by the little fish."

Shaniya winced. "Maybe. The flower is named after Narcissus. Supposedly, these flowers grew where he died."

"They look like happy little flowers," Vera said, smiling. "I guess it makes sense. He was so happy looking at his reflection that these delightful little blossoms sprung up."

Shaniya stopped fiddling with the flowers and took a step back, examining them. "I don't think Narcissus was happy with himself. It makes more sense that he was afraid when he studied his reflection. Most narcissists are." She turned away, adding: "I'm going to put a coaster under it. I'm not used to having expensive furniture; I don't want to wreck the wood."

She walked out to the living room. Lily heard the sliding of a drawer, the clunk of the heavy coasters. Shaniya returned and lifted the vase, sliding the felt-backed stone slab beneath it. "I don't think that myth is actually about self-love," she said. "People who love and accept themselves are usually able to be with other people. Self-obsession, or never being able to get enough from other people, or being unable to see from other people's perspectives—that's not self-love. Maybe Narcissus stared at his reflection because he was afraid of risking himself with someone else. Those kinds of people put barriers around themselves. They're more likely to end up alone."

"Do you know people like that?"

Lily looked up, her gaze riveted on Shaniya's face. She felt certain, now, that this was it: the perfect chance for Shaniya to complain. *Yes, Lily is so like that. Let me give you multiple examples.* She could already hear Shaniya's criticisms in her mind. Instead of anger, though, she felt a cold fear.

Shaniya gazed at the flowers and smiled—a small, forced smile. "Don't we all? Even if we're not full-blown, I think we're all like that to some extent."

Vera glanced around. "Where's Lily? Still at work?"

"No. She . . . went out of town."

Lily braced herself. Here it comes: *My girlfriend is gone, so let's screw around. I really like you and think you're so amazing and you have great tits, too.*

But the conversation remained bland and trifling: how the weather had been, how their families were doing—and, of course, the families were all "good."

The only bit of spice in the exchange came when Vera talked about her husband. "Gary's a good guy. We have been through a couple rough times, especially when his parents were in hospice. He was really stressed out, and he would lose his temper at the drop of a hat—but we're okay now. How are things with you and Lily?"

A deep, aching hole seemed to form in Lily's belly. *Here it comes, she thought. Things aren't that great. I'm petty, I'm difficult, I'm jealous.*

"They're fine," Shaniya said.

"Just fine?"

She shrugged. "We're still settling in. It isn't our first time living together, but we still have things to figure out. The property taxes on this place are pretty high, but we'll be able to stay a few years, at least. . . ."

She rambled on about taxes and relatives and *We live even farther away from Lily's family* and *She has a shorter commute to work, and she likes that* and *There are some really nice bike trails nearby.*

And Vera, too, talked about commutes and leisure, and then about food. "I really want to get the recipe for that cheese spread," she said. "That was divine."

"That's Lily's recipe," Shaniya replied. "All those recipes are hers. She's a great cook. She has them stashed in a cookbook somewhere. I can have her forward them to you." The banter went on in like fashion: *Lily is a great gardener. Lily is good at sports; we go skiing and ice skating in the winter, and in summer we play tennis and go hiking and canoeing. . . .*

Lily felt her breath becoming labored. Her eyes began to sting. She felt hot, yet she shivered suddenly.

She moved backwards, stepping away from the mirror until the sofa pressed against her calves. She slumped onto the seat and looked at the floor.

Vera was leaving. The cliché goodbyes, the *Thanks so much for the gifts* and *I'll see you at work* and *We'll have to plan a day to get together* drifted though the speakers and into Shaniya's ears, but she hardly registered them. She stared into the puddle of dirty water as a drop fell from somewhere and disrupted the calm surface.

The house went silent except for the sound of Shaniya's steps, retreating up the staircase.

Lily laid on the sofa, still facing the mirror—but she didn't look there. She looked into the puddle, thoughtless and numb.

And then the anger surged again, and she whispered: "Bitch."

Of course she says nothing but nice things about me, because that makes me look like even more of an asshole.

Her teeth clenched. In her belly, though, rather than anger, she felt a growing unease—a terror, maybe, one that hadn't yet risen fully into consciousness. Lily's anxiety about getting caught spying on Shaniya had mutated into something else, had shifted its focus to something more frightening. She realized, then, that she didn't know what to do when she left the hidden room. Shaniya had asked her to change. Lily didn't know if she could—or should. *She's asking me to change my personality—selfish, insulting, arrogant. Who asks their partner to do something like that? If I annoy her so much, why start living with me in the first place? Why take it this far?*

She looked up at the mirror, at the narcissus minnows framed at the bottom—the wispy, fragile-looking petals, the sunshine-tinted cups protecting shy-looking stamens and the ovary tucked deep and safe. Those bright flowers reminded her of the better times in her childhood, of acceptance and warmth and love. And they reminded her of Shaniya, who had brought her happiness along with anxiety, who provided a warm contrast to the seemingly empty relationships in her life: the banal co-workers, the indifferent friends, the distant family that Lily saw less and less of. Shaniya was good, kind-hearted—too good to stay with someone like Lily. Perhaps she stayed out of a condescending pity. In her romantic endeavors, no one had been able to continue loving Lily. They left quietly, without bothering to explain why.

But Lily knew why.

Even after Shaniya left the house, even after she returned later and long after she went to bed, Lily didn't move from the sofa. In the morning she still lay there in a seeming paralysis, awake and unblinking. Her eyelids barely moved even as she drifted in and out of sleep. She stared into the puddle until the light bulb burned out and left her in darkness.

Another Black Cat

Another Black Cat

"You meet all kinds of people that help put life in perspective and turn the horror into some kind of lesson or avenue of awakening that lives with you all your days."
-Ruby Dee

Ryan O'Grady knew his cat would die soon. She was seventeen years old with feline leukemia, and he often anticipated waking up to find her lying lifeless in the cat bed. Instead, he discovered her in the front porch with her throat slashed.

"Regan," he whispered, gently examining the wound. The blood had long since dried on her black fur and on the wood-slatted floor where it had pooled, and she had clearly been dead for hours—but Ryan found himself searching for signs of life within her half-open eyes as he whispered sympathies and curses under his breath. "Who the hell did this to you?"

The window next to the porch door had been shattered. Someone had placed duct tape over the glass before breaking it, presumably to prevent the noise of the shards falling to the floor. Ryan found the strips of tape still adhered to the broken glass on the front lawn.

He conducted a somber burial in the backyard. As he dug the hole, Ryan's eyes repeatedly drifted to the fleece blanket in which he'd wrapped Regan's body. It was unfair, he thought, that his grief should be escalated by rage. From now on, he would have no one to come home to, no one to take care of or sit with, and in the expectation of that emptiness writhed the angry, obsessive wondering: Who had done this, and why? Was it something personal? Someone he'd arrested, or ticketed? Someone who hated cops?

Ryan lowered the bundle into the earth and placed a palm against the soft blanket. "I love you, Regan," he whispered.

He covered the blanket with handfuls of dirt before picking up the shovel. When the hole had been filled, Ryan went inside and checked the security footage for his front yard and the north-facing side of the house. He'd set up the cameras only days ago, after someone had broken the basement window. The footage showed a hulking figure approaching the porch just after midnight. The camera didn't capture much detail. There was only the hooded figure, hurrying through the foggy night, head bowed and face hidden from the motion-triggered light. The figure came and left within a five-minute time span. As the figure retreated, Ryan noticed that the hood had been removed, revealing some other strange hat beneath—a hat with two protrusions on top, like devil's horns.

The intruder stopped, turning for a moment to look at the house. Ryan drew in a sharp breath and uttered: "Jesus!"

The man—definitely a man, Ryan decided—wore a mask over his face, a ghastly white thing that resembled a cat's skull. The porch light gave little illumination, but Ryan caught a glimpse of an eye peeking through the skull, and even in the grainy video, he thought he saw a perverse triumph in that eye.

Ryan placed a rush order for three more cameras: one for the porch, two for the rear and south sides of the house.

He installed them as soon as they arrived, keeping his eyes on the street as he worked, looking for any suspicious activity: anyone lurking, anyone watching. He'd barely finished with the porch camera when a rusty white car stopped on the street in front of the house. Ryan had noticed it before: an old Buick with a busted taillight. The young woman who drove it tended to park in that same spot. Ryan had never thought much of it. The apartment buildings in the neighborhood had small, expensive lots, leaving most residents to park along the street—yet this woman had become a regular, consistently parking in front of Ryan's house.

The woman turned off the ignition and grabbed a bag from the passenger seat. She froze for a moment when she saw Ryan watching her. Then she twisted around, peering up and down the street before getting out of the car. She slung the large purse over her shoulder and hurried across the neighbor's property, into the backyard—nearly running, but not quite. Ryan walked to the corner of the house. The woman glanced back, saw him still watching, and continued towards the apartment complex behind Ryan's yard.

Something about her nagged at him. He'd met her somewhere; he felt sure of it. She was a young Black woman, perhaps twenty, with braided hair extensions that began in a dark purple shade and faded to a light violet. A little over five feet tall, with serious, nervous eyes. Ryan racked his brain, trying to come up with some reason that she might be the culprit. Had he arrested her? Had she been watching his house, looking for the right time and method for revenge?

It was only later that night, during a failed effort to fall asleep, that he remembered.

Ryan sat up in bed. "Shit," he whispered.

He saw her again the next day, after he'd finished his shift. Ryan had a routine that he went through when he returned from duty. It had always involved Regan, but became meager in her absence: he simply put on fresh clothes, made a cup of chai, switched on the living room stereo, and tried to stop thinking about the events of the day. The last part wasn't hard this time; Regan's fate remained at the forefront of his mind. Ryan stayed near the front window, watching for the Buick with the busted light.

The moment the car pulled up, Ryan went out to meet the driver. He confronted the woman as she stepped onto the curb.

"Hey," he called sharply.

She looked at him and slowed, but didn't stop. Her face was drawn and weary, the flesh puffy beneath the eyes, her shoulders slumped beneath the weight of her bag.

"What are you doing on my property?" Ryan demanded.

The woman replied coolly: "I'm on your neighbor's property."

He walked beside her across the lawn. "What are you doing on my neighbor's property? This is private land you're on."

She stopped then, facing him, and gestured to the backyard. "I live in the apartment complex over there. Mary lets me cut through her yard so I don't have to walk three blocks to get home."

"Oh, you got to know Mary, did you? That's convenient, but you don't live back there. I remember you. You live on the east side, off Lake Street. I came to your apartment to investigate a break-in."

"You came to my apartment," she replied tersely, "but I don't recall an investigation. Do you remember me saying I was having problems with a stalker?"

Ryan hesitated. "Yeah, I remember something about that."

"Well, that's why I moved. Again. He hasn't found out where I live yet, but I'll let the police know when the trouble starts. Again."

She started to walk on, but Ryan angled ahead of her. "Is there some particular reason you keep parking in front of my house?"

Her dark eyes focused intently on Ryan. "Why? Did something happen?"

Ryan regarded her with equal scrutiny. "Like what?"

She gave a small shrug. "It's true, I park in front of your house most days. In fact, I wouldn't be surprised if Frank thinks I live here. You know—Frank, the guy who broke in and stole my work to get me in trouble with my boss, and who pissed in my food and killed my cat." She stared at Ryan, letting the words sink in before turning to leave. "See you around," she called.

Ryan stopped at the department gym before his shift. His treadmill routine seemed to pass more slowly than usual; he spent most of it fixated on the woman in the white Buick. Later, after he'd showered and strapped on his belt and vest, someone finally commented on his vacant expression: Ari, another rookie who stood a couple of lockers down. The two men exchanged the usual greetings, but Ari's gaze lingered on Ryan. "You all right? You seem a little out of it," Ari said, and then caught himself. "Oh, that's right. I forgot about your cat."

"Yeah. It's not just my cat, though."

"What do you mean?"

Ryan hesitated. "Listen, I need your opinion on something. There's this girl who called the police a while ago to report a break-in. I went over and looked around, and she told me she had a stalker, some guy at work who she dated for a few weeks. Well, now she's living at the apartments behind my house, and she keeps parking her car right in front of my place. And I've been having these incidents—a couple of broken windows, and . . . my cat. I confronted her yesterday, and I think she tricked her stalker into thinking she lives at my house—and now he's targeting me instead of her."

"Well, that's original. How sure are you?"

"She said she wouldn't be surprised if he thinks she lives there. If it's true, think about how messed up that is. I investigated the break-in, and then she moved right behind my house. It's like she did it on purpose—like she planned to trick this guy into stalking me. I gave her my card. She could have looked me up and found out where I live."

"Does she have any reason to be angry at you?"

"No. I mean, I couldn't find anything to catch the perp, but I dusted for prints, I interviewed her, I made the report. And now she's targeting me."

"Well, *he* might be targeting you. Do you know who he is?"

"No."

"You should find out from her."

"Yeah, I can do that, but I need this whack job to stop parking in front of my house."

Ari considered that for some moments. His eyes looked troubled. "The street isn't your property," he replied quietly.

"Maybe a restraining order," Ryan mused.

"Against him, or her?"

"Her."

Ari gave him a pointed look. "Based on what incident?"

"Well, she insinuated that she was leading him to my house on purpose."

A frown touched Ari's lips. "I don't know, man."

It wasn't what Ryan wanted to hear. Though he tried to put aside his own problems for the day, he had to make extra efforts to focus during the morning's roll call and briefing. His thoughts kept straying to Regan's cloudy, lifeless eyes and the hooded figure in the security feed.

The Buick was back that night. Ryan missed his chance to confront the driver; a fatal auto collision and its aftermath had kept him busy for more than three hours after his shift was supposed to end, and he arrived home with strains of sadness still washing through him. He fell asleep quickly that night, but the hooded figure didn't leave his thoughts. The mystery intruder and the day's deaths crept into his dreams, and he woke in the early morning hours thinking that the intruder had returned, that he could feel its heavy breath as it loomed over him. Ryan jumped out of bed in a sudden panic. A moment later he was sprawled on the floor, gasping in pain.

"Damn," he whispered.

He wrapped an ice pack and pressed it to his ankle, watching as the flesh began to swell. The injury didn't seem serious, but it would keep him from any foot pursuits.

He made it through his next shift with some help from an elastic bandage, and arrived home in time to catch the Buick driver. She was dressed neatly in gray slacks, a purple button-down shirt, and a multi-colored scarf, and carried the same large bag on her shoulder. Her face didn't look as lively as her clothes; Ryan saw the weariness in her gait, and even from a distance, her eyes conveyed a certain hauntedness.

He confronted her in the same way as before, calling: "Hey."

She glanced at him and kept walking.

"Hold up a second," Ryan implored her, moving closer. "Listen, I really need you to tell me about this guy who stalked you. I think he came to my house a few days ago and . . . killed my cat."

The woman slowed to a stop, her face full of sudden surprise—and perhaps a trace of regret. "Are you serious?" she asked, and then shook her head. "Of course you're serious. I'm really sorry."

"Right, now you're sorry," Ryan said dryly. "You didn't think about that possibility when you tricked him into coming to my house?"

"I didn't harm your cat."

Ryan tried to keep his voice even, though her words plucked a string of rage within him. "No, but you didn't warn me either. If you know he kills animals, why lead him here? My cat can get into the porch any time she wants through the pet door. You must've seen her sitting in the window."

"I didn't know you had a cat. I hardly look at your place. I run to my own place, and leave my car where Frank can see it, and that's all."

"That's all?" Ryan studied her haggard face, remembering how she'd looked on their first encounter: tired, frightened, defeated. Time hadn't improved her condition. She was thinner, much skinnier than he remembered, a change that created a gauntness in her face. "What's your name? I couldn't look up your case. I didn't have the date, and couldn't remember which address—"

"Iesha Lamont," she said. "There's no need to look anything up. I can tell you whatever you need to know."

"Right. So, who is this guy?"

"His name's Frank Marsh. I know his address, his date of birth, his employer. You want to take notes?"

Ryan hesitated. "I guess I'll have to. But don't think I'm going after him because of anything he did to you."

She nodded. "I'm used to hearing that."

"I'm not interested in your story," Ryan said. "My cat was killed because of you. That piece of shit boyfriend of yours came to my house and slit her throat."

"None of this is because of me," she replied sharply. "It's because of Frank. And he's not my boyfriend, and yeah, I can empathize. He killed my cat too, remember? I had Leo since I was a kid. He was my only friend while I was going through all of this. I still imagine Frank standing over him and . . . ."

Ryan saw the sudden wetness in Iesha's eyes, the swell of grief. "What does this guy have against you?" he asked.

"Oh, you know. Ego issues. Some guys don't like feeling rejected or judged—but Frank takes it to another level." Iesha wiped at her eyes and sniffled. "So . . . are you going to help me get him?"

Ryan let out a small sigh. His initial impulse was to say no, to accuse and condemn—but he said, "Come inside. I'll see what I can do."

She followed him through the porch, past the small bloodstain that Ryan had been unable to scrub from the floorboards. "Take your shoes off, please," Ryan said. "I'm going to make some tea. Do you want any? I have chai and spiced lemon."

"Chai is fine," she replied, slipping off her boots. "Thanks."

In the kitchen, Iesha became suddenly tense. She stood at the threshold with her arms folded, looking around as if to scope out any potential dangers. Her gaze drifted to the photo magnets on the refrigerator, and she moved closer, bending to look at an image of Regan perched on the back of the couch with her paws on Ryan's shoulder. "This is your kitty?" she asked. "Looks just like my Leo. Black, with a white spot on the forehead."

Ryan stood at the sink, filling two coffee mugs with water. He didn't reply.

"I really am sorry that Frank hurt your cat," Iesha said, relaxing and unfolding her arms. "I can almost guarantee you, he's the one who did it. He probably saw another black cat with a white spot on its head and assumed that Leo didn't die, or that I adopted one of Leo's siblings. And if he still thinks I live in this house, he'll come back.”

“Why?” Ryan asked. “What did you do to piss him off so much?”

She gave him a tired but scathing look. “I didn’t ‘do’ anything. We dated for a little while, and he had an inferiority complex. My friends perceive me as a strong person, and his friends perceive him as a poor soul with a bad childhood who needs sympathy and help. That always got under his skin. He does this to show me he’s more powerful than I am.”

Ryan let out a small scoffing sound as he placed the mugs in the microwave. “That seems a weak reason.”

“Nevertheless, that’s the reason.” Iesha went to the table, sighing as she sat down. “He’s sick. And there’s plenty of evidence of it, but he’s good at getting people to feel sorry for him and let him off the hook. And it works to his advantage, but it also bothers him because he doesn’t like to be perceived as weak.”

Ryan glanced at her, at the weariness in her young face. “So, what happened to him? What ‘bad childhood’ made him this way?”

Iesha shook her head. “Nothing too specific. He likes to give speeches about how his mom didn’t give him enough affection.”

“How long has he been stalking you?”

“A year and a half.”

“And how long did you date?”

“A few weeks.”

“And he’s been after you for a year and a half? You sure nothing else happened, nothing specific that you did . . . .”

“No, sir, there’s—sorry, I don’t know your name.”

“Call me Ryan.”

“Ryan. Once again, I didn’t ‘do’ anything. Frank stalks me because he’s sick. I got that old junker out there because he kept vandalizing my car. First it was childish stuff like putting garbage on it, and then it was scratches and dents, and then he slashed my tires. I bought this car and parked blocks away from work so he wouldn’t see which one was mine, but he saw me driving it and took a photo with his phone, and then the vandalism started again. He already busted my taillight and drove a nail into my tire, and some day you’ll come outside and see that he’s done something worse. People have seen him vandalizing my car, but if they catch him crouching by it, he says he dropped something. He's not supposed to come into the office when I'm alone, but he does it anyway and says he doesn't know my schedule, even though our schedules haven't changed all year. Last week he snuck up behind me, grabbed me, and rubbed his dick against me. I reported it, and the Human Resources director said, 'Well, he didn't know it was you until he got close, and he brushed up against you by accident.' He didn't 'brush up' against me. He—"

"Wait, wait," Ryan interrupted. "You're still working at the same place? If he's so dangerous, why don't you leave?"

"Because we work at a campus building, and I figured this was the only way I could stay safe while I finish school: make sure we're at a place where people know what's going on, where someone's watching, where his superiors are putting pressure on him. But all they've done is let him know that he can do whatever he wants and get away with it. And if anything worse happens, they'll probably cover it up to save their own asses."

"But he still has to see you every day at work. Don't you think that if you left, he would find something else to obsess over?"

She let out a small, sardonic laugh. "Of course. He would find some other woman to harass, and no one would stop him then, either. Other women have already quit because of him. Should I just pass him on to someone else?"

Ryan set Iesha's tea on the table. He sat across from her, thinking over the evidence he'd collected: the duct tape and broken glass, none of which had turned up fingerprints, and the shadowed figure on the security feed. "He seems meticulous. Did he just assume you live here because your car is out front, or did you do other things to make him think you lived here?"

Iesha lowered her eyes. "I invited some of my co-workers to a housewarming party. I listed your address on the invitations."

Ryan stared at her. "What?"

She nodded. "Yeah, I did that."

Slowly, he dropped his head into his hands. He shook his head, letting it roll back and forth across his palms. "That is messed up. Why would you do that to me, knowing what he's like?"

"I haven't done anything to you."

"Bullshit!" He looked up, glared at her. "You intentionally led him to my house.”

“Did I?” she asked. “Everyone’s always pointing at me. I somehow instigated all this. And then I was too aggressive in defending myself, or I wasn’t aggressive enough, or I did this or that wrong, or it’s my fault because I won’t quit my job or because I dated him. No one is pointing at him. I didn’t have to lead Frank Marsh anywhere. He stalked me here.” Iesha tilted her head to one side, giving Ryan a knowing look. “I bet no one showed up to that party. Did any college kids show up here, looking for me?”

“No.”

“No, of course not. Before Frank started stalking me, they would have. But now my old ‘friends’ avoid me. My mom tells me I’m an embarrassment and a troublemaker, and she made me promise not to tell our relatives that I filed a sexual harassment report, because she doesn’t want people to find out that I’m ‘one of those women.’ My dad thinks I’m being hysterical, and when I’m at work and people see Frank sidling up to me, they duck their heads and look the other way so they can pretend they didn’t witness anything.” She stared steadily at Ryan, her eyes hard, almost accusatory. “But it’s hard to duck your head when it’s happening to you, isn’t it?”

“Don’t fucking accuse me, or complain to me about your social life,” he said. “Why me? What did I do?”

“You’re a cop. If he comes after you, you can catch him.”

Ryan scoffed. “Is that the only reason? It’s not revenge? I seem to remember that you weren’t happy with the way I handled things at your apartment.”

Iesha wrapped her hands around the warm mug, staring into it as she spoke. “I’m unhappy with the system. People who are being stalked hear the words ‘There’s nothing we can do’ more than any other phrase. Seems like there’s nothing the justice system can do until we’re already dead, or close to it. Do you know how many times you said those words to me?”

“No.”

“Neither do I, because I lost count.”

“I know it might seem like I was dismissive,” Ryan said, “but cops come face to face with things that make a non-violent break-in seem like it’s not that big of a deal.”

"Non-violent break-in? Was slashing my cat's throat not violence?"

Ryan felt his face flushing. He remembered, suddenly, the smears of blood on Iesha's kitchen floor. She, too, had wrapped her cat's body in a blanket by the time he'd arrived on the scene. He had seen the blood, but had no memory of the cat. "Sorry, I didn't mean that," he said. "I just mean that when you actually see the violence . . . like, yesterday, I was called to the scene of a traffic accident, and I ended up having to go to some guy's house and tell him that his husband died. They had just adopted a child. The dead bodies, and the look on people's faces when you tell them . . . it washes away everything else. If you're dealing with corpses, and helping people who have just found out that the person they love the most is dead, and when you're dealing with shootings, beatings, rapes—"

"Frank did beat me," Iesha interrupted. "At work. I had bruises all up my legs and on my upper arms from where he kicked and punched me." She raised her eyebrows and gave a slight shake of her head. "Just saying. You keep talking about my case like it doesn't involve assault."

"You really should quit your job. Move somewhere farther away. This guy can't—"

"Just move farther away? What, a woman should give up her community and home, her job and everything she's worked for, and start all over again 'somewhere else,' just so you don't have to do your job?"

"Don't make this about me," Frank snapped.

"It's not just about you," she replied dully. "Everyone else is doing it, too."

"You don't have to start over. If his motivation is really that petty and he just wants to feel powerful, then let him feel like he won. You can find someplace better, finish at a different school, get a job in your field. Don't stay just to prove that you're stronger than him."

"I can't afford that," Iesha said, "and there isn't someplace better. People always say 'You can just go somewhere better,' but there isn't somewhere that's different. This shit happens everywhere. People duck their heads everywhere. You imagine that my leaving will make things better because then *you* won't have to deal with it.

Frank has done this shit to other people, for who knows how many years, and it's right out there in the open, but no one will hold him accountable. It's not about proving that I'm strong. It's about addressing the actual fucking problem." She took a small sip from the cup and set it on the table. Her gaze focused steadily on Ryan. "Help me nail this guy," she said quietly.

He leaned back in his chair.

"No one else will help me," she said. "My own family and friends didn't help. Frank killed Leo, and still. No one. Nothing."

"Then why do you think I can help?"

"You're the only one who has something to gain by catching him."

He shook his head. "This is messed up."

"Yeah. I've been dealing with it for a year and a half, so I know exactly how messed up it is."

"Haven't you tried getting evidence?"

Irritation rang in Iesha's voice. "Yes, I did that. I recorded him sexually harassing me, and he said I set him up by encouraging him, and that he thought we were just playing around. I recorded him telling me that I'm not as strong as I think, and that it would be easy for him to overpower me because he's been working out, and that he could easily smother someone with one hand—but it 'wasn't specific enough.' Frank said I made the bruises myself and that I made the recordings because I'm 'obsessed' with him. Now it's mostly property damage. I haven't been able to record that. And the other sick things he does, the tampering with my food, the *looks* he gives me, the gestures he makes—I haven't been able to record most of that, not that I haven't tried. I got a couple of his threatening gestures on a mini camera, but the HR lady said, 'Well, he was mad because you keep reporting him' and 'He was gesturing to someone else.'"

"What about a dash cam? If he's coming here and messing with your car . . . ."

"I've tried that. I've spent money, I've stayed awake, I've set traps. It takes a toll. I don't have any money or energy left. Even if this guy doesn't literally murder me, he's ruining my health. It may not be a visible assault to you, but I feel like he is slowly killing me."

"No, I get it." Ryan fiddled with the mug, turning it in slow circles on the table as he debated his next words. "I do want to catch him. I became a cop to catch people like him—people who have no respect for other humans."

A faint smile touched her lips. "Did you? Your childhood dream, was it?"

"Well, my dad was a cop. We had a bar in the basement, and his cop buddies used to come over and hang out. Some of them were okay."

"Some of them?" she repeated, in a sardonic tone. "What about your dad? He was your role model?"

Ryan let out a bitter laugh. "No. My dad wasn't a good man. He was cruel to my mom, and cruel to me and my sister, and I'm sure he wasn't a good cop. I wanted to become a better police officer to make up for the things he did. Well, that, and I wanted to catch bad guys and put them away."

"Then help me catch this one," Iesha said.

He thought back to the incidents thus far: the broken basement window, Regan's body on the porch floor. The shock and horror of seeing her there, the rage, the strain of guilt that coursed through all of it. "I did catch an image of him outside the house," he said, "but . . . he was wearing a mask. A damned creepy mask. I'm going to get some stronger floodlights for the yard and the porch, and I have a friend who can help me set the motion range, so the perp will be well onto the property when the lights are activated. We can get a better shot of him on camera. I can work with the neighbors, too, and see if they'll let me set up security feed on their property. And I know where there's CCTV in the neighborhood. We might be able to catch him coming or going. Do you know what he drives?"

"Of course. A gray Ford. I can give you the plate number."

"Does he ride anything else? A bike, or—"

"No, no bike. He doesn't take taxis or the bus either. Just the car. He's more likely to drive here and park a couple blocks away than to take a bus."

Ryan got to his feet. "All right. I'm going to start taking those notes."

He grabbed a pad and pen from beside the kitchen phone. Iesha wasn't exaggerating about the details she had memorized; she provided a full description, starting with Frank's full name, nicknames, birth date, address, and physical characteristics, including his exact height, weight, and shoe size. She went on to list his previous jobs, his reasons for getting fired, and names of former co-workers who would be willing to talk to police. "He went by other names at some of his jobs—maybe so people don't make the connections between what he did before and what he's doing now. He was Big Fred at his last job, and now people call him Sonny."

"And these other people, they're all people who have been harassed by him, or seen the harassment?" Ryan asked.

"They've all seen *something*. Frank doesn't just harass. He supplements his income by stealing things and selling them online. He got caught by a couple of my co-workers, but after seeing what happened to me, they didn't want to report it."

"We need evidence," Frank replied. "Hearsay won't cut it."

"Well, what else can we do? I wanted to set up gopher traps outside my bedroom window at my last place, but the landlord wouldn't let me."

"We have to be careful about setting up secret traps," Ryan replied. "A few years ago, a guy set up a trap by his yard signs because someone kept vandalizing them. Well, a ten-year-old kid stepped on it. Sent a spike right through his foot. The kid's dad sued the shit out of this guy. He won, too."

"Yes, but you have a serious problem with gophers," Iesha said. "A very serious problem. And gopher traps aren't illegal."

"I can't do it. What if Mary or someone else comes over? And even if I warn her, there isn't a single gopher hole on my lawn."

She shrugged. "So, let's make one."

Ryan glanced at the photo magnet again, the selfie he'd taken on the couch with Regan, and then looked back at Iesha's haggard face. It struck him again: the extreme measure she'd taken by baiting Frank to this house. The seeming perversion of it. And it sank in for the first time: Iesha wasn't doing this for revenge. She was doing it to live. And, likely, to prevent another woman or another black cat from becoming Frank's next fatality.

"All right," he said at last. "I'm going to make a few phone calls. Let's nail this guy."

He expected Iesha to looked relieved, but she stared at the table with a strange, empty-eyed look. "Do you mean that?" she asked.

"Yeah, I mean it. Let's get the bastard who killed our cats."

She raised her eyes, and Ryan saw a new hauntedness in her face. "Even when you tell your cop friends, or your family, about what I did, and they say I'm a crazy bitch who should be punished, you'll still help me?"

Ryan looked at her in surprise. "I think," he said, "Frank is the crazy bitch who should be caught and punished."

Iesha lowered her gaze again, and once more, Ryan anticipated a look of relief—but Iesha's face crumpled. She leaned forward, covering her face, racked with sudden sobs.

"Hey," Ryan said, half-standing.

She didn't respond, but continued to wail—a string of tortured, almost inhuman sounds. "I'm sorry," she rasped, and took a shuddering breath. "It's just—"

"Hey," Ryan said again. He went to her side, awkward and uncertain, and rested a hand on her quivering shoulder. "Cry as much as you want, but don't worry anymore. I meant what I said. Let's nail this guy."

Goodnight, Custodian

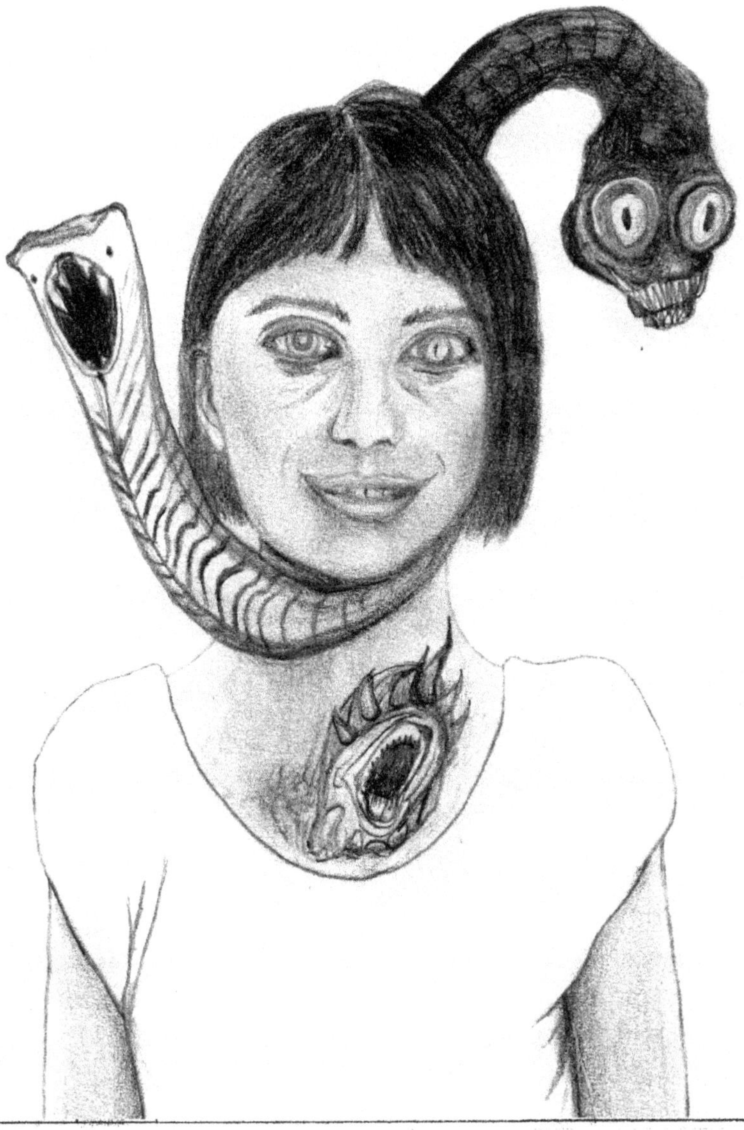

Goodnight, Custodian

*" . . . if they're so successful, why haven't parasites taken over the
world? The answer is simple: they have. We just haven't noticed.
That's because successful parasites don't kill us; they become part of
us, making us perform all the work to keep them alive and help them
reproduce."*
-Daniel Suarez, *Daemon*

"Well, Loria, I'm interested to see your work. I know you're
just a janitor, but all of your employers described you in glowing
terms." Adhira peers at me over the top of her glasses, curiosity
lingering on her face as she sets down my résumé.

I decide to ignore the "just a janitor" remark. She's impressed,
both by my enthusiasm and my slew of positive references. The
people I've worked for feel incredibly grateful to me without really
knowing why. "Thank you," I reply. "I look forward to being part of
the team."

"Well, we're not really a *team*." Adhira scratches her neck and
lets out a small laugh. "Actually, on that note . . . ." She opens a desk
drawer. "I'm giving you a master key to all the offices—but make
sure you only use it during work hours. We've had some thefts in the
building, so we're on the lookout for anything suspicious."

As I place the key in my pocket, Adhira yawns and scratches
again at her neck. The flesh there is slightly discolored, red-and-pale
splotches cascading across light brown skin. Though I'm not looking
directly at her, I can see what's bothering her: a large worm, coiled
around her throat like a collar, with two tiny black eyes at the head.
Two large teeth gleam in the fluorescent light, contrasting the
darkness of the gargantuan mouth, just visible above the point where
they've hooked into Adhira's neck.

"I'll keep an eye out," I reply.

My new custodial gig is at Millis Hall, a one-story building in
the center of a sprawling college campus. I'm tasked with cleaning
six restrooms, a number of offices, and a hideously outdated
bookstore. Across the store's length is a shag carpet streaked with
mismatched shades of brown, green, purple, and orange, collecting

dirt and dust around the edges of every bookshelf. I show up at closing time, armed with a vacuum cleaner, a cart full of supplies, and a backpack slung over my shoulder. The employees are mostly college kids. They're friendly enough, especially when they find out that I teach music lessons and occasionally perform at campus clubs. After a short time I'm no longer shunned as "just a janitor;" I'm welcomed as "a really talented musician."

Colleen, the store manager, is a small, smartly dressed woman who loves Beethoven and Rachmaninov. I connect with her over our mutual love for classical music. At day's end she finishes balancing the cash drawers and moves toward a stack of returned textbooks. I switch off the vacuum and drift toward her, humming softly as I pull a roll of trash bags from the cart. My eyes rest on the red and rust-brown patterns of Colleen's sweater. I pause a few feet from her, pretending to have a hard time finding the perforation between the plastic bags.

Colleen glances back and smiles—a genuine smile, mismatched by the gray hues in her face and the pink swell of her eyelids. "What are you humming?"

"It's a song I'm working on. I'm figuring out the lyrics."

"I wish I could write music." She slides a stack of books onto the counter. "I write poetry, though. When I'm here alone, I go on auto-pilot and compose while I'm working."

I've tucked the roll of trash bags under one arm, lowering my opposite shoulder and shifting my backpack onto my hip. Everything is in position: a half melon, resting face-up like a bowl, the other half lodged neatly beside it. "I do the same thing. I used to . . . hey, hold still a minute. You've got a spider on your back."

She gasps, shudders. "Ohh, get it off! I *hate* spiders!"

"This is a really ugly one," I murmur. "Don't worry, it's dead. You must've leaned back and squashed it." I resume humming in my seemingly absent-minded way as I probe the wool fibers.

The spider isn't dead. Its thick, furry legs are already protruding through the knitting. Next comes the torso, a sightless clump of hair and slime. The creature is more than three inches across, legs and all; it seeks me in a stupor, groping with trance-like determination, its feeding interrupted by my compelling, invasive tones.

I pluck it loose by one bent leg and drop it into my bag, where it falls into the half melon. Another second and it's trapped inside the two halves.

Colleen never notices. She stands frozen, her hair clutched safely above her shoulders, until I say: "Damn, I dropped it." I pretend to look for the dead spider, but quickly give up. "I'll get it with the vacuum. We'll never find it in a carpet that looks like a menagerie of squashed bugs."

She laughs, her eyes still bright with spider-on-your-back anxiety. "Yeah, this building is a nightmare from the seventies." She releases a long sigh. I can see tension melting from her shoulders, healthy color returning to her face. "Thanks, Loria."

Heartfelt gratitude rings in her voice. Subconsciously, she must know what I've done—what she's actually thanking me for.

At home, I bury the melon in the backyard. Winter has frozen the ground, but I've prepared well. The yard is dotted with holes, little burial sites to last me through the season. I consider what I've seen at Millis and wonder if I've dug enough of them.

I didn't get the janitor job to clean floors and toilets, though that has its own purpose: Removing the day's stresses, and creating a clean space for the next day to begin anew, has healing qualities. But Millis Hall, for some reason I haven't yet fathomed, has worse problems than soiled floors. It's teeming with energetic parasites. I walked past the hall countless times in the summer, and it was only this past autumn that I sensed its heavy energy. Sitting on the low stone wall outside the building, I turned my mind, letting my vision come through those other powers I've developed. At first I didn't notice much—just the usual parasites people carry, small and relatively easy to deal with. As I stood, I passed a young woman on her way to the bookstore. A long, hook-legged worm had coiled around her shoulders. She rubbed anxiously at the area, not knowing the cause of her discomfort. I followed her to the hall, found another monstrous parasite near the entrance, spotted one through an office window, and in the bookstore saw three more: venomous lizards and spiders, latched snugly into the energetic bodies of their hosts.

I decided right then to get a new job. I called my mentor for help, and we did some work with our songs and mesas. Soon the janitor at Millis received a new offer and moved on, leaving a position for me to fill.

Bending over the half-buried melon, I punctuate my singing with occasional puffs of tobacco smoke. The song's meaning is hard to convey in English. In my way, I'm persuading this creature to consume organic food—to be a true creature of the earth, a thing that lives and dies and returns to the soil. The earth will transmute it and make its energy into something useful.

The snow crunches softly, rhythmically, behind me: the sound of an animal approaching, likely one of the stray cats who stop by to see if I've left food on the porch step. I expect the aggressive one I've named Marcie, but instead I find a small black kitten. This one is bold. She strides right up to the melon, sniffs, and looks inquisitively at me. Her turquoise eyes reflect the porch light.

As with the others, I immediately name her. "Yanakoya! You've got creepy eyes." Yanakoya allows me to run a hand along her back, arching against my hand and turning around for another rub. She inspects the cantaloupe again, then steps back and gives me another penetrating stare. I wonder if she can sense the entity inside.

The being inside the melon isn't really a spider; nor is the lizard a lizard, nor the worm an actual worm. They appear as such so that I recognize their nature. They're parasites, but they appear as venomous creatures because while they feed, they must also poison their hosts and create imbalances. A healthy host would discover the parasite and reject it. The venom, then, becomes the larger problem.

Or so my mentor says. I'm still a novice, trying to be a custodian in all senses of the word: cleanser, caregiver, guardian.

Sometimes, though, I wonder if I'm merely imagining the entities. I consider the possibility that my mentor is a confident and persuasive nutcase, and I myself am less than lucid.

I finish the burial with a blessing to the creature inside the melon and to the higher entities helping it, and return with my empty sack to the run-down house. Inside, I step over a foot-long hole in the kitchen floor. The bathroom ceiling leaks, the oven doesn't work, and the house has tipped slightly forward. My landlord has leased the property "as is" in an attempt to avoid responsibility for its broken and missing amenities—but the rent is cheap, and here I have privacy and a good-sized yard. If my landlord complains about the holes, I can always bring up her illegal lease conditions.

By the second week, Colleen has taken such a liking to me that she invites me to the annual staff party. After closing the store, she covers the counter with appetizers and a crock pot full of barbecued chicken. I spot more critters as I watch employees lining up to eat: a snake, another spider, something that looks like a cross between a lizard and a toad. It's unusual to see so many substantial parasites in such an unambiguous place. If I was at a trauma center, or rehab, the phenomenon wouldn't surprise me. My mentor has warned me that when so many parasites convene in a random place, it's usually because a larger and older parasite has started the chain of sickness. But none of these creatures looks more significant than the others.

Before I can grab a bite to eat, Colleen asks: "Have you seen Jill? She's interested in violin lessons. I think she's in the back, if you want to talk to her."

As I draw near the corridor, voices drift from the farthest room: a deep, male voice, and another voice I recognize as Jill's. The door is halfway open. I pause at the sight of a man, tall and light-haired, his pale-brown eyes brimming with sadness. "I try not to get serious about girlfriends." He says the words in a moping tone. "They never end up being loyal anyway; so I figure, why get attached?"

Jill smiles up at him, all sympathy and comfort. "You just need to find the right one."

"Thanks. You know, you're a lot nicer than other people who work here. There's a lot of gossip here, a lot of people who think they're better than everyone else. People like to look down on Brad, the manager who was here before; they're always gossiping about his problems, but you always stay out of it."

"Well, everyone has problems."

"That's what I say," the young man replies. "Sure, he made some bad decisions, but who am *I* to judge?" Suddenly he sees me, and his face contorts in a momentary spasm of anger—but he controls himself and relaxes. "We have an eavesdropper."

I step forward. "Hi, Jill. Colleen said you were interested in violin lessons."

We talk for a few minutes while the young man returns to the party. When I finally get a chance to eat, he's standing at the counter, eating a meaty piece of barbecued chicken. He greets me warmly. "So you're a musician. Are you in any bands?"

"Sometimes. I'm not working with any bands right now."

"Well, I'm Sonny Marsh. My name's Frank, but everyone calls me Sonny."

"Loria." I reach out to shake his hand. Sonny's grip is firm and slightly damp.

"I have a lot of connections in the music scene. I used to work at a club." Sonny leans closer. "If there's anyone you want to meet, or a band you want to see, I can hook you up."

"Which club?"

He averts his gaze. His tone thickens. "The one on the corner of eighty-fourth."

While Sonny's focus is elsewhere I begin to turn my mind, looking for any impressions of a parasite, but in that first superficial glimpse I see nothing moving in him—and then Colleen interrupts, squeezing Sonny's arm. "Sonny's into the music scene, too." She reaches around him and grabs another chicken wing. "He can introduce you to anyone."

Sonny isn't listening. He's staring at one of the tables, where the staff have piled coats, backpacks, and purses. "Oh, I just remembered I was going to loan some CDs to Dan." He tosses his empty paper plate into a trash can. "I better do it before I forget." I watch him in puzzlement as he wanders away. Something odd about that man. Something in his tone.

I'm still standing with Colleen when Sonny places the CD on the table. His fingers slide off the plastic case, and then they're pushing into an open purse, rifling through its contents. Within seconds he's sliding a handful of bills into his pants pocket. Without a word of good-bye, he leaves the bookstore. The departure is quick and quiet—but not quick enough.

I turn away from Colleen and let a certain power course through my body, shaking off enough of my humanness to surpass the limits of ordinary vision. My heart races, first with the challenge of altered being, then with the fright of what I see: a lizard-like creature, standing six feet tall and covered with rough, spotted scales. It frightens me because that's *all* I see.

The lizard hesitates beyond the doorway. It turns, and I know that I should look away, that I should feign ignorance, but the shock is too great. Sonny Marsh makes eye contact. His inhuman eyes widen in fear, as if he *sees* me looking into him; then the chin lifts, and the eyes narrow defiantly—and he gives me a look of raw, trembling hatred.

"Colleen . . . ." I try to relax, to slow my heartbeat and speak in a steady voice. "Listen, I know we've been having issues with theft, and . . . I'm pretty sure I just saw Sonny take money from one of those purses."

"Oh, don't worry. I saw that, but I'm sure it was nothing. *Sonny* wouldn't do that."

"You saw him?"

"Well, I didn't see him *take* anything. He was probably just looking for something. Sonny is always losing things. He's nice, but he's absent-minded."

She smiles and walks away, and suddenly everything seems to make sense: the plethora of parasites, my failure to see any critter-like entities living discreetly within Sonny's energetic body. Sonny Marsh doesn't have a parasite. He *is* the parasite.

On Friday I loiter near Jill while she hoists the last of the new books onto metal slats. Fatigue has created puffy red sacs below her eyes, and she seems grateful when I offer to stock the higher shelves. I hum as I work, pausing to complain about the dry winter air and the tiny red cracks forming on my fingers. I shake my near-empty lotion bottle as Jill heaves a gargantuan psychology text.

"Damn . . . I accidentally splattered lotion on your back. Let me wipe it off."

I resume humming as I pull a small, oily snake from between her shoulder blades. In a flash the snake and lotion bottle drop together into my backpack, right into the half coconut. I slam the other half in place, but Jill has already turned. She stares into the bag with a furrowed brow.

"What's *that*?" Her tone is curious, unconcerned.

"Oh, it's a coconut purse. My uncle picked it up on his Bahamas cruise. Have you ever been to the Bahamas?"

A deep voice replies: "I've been to the Bahamas."

Sonny is standing at the edge of the stacks. His gaze is hard, challenging, and there's a feigned friendliness in his tone that should have been obvious even to Jill. "I have a coconut purse just like that," he adds, coming toward us.

I put my hands protectively around my pack.

"Can I see it?" He reaches out, but I quickly grab his wrist.

"Stop," I insist.

"What's the matter? Got something in there you don't want people to see?" Sonny says it in a half-joking manner, but his pale-brown eyes are menacing. I keep a hold on his gaze as the surrounding flesh contorts into a scaly, reptilian mass. I'm *seeing* him, connecting with an aura that flows with anger, hate, arrogance—but also terror, even grief. That energy flows into me, tries to manifest. I channel it into my gut. From there it divides: One half of the sickness is to be meticulously digested, both purified and expelled as waste. The other half has a more immediate outcome.

Sonny wrenches his arm from my grip. "Oh, you're hiding it. You know, we're supposed to keep an eye out for anything sus—"

I lean forward and vomit all over Sonny's shoes.

"Oh my God!" Jill says, as Sonny scrambles backward.

I heave again, then spit and reach for a tissue. "Sorry," I gasp. "Stomach problems. I should have warned you."

That evening, I wonder what I'll do if my yard runs out of room. I could move, but how would I explain the dug-up yard? And how many parasites would the landlord or new tenants release as they poked around in the soil? The thought brings a half-amused smile to my lips as I perform the ritual burial of coconut, snake, and lotion bottle. I contemplate once again how I should handle Sonny. I certainly can't put him in a melon and bury him.

At the next day's closing, I'm not surprised to find a spiny worm tucked beneath Jill's shoulder blade. She sees me and grins. Her eyes are bright but slightly glazed, and there's something sagging in her face, as though smiling takes effort. "Loria! Are you feeling better?"

"I'm fine," I reply.

"It turns out I won't need violin lessons after all. Sonny found someone who can teach me. She lives right by me, and she'll do it for a discount."

I have to think quickly. "Sure, but let me know if you change your mind. I was about to offer a couple of free lessons. Colleen said you give really great haircuts, and I need one."

The smile falters. "Well . . . maybe. I kind of want to help

Sonny's friend. She really needs the money."

Damn. Sonny must have anticipated me. "That's kind of you."

"Sonny is trying really hard to help her get by. I think it's really sweet of him, since he's having trouble too."

"That's too bad. What kind of trouble?"

She shrugs and ducks her head. "Well . . . I stayed and talked to him last night, and his landlord called, and . . . it's really none of my business. But I know Sonny has had it rough, especially this past year. He got fired from his dream job because some jerk kept harassing him."

A male voice speaks up: "That's not true." It's Amin, one of the cashiers. He comes to the counter and sorts through textbooks. The fluorescent glare on his glasses hides his eyes, but I hear the mockery in his voice. "Chris fired him because he kept showing up late and 'losing' equipment and merchandise."

"Fine, but Chris shouldn't have accused him of stealing. Sonny misplaces things because he's absent-minded." Jill looks at me for sympathy, and adds quietly: "Sonny's girlfriend had just committed suicide. And he was the one who found—"

"Holly *supposedly* committed suicide," Amin interrupts. "Her throat was cut. I think it's unlikely that she did it herself."

"She left a suicide note. Anyway, she had problems. She—"

"It was a diary page." Amin's voice drips with impatience. "Someone ripped it from her diary."

They argue about the circumstances of Holly's death while I try to ease my pounding heart. *Maybe he's not just a thief. He could be a murderer.*

The conversation stops as Sonny enters the store. His pace slows; his face is suddenly pale, his eyes frightened—but he quickly recovers and strides to the counter. "Oh, I'm kind of late," he murmurs. "I had to meet with one of my teachers about a group project." He looks at Jill, tipping his head to one side and frowning sadly. "School has been pretty tough. I'm starting to worry that I won't get through it."

Jill's strawberry-blonde ponytail bobs up and down as she nods her understanding. "Oh, I know. It's tough for me too. Hey, if you ever need a study partner, let me know."

The frown vanishes. "Yeah, maybe I'll do that. By the way,

Amin, I saw your post about the paint-a-thon at the mosque."
Sonny's chin lifts slightly. "Do you go to services there?"

Amin busies himself with the stack of returned books. "Yes."

"It surprises me that someone can be in college, and still believe in things like that."

"Like what?"

Sonny shrugs. "Oh, you know . . . like thinking you'll be protected if you pray."

For just a second, Amin's hands stop moving.

"Adhira goes to a temple," Sonny adds, "and she still got her purse stolen. Her husband still got cancer."

"That's not why people pray," Amin replies gently. "They might be praying to stay connected to their creator, or to remember compassion and gratitude."

Sonny emits a puff of air through his teeth.

"It beats becoming selfish and miserable," Amin adds. His tone infers that he meant it as a self-reflection, not as a jab—but Sonny lifts his chin again and clenches his teeth, and his pale-brown eyes seem suddenly dark.

At home that night, I climb into bed and lie on my back, eyes closed, arms straight at my sides. I slip into a relaxed resolve, assuring myself that I am protected; I am prepared. Sonny's energies are being slowly picked apart within me, processed according to their use. My new enzymes break the energy down into small bits of information; they become absorbed into my consciousness the way nutrition is absorbed into the bloodstream, and I explore the digested material, seeking answers to my questions. Who is Sonny? What happened to him? What am I supposed to do?

I'm still wondering as I drift off to sleep. Night is a high but sometimes difficult time for shamans and their apprentices; in darkness we can ignore the world around us and go deep within ourselves, exploring hidden nooks, including the places affected by others—those who inspire us to courage and terror. In the jungle, whenever the darkness began to deepen and the night's ceremony was ready to commence, doña Rosana would always wish me a good journey with tender words: *Good night, custodian.* To her I was already a guardian, already a cleanser and a seer.

Tonight, sleep is my ceremony. I dream about a small wooden

box sitting in the middle of a desert. Inside is a dark void, shrieking with powerful wind. Bits of rough sand swirl within the darkness. If I dipped my finger inside, that sand would burn away flesh and bone; it would obliterate my very soul.

"Loria, did you see anyone suspicious around the bookstore last night? Someone stole Amin's wallet. He said it happened between closing time and the end of his shift."

Adhira is standing in the hallway, fumbling with a stack of papers. She shoves them into a folder and straightens herself to face me. Her eyes are dim and red. For just a moment I let myself *see* her—her, and the two hookworms curled into her neck.

"Just the usual," I reply, pulling the vacuum cleaner from the custodial closet. "Sonny was there . . . and Jill. It was just us four." I pause. "Sonny did make a weird comment about Amin. He was ridiculing him for going to a mosque. He warned him that praying wouldn't protect people from theft."

"Hmm. You didn't notice anyone else?"

"No. How come this place doesn't have security cameras? It would be worth the cost if it prevents more thefts."

"I *have* been thinking that. There are budget issues, but I think you're right: the thefts justify the expense. I'll make another appeal. Maybe someone in the building has a connection and can get us a discount."

"You can't tell anyone in the building," I remind her. "The thief is probably one of us."

"Well, I suppose so. That's disappointing, but probably true."

The bookstore is nearly empty; Colleen is alone in the front. Beneath her smile of greeting, another spider is creeping its way into her chest. I try to remain neutral. My mentor warned me not to take these things personally, not to let them get under my skin. As I run the vacuum, I delve deep into memories of doña Rosana's teachings. *The sickness becomes contagious, because a parasite and host will treat others according to their own sickness, and the problem is less likely to be noticed by others who are ill. In such an environment, energies attach and grow, and take on lives of their own.*

Adhira, Colleen, and Jill collect parasites easily. So do Bill and Dan, two student employees who I haven't had a chance to meet.

I've only seen them wandering around with lizards in their chests. Doña Rosana would have pointed out that they are vulnerable for a reason; their energies are riddled with empty spaces that yearn to be filled. My peers unwittingly draw parasites into those spaces, much like this vacuum: The cleaner draws in dirt and debris because of the pressure created by its emptiness, and it only stops when the void has been filled. It doesn't matter if it's filled with trash or treasure. A parasite can feel like treasured company. It seems to appreciate you; it clings, it desires, it thinks you're delicious.

Colleen calls to me as I'm wheeling the vacuum away. "Loria, want some coffee? It's fresh, but no one's here to drink it."

"Sure."

She pours some dark roast into a chipped mug. "There: some energy to get you through your shift. Sorry, but the bathrooms are really gross today."

I brace myself as I swap the vacuum cleaner for the custodial cart. Outside the women's room, I stop to sip coffee.

"Time to clean the bathrooms?"

Sonny has sidled up behind me. He stops to peer into my cart. "It's sad, isn't it, that we have jobs that just consist of cleaning up other people's shit."

"I can think of sadder things."

He raises his eyebrows. "Oh, *touchy*. Well, I'm off to take a dump." Sonny turns his back and saunters slowly toward the men's room, swaying his hips as he goes. Suddenly he stops and turns. "I'll try not to make too much of a mess." His lips tremble as he restrains a grin. "Or maybe I'll make as much of a mess as I want. You should spend some time cleaning up my messes, since I had to clean your vomit off my shoes."

I grab the glass cleaner from my cart. "That's mature."

The women's room isn't as bad as I expected. The floor is littered with toilet paper, and the bowls need cleansing, but a smell of soap and disinfectant still lingers in the air. Normally I hum while I clean; the bathroom may not be the best space to take a deep breath and belt out a tune, but it has a great echo. This time, though, I'm listening for Sonny's departure. When I've finished cleaning the toilets, he still hasn't emerged, and I wonder: *Would he really?*

I finally hear the sound of flushing. Sonny appears seconds

later. Without a word, he pauses beside my cart and dips his index finger into my coffee. "So you live out by the border," he says.

I stand with my arms full of toilet paper, staring at the mug.

"Jill showed me your address," he continues casually. "Sounds like a pretty remote spot. That's a long way to drive for violin lessons, but I found her someone a lot closer."

"I guess I won't be drinking that," I reply.

"I'm surprised you'd live way out there by yourself. It doesn't seem like the safest place for a young woman living alone."

"We have a good neighborhood watch."

Sonny lets out a small, airy laugh. "So you think. You don't really know people. Take this place, for instance. Everyone seems really friendly, but we have all these thefts. It could be anyone. Adhira said you thought it might be me." He leans his weight into one hip, lifting his chin to give the impression of looking down on me. "I guess I can see why you'd think that. It's not hard to get ahold of a master key. Colleen keeps hers in her desk drawer. I'm here late at night doing database entries, with no one else around, and *I* could take the key. Not that anyone else would suspect me." His eyes are smug, challenging. There are no absent-minded airs in them, no pretense at innocence.

He knows that I know. Probably knows I'm a custodian, too.

"Of course," I reply smoothly. "Because everyone knows you wouldn't do something like that." I can't help adding: "Even after they've *seen* you do it."

It's a dumb thing to say—a stubborn, self-righteous challenge. He was waiting for it, and now he looks pleased, his expression conveying unperturbed triumph. "I'll let you get back to cleaning . . . not that it matters much. It must get frustrating, cleaning people's crap day after day, only to have them come back and make the exact same messes."

"Not at all. It keeps the dirt from over-accumulating."

Sonny narrows his eyes and starts down the hall, swaying his hips in a peculiar manner, as though he thinks he's on a fashion runway. After a few steps he pauses and gives me a sinister look. He says in a strange, deep voice: "Goodnight, custodian."

Maybe I can't convince anyone that Sonny is capable of murder.

Hell, I don't know whether he's guilty. But he is a thief. That, at least, I could prove.

Yet I can't help thinking that even if everyone at Millis saw him committing the thefts, they would still make excuses. *He's absent-minded. He just did it this once because he was about to get evicted. Things have been tough for him.* Someone else, though—the University President, the campus police—someone will hold him accountable.

Adhira shakes her head when I ask if she ordered the security cameras. "We had to make some adjustments in the budget first. But we're making progress."

"We?"

"Oh, don't worry. I haven't mentioned it to anyone—except Sonny. He has so many connections, I figured he'd know someone who can do it cheap." She smiles, still glowing from what must have been a recent conversation.

It takes great effort to control my tone. "If you've told even one person, the whole thing is pointless."

"He won't mention it to anyone. I told him not to."

"It might look bad on him if the thefts suddenly stop. He knows he's being watched."

"Oh, I don't think *Sonny* is the culprit."

"But we've all seen him going through other people's things. And . . . it sounds like he's in a tough financial spot."

"Well, he is, but Sonny is harmless." The stars in Adhira's eyes dim ever so slightly. "I mean, people have mentioned that he does some odd things, but . . . we all have our issues, you know? Who am *I* to judge?"

Silvery flakes brush past my windshield on the drive home. I arrive to find the front yard looking prettier than usual, the curbside grime covered with a clean white blanket and the bushes neatly capped with snow—except for the shrubs below my bedroom window. From where I stand I can see bare spots on top, clumps of snowflakes shaken loose and heaped around large footprints. My gaze follows the prints from the bushes to the street and back, and then around the side of the house, into the backyard.

A dark lump sits on the concrete beside the back porch. It's the corpse of an animal—too dark to be Marcie, too large to be

Yanakoya. It isn't until I'm standing next to it that I realize what it is: an opossum, soaked in blood, a gaping wound across its throat.

I stare in puzzlement, and then go inside to gather tobacco, sage, and a garden glove.

The opossum is frozen to the concrete. Fur and flesh tear as I try to pull it away.

"Shit," I whisper.

I try different tactics to free the corpse: hot water, gentle nudges with a shovel. The legs remain frozen solid, but the head is thawing; the force of the shovel pushes it away from the lower jaw, so that the opossum appears to cry out in silent agony. Steam from the boiling water is still visible in the air, and a familiar smell makes its way to my nostrils: the smell of heat, blood, and putrid flesh.

I stumble away, using the shovel like a crutch, and try to compose myself. The animal's wound is neat; the body is otherwise unmarked. It doesn't seem to have been killed in self-defense, or as food. My guess is that it was killed and dumped there by the person who trespassed on my porch, perhaps as a warning.

Her throat was cut.

Jill showed me your address. Sounds like a pretty remote spot.

I quietly lean the shovel against the house. My cell phone shows me a promising forecast for the following day: warmer, sunny. Perhaps I'll have better luck then.

"Sorry, buddy," I whisper. "We'll do your burial tomorrow."

The nightmares begin that night. I'm sleeping on the living room couch when I hear the sound of breaking glass. I'm sluggish; I can't quite wake up, can't even turn to see what's happening, but my peripheral vision catches a dark figure entering through the shattered front window. The silhouette of Sonny Marsh stands over me. I recognize the heavy sound of his breathing. It intensifies, pours its essence over me—and it draws in a long, shuddering breath.

Sonny Marsh is sucking out my soul.

Panic overpowers the paralysis. I leap from the couch and run. I've made it across the kitchen before I realize that I was only dreaming—that there is no specter, that I am alone and safe.

Except I'm not. Dreaming is a most basic form of altered consciousness, and I've learned how spirits can traverse the dreamscape, entering the bounds of energetic neighborhoods and seeking those who sleep, often stirring up trouble for the sleeper. I've done it myself: traveled the dreamscape to meet others, most often doña Rosana. I know the difference between an anxious nightmare and a malicious entity. An entity leaves its energy lingering in the room around you, almost like a physical intruder leaves dusty footprints and oily fingerprints. A question nags at me: *How does Sonny Marsh know how to do that?*

Details swirl through my mind: the micro-aggressions, the secret thefts, the subtle mind games. Again I remember Rosana's warnings: *The parasite plays tricks to make us feel disempowered. We become vulnerable through such feelings; they create insecurities and self-defeating moods, weak spots on which the parasite can attach and feed.*

For some time I stand there, catching my breath, considering my own weak spots. I'm starting to suspect that Sonny Marsh knows them—perhaps better than I do. He wants to scare me. And I *am* afraid, because I don't think Sonny Marsh just wants to stop me. He wants to consume me.

Perhaps I've gotten in over my head.

When I'm Dead

When I'm Dead

"When written in Chinese, the word 'crisis' is composed of two characters. One represents danger and one represents opportunity."
-John F. Kennedy, 1959 UNCF speech (in which he incorrectly translates a Chinese character)

I pull my tales from the lives of those around me. For this, I am unfailingly rewarded with threats: "Write another word about me, even in disguise, and I'll stop your allowance." "Mind that you only write because I let you live here rent free." "One more word about my wife and I'll break every bone in your meddling hands."

It happened again in the spring, but with a crucial difference: this threat inspired. My mother, upset by some narrative I'd drawn from her brother's opium addiction, wore a deepening frown as she paged through my manuscript. It was all there: the lost job, the ruined marriage, the failed attempt to quit the drug; the agonizing withdrawal, the paranoia, the baseless accusations and assaults that left him ostracized by the town. In a shanty he aged alone, a charity case, unable to regain his stature. The story had everything: drama, sympathy, action, moral consequence. For my mother, it was a fresh knife in an old wound.

"Don't you dare throw this on him!" she raged.

"It's not about him. I changed the names."

"You think people are simple enough they won't see through a name? You're supposed to write fiction—so learn how to make things up!"

"You say the same thing about all of my works! They're bound to offend someone. Uncle, at least, I can afford to offend."

"At least have the decency to wait until he's dead. The way he looks now, you won't have to wait long." She flung the manuscript on the desk. "And do me the same courtesy. I don't want to wake up one day and find that my son has strewn my dirty laundry across the pages of some low-brow journal."

Those words set my mind stirring. For days, nights, they were an impetus pushing me closer to action. I desperately needed to print the man's story—but if he wouldn't last long in the world, perhaps I could afford to wait. Ultimately, I decided to call on him and get some sense of his vitality. It was an act of kindness.

As it happened, he called on me first. Uncle, unlike other visitors, did not look on my living conditions with a grimace, for he too was bound by dependence. And while he lived in squalor, my own poverty had style. The creaking floors, the salvaged antique furnishings, the cracked windows, the warped steps leading up to my rooms, the shelves stained with candle wax—these were means of inspiration. When I needed a setting for dark and dreary tales, all I needed was to look around me.

I invited Uncle to sit while I boiled some tea leaves that hadn't fallen victim to moisture. We spent a good hour in strained conversation, our lengthy pauses disturbed by familiar crumblings in the walls. As evening approached, he made his way down the rickety staircase. I watched his stiff, clumsy gait as I uttered my congenialities. Remembering that the front door was locked, I excused myself and passed by him with the key.

He fell—through no fault of mine. I did not push him. A bump, maybe, as I hurried by. Such a bump was bound to happen at any time. If he'd been younger, if his body had meant to heal and live and push on through this life, he would not have died—but after my panicked dash for help, the sanatorium and pneumonia took him. He died mere days later. And I sent out two manuscripts.

But what are two stories? Only one, the opium piece, was published—and in a lesser-known journal, at that. Other friends and family were the subjects of my better works. The potential lied in those with whom I was most involved, whose dark secrets I knew best.

I remembered my mother's words: *Do me the same courtesy*! I couldn't restrain a sordid grin—but don't believe that I seriously entertained the idea of harming my mother. It was just a thought. A plot, perhaps, for a good story.

I remembered Uncle's gaunt figure in the candlelight, his difficult movements on the stair. The sound of his cry as his balance faltered, a glimpse of his horrified face as he cracked and thumped toward the landing. I tried to make the event into a fine murder mystery, but could not craft the tale without seeming to incriminate myself. It kept coming out as a story about a loose-lipped writer who avoided revenge by murdering his relatives. That is not what happened with Uncle—I swear it—but it was all I could think to write.

The tale sat unfinished. I did not think of it again until Mother's next visit. She lived in a country home, a fine place to entertain guests, yet I was rarely invited. Sometimes I believed that she felt ashamed of me, that she tired of explaining my circumstances. I was kept hidden away like some vexing secret, never to enter her realm, always visited on the sly. She claimed she would not suffer me the cost of travel. Each month, we visited in the obscurity of my rooms.

In the waning afternoon light, I watched her climb those unsteady stairs. I scrutinized her bony grip on the railing. The gap below the rail had always concerned me. From the high stairs, a fall through that gap would mean a long drop to the hard landing below. Rather than tumble down each forbidding step, a thin woman like Mother might slip through and meet a quick end. Mere fantasy, of course. Mere fodder for story.

She drew her restless gaze across my scattered papers, uttered distressed sighs, laid out criticisms. So I had published one more piece—but had my writing ever supported me? When would I stop driveling about the generous sponsors of great authors, who could devote their full time and energy to the art? When would I work for my own sustenance?

She believed she had reason to judge. My living depended partly on Mother's allowances. Much of my writing depended on her as well: she was the subject of many stories, but love and duty kept me from publishing them while she lived.

Though she would not acknowledge it, I was certain my mother had willed her estate to me. If she did expire, I would inherit. And I would publish. Mother's age showed in her thin, snow-white hair and sagging, spotted flesh. She was several years older than my uncle. Rheumatism warped her fingers, and a bad stomach kept the fat from her bones. An accident such as Uncle's might just send her on her way—kindly, benevolently.

I looked again, and doubted. Mother had a determined spark in her eyes. She had energy and directness. But those words! *Do me the same courtesy.* An unconscious wish, perhaps. She had spoken as though her death must precede my success. What love, what a sacrifice to make for one's child!

Again, I swear: I never intended this route, not at the beginning. With Uncle, it was an accident. With Mother, it was . . . an accident. And yet it also seemed an ignoble but necessary favor. Selfless, even, for I would have to bear the guilt, while she obtained freedom from pain. I saw that pain acutely as I watched her on the stairs. She moved slowly, stopped and gasped at some sudden ache.

"Mother!" I hurried after her. "The door—it's locked. Let me . . . ."

In a frenzy, I rushed past her. She cried out as I knocked her over. Mother's bony hands clutched the railing and held her from the fatal drop. "Good Lord!" she cried, in disbelief rather than fear. "Clumsy ox! Are you trying to kill me?"

"I'm so sorry! Here—let me help you up. Here, Mother."

My body trembled. I was overcome by a strange feverishness, and in that unsteady state I stumbled and pitched forward, knocking Mother off the stair. Her grip was too weak to hold her full weight in mid-air. The rheumatic fingers slipped from the rail, and she fell to the landing below. I heard her skull knock against the rotted floor, the boards cracking beneath her. She lay motionless while I stared from above. My own white-knuckled fingers gripped the railing. Fear, remorse, all emotion was driven from me by pure shock. Thought plagued my mind, but I muted it, refused to let it in. I could not think—not now, seeing what I had done. I could not consider anything at all.

At last I had to descend.

"I'm sorry," I whispered. She was lifeless, already dead by my own hand. "I'm sorry . . . I'm sorry . . . ."

For hours, long into the night and when I woke the next day, I maintained my senseless apologies. For Mother, I made no panicked attempts to get help. The smell of a body beginning to rot—that's what drove me out. I could not bear it. A neighbor found me wandering. I must have given some confused reply to his questions. I still could not allow myself a coherent thought, could not acknowledge what I had become.

But what better place than a funeral for such dark thoughts to reconvene? That, and the shock of my mother's will, brought me to my senses. She had not left me much at all, but had willed most of the estate away to her youngest sister. Her *sister*! I could not comfort myself with the notion that the will was old, perhaps drawn up some fifty years ago, before my birth. The woman had included me, but had afforded me so little—just my allowance and some petty household items. The judgment stung with the power of a lifetime's worth of criticisms.

It seemed that I was avoided at the funeral service. At first, I believed people felt uncomfortable about my status in the will, but a cousin—a father of three, on my mother's side—gave me a different idea. Just as the viewing room opened, he stopped and gave me a queer look. "A bit of a coincidence, isn't it? Two people fall to their deaths on your staircase, within the same month."

I was shocked. Why hadn't I thought of it? Two dying by the same method—of course it would look suspicious. Could I not have contrived some other way?

My initial reaction gave way to anger. What an accusation to make, in front of my mother's body, at the moment the coffin appeared! "How dare you," I began. "How dare you suggest I had anything to do with . . . ."

He looked surprised. "Oh, for heaven's sake, I didn't mean that. I meant that the stairs in that old house can't be safe. You really should look for some other place to rent."

"Rent, with what? Did you not hear my part of the will? I have an allowance—a minuscule, unlivable *allowance!*"

His wife, alerted by my tone, drew near us. With her were the children: a handsome boy and two girls, one of whom was small and pale, her legs in braces, her spirit dulled by disease. I shuddered with sudden fear and revulsion, and knew that I should look away. But as I said, what better event than a funeral for the fostering of morbid thoughts? I looked on that pale, listless girl, and the words spilled out unbidden: "Ah, she's sickly. It will make for a hard time, when you lose that little one."

Her mother's horrified face, and the other looks of astonishment and anger, silenced me. To have such thoughts is one thing; we must allow ourselves to be creative; but to say them out loud!

My cousin's eyes gleamed with disgust. He leaned over and spoke in my ear: "Kindly refrain from speaking about my children." After a pause, he added: "Ever again."

But I couldn't stop the flood of words. I trembled, overcome by some feeling I could not name. "What else would you expect me to say? It's everywhere, now. You're all so frail, and I'm doomed to stay where I am—in that pathetic state, at that damnable house, a place where accidents happen—a stair that stands like a gaping maw, just waiting to swallow you up!"

The minister took my arm. "Gently, now. Let's go outside, shall we?"

As we left, I heard someone say "Poor man. He's beside himself."

I think some of them pitied me, then.

At home, I pulled out a blank sheet and wrote: *The staircase stood like a gaping maw, ready to swallow them up.*

And I submitted thirteen stories.

Waiting for any response proved a gloomy task. The weather matched my mood, sending bleak mists that obscured the sun and made the world smell of damp and mold. For days, I sat with pen in hand, unleashing wild and mixed emotions onto paper, emitting tragic scenes of dust and blood. It seemed strange how many turns a mind can take when perturbed by the countless implications and unknown consequences of a single, evil misdeed. And strange how, in that disturbed state, a room can reveal details never before noticed—line and color that come alive for one who looks with a haunted eye. I never noticed how the patterns in the wood grain curved into distinct figures until they became my mother's face peering at me—twisted in horror one moment, burning with accusation the next. I shuddered, but still I wrote. No matter that she'd left me unsupported; now, I had inspiration. Vivid scenes of fright and misery crept out of that cursed room with such ferocity that I could hardly write fast enough to record them. And then I would see Mother's eyes glaring again with rage, her mouth opening with silent charges. I could not glance up without seeing her in the wood grain. My hand shook so that the letters became indecipherable. The ink spilled; the vial crashed, breaking like bone and splashing its dark blood across the floor.

I took my satchel with ink, pen, and paper, and walked out to the receding mists, desperate for relief from that cursed illusion. My clothes were damp by the time I reached my destination. A small range of rocks braced the far side of the valley, jutting high above

the trees, with narrow trails cut across and leading to the highest
peak. This vantage point was scarcely visited, and there I hoped to
find peace enough to write. On the way I crossed a bridge—a few
planks, rather, with twisted branches for rails on either side, leading
me over a furrow in the earth. The drop was not deep. I could have
stood at the bottom and rested both arms upon the planks. But I
looked through the gap beneath the rail and shuddered, hurrying
over the slick wood on unsteady limbs.

Beyond that disturbing pass, I ascended toward the cliffs. They
gave me no relief, for rocks also have line and form, and when I
looked up I felt terror at the monstrous faces that gaped down at me.
I kept my gaze low as I walked, until at last I reached the summit.
That point revealed a distant horizon and vast glimpse of sky. A blue
patch broke far beyond the abysmal gray, with bits of cloud seared
white by sunlight.

I stood, nearly spellbound by that beauty, and turned away
before the spell could take me. That vista offered its own horror: that
of a heaven I could no longer hope for. I descended back into the
stony swarm of stony eyes and agonized mouths.

At the bridge, I set my gaze toward the crossing. I stopped with
a gasp as I encountered a familiar face—the pallid face and pale blue
eyes of my cousin's youngest daughter. She stood halfway across the
planks, silently watching my approach. Lusterless braces poked
below the hem of her gray dress, and a scarf was draped across her
shoulders. I felt sudden disgust and awe at the sight of her—disgust
at her family, for letting her alone on this perilous crossing, and awe
at the picture of her, the crimson of her scarf against the endless gray
backdrop, two crimson eyelids over faded blue eyes that regarded
me with startling severity. I had always thought her an ugly child.
She was gaunt, with circles darkening the flesh below her almost
colorless eyes, the irritated lids always drooping down and making
her look half-asleep—but now the look seemed shrewd and
suspicious. The defined cheekbones and sleepy lids gave her an
other-worldly, pixie-like quality. Strength and vulnerability claimed
an equal presence in her face, her posture, her placement on the
bridge. The scarf fluttered in the breeze as she stood above the
trench, framed by endless cloud, like a flickering stream of life-
blood about to be swept forever into that swath of gray. I heard my

own voice murmuring low: "Like a gaping maw, waiting to swallow her . . . ."

My own remorseful tone took me by surprise. The girl's eyes shifted to the gully below, then back to me, bright with consternation. Her voice came forth soft but steady: "You're the man who said I was going to die."

Those words sounded like prophecy.

I stepped forward. "What would you have me say?" I demanded in a whisper. "What compelled you to come here—to stand with those feeble legs on rotting boards, above those jagged rocks? I could write volumes about what will pass—and don't you see how you stand in my way?" My voice rose, and I sputtered on, unable to stop the words from coming. "I'm a sick man. You don't know the things I think—the things I'm thinking right now. Your scarf, like blood across the sky! A broken bird fluttering into a river of gray! See this rail?" I rapped my knuckles on the slick wood. The girl flinched, and her sleepy eyes widened. "It seems sturdy—but next to you, the picture of death, it can never be thick enough! This gap underneath, large enough for a child to fall through! And me, a man who pushes people in, sickly people like you—do you know I pushed my own mother? My mother, my uncle—I watched them fall, and used it for my own gain! And your thin and frail body, so powerless to resist a wretched killer like me! To see you lying below, broken and at rest on those gray rocks . . . to see it, smell it . . . the sweet-sour rotting . . . my mother's life-blood—"

Terror may have struck her into a stupor while I rambled, but suddenly she drew back, her lips parting as if in the beginning of a cry. She gripped the rail for support. I saw her fingers slip, watched one unsteady leg slide toward the edge.

"Don't!" I cried. "I won't do it again. Mercy—that is also artful, also intriguing. Saving grace is also compelling! I haven't written a word. It isn't me—it's the rail—a gaping maw!"

She was sliding, faltering, and the space below us seemed to stretch unfathomably, the rocks to sharpen to razor points. I reached out to save her. I swear that's what I did. She cowered from my clutching fingers, and she fell. I heard a thump, then a scream. But the voice wasn't hers. It was mine.

I ran. On my panicked flight home, I was assailed by images of the sickly girl lying in that shallow gully, her pale eyes glazed peacefully beneath the rough-red lids, the now-useless metal supporting her thin legs. She couldn't be dead, of course. A few scrapes and bruises, nothing more. And if she was dead—well, no fault of mine! I had other reasons for running. So many different stories I could tell, so many directions could I wander through! The fear of incrimination, the stress of my mother's—

Mother!

I froze at the bottom of my stair, remembering with horror what I'd revealed. *I pushed my own mother . . . I watched them fall, and used it for my own gain . . . a wretched killer like me!*

The girl would tell her father, of course. She would tell everyone. Word spread fast. It had spread fast for my uncle's undoing, and would spread faster for mine. The town would do more than shun me. They would come after me as a mob.

I set aside the damp satchel and placed another vial of ink at the table. My mother's face sneered at me from the shadows. I saw her in every dim corner, every meandering curve, mocking me, warning me of punishment to come. I lit every candle to snuff out the shadows, made the room clear and bright. It was imperative that I write about this girl—her decay, her innocence, her strength! The rotting bridge, the mist and enveloping death! I penned the words even as the flickering light created new shadows, new specters that taunted me from the walls.

I wrote, and still write—and there they are! I hear them, the mob, rapping at the door! And my mother's form is still waving its thin, shadowy arms, dancing above the candle flames as if to illustrate some fiery hell that awaits my soul. Now I've put out the candles, knocked them over in a rage, and they spill wax like life-blood.

Still they knock, and still I write. Now I smell smoke—they've come with torches, a real mob, come with vengeance to burn my all to the ground! The landing is always damp. Perhaps the seeping water will hold off the flames, and I'll escape yet.

No, the fire is already here, consuming the curtains and the ancient woodwork. Did I set it myself, or have they hurled the torches? The cracked panes have burst, and how quickly the chilled breeze ushers flame toward the door—fire and ice twining in deadly connivance! Smoke stings as I look with dismay on the stories scattered around me. So much material—and so many materials unfinished! And my final work is in its roughest phase. I haven't even killed my darlings.

The satchel is still damp. There, my works might have refuge enough to survive this fiery onslaught. It sears my lungs, tortures my eyes, but what a finale! I realize now: death must precede success. Great writers are unrenowned in their lives, only to surge to fame much later, in death. The living devour whatever is morbid. They will feast on my miserable fate.

Mother's admonishments mock me from the shadows: I failed to achieve all that I sought. Instead of a rise to glory, a descent to the fires of hell! But no matter; I'll be admired in death. My final act will ensure it. It's all about me now—heat, smoke, flame!

XI

Consequences

Consequences

"Sometimes when I consider what tremendous consequences come from little things . . . I am tempted to think . . . there are no little things."
-Bruce Barton

My dad knew he was dying. He came home one day, crowing about a ceramic vase he'd found at the thrift shop: "Lady and gent, let me introduce you to my tomb. Put my ashes in this, and you won't be strong-armed into debt for a patch of earth or a big damn coffin."

The vase was shiny black, with little red flowers scrawled across it and a loose-fitting lid. Dad held it with thin fingers that matched the rest of his wasted body. Over the months I'd watched the fat and muscle melt away under dry, cracking skin. He chugged water but dried out like a raisin, his eyes always pink and stinging, the folds in his hands and face cracking open. I wanted to say: *Pretty soon you'll be so small and dry, we won't need to cremate you. We'll just crumble you up and sweep you into the urn.*

We didn't know what was wrong with him. The only way Dad would go to a hospital was if he was dead or passed out—or too weak and delirious to fight the neighbors who carried him down six flights of stairs. That's how he went. They laid him on the curb while they waited for one of the guys to bring a car around.

I sat on a banged-up desk that had been left on the curb as trash. Dad was unconscious now, and naked except for his underwear, which was blood-spattered in the back. He stopped breathing, then drew one ragged breath, then stopped again. His eyes shone through half-closed lids. The neighbors debated using "mouth-to-mouth," and then the car pulled up and they shoved Dad's limp body into the back seat. As the junker sputtered away, Mom threw her arms around me and pressed her tear-streaked face to mine, crying: "Jacob, what are we going to *do?*"

I'd spent weeks thinking about what I would do: study hard and find a job. Most people would've laughed at that. Kids in my building didn't get much from studying. They got ahead by fighting. They got cash by committing petty crimes, selling weed, fighting over scraps. I didn't want to go that route. If I did, then someday, maybe in a year or two, the older guys would corner me, give me an ultimatum, force me to commit acts that could never be undone or forgiven.

The desk was still on the curb two days after Dad died. My buddy Rich helped me drag it upstairs and stow it against the wall of my room. The drawers flopped down every time I pulled them out because the tracks weren't screwed in. I took the screws from the leg of my bed frame and got the desk working right, and dragged in the extra kitchen chair—the one Dad used to sit in.

Mom laughed when she saw it. "You gonna be a scholar now?"

"Don't laugh," I said. "Everyone else can laugh, but not you."

Her smile vanished. "No, I won't. You do your thing."

"I'm going to Strohm's tomorrow. Rich said he might give me a job."

"Who's Strohm?"

"He owns a record shop. Don't worry, it's legit."

"Anything's legit now," she murmured.

"No it isn't," I replied sharply.

I didn't ask what she would do to make up for Dad's absence. Even in his sickness, he'd brought money home. Mom was pretty, she had a nice figure, and the guys in our building liked her. I didn't want her to end up like the prostitutes who lived in our building. As soon as they made money, they bought heroin to chase the ugliness away. We watched them shrink and wither into nothing.

I couldn't keep an eye on Mom during the day. At night, I slept with the bedroom door open so I would know if she went out or had late-night visitors.

That first night with the desk, strange things began happening in my room. I was lying in bed when a movement caught my eye: a dim patch of light, coming around the door frame. It looked like a small, luminescent hand. One second the doorway was empty, and the next, the transparent figure of a little girl peeked into the room.

My heart pounded as I sat up.

The figure became clearer, the eyes more visible, as she approached the bed: a little girl with pigtails. She was looking at the floor, and as she drew close, she stretched out her arms.

I lurched backward. The movement made the unscrewed leg slip out from beneath the frame, and the corner of the bed crashed to the floor. The apparition disappeared—as if the noise had frightened it away.

"What the hell's going on?" Mom stood in the doorway, hands on hips.

"Mom, something was in my room!"

"What? A rat?"

"No. I . . . I don't know." What could I say? Guys like me didn't believe in, or talk about, ghosts. "I musta been dreaming."

"What happened to the bed?"

"The leg came out." I stood, trembling, lifting the bed so I could slide the leg into place. "It just needs screws. I'll fix it tomorrow."

It didn't get fixed, because the next day I took the city bus to Strohm's. The University was on the eastern end of the route, and the bus was packed with college kids. They were easy to spot. It showed in the way they dressed, the way they walked, the things they talked about. A guy behind us tried to impress his girl with philosophy: You can slow the aging process by "thinking young," you can attract good things by expecting them, time travel is a matter of perspective, and blah, blah. "From a cosmic perspective, there's no such thing as time. Everything is happening at once, but we see events in a linear way so we can learn action and consequence. It's crucial to the experience of being human."

"You hearing this?" Rich asked, elbowing me. "Where do people find the time to think up this shit?"

Strohm's faced a busy street. It stood between a family planning clinic and a crowded ice cream parlor with a line trailing out the door. A small circle of protesters milled on the sidewalk by the clinic, wearing badges that said "Guardians of the vulnerable." We watched as the two girls in front of us pushed their way through, insisting "We're going to the record shop," and then we did the same, though there was no need. Strohm's was already bustling. About twenty other customers were already inside the little shop, mostly young folks and middle-aged white men in band T-shirts. They looked like they had money to spend. I felt good about my chances of taking care of me and Mom, but Strohm took one look at me and scowled. "How old are you?"

"Fifteen."

"You sure?"

Rich rolled his eyes. "He's the same age as me. Hire him already."

Strohm was ugly and out of shape, with long stringy hair and bags under his eyes, but he looked me over like I was no better than dirt. "Can you alphabetize?"

I needed the job, so I didn't say the first thing that came to mind. "I am outraged, sir," I said, straight-faced. "I'm fifteen, not five."

He smiled and handed me a job application. "Starting wage is eight-fifty an hour."

I couldn't restrain my disappointment. My mouth hung open. "Eight-fifty?"

"Take it or leave it."

I persisted: "Isn't that below minimum wage?"

"No, smart-ass, it's above, and you won't find better around here. What does a fifteen-year-old need more than eight-fifty for? You going to buy a house?"

Out on the sidewalk, I muttered my anger. I gestured to one of the protesters, an older woman holding a plastic Starbucks cup with a whipped cream-topped drink inside of it. "She probably paid eight-fifty for that fancy coffee," I said, and mimicked in a whiny voice: "'What's a fifteen-year-old need more than eight-fifty for?' Arrogant prick. I got to take care of my mom and me, that's what. Seriously, there isn't another place around here that pays more than eight dollars?"

"Not to a kid," Rich said. "You can try taking the bus to the suburbs, and see if someone will give you a lawn mowing job. But even if they pay twenty an hour, that's only gonna be twenty bucks total."

On the bus ride, I was still stewing. Rich didn't mind. He fixated on the two college girls across the aisle. The olive-skinned girl had long, straight hair and smooth, slender legs. She crossed one leg over the other and bounced it as she talked about the bar they were headed to. "It's not my favorite venue, but the drinks are cheap. Watch out for the guys, though. Beth dresses like a slob and puts grease in her hair when she plays, because she doesn't want her own fans hitting on her."

Rich stared at the olive-skinned girl and said: "I think about sex whenever I ride the bus."

"Don't start that crap," I warned him.

"It's true. I see beautiful women and I think about doing them."

The girl gave him a disgusted look, but he kept staring.

"Keep dreaming," I said, "because that's as far as you're gonna get."

The bus pulled to a stop. The olive-skinned girl stood, and the blond one looked out the window and frowned. "Is it right there? I didn't realize it was so close to the crack stacks."

I walked slow behind them, giving them some distance from Rich. They stopped at the corner bar where a bunch of guys hung around the doorway, pretending to be bouncers. A greasy, middle-aged man took the blond girl's ID and smirked. "Twenty-one. Sorry, honey, too young for me."

A block down, we pushed through a busted door and climbed the stairs to our apartments. College kids called this place the crack stacks, but the drug of choice in our building wasn't crack. It was heroin.

"Get me my goddamn fix!" Caesar stood near the sixth-floor landing, waving and screaming at three other guys. Everyone knew Caesar. He was loud, fierce, and ghastly. He stood tall and lean, and his loose-fitting clothes made him look dangerously thin. The bright, sunken eyes and too-thin body reminded me of death. "When you tell me there's gonna be a fix, there better be a fix!"

"We said we'll take care of it," Chaz replied. "Yelling down the hall ain't gonna fix your problem."

"I'm yelling? THIS IS MY TALKING VOICE, YOU DON'T TELL ME TO SHUT UP."

Halfway down the hall was a metal trash bin with an ashtray on top. A four-year-old girl peeked from behind it. Caesar's daughter, Miri. Caesar raised her alone, had done so since the mother died. I saw Miri cowering and thought of the little ghost girl in my room, wondering what she was, if she was anything at all, and thinking of stories I'd heard. Folks always said that ghosts were the spirits of the dead—people so traumatized that they couldn't really die, because they were still looking for ways to fix whatever tormented them. If it was true, this place should've been full of ghosts.

"Shut up already," Kent demanded. "Everyone's tired of your screaming, it goes on all damn day. You keep screaming and waving that gun, the police or some social services bitch are gonna show up to take your girl away."

A wild look came into Caesar's eyes. "You threatening me?"

"No, man, I—"

Caesar pulled a handgun from his waistband and waved it fiercely, but kept it pointed at the ceiling. "You try to take my girl, you die. Understand? I will kill you. She's all I got in this world. I don't get out of bed for any other reason."

Kent rolled his eyes, turning away with a wave of his hand. The other neighbors followed, unconcerned. Caesar pulled his gun nearly every day, but he never fired. The grown-ups always assured themselves that it wasn't loaded.

I reached for the doorknob to my own place, but stopped when Miri peeked out and smiled at me. My breath caught as I looked at that little girl, her large brown eyes shining with all the hope and innocence of childhood. Seeing that look on kids' faces always pained me because I knew how it would get crushed. Pretty soon there would be nothing in those eyes but despair, or a sort of dullness that came from trying to drown everything out. Miri would probably hold out longer than other kids. In our building we had kids who were beat more often than they were bathed. Caesar never hit his girl—but his screaming, his threats, frightened her.

"Give me fifteen minutes," Dean said.

"Fifteen." Caesar turned away, lightly ruffling Miri's hair as he went. "Come on, girl."

Rich leaned toward me and murmured: "That one's gonna turn out fine."

"What?"

"Miri. That girl's gonna be a fine one, when she's grown. Don't act like you don't know. I seen you staring."

"You jackass. That's not what I was thinking. I'm just wondering how kids can stay so resilient."

"*Resilient?*"

"Yeah. Like, with all the . . . never mind."

Mom didn't hear me come in. The radio was playing in the kitchen, and she hummed as she cooked. I walked past her, still nervous about the "ghost," afraid I'd see it again—but I opened my door and found something worse: a grown man, fully clothed and lying on my bed. A neighbor from another floor.

I went back to the kitchen. "What is that asshole doing in my room?"

"Don't worry, he's just sleeping it off."

"What'd you do? Mom—"

"Mind your business," Mom snapped.

"It *is* my business, he's on my bed!"

"I put a sheet over it."

"A sheet. That makes it okay?"

"You know we need money," she said. "I sold some stuff to him and gave him a place to lie down. That's all."

"Where'd you get it? Did Mitch get you?"

"Mind your business!"

"He'll corner you," I said. "He'll make you do other things. You know he will."

Her eyes dulled. She looked away. "It's not Mitch. It was your dad's."

"I told you I was getting a job."

"Well you didn't bring a paycheck, what was I supposed to do?" She turned to the pan of Hamburger Helper on the stove, gave it a vicious stir, and then turned the burner off. "You didn't get that job at the record shop, right?"

"I just applied for it."

"Right there at the shop? Did he see your address?"

"Yeah, he looked at it."

She turned to me, looked me searchingly in the eyes. "I know that what I'm doing isn't right," she said, "but we need it. You want to go back to being homeless? Dumpster diving, washing up in the bathroom sink at Hardee's, having to sleep in a room with all those crazies?"

My anger ebbed—just a tiny bit.

"People don't hire folks like us," Mom said. "To them, we're just a risk. Believe me, I've tried doing something else, too. But they look at my clothes and my cheap-ass makeup, and they see my address, and they say, 'Oh, you live *there*?'" Mom turned away again, standing with her hands on the edge of the stove. "You shouldn't be living in a place like this. We got to get enough money to get out of here, but we barely have enough to keep this place."

I watched as she stood there, frozen like a statue. Hesitantly, I asked: "What about your parents? I know you haven't talked to them in forever, but—"

"No, no, noooo," she said, shaking her head. "Not them. Yeah, they got some money, but we can't involve ourselves with them. They're not *good*, Jacob. They're filth. They're my parents, but even filth can have kids. No way in hell I'm letting them near you." She glanced over her shoulder at me. "It's you and me, Jacob, and that's it. Your dad checked out, and if other people offer a hand, it's only for their own good. It always is. Don't let anyone tell you different."

That night I saw the ghost girl again—only this time, I wasn't in bed. She got there first. I was reaching for the light switch when I noticed a face watching me from beneath the bed frame. The girl was lying on her back, looking right at me, her pale arm visible against the floor. She turned away and vanished.

"God damn it," I muttered.

I sat at the desk for a while, staring at the empty space under the bed. At some point I realized that the girl had started appearing after I'd brought the desk up, and I wondered if it was haunted. That made me stand up quick. I didn't want to be on the bed either, but I was tired.

Sleep didn't come easy. I heard the shower going, and after a while, Mom walked by. I saw her out of the corner of my eye, standing in the open doorway, a white towel wrapped around her hair. She crouched, then stood again.

"What are you doing?" I asked.

I rolled over and felt a shock: the figure wasn't Mom. It stood tall and slender, like her, but the dimly glowing body didn't have a head. Instead, a bright white orb shone above the neck.

The figure rushed toward me.

"*Mom!*"

Mom came running. She wore a long T-shirt and a blue towel around her head. "What the hell, Jacob?"

The ghost had vanished as soon as I yelled. Once again, I didn't know what to say. Ghosts in my room didn't make sense. In the movies, hauntings always happened in mansions, or to middle-class suburban people who moved into the wrong house. In the end they found out that someone died a horrible death in that place, and then they packed up their families and drove away in SUVs and got a different house.

When people died in the stacks, they didn't become ghosts. And we couldn't pack up and leave.

"Nothing," I said. "I was having a nightmare."

And so it went. First the ghosts, then the addicts, showed up at my bed.

I kept my door closed, but the little girl showed up the next night, walking right through it and reaching for the bed. A few hours later, the figure with the white orb rushed at me. I gave up trying to sleep in my room and spent the night on the living room couch.

On the way back to Strohm's, I asked Rich: "You know who that desk belonged to?"

"Why, what'd you find in it?"

"Nothing. It's just . . . I seen strange things in my room since I got it."

"Like what?"

"Like, I don't know. Things."

"Bed bugs?"

"No. It looks like . . . I mean, I know I'm imagining it, but I've seen . . . *things*. Figures that look like people, showing up in my room."

He looked blank. "What?"

"I mean that ever since we brought up the desk, I've been seeing things that look like ghosts."

"Doing what?"

"Walking. Lying on the floor."

"And you're still clean?"

"Yeah."

"Then you need to start using." He laughed.

"If you find out whose desk, tell me."

"Why, what you going to ask? If they trashed the desk because it was haunted? Or maybe they killed someone and the spirit got trapped in the drawers?" Rich glanced aside, listening for a while to another conversation. "Everyone's talking supernatural today."

The "no such thing as time" guy was across the aisle, still trying to babble about philosophy, but to a different girl. This one looked older, with close-cropped hair and glasses, and had dared to interrupt his rambling speech. "Actual mediums are rare," she said. "There are so many frauds because people think that being a channel is really fun and fascinating, but it's not like that at all. It's tough. It's embarrassing. You're always getting pulled away from yourself by someone else's intentions." She looked away and saw Rich staring at her.

Rich was mean-eyed and creepy. People usually took one look at him and kept their distance, but not this girl. She looked right at him and smiled. "Are you interested in channeling?"

He looked around, confused. "You talking to me?"

"Yes, you. You looked interested."

"Well, I got this guy over here who thinks he's seeing ghosts." Rich jabbed a thumb at me. "Says he brought home a haunted desk, and now he has ghosts walking around in his room."

The girl looked fascinated, but I wasn't talking. She introduced herself and offered her hand: "I'm Dixie Simon. I'm a channeler. I get people talking to me about these things all the time, so it's not unusual to me."

I shook her hand and kept my mouth shut. Rich talked to her instead. They talked about ghosts and channeling all the way to Strohm's, while I looked around to see who was listening, and the "no such thing as time" guy sat by the window looking annoyed.

The bus slowed for our stop. I stood, and Dixie said: "If you're seeing ghosts, they're trying to tell you something—and it's something important. Ask them to show you what they want. Do it soon, because sometimes we get these messages but we don't figure them out in time, and we have to deal with the consequences. If you can't communicate, I'd say get rid of the desk. You could've caused some kind of imbalance by moving it into your room. Put everything back where you found it. If that solves it, the ghosts won't show up again."

I didn't want to trash the desk. It helped me study and gave me a place to keep my books. The lower drawers were stuffed with clothes, but in the top I kept pens and notebooks, and whatever books I could find to read. We didn't have a library close by, but six blocks away was one of those "leave a book, take a book" cabinets.

I'd run the six blocks and back just on the chance I'd find a good read. The last books I'd picked up were *Nobody's Child* and *The Complete Sherlock Holmes*, and I was reading them cover to cover. I'd read anything fit for an adult. It helped me learn to write. In school I was mostly a C student, but in English I could get As and Bs.

Strohm gave me the job. He said to come back Saturday at noon.

When I got home, Miri was sitting at my kitchen table, doodling with a pen. I knew what it meant: Caesar was doped-up on my bed. "What the hell, Mom! How many . . . ."

I was going to say *How many assholes you going to bring in here*, but Miri looked up at me with wide eyes and I changed my tone. "Hey, Miri."

"I have flowers like those," she said, pointing to Dad's urn. It sat on a kitchen shelf, surrounded by tins and spice boxes. The county had paid for Dad's cremation and offered us a "flawed" urn, but Mom wanted the one from the thrift shop. It was one of the last things Dad seemed excited about.

The red flowers reminded me of the red spattered across the back of Dad's underwear. It was all I could think of when I looked at the urn: the way he'd let himself die, the way he'd left Mom to fend for herself, knowing she wouldn't be safe without a man. *A man's born to die*, he'd said. *If it's my time, just let me die.*

Mom stood at the counter, fixing sandwiches. "You want one?"

"Sure." I looked away, studied Miri's drawings: scribbles and heart shapes. I frowned, recognizing the pen she was using. "Is that my notebook?"

"I got it from your desk. She needed something to do."

"My stuff's in there. Hang on, Miri." I tore a few sheets out and set them down, tucking the notebook under my arm.

Mom gestured to the bedroom. "I had to fix him up. He was in the hall, throwing a fit."

"Why use my bed? Why not—" Again I stopped. I knew what she'd say. Not the living room couch, it wasn't private enough. Not her room, because she didn't want those men in her bed—and neither did I.

Miri pointed at the urn again. "Daddy got me red flowers like that.”

"Red flowers, huh?" I wasn't good with kids. I never knew what to say to them, and as I looked at the urn I forgot about Miri. "Mom . . . how long you been letting people use my bed?"

"Just since Dad died. I never did it until I needed to."

"But, when was the first time? Was it a couple days after Dad died?"

"I don't know. Maybe."

"Shit." *It isn't the damn desk. It's the heroin.*

"What?"

"You got to stop it. I been seeing things in my room since Dad died."

She turned away, wrapped up the bread. "You've been having nightmares. I have them too."

"Not like mine."

"No," she said bitterly. "Not like yours. You get that job?"

"I start Monday."

"Good. Then I won't need the bed much longer. If it bothers you, sleep on the couch."

But I didn't. I wanted to sleep in my own bed that night, to see if the ghosts would "communicate" with me.

Nothing happened for the first couple hours—and then, when I was half-asleep, a figure appeared at the door. *Mom,* I thought, but as the white orb flashed above the dim neck I realized I was seeing the ghost.

"What you want?" I asked drowsily.

The image flickered, faded—and I heard a shrill, terrified cry. *Help! Help!*

I sat up, wide awake, but the figure was gone.

"Mom?"

I said it quietly, not wanting to wake Mom if she was asleep. I got up and checked her room. She was lying with her eyes closed, breathing deep.

I whispered: "What the hell is happening?"

My first day at Strohm's was okay. He ordered me to do all the boring stuff, and I found out I didn't know a damn thing about music. I came home around six o'clock and found Caesar in the

kitchen, talking about his rich cousin in California while Mom
opened the bottom cabinets. "He buys them all up, comes back here
and sells them for twenty times the price. And some of it's shit.
But—what, she's not there? Damn, woman, you were supposed to
be watching her!"

Mom stood up. "I thought she went back to your apartment."

"It's locked. No, she's hiding somewhere, that's what she does."

"What's going on?" I asked.

"I'm just on my way out," Caesar replied. "Me and Miri came
to visit." He pointed a finger at me. "Boy, you got to fix that bed. It
crashed down on one side as soon as I laid down."

"The leg came loose," Mom said. "He'll fix it."

"*Miri!* Where you hiding, girl? We got to go." Caesar frowned.
"She hides when I get mean. I don't like to get mean, you know I
love that girl. But, nothing I can do about it. *Miri, get out here
before I get mad again!*"

Mom gave me a shove. "Jacob, go look in your room."

It didn't make sense to look there, but I went anyway. Through
the open doorway I scanned the room. The bed was still tipped, one
corner low to the floor, and I was about to call out when I caught
sight of something beneath it: a brown pigtail and a child-sized arm.

My voice came out quiet: "Miri?"

She didn't move. Neither did I. I knew I should hurry to check
on her, but suddenly I understood that what I'd been seeing all those
nights was not a ghost girl who just happened to looked like Miri.
All at once, I understood why I shouldn't have taken those screws
out of the bed frame.

"Miri?" I said again, louder. *Please get up. Please.*

"She in there?" Caesar asked. "Miri, come on!"

I walked back to the kitchen.

"What's wrong?" Mom asked.

Caesar brushed past me. I stared at Mom and thought of the
little ghost girl—peeking into my room, walking to the bed. *Miri.*
The little face looking at me from under the frame before it
vanished.

And the other figure—the tall, thin one with the missing head. I
remembered Caesar's threats: *You try to take my girl, you die.
Understand? I will kill you.*

Dixie Simon's words floated back to me, too. *Sometimes we get these messages but we don't figure them out in time, and we have to deal with the consequences.* Miri must have been the first ghost. Mom would be the second.

"Mom, you have to leave." I pushed her toward the door. "I think Caesar's gonna shoot you."

"What?"

Caesar's voice rose: "Miri!" Footsteps rushed across the bedroom. Grief-stricken cries pierced the air.

Mom's eyes went wide. "Jake, what's going on?"

"Miri died. She got crushed under the—"

"*Help!*" Caesar cried. "*Help!*"

Mom pulled away, heading for the bedroom. "Oh my God. Jake, let go."

"Don't go, Mom, he has a gun, this time he's gonna shoot you. Get out."

"Jacob—"

Caesar's voice came loud and shrill: "*She wasn't supposed to be in here! My poor girl . . . my poor girl's gone! Bitch, you let her die!*"

Mom stopped resisting. For a moment we both froze, our gazes locked in terror as Caesar's cries gave way to tortured moans. Then we were running through the door, down the stairs—but we stopped at the sound of a gunshot.

"What's he firing at?" Mom asked. "Jacob, what the hell happened?"

"Miri was hiding under the bed when it broke. Caesar . . . ." I couldn't finish.

My mom covered her own face, her fingers parted so that her eyes looked up into the stairway.

One of the neighbors, Mrs. Simmons, dared to peek out of her apartment. She saw us on the landing and waved us closer, whispering: "What's going on?"

"Caesar's in my apartment," Mom said. "Miri got hurt. I think . . . she died."

"Miri? He shot her?"

"No. She . . . had an accident."

We listened, but the building was quiet except for the blare of

TVs and radios. It wasn't like Caesar to be quiet when he was upset. He was a screamer.

I thought of how Mom and Caesar had looked standing side by side. They were the same height, both tall and slender.

Miri's all I got in this world.

I imagined him standing in the doorway, seeing his daughter's arm under the bed frame. Rushing to help her. *I don't get out of bed for any other reason.*

"Mom, I think he shot himself. We gotta call the cops."

"No! No cops, not yet! He shot up in there, I got things I need to get rid of!"

"Then get rid of them."

Caesar didn't answer when we called out. We cleaned up the rest of the apartment, never daring to glance at my bedroom. Finally Mom stuck her head into the hallway and yelled: "We got to call the cops. Caesar used his gun."

A few of the neighbors peeked in. They debated what to do. No one wanted cops inside, but this time they'd have to come. "You can't move Caesar," someone said, "and we need the cops to know it wasn't one of us."

Mom put an arm around me. She tightened her grip, and I whispered: "I hate this place. God, I hate this place."

I should have listened to that "no such thing as time" guy. If I'd figured it out in time—that the ghosts weren't dead yet, that they were haunting me from the future—Miri might still be alive. *If.* If I'd put everything back, like Dixie said. If Dad hadn't died, if Mom hadn't needed money, if I hadn't been at Strohm's.

We heard voices on the stairs. Someone had let the cops in.

"I don't wanna to go to jail," Mom whispered in my ear. "I've been having nightmares, too. Your dad, telling me not to sell. I should've known there'd be consequences."

XII

Yanakoya

Yanakoya

"We patronize the animals for their incompleteness, for their tragic fate of having taken form so far below ourselves. And therein we err, and greatly err. . . . In a world older and more complete than ours, they move finished and complete, gifted with extensions of the senses we have lost or never attained, living by voices we shall never hear."
-Henry Beston, *The Outermost House: A Year of Life on the Great Beach of Cape Cod*

The forest feels different now that the jaguars are gone. Every now and then, a sighting is reported in some distant patch of wilderness, but near the ranches and plantations they are shot on sight. The landscape is changing, and I no longer recognize my neighbors. Their faces are unfamiliar as their customs. Many have taken up the tools of the newcomers and adopted their ways. They tell new stories of dangerous beasts that live in the thickness of the trees: powerful, venomous, lethal as oblivion.

Those who still live in the forest tell similar tales, but the beasts they fear are human. These are merciless destroyers, fast and powerful, filling the earth with venom, tearing away vast forests with the powerful jaws of their machines. They level the land and kill the spirit animals who were once revered.

My own people remember when the black jaguar emerged from those woods, carrying a small child on its back. As the child grew into a young woman, she learned the jaguar medicines and the secrets of other forest creatures. Those who weren't there, the outsiders and all those who didn't see, laugh it off as a myth—but I know the story because I was that child.

Before the jaguar took me, I lived with my grandmother. On the day I received my first jaguar medicine, I was only as high as my grandmother's waist, too small to prepare medicines or food—but I helped in the new ways. I sat at the end of the worn path that led from our village to the new plaza, watching the foreigners and their money. These foreigners paid to have their meals fetched and prepared. They paid others to wash their heaps of clothes, which they sweated through every day and sent for washing again. Sometimes they would pay for woven baskets and necklaces and other things made from the jungle.

I chose a shady spot along the path to lay out my blanket and my goods—necklaces and arm bands decorated with shells, teeth, and seeds. Behind me, four boys crowded beneath the fronds of a huicungo tree, listening to a man who murmured English words. Once, after the Spanish invaded, men had gathered here to learn Spanish; now, they needed English. *"Oro se llama 'gold.' Chuqi, chuqi suti 'gold.' Dicen: This is gold."* The man spoke quietly, as if he didn't want the foreigners to hear the words he was teaching. I knew only a few phrases in English, but the children in my village had learned Spanish along with our own language, and I understood most of what was said—or so I thought.

I turned my attention to the tourists. Children milled around the restaurant like predators. Sometimes, through the barking children, I heard talk from the rich foreigners. I mostly heard a loud woman with sunglasses and dark hair shaved close to her head, using English words I knew: *rainforest* and *company* and *gold* and *oil*. She sat with a light-haired woman who held a big camera, the kind that people use when they want to put their pictures in books. A foreigner had lived in our village for some time, using her big camera to take pictures for the book she was making. She said it was important to write about us and take pictures of the village, so that her people wouldn't tear up our forest and poison the water. "They won't care unless they can see you. If they don't see you, you don't exist."

The woman with the camera took out her money, and the barking children lunged at her, shouting and shoving to get close. The empty-handed ones held out dirty palms, chanting "Please, I hungry!" while the ones with bracelets shouted their bargains: "Only three soles! Look, look!"

"Get out of here! *Váyase!*" The short-haired woman thrust out an arm, and the children scattered.

The big camera woman didn't say anything. I sat with my head bowed, quietly weaving as the two women approached on the boardwalk. When they came close, I looked up at the big camera woman and smiled my happiest smile. I held up a bracelet of acai seeds and brown tagua nuts, earthy tones that matched her clothes. "Hi," I said meekly. "Do you like this?"

The camera woman smiled at me. She didn't wear sunglasses, and I saw a familiar affection in her eyes. Foreigners looked that way at kids who didn't bark and lunge. She slowed and looked at the bracelets on my blanket. "How much?"

I held up three fingers.

"Three soles? Sure, I'll take it."

We made our exchange. Later, as I walked back to the village, the boardwalk gave way to a dirt path, and in that dirt I spotted the ring of acai and tagua. The sight wasn't unexpected. I made the clasps loose, and the bracelets often fell off. I picked them up and put them back in my bag, to sell again later.

At the village, I went straight to my uncle Kashayawri. His hut, which he had made strange and foreboding, had drawn the attention of tourists. A first glimpse of it seemed to reveal a menagerie of alien beasts: the mud-brick walls were decorated to look like giant animals, with large mouths carved from wood and stone, and frightening eyes that never blinked. Hides and grasses became the creatures' skin and fur, and the legs were spiked with thorns and needles, each ending in a clump of wild pigs' feet gathered to look like one large hoof—and even the tools hanging on the walls inside the hut were sometimes arranged to look like dangerous critters. This, Kasha claimed, was what would keep his domain safe from invaders—not because it frightened them off, but because it brought attention and money.

After I had given all of my soles to Kasha, I went out to my grandmother Nina. She stood alone at the fire, stirring a pungent green liquid in a cast iron pot, murmuring songs as she released sustenance into the bubbling brew. Drops of sweat clung to the strings of huayruro and pona beads around her neck and trailed to the woven cloth at her waist.

When the brew had thickened, she ladled some of it into a tiny cup and let it cool. "You will only have a swallow of it, but this is a strong medicine," she warned me. "It will help you open up to the jaguar medicine. If you get scared, remember that you are Illari, a strong girl, and that your family is here to protect you. And if you need to vomit, go and do it in the trees over there."

My grandmother held a strand of beads in her palm, deep red beads with black spots. In the dying light, they looked like a mass of shining blood, grit, and teeth. The necklace unraveled as she held it out to me: huayruro beads and a peccary tooth. "This place is a part of you," she said, placing the beads around my neck. "The plants, the animals, the water, all of it. It's already in you, so just let it be, and learn from it."

The big camera lady showed up as I swallowed the brew. She came down the tourist path, the one that led to the boardwalk and the busy street with its shops and restaurants. She recognized me and smiled—that warm smile that grown-ups give to children they are enchanted by. "Do you have any more bracelets like the one you sold me?" she asked. "I lost mine."

I didn't cringe at the pungent taste of the medicine. I held my head up, nodded, and sold her the same bracelet. Then she asked to take my picture with Nina and Kasha in front of the strange hut.

Kasha smiled. He said yes, she could a take photo, and he would appreciate a small fee to help support our village. "It is appreciated," he repeated, still smiling as he held out his hand.

Nina rolled her eyes, but she waited while Kasha chatted with the light-haired camera lady. He asked questions, showed her our chicken pens and our storage shed, our sugar cane mill and other tools that lined the central plaza. He led her around to the other little houses, some new, others crumbling—but none were remarkable like Kasha's hut.

After the tour, Kasha joined me and Nina in front of his hut. My grandmother stood behind me, her hands on my shoulders. I had begun to feel the medicine by then. Some strange power coursed me, some force I did not understand—and, even with Nina's protective hands on my shoulders, I looked into the camera and felt afraid.

The woman took the picture and left. That was a bad thing, but we didn't know it yet. We didn't know what pictures could do.

Later, when Nina scolded him about his love of money, Kasha gave his speech about the new ways: "We won't live like this when the forest is gone. Even if we resist, we must learn to live from money. We have already started to change." He gestured to me. I suppose he was pointing to my clothes. We often traded with the tourists, and they gave us Western clothes in exchange for our bast-woven skirts, forest beads, and blow guns. They usually didn't bring children's clothes, but it happened sometimes—and now I was dressed in tattered denim shorts and a Western-style pink T-shirt with the word "LOVE" across the front.

"It's time to live like the jaguar," Kasha continued, "knowing the ways of our surroundings and adapting to them. Isn't that what we learned: that we must watch and conform in order to live?"

Nina sat near the fire pit, crushing a handful of coarse beans against a flat stone. This was the jaguar medicine, the snuff that would help me to know the spirit of the jaguar—an idea that I could not yet comprehend. My grandmother beckoned me, and I came to her obediently, kneeling on the ground and waiting as she brushed the bean powder into two small piles. Nina handed me a pair of hollow, brittle stems. "Maybe Illari will see the answer to that," she said to Kasha. Then she spoke to me: "Don't sniff too hard. You just want it in your nostrils, not in your lungs."

The effects of the brew still hadn't worn off, and the bean powder made me nervous. I worried that it would be too much. Nina guessed my thoughts and reassured me: "It's okay to be overwhelmed. If you're not overcome by the medicine, you won't be able to learn from it."

I stuck the tubes into my nostrils and sniffed. For a few moments, I felt nothing aside from the slightest burn—and then I was retching, my nostrils filling with snot that spewed onto the ground along with vomit and tears. Frantically, I pulled off my shirt and blew my nose into it, trying to get rid of the terrible snuff.

When the retching subsided, I lay on a clean space on the ground. The earth was cool against my skin. My eyes closed, and suddenly I wasn't on the ground anymore. I seemed to have shrunk, becoming tiny like a grain of bean powder, shuttling along the snuff tube and up into some strange, dark portal. At the top of the tube I stopped. A dark figure seemed to look down at me from the edge. It was black and featureless, like a shadow, but if I didn't look directly at it, it seemed to glow brightly.

I asked: "Can I come up there?"

The figure seemed to smile at me—a smile that was felt rather than seen, and then I was shuttling downward again, back to my place on the ground.

Nina and Kasha stood watching me. I sat up and blew my nose again, and rubbed at my arm where ants had bitten me.

"I will wash that shirt when you're done," Nina promised. "Did something happen?"

I explained my brief venture into the mysterious portal, and Nina smiled faintly.

"I didn't see the jaguar," I complained.

"You will," she replied quietly, and her smile faded.

As Nina helped me clean up, Kasha continued to argue his point. "Even if we don't want to live by the new ways, we have to know them," he said. "These people fight with money, and they win with money, and we can only fight back with money."

Nina regarded him coolly. "You use the new ways if you must," she said, "but I will fight in my own way."

I did not know who "these people" were. Kaska sometimes said they were white people, but he also said they were our own people. He said they were foreigners, yet he encouraged foreigners to visit our village. Nor did I understand the troubles around us, though I caught a few details from the frightened murmurs of grown-ups. Village leaders and healers had begun to vanish. If their bodies were found, they were sometimes found shot, but usually they had been hacked to pieces—and this, Kasha said, was evidence that our own people were guilty. Few of our people had bullets, but everyone had machetes.

Now, the children were vanishing as well. An old man, the *apo* in a neighboring village, had been found butchered, and his grandson had gone missing. My uncle was deeply upset by the news. He left our village with two of the other men. They went away angry and never returned.

Without Kasha, Nina was left to fight in her own way.

Nina's way was with the jaguar. She worked with many medicines, but the jaguar medicine was part of every ritual. In Nina's time, my people feared and revered the great cat. It was strong and fast, resistant to our poisons, and every parent worried that it would sneak from the village with a child hanging limp between its jaws. Yet, we looked to the cat for wisdom and healing, for it was the jaguar who first led us to the medicines of the misk'i tree, and through whose eyes we gained another view of the forest.

When I first saw the misk'i tree, I was disappointed by its ugliness.
It was a pale tree covered with dark, scabby-looking horns that made
it look sickly and rough. "Perhaps it is meant to remind you of
disease," Nina said in reply to my complaints, "because it is here to
heal disease." We used misk'i sap in our food and medicines. It was
good for cooking, and it strengthened our bodies and treated many
ailments. Its bark made a curative tea. Late in the year, its flowers
bloomed: white, fluffy spheres that always seemed in mid-burst.
Then, it didn't look so ugly.

Along with the flowers came the bean pods, hairy green-and-
brown things that looked like giant caterpillar cocoons. Nina said
that those beans held magic. Though we were wingless, misk'i beans
allowed us to fly.

Nina was just a child, like me, when she swallowed her first
ceremonial medicine and took the snuff from the misk'i beans. Her
own mother brought her to the tree. It was there that Nina and her
mother ground the beans into a powder. It burned her nostrils and
stung her eyes—and then Nina blinked away her tears and found
herself lying on her back, staring into the branches of the tree. The
ugly, horny nubs along the branches no longer looked like sores or
blemishes. They were rosettes, she realized, like the rosettes of the
jaguar. The branches looked just like the veins of her own body,
ripped out and stretched above her, reaching out to join the branches
of other trees, connecting the whole jungle. Nina shuttled along
those veins, across the forest to where a golden jaguar ran. Blood
seemed to pulse within the misk'i branches. Nina felt the rhythm,
saw its pace in the wildcat's steps. Its paws hit the ground in time
with the magnificent heartbeat. The beat became more distinct as
Nina descended toward the cat, connecting with its rhythm,
indulging in the cat's senses. For a moment, Nina knew the jungle as
the jaguar knew it. And of all the new and strange things she saw
before her, the thing that awed her the most was the misk'i tree—
pulsing and alive, and all of its parts filled with medicines.

It was only in her older age, in the years after I was born, that
Nina began to run with a legendary wildcat, the black jaguar called
Yanakoya. Yanakoya was the only black jaguar in our woods. The
few who saw her knew her at once, and others in our villages knew
of her as a legend. Yanakoya's face was dark as a midnight forest

under the densest canopy of leaves. Her black flanks shimmered with dark golden rosettes, so subtle they could only be seen in a certain degree of light, and her coat shifted beautifully as she moved through the sparse sunbeams. I, too, would see this cat and know her.

On the day that Kasha left, Nina went to her hut and prepared for herself the bean snuff. As she began to fly along the misk'i branches, she spotted a few ranchers scouting the forest. They had stopped near the spot where Yanakoya nursed her two young cubs. They heard the delighted cries of her cubs. They carried guns. Nina knew that the ranchers were likely to shoot.

Quickly, my grandmother flew to Yanakoya. She put the warning in the black jaguar's head. Yanakoya leapt up to carry her cubs away, but no sooner had she started off with the first cub than a shot was fired into her flank. She was felled, and as the shots continued, a powerful surge of resistance tore my grandmother's spirit from Yanakoya's body. She rose into the air above the gunmen, roaring with all her might at their atrocity.

The ranchers reared back in horror. She knew not what they saw, but they shot wildly in her direction, at some phantom figure that loomed over them. Their bullets were ineffective against the illusion, and they ran off, leaving the bleeding wildcats to their fates.

The black jaguar laid on the ground, eyes closed in mourning. She would survive, but for the little ones it was too late. Yanakoya's cubs were dead.

My grandmother spent the rest of the day in a bad state. I watched her slump on the floor, weak with grief. She wept so painfully that at last I began to understand how she had merged with Yanakoya. She lowered her head, dripping tears and murmuring, "My babies."

She received a small consolation in helping to heal the black jaguar's wounds. When Nina approached Yanakoya, in her own body and on foot, the jaguar seemed to recognize her. Yanakoya was alert, but never withdrew from my grandmother's hands. Nina pried one of the bullets free and did what she could with salves and sacred songs.

I stayed in the village and waited for Kasha's return. No one had news of him—not in the other villages, not in the tourist area. Day after day, I looked at the path to our little village and hoped to see his face. Instead, after many days, we were visited by a small, thin man with a gaunt face and sunken eyes. Walberto was a plantation owner with big plans for the new ways. He had come to plead with the village leaders to give up the lands near the edge of the forest.

The foreigners who had advocated for us, those who had talked and laughed with my uncle, didn't stay to discover our fate. They went home with their writings and photographs. Another village leader disappeared, and then another. It was rumored that Walberto was paying poor farmers to kill those who stood in the way of his aims, and that his men stole the children of the dead. The children would be sold as slaves, or a witch might pull out their organs and put them in someone else's body.

Gruesome images began to haunt my dreams: My neighbors found bloody and dismembered outside their huts, their arms and legs strewn in the small plaza. Child slaves with eyes as dull as the dead, mutely fulfilling the commands of some unseen enemy.

We hardly had time to prepare ourselves against such nightmares before they struck our village. Walberto's men had no trouble finding the little hut where my grandmother lived. I was sitting on the palm-plank floor, weaving bracelets, when the men burst inside.

The men with guns and machetes moved so fast that I didn't know which one was shouting. They looked around wildly, as if to discover Nina hiding along the walls of the near-empty hut, or veiled somehow behind the mosquito net. One of them descended on me and grabbed my arm. In Spanish, he said: "Take her. It's the girl in the picture. She's the granddaughter."

I remembered the rumors. I screamed for my grandmother as the men dragged me from my home. Nina was foraging nearby, and as she raced to my aid, the men raised their rifles. Shot after shot rang out as my grandmother dove back into the trees. She ran for her life, down the paths she knew would be hardest to follow. And then she could only cower in the forest while I cried her name.

Desperation rose in her. If only she had been with the misk'i tree at that moment. If only she could turn back into a terrible specter and scare off these men the way she had terrified the ranchers. Not knowing where else to turn, Nina fled to the misk'i tree, whispering songs and prayers as she hurried to pound out the black powder.

Yanakoya, who knew the jungle, met my grandmother's spirit. With Nina's silent will pressing into her mind, Yanakoya sprang to her feet. She remembered her own cubs and their ruined bodies, their warmth vanishing into cold stiffness. Her thoughts merged with Nina's memories. She saw the woman's tears, heard her mournful cry: *My babies . . . .*

Don't let them take my little Illari, my grandmother begged. *I can't reach her in time, and I can't carry her away safely, but you might. Yanakoya, please protect our child . . . .*

With the racing heartbeat of the misk'i tree driving her pace, Yanakoya shot through the forest. Faster than the man who dragged me in the crook of his arm, and faster than the van that bumped along toward Walberto's ranch, the black jaguar ran the line toward the edge of the woods.

In the back of the van I sat frightened and motionless, listening to the men over my own ragged breath. They spoke freely in Spanish, and from their words I learned of my uncle's fate. "Finding the son was easy," one man said. "He took pictures with every tourist who came this way, and everyone knows where his family lives. We got rid of him and the other troublemakers, but we have a few more shamans to take care of."

As I sat trying to suppress my tears, the men went on to rationalize their violence: shamans drew the wrong types foreigners to our villages, foreigners who meddled and interfered with Walberto's aims. They had taken me to lure Nina, and when they found her, they would "get rid of" her, too.

The van stopped. I was dumped into a small, damp room. The concrete floor felt hard and pitiless under my bottom and bare feet. Before the door closed, I looked up and recognized Walberto's face: sunken like that of a dead man, the eyes perpetually bloodshot and framed by folds of dry, weathered flesh. A frame so thin as to evoke thoughts of ghouls and ghosts. I have seen evil men who are handsome, whose charming smiles and shining eyes add power to their charisma, but Walberto was not one of those. His mouth twisted into an ugly grin. Though he only looked at me for a moment, his thoughts flashed in his eyes: *You are nothing. You are part of a dying tribe. I have power, but you have none, and your people have none—and no one will come to save you.*

Yet, in a way, my people came to my aid. Walberto had hired men from a neighboring tribe to guard the compound. Their work was cheap, which was agreeable to Walberto, but they followed the old ways, and none would shoot the black jaguar. And so my grandmother compelled Yakanoya to creep into the compound, unassailed, her watchful eye fixed on five men who stared back in awe. Five guns stayed at rest on the men's shoulders. No one dared take aim.

I sat alone on the bare concrete floor, huddled in the corner, when the black jaguar stole into my room. With her claws, she unlatched the door. She pushed through with her massive form. For a moment I could only stare in terror, wondering if this powerful beast had come to feast on my flesh. Yanakoya stood in the light that streamed from behind, her eyes glowing strangely in the shadow of her dark face, and in those eyes I somehow recognized the gaze of my grandmother. She looked at me intensely, trying to communicate what she could not say with words. Then she turned aside and crouched low, glancing at me as if to say: *Get on.*

Every magical tale of the jaguars and the misk'i tree swam to the surface of my thoughts and turned my despair to relief. I climbed onto Yanakoya's back, wrapping my arms around her body and hugging her to my chest. In a moment, we were racing through the sunlit clearing. I saw the alarmed faces of the guards, heard their shouts as the black cat fled into the trees with Walberto's prized possession clinging to its back.

After some distance, Yanakoya slowed enough that I could sit up. The jungle had never seemed so grand. I could barely hear the sound of the jaguar's feet padding along the ground. She was swift and gentle, fierce and cautious, and if any animal saw us passing by, they didn't dare stand in our way. We became bound in that journey: a mother without a cub, a cub without a mother. I no longer feared fanged beasts or poisonous critters. There was power in the wood, and it existed to protect me.

As the setting sun deepened the forest hues, Yanakoya came to a halt. Something had changed. A disturbed aura hung about us now, and I realized that I could no longer sense my grandmother's presence. *The snuff is all finished*, I thought nervously, and lowered my eyes to the bulge of Yanakoya's tense muscles. I stayed perched on her back, waiting to see how she would react.

She turned her head towards me, made a soft snuffling sound, and went on.

A few villagers had gathered near Nina's hut when Yanakoya emerged from the jungle. At the sight of my neighbors, I slid from her back and ran into one of the older women's arms. The jaguar slipped back into the trees before I could turn around. And I didn't turn, because when I looked to the other side of the clearing, I saw the villagers carrying pieces of my grandmother's body.

At the base of the misk'i tree, as Nina guided Yanakoya back to the village, the men had hacked her with machetes. I saw the gore hanging from a severed limb, the blood-red huayruro beads strung beneath a ruined throat—and I understood. The men had finished her.

My elder neighbor tried to comfort me. She turned me gently away from the sight. In the trees, I saw two eyes watching me— mottled green and brown eyes that seemed to glow in the shadow of the forest. I saw traces of my grandmother in those eyes. They comforted me more than the woman's embrace. I tore away and ran to Yanakoya.

From then on, we traveled the wood as mother and daughter. Nina's hut was abandoned, and Kasha's hut crumbled to pieces, its fabricated creatures slumping to the ground in a slow death. My people fragmented. Some left for the cities. Others retreated deeper into the wood, and I went furthest of all. Yanakoya led me to the misk'i tree and watched over me during my journeys. There in the jaguar's mind, Nina's memories lived on. They merged with my own and forced me to know life the way my grandmother knew it. My head burned with misk'i powder, and my spirit was seared by grown-up ideas, by the burden of growing up so soon. But my survival depended on it. My innocence died—and in the deep of the jungle, Yanakoya and I became one.

Walberto's pace never slowed. I wanted to leap on him and his men, to slay them all in one blow and stop their hands from further destruction—but I couldn't do anything yet. I waited.

During my waiting, I learned those things which I needed most.

251

Yanakoya taught me to swim, first in the smaller, gentler streams, and then in the deep and fast waters, when I was strong enough not to get swept away. She taught me to avoid being seen by Walberto's men. They often came to hunt peccaries, rodents, and the red-throated guans who nested in the misk'i trees. Their methods were sloppy, and they crippled more animals than they killed. Yanakoya was a wait-and-ambush hunter who secretly watched her prey, who learned the best place to lie in wait, and who killed quickly, often before the prey had any notion of its fate—and it was she who taught me to hunt.

Walberto had also learned to swim, but he never became a great hunter. In the evenings, he sometimes relaxed in the private lagoon behind his ranch. At other times, he and his men stayed inside, entertaining themselves with women and girls. I watched them from the woods, learning and waiting.

I waited until hair grew between my legs and the beginnings of breasts swelled on my chest, until my nipples protruded like little round bullets. And then I went swimming.

I was already in the water when Walberto and two of his men came to swim in the lagoon. I stood on the far side, waist-deep and naked, without moving. I was turned slightly away from the men, yet still facing them. My eyes were on Walberto.

He saw me first. He started to shout in anger, but his words faltered. For some time, the only sounds were those of the rainforest: the evening songs of birds and insects, the rustling leaves and distant howls of monkeys. Then the other men began murmuring, debating with one another about what they should do.

Walberto shooed them away. "I will handle it," he assured them. He started into the water, asking in Spanish: "What are you doing in my lagoon?" The words didn't carry the faintest trace of anger.

Slowly, I moved away. I ascended to the shallow edge, letting my backside rise above the water. Near the edge of the lagoon, I stopped and looked back at him, turning so that one breast was visible again. On my face I wore a mixture of curiosity and fear.

The other men hadn't moved. Walberto turned around and waved them away. "Go on, get out of here," he said. "You're scaring her."

The men left quietly. Walberto waited until they were gone

before he looked at me again. He stared like a man who had stumbled upon some beguiling, harmless mystery. "Who are you?" he asked.

I didn't respond. I waited.

He moved closer, sinking deeper into the water. "Do you live near here?" he asked.

"Yes," I replied, meekly.

"Do your parents know you're out here?"

"I don't have parents." My voice was breathy, soft, fragile.

He moved closer.

I ascended from the lagoon, loosely hugging my arms across my chest. "I needed a place to bathe," I said. "I've been living out here in the woods."

Nothing I said was a lie.

Walberto came closer. "This is private property. If you want to swim here, you have to ask." He hesitated, remaining shoulder-deep in the lagoon. "See that house over there? Next time you want to bathe, come and ask me. Make sure you talk to me first." He inched closer. "Usually, people pay to use this pool, but I can make an exception for you."

I didn't respond. I waited, and eventually he rose from the water. "What else do you want? Are you hungry?"

I turned my face away, meekly, and took a few more steps. Walberto stopped—but I uttered a soft "Yes," and he came closer.

Each time he stopped, I waited. Each time I waited, he wanted, and followed. I waited until he had followed me into the cover of the woods.

When the trees had closed around us, when the shadows had converged, Yanakoya emerged. Her powerful figure was barely visible in the cover of dark. It seemed to me, as I watched, that an invisible shadow with glowing eyes leapt at Walberto. It started with the thin flesh of his throat, and in seconds, the shadow tore him to pieces.

The villagers say it was a witch who killed him—a sorceress whose power is to shape-shift into wild beasts. They began to tell tales of the *runa-uturuncu*: the half-human, half-wildcat who prowls the forest at night, looking for outsiders to devour, living on even as the other jaguars vanish. And they have vanished, along with the wild pigs and the red-throated guans. Yanakoya aged well, and lived the full breadth of her life, and she has vanished too.

The big roads come ever closer, like poisoned veins, and the forests around those roads become devastated. The animals look small and starved, and when they die, their corpses are already full of worms. The fruit rots before it can ripen, and the waters often flow with poisons that sting our insides. Even the sun seems more intense these days, wearing us down and burning our flesh.

And the children continue to vanish. I cannot leap and save them all, but at least I am learning to leap. I hunt like the jaguar, quiet, patient, and focused. With the misk'i guiding me, I prowl in the air and lurk beneath the branches, like some strange phantom that cannot be felled by bullets and machetes—and if people see me, their eyes fill with terror, though I know not what they see. On foot, I prowl with a sharp claw or some other forest instrument honed down to a small, lethal blade. I am changing. Sometimes I make myself visible, beckoning with an innocent gaze, hiding a clawed hand that no longer looks completely human. Stealth and deception can beat bullets, and I have learned both. My weapons are easier to carry than machetes, and with practice, they will be faster and deadlier. In that, I am not ready yet—but it is no matter. I will wait.

To the Solemn Graves

To the Solemn Graves

"Time is fleeting, And our hearts, though stout and brave, Still, like muffled drums, are beating Funeral marches to the grave."
-Henry Longfellow, "A Psalm of Life"

The disturbances began the same day Mona stumbled across the decrepit cemetery. She had already lived in the backwoods cottage for a few days, taking time to put the place in order before venturing into the forest. A well-worn path led into the trees, but the realtor had warned Mona not to stray too far. The swamps were not far from the house, and the trees were thick enough that it was easy to get lost among them. And then there were the snakes, and the alligators, and even bobcats and bears. Mona kept keen eyes and ears during her brief trek into the woods, pausing countless times to listen, stopping when the cypress trees appeared and a thick, pungent scent wafted past her—sure signs of the swamp. As she began to turn back, something caught her eye: a gray streak, out of place in the brown and green drapery.

Mona ventured farther, following the curve of the path until the figure came into view, and her breath caught. A woman was sitting there. A woman in a flowing gray dress, her hands and feet the exact same shade as her clothes. Her eyes were closed, and her stony face wore a peaceful expression.

Other splotches of gray were visible beyond the figure, now, as Mona drew closer: headstones arranged in a haphazard spread behind the statue, some crumbling around the edges. The woman was seated on a large stone base. On one side it bore a memorial inscription, beginning with a name: Adelaide Magdalene Dumaine. The dates showed that she had died young, aged only thirty, a few years ago. On the opposite side was the phrase: *Our time here is short, but our arts and our hearts are eternal.*

Mona marveled over the finely sculpted face and the details of the close-cropped hair. The statue exuded peace; its expression washed Mona in a strange sense of calm. Gingerly, she brushed the woman's cheek with a fingertip. *Someone loved this woman. Someone knew her and loved her.*

The other stones were unremarkable. A few were even illegible, the engravings worn away by time and weather. Several bore the family name Hugon. There was a sole Bonin, a rough stone marker for a "beloved dog" named Hero, and one more Dumaine: Marcela Therese Dumaine. Her stone was a flat plaque set into the ground, and though the moss and other greenery had encroached on the edges, it looked like it had been cared for. The stone in the worst shape had been knocked from its base, and was now encased in mud, moss, and slime. Mona crouched beside the granite slab and peered at it. The surface was blank; the inscription was likely on the other side.

Mona dug her fingers beneath the slab and hefted it upright. She raised one side, then the other, edging it back onto the broken base until it stood in its original position.

Slowly, she released her grip. "Stay," she whispered.

The headstone remained in place. Mona watched it for a few seconds more, then gently brushed dirt from the grooves of the writing. The given name was Louis, or maybe Louie, born in 1938—that was all she could make out. Mona stood up and headed home, holding her muddy arms away from her sides. Her flesh had begun to itch. In the bathroom, she turned on the faucet and scrubbed the green and brown slime from her skin.

Mona wandered through the house, making yet another mental list of what needed to be done. The living room walls had already been painted, the dull gray planks transformed to an earthy shade of beige that complimented the brown sofa and espresso furniture. The rest of the cottage suited Mona's tastes and needed only a little more work, mostly in the bathroom. Mona had already made the necessary trip to the hardware store, but put off the repairs for the next day. She turned on the living room stereo and sat at her computer, trying to work with the area's spotty Wi-Fi. Though she was in no need of a paycheck and had wanted to take a break, Mona found herself perusing local job openings in her fields of experience: translating and teaching.

She kept the music going until late evening, when the night creatures started their own songs: the insistent chirps of frogs and crickets, and now and then the hoot of an owl. Mona kept the windows open and listened with an air of relief. During the day, the heat and the silence got under her skin. Night offered a welcome refreshment. She went out to the wide gallery porch at the front of the house, lighting the citronella torches she'd set up that morning and seating herself in the new rocker. Overhead, the stars shone like a fragmented burst of light across the dark—many more stars than she's been accustomed to seeing as a child, though the ensuing years had given her opportunities to see them from different spots on the globe, and in darker places that allowed her to see so much more in the vastness of space. Mona gazed upward and thought of those times past: late-night gatherings in the dark night, the occasional bonfire, the murmuring voices that sometimes broke into song—all those times she had sat looking at the night sky before falling exhausted into bed, in all those different places, with so many different people, so many of them now dead or estranged. A memory tugged at her mind: children's wide eyes gleaming in the moonlight.

The image was shattered by the buzz of a mosquito in her ear. She shooed it away, then extinguished the torches and went to bed.

The drone of the ceiling fan lulled her to sleep, but only for a moment. Mona found herself disturbed by a sound, some kind of cry rising above the cacophony of croaking and chirping, like the mewl of a cat. A stray, perhaps, that had wandered onto the property. It might have taken shelter in the space beneath the house.

Mona sat up. She switched on the bedside lamp, then went to the window and closed it She switched off the fan and stood listening.

The sound came again: a voice, soft and mournful, like a child weeping. It sounded like it was coming from above. The upstairs rooms. Maybe an animal had become trapped there.

The floorboards creaked under her feet as she went to investigate. Mona only braved to go as far as the foot of the stairs. From there she heard the cries, soft and mournful, somewhere on the upper floor.

The voice didn't belong to an animal. It uttered words, indistinguishable, but with a definite cadence.

"Hey," Mona called out sharply, and paused to listen. "Who's up there?"

The voice uttered a final syllable. It sounded like "*Stop*"—and then the stairwell fell into silence.

Mona stood for some time, listening to the muted chirpings of wildlife. She dared to ascend a few steps, but changed her mind and returned to the bedroom.

She had likely been mistaken. The sound had probably come from the roof, and was the call of some night bird, maybe an owl. Maybe the discovery of the graveyard had perturbed her. She was rattled; she was imagining things. Her nightmares had crept their way into the waking state.

Though the sounds had ceased, Mona's anxiety didn't. She lay in the bed with eyes open, thinking about the things that might be haunting her. That single word, *Stop*, echoed in her mind. Eventually, anxiety muted into grief. She rolled over and sobbed into the pillow.

The morning was spent on the last of the repairs: replacing the rusted-out bathroom faucet and scrubbing away the dark yellow toilet ring. Baking soda and vinegar had failed to accomplish the latter, but the hardware clerk had schooled Mona on both tasks and supplied her with the proper products. She finished quickly and found herself with the whole day still ahead of her.

She scrolled through job sites on the internet. The local schools were desperate for substitutes, as schools tended to be. *No harm in applying*, Mona thought. She might even sub once a week, just for something to do.

As a teacher applicant she'd had to take tests, write essays, and submit numerous records and letters of recommendation, investing half a day for each job, but a sub position didn't require much input. Mona finished her application and once again found herself with empty hours ahead. She read a book, made a batch of pickled cauliflower, and wiled away the time until the afternoon. Then she put on her boots and trekked back into the woods, toting her digital camera.

After snapping a few photos from the front of the statue, Mona circumnavigated and explored other angles. On the opposite side, she saw that the broken tombstone was once again dislodged, nestled into the dirt beside its base. Mona sighed and crouched beside it, running a fingertip along the jagged edge. "Nothing a little mortar can't fix," she muttered. "Maybe then . . . ." The words trailed off. A footprint was visible on the face of the stone, as if someone had kicked it over. Around the gravestones, too, Mona saw two sets of prints in the soil—small ones, somewhat smaller than her own feet.

As she began to stand, something else caught her eye. Marcela Dumaine's grave marker had been pruned. The flat stone had already been noticeably cleaner than the others, but the weeds and moss around the edges had been recently shorn, the clippings brushed back from the stone.

"So," she murmured. "You've had visitors."

She skirted the edges of the graveyard, peering closely at the surrounding woods, but found no other paths than the one that led to her own house. It was possible that another property bordered this land, and that the inhabitants were coming to visit—or to vandalize. But why care for one stone, and kick down the other?

Mona puzzled over the prints. She noticed traces of them on the path back to the cottage, though they didn't make deep impressions, and some had likely been obliterated by her own feet. As she walked, her thoughts strayed from the mystery of the cemetery to the shortcomings of the cottage. The important repairs had been finished, but there were other, superficial details that could use some attention—other things Mona could fix, if only to occupy her time. The bathroom and bedrooms could use some fresh paint; a few floorboards in the porch could use replacing; the empty wooden frame in the backyard, which had probably been a dog kennel, was something of an eyesore. It could be torn down easily, but over time it had developed an aesthetic advantage. Numerous strands of ivy and morning glory vines had twined their way up the frame, and the flowers had blossomed into striking violet trumpets.

As she emerged from the woods, Mona cast a critical eye at the frame. She was surprised to see two children crouching behind it. They ducked low, behind the thickest array of vines, peering at the house and whispering to each other. The older one, a girl, wore two braids that hung to the shoulders of her bright red T-shirt. She looked about thirteen, while the boy was a few years younger. He was better disguised in a green shirt and tan shorts. Mona approached them slowly, debating how to address them. Finally, she greeted them with a simple "Hi."

The kids jumped. The youngest one let out a yelp, and they whirled to face her with twin expressions of terror.

Mona chuckled. "Sorry, did I startle you?"

Their wide eyes answered for them.

"You live around here?" she asked.

The girl shifted, looked from left to right, tried to get her bearings. "We . . . we just wanted to see the haunted house," she said.

"What haunted house?"

The girl pointed to the cottage. "This one."

Mona glanced up at the sand- and reddish-brown siding, at the striations and tiny holes visible in the cypress planks. The house was rustic, for sure, and had originally been built in the early 1900s. Plenty of time to accumulate ghosts.

She replied casually: "Oh, it's haunted, is it? I live in that house."

The girl pursed her lips, as if debating whether to speak. "You probably won't live there very long," she blurted. "Whenever someone moves in, they move out right away because of the ghost."

"Hmm. Well, I haven't noticed any ghosts."

"You haven't?" The girl's face set into a vague frown. She peered at Mona with perplexed curiosity.

"Nope."

"Not even at night?"

"Why, is that when the ghost comes out?"

The children exchanged uncomfortable glances.

"So, what kind of ghost is it?" Mona asked. "Is it a girl ghost, a boy ghost, is it old or young, does it move stuff around or make noises . . . ."

Again, the pair looked at each other. They were siblings, Mona supposed. They had the same large brown eyes and long lashes, the same arched eyebrows and narrow, protruding chins, the same shade of dark brown skin. She glanced down at their muddy shoes.

"It's a mean ghost," the boy said. "It doesn't want you to live there. It gets mad when people change things."

"How do you know it's a mean ghost?"

"It does bad things," the boy replied.

"Like what?"

The boy lowered his eyes. He seemed to be trying to think of an answer, but the girl nudged him and grabbed his arm. "Let's go," she whispered.

They mumbled goodbyes and hurried away toward the road. Mona didn't follow to see where they went. She went back inside to check her email. She'd already gotten a response to her job application. The school district wanted to know when she could interview.

That night, in bed, Mona heard the sounds again. Within the harmonious blanket of chirping and croaking, a soft weeping reached her ears. She got up to investigate, stood at the foot of the stairs and listened. The same voice. The same cry.

"I'm coming up," she announced, and began the ascent.

The planks groaned beneath her bare feet. On the topmost step, Mona reached out and switched on the hallway light. The top floor had much less square footage than the main floor. It had a single bedroom on each side, another at the end of the hall. She knew immediately that the sound was coming from the farthest bedroom.

Silently, Mona encouraged herself onward. At the threshold of the open doorway she paused, leaning forward to peek inside, half expecting to see a luminescent figure standing somewhere in the empty room. A voice spoke softly: " . . . *killing me. Leave it alone.*"

"Is someone in here?" Mona asked.

The room was bare. It hadn't yet been furnished. Mona had considered making it into a library—or maybe buying a piano, and taking up playing again after a decade-long hiatus. Anything to make the house feel less empty.

Another mournful sob came from somewhere in the room. Mona stepped carefully inside. The closet, too, was open, and just as bare. A floorboard creaked loudly beneath Ella's foot as she reached the center of the room. She stopped and half-turned in sudden confusion. The voice seemed to come from behind her now, as though it had moved to the doorway. It uttered a final plea: "*Stop.*"

Mona stood motionless for some time, listening to her own breathing.

"Well," she said at last, "The house is haunted, or I'm going crazy. Fine. Whatever." She scoffed, went back down the stairs to the bathroom, and dug around in one of the drawers until she found a packet of foam earplugs. Mona shoved them into her ears and went back to bed.

The day had worn her out. She didn't stay awake. Nor did she cry. Sometimes, at night, grief visited her like a phantom and washed her in tears, but a haunted house with a single ghost didn't seem particularly scary. Mona had experienced scarier things, and she had learned to live with ghosts.

The local school district hired her right away. Her first class was eleventh grade chemistry—a lucky assignment, she thought. She had worked as a chemistry para for two years before becoming an English teacher. Subbing was much like being a first-day para. The kids didn't take her seriously, and if they looked at her at all, they tended to do so with detached and distrustful gazes. Eventually, if she kept showing up, and found ways to connect, some of those looks would become warm and eager, and even the uninvested students might find something to be enthused about. She missed that about teaching, about human contact in general.

As the first period started, Mona scanned the attendance sheet for hard-to-pronounce names. The first was the toughest: Breaux Chefdhomme-Boisblanc. She stuck to the given name, pronounced it like "Bro."

"Wow, she got it," a boy in the front row replied. "Yeah, that's me."

"All right. I won't do as well with your last name. Marcela? Marcela Du . . . ." Mona trailed off.

"Dumaine," a voice replied.

Mona's gaze flicked to the source: a girl with large, deep brown eyes, arched eyebrows, and a narrow, protruding chin. Her gaze bored into Mona with the vaguely defiant look that so many students gave her at first.

Quietly, Mona checked off the girl's name. She continued the roll call.

The class spent most of the period quietly practicing equations. Mona's curiosity about the girl maintained a hold. She kept an eye on the girl, but tried not to stare while the students worked.

A teacher from a neighboring classroom came in to check on Mona halfway through the school day. The fourth hour class had just ended, and one of the teenage boys was having fun teasing the sub in front of his friends, pleading with Mona to be his homecoming date.

"I'm an old lady," she replied in a bored tone.

"Ah, you can't be that old," the kid replied with a grin. "How old are you? Twenty-five?"

"Thirty-seven."

A howl of surprised laughter rose up from his friends. The other teacher walked in then—Mr. Lind, the physics and astronomy teacher, younger than most of the other staff. "Class is over, guys," he said, waving the students away. "Go eat. It's not a half-bad meal today."

The boys trailed out of the room, still hooting with laughter.

Mr. Lind smiled, asked Mona the standard questions about how the day had gone, made the standard comments about how students could be hard on subs. He'd chatted with her in the morning, too, almost until the first bell, so that she'd barely had enough time to prepare for class. Mona glanced at the clock, anxious about missing lunch, but couldn't resist prolonging the conversation.

"I was wondering if you know Marcela Dumaine," she cut in. "I think I might be her neighbor."

"Yeah, I know Marcela," Lind replied. "She's not in my classes anymore, but she's on the robotics team. I see her every Wednesday after school. Smart as a whip. Her programming skills basically got us the state championship last year. Do you live in town?"

"No. I'm out in the boonies, actually."

"Then you wouldn't be neighbors. She lives in one of the apartments on the other side of town."

Mona frowned. "Oh. I just thought . . . there's a cemetery in my backyard, and one of the tombstones says Marcela Therese Dumaine. I thought it might be a relative of hers."

"Could be her grandma," Lind said. "Marcela was named after her."

"Ah. I wonder if she has relatives in my neighborhood. I've seen some kids hanging around the house. It looked like they were visiting the cemetery."

"Did you notice any of the other names? In the cemetery, I mean."

"Hugon," she replied. "And Bonin."

"Marcela's grandma was a Hugon before she got married. You probably live in Marcela's old neighborhood. I'm sure they have relatives buried in that area. Her family just moved into town a couple of years ago." He, too, glanced up at the wall clock. "Listen, I'm looking for a sub for next Wednesday, if you're interested. I'd rather have someone who knows the curriculum. You could stay and host the robotics club, too, or I can just cancel it."

"Yeah, I can pick up your class. I would like to check out the club, too."

"We're meeting after school today, if you can hang around. We meet next-door, in my classroom."

Lind chatted for another minute about sub plans, and then hurried off to lunch. Mona didn't see him again until after school, when she walked into his classroom and found him talking with Marcela and two other students. The group was relaxed, smiling—but when Marcela caught sight of Mona, her smile vanished. She looked at Mona with cautious intensity.

Mr. Lind introduced Mona to the students and gave a brief background on the club. "The students organized a fundraiser to get us some 3D printers last year," he added. "We had a hell of a time getting the parts we needed, so we had a lot of limitations. Now, for the parts we can't get, we can make them ourselves."

A few more students joined the group as the materials were being set up on the lab tables. The kids carried equipment from the storage closet between the classrooms, chatting and laughing—except for Marcela, who remained subdued.

One of the girls from the first-period chemistry class filled Mona in on their current project: a machine that could help clean up potentially hazardous spills. She showed Mona how they were fitting it with a sensor to prevent the waste reservoir from over-filling, and how they logged their progress, problems, and ideas for improvement.

"For last year's competition we had to build a robot that moved boxes and stacked them up," she said, "but Marcela decided we should build a robot that was in two separate pieces, and could stack itself. Like, we started out with one robot going around and stacking, but when the boxes got too high, the robot came back and stacked the second piece onto itself. The grooves for the lifting platform matched up on both pieces so that it could lift the boxes even higher."

Lind gave Marcela an approving look. "It was genius. Marcela wasn't satisfied with it, though. She wants to design something that there's more of a public need for. She's a bit of a philanthropist."

Marcela replied with a quick glance and a vague smile, keeping her head lowered. For the rest of the session, she kept much the same demeanor: tense, preoccupied, and never meeting Mona's gaze.

"You're quiet today," Lind told her as the students began to work. "Everything all right?"

Marcela shrugged. "Yeah. Fine."

Mona excused herself and headed for the parking lot. She felt sure, by then, that she was living in the girl's old house. That was, perhaps, a source of the girl's discomfort. But what else might be adding to her unease? Was it something to do with the strange sounds in the house, the supposed "ghost" that the other kids had warned her about?

Nothing unusual happened that night. On Friday, though, when Mona took a stroll to the graveyard, she found that the headstone she'd repaired had been knocked down again. She stood with her hands on her hips, looking at the crust of mortar she'd used to keep the stone in place. "Now I have to scrape it off and do it all over again," she muttered.

Once again, two sets of footprints trailed along the dirt path, to the cemetery and back toward the house: two sets of roughly the same size, one perhaps slightly larger than the other.

"Two kids," Mona murmured. "Ah. Detective Mona is on to you."

Two sneaky children, though, couldn't account for what happened at night. Mona didn't bother with the ear plugs. She kept the windows open and let the soft breezes and the faint chirps of frogs and crickets lull her to sleep. She had hardly drifted off when the noises began.

It began the same way as before: a sound like a child crying. Mona roused herself, sitting up in bed and listening intently.

"What the hell," she said.

She turned on the lights as she made her way through the house. At the top of the stairs she slowed, following the sound to the bedroom at the end of the hall. The mournful voice was speaking, and as Mona moved closer, the words became distinct: "*Stop wrecking my house. You're killing me.*"

The bedroom door was already wide open. Slowly, Mona crept toward the threshold, holding her breath as she peered around the door frame.

"*Leave it alone,*" the voice commanded.

The light from the hallway illuminated most of the room. It was easy to see that the room was empty. Mona had barely furnished it since the last encounter. Inside was a wicker rocking chair and a single bookcase.

The closet, however, was closed. And the voice sounded as if it was coming from that direction—until Mona was standing in the middle of the room, and heard a sobbing sound behind her.

She half-turned, peering at the doorway. "Is anyone here?"

The voice replied: "*Stop.*"

Mona was still debating whether she should check the closet when she was startled by another sound: a loud, shrill scream. It came from farther away, from the hall or one of the other bedrooms—and then, a terrible crash, and a booming, outraged voice: "*Get out. I said GET OUT!*"

Mona heard her own cry as she hurried to slam the door shut. It didn't matter to her, then, that there had been a sad little voice in the closet just across the room. Better to take her chances with that one, than to deal with the volatile force outside the room. She stood with her back to the door, feet planted firmly on the floor, and waited.

The house was silent.

It was perhaps an hour later that she worked up the nerve to move from her place. First she turned on the light. Even with the supposed specter in the closet, she had been too afraid to reach out and flip the wall switch. Now, though, with the room illuminated and looking perfectly ordinary, Mona tiptoed across the room and grasped the handle of the closet door.

She opened it slowly, bracing it with the ball of her foot, just in case someone tried to shove the door from inside.

The closet was empty, except for some paint cans and a couple of quilts Mona had placed on the shelves.

"Okay," she whispered. "It's ghosts."

The following night, even though she stuffed earplugs into her ears, she heard the same crash and screams again—but she wrapped the pillow around her head, pressing it against her ears, and stayed curled up in the bed. "Screw you," she muttered. "I'm not getting up."

Her next teaching gig was an English Language Arts assignment at the local middle school. The sixth graders were reading *Where the Red Fern Grows*, and Mona spent the first period reading excerpts from the last couple of chapters. She heard the tremor in her voice as she narrated the violent death of Old Dan, the redbone hound dog, and then the grief-driven wasting away and death of his sister Little Ann. Mona struggled to focus on the text as her eyes teared up and the book trembled in her hands.

It's just a bunch of words, she told herself. *Nothing bad is happening. Just blank out your emotions and read the words.*

She made it through the passages and calmly asked the analysis questions. The kids didn't seem to notice her anguish—or maybe they felt the same way. A boy in the class hadn't been able to restrain his tears. He explained in embarrassed tones that his own dog had died in his arms after being attacked by a larger dog. His story, too, stirred the vast grief that haunted Mona's soul. She uttered practical assurances and tried to control her emotions, to bury them deep inside her, too deep to be accessed any time soon.

After class, though, she hurried to the staff bathroom. Once inside, she locked the door and shuddered with weeping. She had only a minute to cry. Then she had to wipe her face and go back to class, and do the same readings all over again.

In the second group of sixth graders, she saw a familiar face: the boy she'd caught crouching in her backyard. His name was Thomas Dumaine.

After the readings and class discussions, as the kids sat quietly writing their reflection paragraphs, Mona stopped by Thomas' desk. In a casual voice she said: "I think I know your sister. Marcela Dumaine. Right?"

He looked up at Mona with terrified eyes.

"I went to her robotics club last week," Mona added. "She's a nice kid. Good with technology, too."

Thomas' brown eyes widened. He didn't say a word.

The next day, Mona returned to the high school to sit in for Mr. Lind. The robotics club meeting began much the same way it had the previous week, with most students smiling and eager, and Marcela becoming quiet and distracted. Mona tried to let Marcela alone. She spent the beginning of the session with Ty and Samantha, who were working at one of the lab tables while the other students moved desks to make space for the robot. "We're designing our robot so that it can attach its own tubes," Samantha explained, "but if we can't get it to work, we'll just disable that function and attach them ourselves. But I hope it will work. It will give us an edge."

Marcela was working alone at another table. Mona's curiosity got the better of her, and she sidled over, watching as Marcela organized her supplies.

"I think I know your brother and sister," she said casually. "I've seen them around my neighborhood, and I taught their English classes yesterday. Thomas, and . . . ." Mona hesitated, waiting for Marcela to fill in the blank, but Marcela just looked at her.

"Sophie," Mona finished. "Right?"

Marcela nodded. "Yeah," she said huskily, and turned away.

A sudden commotion sounded from the floor. The robot's sweeping function had come to a sudden halt; the broom had stopped in mid-sweep, jerking uselessly as the robot erupted into a series of loud, staccato pops.

"Shit," someone said. "Turn it off."

A sudden pain racked Mona's head. The ache was accompanied by a strange sound: an electronic zapping, as though someone had sent a jolt of electricity through her brain. Mona reached for the lab table.

She heard the vague murmurings of the students: "*. . . jammed. . . take it out . . . don't . . . .*" And then her own name: "*. . . Koske? . . . Ms. Koske?*"

Mona realized that she had closed her eyes. She blinked and tried to focus.

The lab table came into view. Mona's saw her own fingers grasping the edge, clenched tight and trembling.

"Are you all right?"

She looked toward the source of the voice. Marcela stood there, her face fraught with concern.

"I'm . . . fine," Mona said. "I just felt faint for a second." She made an effort to stand up straight, to speak in a steady voice. "I'm just going to step outside the classroom for a minute."

In the hall, Mona stood with her back to the wall and tried to catch her breath. Her heart raced for some time, but eventually it resumed its normal pace, and her breathing slowed. *It's just a malfunctioning robot. A harmless robot. Nothing is wrong. We're all safe.*

When she returned to the classroom, Mona found Marcela Dumaine a bit more welcoming. Several times, Mona caught the girl watching her with concern—and when the meeting ended, Marcela bid her farewell with a quiet "Thanks, Ms. Koske."

Another two nights passed without incident. On Friday, though, Mona found herself anticipating another haunting. At first, as she moved about the quiet house, she wondered if some energy had awakened there, some force that would express itself in sobs and shouts that night—if there was, indeed, some presence that she could sense, subtly but surely. The noises always began at the same time at night, like part of some supernatural loop. A traumatic event may have played out in the upstairs rooms. Mona spent a good part of the day trying to search the house's history on the internet, but found nothing. Nor were there any reports of crimes or deaths that could explain what was happening upstairs.

As night approached, Mona found herself glancing repeatedly at the clock. She realized, then, why she was anticipating the noises. They had occurred the previous Friday and Saturday, and the Friday and Saturday before that. They had started up at the same time, around eleven-thirty.

"Why those days?" she murmured to herself. "Ghosts are too tired to work weeknights?"

Despite her jest, Mona felt a building anxiety as the clock hands continued to wind towards night. "Well, I'm not living like this—afraid of ghosts every night," she muttered. "Might as well see what's up. You hear that, ghosts? I'm coming."

At eleven o'clock she went upstairs. She pulled the closet door open and began perusing the volumes in the bookcase, looking for a happy story or two. Until then, she hadn't realized how little light-hearted fare graced her bookshelves. She passed over Kibera's *Voices in the Dark*, then *The Excorcist, Things Fall Apart, Nervous Conditions, Slaughterhouse-Five, Great Ghost Stories of the World* . . . it took Mona some time to find a volume that wasn't creepy, violent, or depressing. She chose a copy of *Love in Colour* and settled into the wicker rocking chair.

Eleven-thirty arrived. With it came the whispering and whimpering.

Mona set the book down and went toward the closet door. She stood and stared up at the frame.

The crying continued, but Mona was listening to another sound, a background noise that she could hear behind the voice. She'd noticed it right away: just before the cries began, a soft burst of noise, like static. As the whimpering drifted into silence, so did the background noise, leaving the room in silence.

And then it began again: the same soft static, followed by about thirty seconds of sobs and whispered pleas. "*Stop wrecking my house! You're killing me. Leave it alone.*" And then, from the bedroom doorway, a sob and another plea: *Stop.*

"What the hell," Mona whispered.

She hurried toward the other bedrooms. When the crashing sounds began, she followed them into the left-hand room, to a similar location: the door frame on the upper left side of the closet. It was uttering its last threat as she placed her finger at the source of the sound: "*Get out! I said GET OUT!*"

She went downstairs and returned a few minutes later with a hammer and a kitchen chair.

Standing on the chair, Mona pried the top of the door frame away from the wall. Beneath it, in the very center, she noticed a wide patch that had been plastered over. Mona picked up the hammer and smashed a hole through the patch. As she pulled away the broken chunks, something became visible in the interior: a small round speaker encased in a circular strip of cardboard. Mona pulled the speaker from the jagged hole and studied it. A pair of wires trailed from the back. One was attached to a nine-volt battery connector, the other to a small vinyl pad encased in a white plastic square. Mona stared at the contraption, dumbfounded.

She stepped down from the chair. She set the speaker down and dragged the chair to the back bedroom. After tearing away the frame panel, Mona found the same plastered-over patch, and another speaker beneath.

Once again, she stood staring at the speaker in her hand. Glimmers of anger began to penetrate her amazement. "Crazy bastards," she whispered. "Who the . . . ."

A realization began to stir in her mind.

By the closet she found two more speakers, both embedded in the wall beneath the frame.

"Not ghosts," she said, and breathed a long sigh of relief. "I'm betting everything on those kids."

Mona made a point of signing up for a sub shift the following Wednesday. Though she hadn't been invited, she stopped by the robotics meeting, making sure to give everyone a big smile and an excuse: "Hey, everyone, how's it going? I subbed for Ms. Elmore today. I thought I'd stop by and see how the project is going."

Lind and the students welcomed her. Mona kept her distance from Marcela until the girl was on her own; when she went to the storage closet, Mona followed quickly, stopping just inside the doorway.

"Marcela," she said quietly.

The girl half-lifted her head, but didn't look at Mona.

Mona held out a hand, revealing the cardboard-encased speaker in her palm. "Does this belong to you? I found a few of them."

Marcela went still. She stared wordlessly, then raised her eyes to meet Mona's gaze.

"I'm not upset," Mona said. "I just want to know why."

"I don't know what that is." Marcela's words were a hard monotone. She grabbed a case from one of the closet shelves and brushed past Mona. She stood stiffly at one of the tables at the other end of the room.

Undaunted, Mona followed her again, coming to stand at her side.

"You sure you don't want to talk about it?" Mona asked. She

leaned her elbows on the table, trying to look casual. "Your brother and sister have been to the house. It sounded like they don't want me to change anything. Is that what it's about?"

Marcela gave her a cold look. She didn't reply, but as she started to turn away, Mona saw tears forming in her eyes.

Mona held up the speaker again. "Is your dad involved in this?"

The girl's head jerked up. Her eyes went wide. "No," she said.

"Okay, okay. I didn't think so." Mona pocketed the speaker. "Just let me know if there's anything else that's going to scare the shit out of me in the middle of the night. I would appreciate that. And I won't change anything in the house, if you don't want me to."

The following afternoon, Mona made a small change in her own routine: She went to volunteer at a local animal shelter. She had signed up with some reluctance, worried that if she set foot inside, she would come home with a cat, or a dog, or one of each. Mona missed having a pet, but wasn't ready for all that came with it: the responsibility, the mess, the grief that lingered long after the animal died.

She had hardly left the driveway when she saw two figures on the roadside. Mona almost missed them. The oaks that lined the street, with their thick, leafy branches curving over the road, shrouded the figures in shadow. Mona glanced in her rear-view mirror and recognized the faces that looked back at her. Sophie and Tom crouched there, inspecting the front wheel of a dirt bike. Behind them, another bike lay on the ground. Mona backed the car up and lowered the passenger window.

"Hey there," she called. "You need any help?"

They looked up, but didn't reply. After a moment they leaned close and spoke to each other in hushed voices.

Mona parked nearby and got out. "Something wrong with the bike?" she asked as she approached. "Ah . . . you have a flat." She frowned at the ruined tire, thinking over the drive to town. Even by car, it wasn't a short journey. "Want a ride? You could have someone get the bikes later."

"We don't ride with strangers," Sophie replied.

"Well, that's wise. How about I let you use my phone? Do you know your dad's number?"

"We can call him at home."

Mona pulled a cell phone from her purse. "Here you go."

Tom took the phone and moved a few steps away, turning his back, as if initiating some secret conversation. Mona restrained an amused smile as she looked down at Sophie. The girl was standing now, facing Mona with brown eyes full of mistrust—a mirror image of her sister's expression.

"Do you two bike out here from school?" Mona asked.

Sophie shrugged. "Sometimes."

"It's a long ride. But I suppose you like coming back to your old neighborhood."

Sophie's jaw clenched. She stared at Mona wordlessly.

Tom was murmuring into the phone, his voice rising as he tried to assure his father. "We know her—kind of," he insisted, turning to glance at Mona. "It's Ms. Koske. She was our substitute teacher . . . and . . . ." The boy's voice lowered a notch, and he turned away again, cradling the phone close to his face. "She lives in our old house."

Sophie hurried over and nudged him. "Don't tell him that," she whispered.

"Too late," Mona said.

Tom hung up and handed the phone back. Mona made a point of looking down at her purse as she placed the phone inside, rather than looking at the kids. "I already know that you used to live in my house," she said casually.

"It's really *our* house," Sophie retorted. "Our family built that house."

"Well, maybe you'll live there again someday. I'll just keep it up for you in the meantime."

"We don't need anyone to keep it up," Sophie insisted. "It's better empty. That house is haunted, anyway. There's a mean ghost who lives there."

"Oh, I know about the ghost," Mona replied. "I found the speakers in the walls. Was Marcela the one who did that?"

Tom gasped.

"She won't admit to it," Mona added, "but she didn't deny it either."

Sophie recovered from her surprise. Her eyes hardened; she folded her arms over her chest. "Deny what? Marcela didn't do nothing."

"Fine, fine. You don't have to answer . . . but I have another question. Are you the ones who keep kicking down that headstone in the cemetery?"

Sophie lifted her chin. "Yeah, we kicked it down," she replied defiantly.

"Why?"

"Don't set it back up," Tom said, and Sophie added: "That man doesn't deserve a headstone. He was a bad person."

"What'd he do?"

The kids exchanged silent glances.

"Did he hurt people?" Mona asked.

"Yes," Sophie replied quietly.

Mona waited, but the kids didn't elaborate. "Let me fix his tombstone," she said. "Not because he deserves it, but . . . for luck. Maybe in his next life, he won't be a broken man."

A deep frown settled into Sophie's face. Again, the kids looked intently into each other's eyes, as if relaying silent messages. They looked like they didn't agree with Mona, but they didn't protest either.

They didn't have long to wait before an old Buick pulled to the side of the road, a portable bike rack strapped to its trunk. The driver could hardly be mistaken for anyone but the children's father. He had the same long-lashed brown eyes, the same cheekbones and nub of a chin, and was so similar in appearance to Tom that he could have been a future version of the boy. He got out of the Buick and came across the road, greeting the children with a warm smile.

"Hey, kids! Let me take a look at that tire. Maybe we can patch it up when we get home." The man turned to Mona, still grinning. "Hi. I'm Joe Dumaine. Thanks for staying with my kids, it's much appreciated."

"No problem."

"Tom says you live in our old house."

"Yes. Actually, I had a few questions about the house. Could I talk to you for a minute?"

He hesitated, his eyes expressing a subtle curiosity. "Sure." Joe turned to the kids and waved them away. "Go on, you two, get in the car. I'll get the bikes."

With sullen faces, Tom and Sophie headed for the car. Joe waited until they were inside before turning back to Mona. "What's up?" he asked.

"Well . . . I'm sure you're not aware of it, but the kids have been trying to scare me away from the house. I think Marcela has done most of the work on that, but anyway, no harm done."

"What do you mean?"

"They tried to make me think it's haunted," she said. "You know . . . telling me there's a dangerous ghost that lives there, setting up timed speakers that play voices and loud noises, things like that."

"Timed speakers," he repeated.

"Yeah. I found these little speaker things in my walls. Marcela's work, I'm guessing. But like I said, no harm done. I talked to them about it, and I think they're just afraid that whoever lives in the house is going to change it. They like the idea that they might move back in someday, and they want it to be the same as how they left it."

Joe ducked his head. He stood like that for a few moments, silent and still, but Mona saw the glisten of tears forming in his eyes. "I'm real sorry about that," he said. "I'll make sure they don't do anything like that again. Their mom died a few years ago, and we ended up losing the house not long after. It's been tough on them."

"Yeah, I've been to the cemetery out back. There's a beautiful statue there."

He nodded. "My wife's memorial. Her family and my mom are buried on that property. Are you the buyer, or are you renting it?"

"I bought it."

"Well, like I said, I'll make sure they don't mess with you again."

"Oh, I don't think they will. And . . . I just want you to know that you and your family are welcome to visit the cemetery any time."

Joe hesitated. "It's hard to get to. The best way is through the yard."

"Yes, and you can cut through the yard any time." Mona gestured to the Buick, where Sophie and Tom sat with their faces close to the windows, intensely watching the exchange. "I've already caught these two in the yard a few times. I really don't mind them being there. Like I said, any time. You won't be interrupting anything."

He looked at her thoughtfully. His eyes, though kind, were uncomfortably penetrating—or so Mona thought at the moment. "Well, I appreciate the invitation," he said. "And I'm sorry the kids messed with you. I'll have a good talk with them."

"All right. Well, I should get going. I have a volunteer shift at the animal shelter. Maybe I'll see you around."

He nodded. "Take care, Ms. . . ."

"Koske. But call me Mona. Please."

"Will do."

She caught sight of Joe's now-familiar features that weekend: the large, long-lashed brown eyes with arched brows, looking warmly at her as he strolled into the backyard. Mona, crouching beside a row of hostas, froze when she saw him.

"Those are some mean-looking blades." Joe gestured to the shears in her hands. "Trimming back the hostas? It's the time of year for it."

"Yeah . . . ." Mona set the garden shears on the ground. She had become unaccustomed to surprise visitors, and found herself struggling for words—especially in this moment, as she tended to the flowers that Joe's family had planted.

"I hope you were serious about letting me come through your yard," he said.

She stood up. Her eyes fell on the contents of Joe's hands. He held a small bouquet of yellow wildflowers and a few small sheets of paper. "Of course," she replied.

"It's been a while since I've gone to the cemetery. I . . . used to bring her flowers and poetry."

Mona moved closer, getting a glimpse of thick paper with charred edges, of handwriting done in neat calligraphy. "Looks like old stationery," she said.

"It's from the art store in town. I burn the edges to make it look . . . intense, I guess. Is it all right if I leave these in the cemetery?"

"Of course! It's your cemetery. You can do whatever you like."

"I just don't want you to feel like you have to clean up after me. Next time I come, or the kids stop by, we'll clean up what we left, and leave something else.”

“Sure.” Mona shifted her gaze to the forest, to the trail that disappeared into the trees. “It’s a beautiful statue you have at her grave site. Is it supposed to be her?”

“Yeah. It’s her. Sculpted it myself.”

“You made that statue? Wow. You’re talented.”

“It’s what I do for a living,” Joe said. “Or . . . used to, anyway. It doesn’t pay the bills nowadays, so I had to switch jobs for a little while. Maybe just until the kids get a little older.”

“Did you write the inscription, too? The one on the statue?”

“Our time here is short, but our arts and our hearts are eternal?” he recited. “It’s adapted from a poem she liked. Charles Baudelaire.” Joe tilted his chin up as he recited: “To lift a weight so heavy, Sisyphus, would take all of your strength. Although we have our heart at work, Art is long and Time is short. Far from famous graves, toward a lonely cemetery, my heart, like a muffled drum, goes beating funeral marches. Many a jewel sleeps buried in darkness and oblivion, far from pickaxes and probes; many a flower pours out, with regret, its sweet scent like a secret in profound solitude.”

Mona mulled over the words. “Charles Baudelaire,” she repeated. “Are you sure? Isn’t that a Longfellow poem?”

“No, it’s Baudelaire.”

“I swear there’s a Longfellow poem that has those same lines: toward a lonely cemetery, like a muffled drum, my heart goes beating funeral marches.”

“Hmm.”

“Well . . . I should let you be on your way,” Mona said. “But, come over any time. Really.”

He returned a few days later. Mona was outdoors again, snipping a few vines from the kennel frame. With its slew of ivy and morning glories, the frame needed a bit of aesthetic pruning. Mona had been spending a lot of time in the yard lately. The interior of the house was finished, and she had promised not to change it—but the yard was alive, shifting and growing all on its own. It needed tending to keep it looking the same.

Or so she told herself. Her gaze kept drifting from the task at hand, scanning the yard for visitors. This time, she heard him before she saw him.

"Ms. Koske!"

She turned. Joe was coming from the trail behind her.

"Hi. Please call me Mona," she reminded him.

"Mona. Hope I didn't startle you."

"Not at all." Mona's gaze dropped to his dirt-smeared T-shirt. His fingers, too, bore traces of dirt. "By the way, I looked up that Longfellow poem. I'm pretty sure Beaudelaire committed a bit of a theft when he wrote his version."

"What?"

"They're almost exactly the same."

"I'll believe it when I see it."

"I can show you. Want to come in for a minute?"

"Sure. I need to wash my hands, too, if you don't mind. I was doing a bit of cleaning up back there."

They walked to the house, debating about the two poets and the time periods during which they crafted their published works. As they stepped through the back door, Joe paused and surveyed the dining room. The space was fairly bare; Mona wasn't much of a decorator, and preferred clean, uncluttered spaces. Only practical items were visible in the room: a table, four chairs, and a small doormat.

"It's strange to be back here," he said.

"Is it all right?"

"Yeah." He slipped his shoes off and went to the kitchen sink to wash up. "All right," he said as he finished, "where is this supposed victim of artistic theft? I want to see this poem."

Mona led him to the living room, where the Longfellow book still lay on the computer desk. "I just looked up the Beaudelaire poem before you got here. If I'm lucky . . . there, it's still up." She pointed to the screen. "'Le Guignon.' I know you probably know it by heart, but here it is anyway. And . . . . ." She opened the Longfellow volume to a bookmarked page. "Here's the Longfellow poem. Look." She pointed to a passage and read aloud: "Art is long, and Time is fleeting, and our hearts, though stout and brave, still, like muffled drums, are beating funeral marches to the grave."

Joe peered closely at the text. "You win. What's the date?"

"Longfellow wrote and published his poem in the 1830s. Baudelaire started writing his collection in the 1840s, and it was published in 1857.”

“I’ll pretend I don’t know that. ‘Le Guignon’ is still a great work.” Joe turned to the screen, scanning the lines of Beaudelaire’s poem. “It’s not a happy poem, but Addy loved it. I managed to find a way to change that second line into a hopeful one: ‘Our time here is short, but . . . .’”

“Our arts and our hearts are eternal,” Mona finished. “What’s Sisyphus?”

“A king who cheated death. Twice. In Greek mythology, the gods punished him by making him roll a boulder up a hillside . . . for eternity.”

“Lovely.”

“Greek gods usually are.” Joe’s gaze shifted to the wall behind the futon. A large antique mirror hung there, flanked by framed portraits. Joe moved close and scrutinized one he recognized: a younger version of Mona, smiling beside another woman. “She looks like you,” he said. “Is that your sister?”

“Yeah.”

“Does she live around here, too?”

Mona hesitated. “She died.”

“Oh. I’m sorry.”

She gestured to one of the other photos: a black-and-white picture of a young woman and man sitting together in a field, the man’s arm draped loosely around the woman’s shoulder. “My parents are gone, too. We’re from Minnesota. Well, Kenya, originally, but I lived in Minnesota since I was four. I don’t have much family left up there—just my mom’s cousin. I haven’t seen him since the funerals.”

“Well, I’m sorry to hear that. Mine are gone, too, but I have a brother in Laplace. It’s not too far from here. Wouldn’t mind having him and his family closer, though.”

They chatted about family until Joe caught a glimpse of the wall clock. “It’s getting on. I better go; I got dinner to cook. Listen, is it all right if I get your number? I’ll call next time and let you know I’m coming through. That way, I won’t sneak up behind you when you’re not expecting it.”

Mona started to protest, but stopped herself before the words came out. It would be good, she told herself, to exchange numbers with Joe. Getting a call would make her feel normal. The silence in the house could be overwhelming: the lack of voices, of life. "Sure," she said. "Is it all right if I get yours too? I don't know anyone out here, and it would make me feel better if I had one person I could call—just in case anything happens with the house, or . . . ." She fumbled for another excuse.

"Sure, sure. Here." He pulled out his phone, and they exchanged numbers.

He didn't call, though, and she thought of no reason to contact him. Mona's routine of bustling quietly around the house and making the occasional trip to the school or shelter remained uninterrupted—until one afternoon as she searched the high school lot for her car, and spotted Joe Dumaine instead. Mona felt a flutter of surprise, then of pleasure.

"If it isn't Ms. Koske," he greeted her. "How're you doing?"

The robotics team, he said, had invited the parents to see their work. The two stood and chatted about the project, about Marcela's talent for engineering. "Say, do you still have those little devices that she put in the walls?" Joe asked.

"I do."

"If it's all right, can I pay you a visit tomorrow? I'd like to see them."

"Sure," Mona said reluctantly. "Maybe I should warn you . . . the recordings are a bit volatile."

He nodded gravely. "I can only imagine."

"But like I said, no harm done."

"Yes, like you said."

After his next visit, Joe Dumaine no longer needed to rely on his imaginings. He stood in the living room, listening with that same grave look on his face as Mona pressed the small, rubber-coated buttons that initiated the haunting sounds. She had removed the timers; the little white boxes lay scattered in the drawer of the computer desk, where they could no longer provoke the sobs and screams into action.

She played the angry recording last. *"Get out,"* the voice demanded. *"I said GET OUT!"*

"Well," Joe said, as the recording switched off, "I'm sorry you had to listen to that every night."

"Oh, it wasn't every night. Just two nights a week."

"Hm. How thoughtful of her to give you a break. Seriously, though, this was an evil thing that she did. She's getting consequences for this one."

Mona laughed. "That's not evil," she said.

"No? It's damned evil in my book. Scaring the hell out of someone in their own home, where they're supposed to feel safe."

She mulled over his words. "Is that what home is supposed to feel like? I guess that's why she wants to come back here so badly."

They continued talking about the kids, about the young ones' losses and fears. Then Mona was offering Joe a drink, and soon they'd made themselves comfortable in the living room, where they sipped tea and lemonade—and the conversation began to turn, not toward the children's fears, but toward their own.

"Honestly, I don't like it when the house is changed, either," Joe said. "The first couple who moved in here, they came when we were still moving out. They started changing things, and it felt like they were erasing my wife. Can't be helped, but . . . most of my memories of Addy are here. Her presence was here, still is here."

Mona nodded. "I don't have big plans for the house. I fixed most of what needs fixing, but otherwise I'll leave everything as it is."

"Even the kennel frame in the back? I'm amazed no one has taken it down."

"Even the hideous kennel frame," Mona assured him.

"Is it hideous? I think it looks pretty with the vines and flowers growing along it." Joe relaxed against the futon, setting his empty lemonade glass on the side table. "Why did you move to this house? It's not a convenient spot for a teacher."

"I wasn't planning to teach when I came here. But I need something to do, and your kids won't let me fix up the property."

"Sophie says you've been to Nigeria."

"Oh . . . yes. We were reading a story by Adichie."

"Never heard of . . . her, or him, but I'm assuming they're Nigerian," Joe said. "Were you a teacher there?"

"No. I worked for some NGOs in West Africa for a while," Mona replied. "Six months, maybe seven. We dealt with a lot of the fallout from Boko Haram—do you know about them? They made headlines in the U.S. after they kidnapped a group of schoolgirls."

"I vaguely remember."

"They kidnap women and kids, and try to recruit them. Especially the kids. Child soldiers, child suicide bombers. So, when people are rescued, they're treated with suspicion. Even if people escape, they end up displaced. Their villages have been destroyed, or the women aren't allowed to come home with children from Boko Haram fathers. I worked for NGOs that tried to help war refugees. The first one I worked for was shut down by the Nigerian military. We provided aid to people who escaped from Boko Haram, so we were accused of helping the terrorists."

"Hm. I was going to ask if substitute teaching is tough, but never mind."

"It didn't get any better," Mona said. "I joined up somewhere else, and we were told that we couldn't help those people without getting approval from the U.S. If we helped people who escaped, we would get shut down—so they would have to wait for approval, and starve, and get sick. Our hands were tied in so many situations." Mona began to scrape her thumbnail along the edge of her tea cup— a nervous, unconscious gesture. "One day I was bringing a group of women and children back to their village, and a few men stopped us on the road and . . . they started killing the kids."

She hesitated, uncertain about whether she should continue. Joe's eyebrows were half-raised. After a moment, he leaned forward and folded his hands. "Listen, I hope you don't mind my mentioning this, but . . . does this have anything to do with how you nearly fainted during robotics? Marcela told me you had to leave the room. My brother was in the marines; he has PTSD, and he gets really anxious whenever he hears anything that sounds like gunshots. Marcela said you reminded her of him."

"Yeah, I get that. I . . . I ended up killing two men that day. Or, I helped kill them." Mona paused again, and continued reluctantly: "That's not what bothers me. I hardly remember doing it. It happened quickly, and . . . at the time, it was easy."

Joe's eyebrows went up again, and she added hastily: "That may sound cold, but if you had seen what they were doing . . . I just needed it to stop."

He nodded.

"Two of the mothers died while they were trying to save their kids. We fought so hard . . . and even though it made me feel like a coward, I came back to the U.S. as soon as I could. I was too confused about the right thing to do. I had doubts about my country's reasons for being there . . . the development loans, resource grabs, other issues. Personal issues. But, all that aside, in the end I couldn't function well enough to do my job. And I was scared. People felt that I had killed innocent men, and I barely managed to get out."

Mona searched Joe's face for signs of concern, of judgment, but he was just as calm as if she had been discussing the day's fine weather.

"Why did you go to West Africa?" he asked. "Why not Kenya?"

She shrugged. "I don't know. I always feel like I'm not doing enough with my life, and I end up going to extremes. You know, like . . . it's not enough to teach kids. There are kids dying, and I have to help save them. That, and I just wanted to get away from my life. West Africa seemed far enough."

"And what drove you away from home?"

"Oh, you know. Death, heartbreak, betrayal. I got divorced, my parents died, my last living grandparent died, my sister committed suicide, and even my cat died. I got a pretty hefty inheritance from my family, so I wasn't concerned about getting work. I just wanted to leave."

Joe was nodding, mutely, but with compassion in his eyes.

"I usually don't tell people that," Mona blurted. "About the inheritance. I'm afraid to. You know, like . . . if people find out I have money, I'll get beaten up and robbed. I've become afraid of violence. I don't trust people. Usually." She picked up a spoon and began to stir her cup of dandelion tea, slowly, though there was nothing to stir. "All of those kids died. We didn't save a single one. I feel like those kids and the two mothers are somehow always . . . nearby. I could go anywhere in the world and they would still be there. I know they're not actually *there*, but I can't forget them. I love them, you know?" She looked up and smiled, and the tears came suddenly; they spilled over her eyelids and down her cheeks. Mona wiped them away and grasped the arm of the desk chair, feeling a sudden anxiety as old sounds and images floated up into her memory. *Nothing bad is happening now*, she assured herself. *I am safe.* "I think I just don't want that day to be my final memory of them. I *want* to be haunted by them." She chuckled suddenly, unexpectedly. "I'm sorry for dropping my life story on you."

He shrugged. "Well, what are other humans there for? It's all right."

"Thanks."

"So you didn't come here to teach. What about Louisiana, then?"

"What about it?"

"Why did you come here?"

Mona shrugged. "It was random. I printed out a map of the U.S. and closed my eyes, and pointed to a place. I landed on Louisiana. So I looked at some properties online, and . . . it was just random." Mona paused. "My plans don't work out. I thought randomness would bring me better fortune. I was doing okay when I first got back to Minnesota, but then it was like . . . a year went by, shit happened, and then I woke up one day and I was convinced that the relatives of the men I killed were going to come all the way to the Midwest to do terrible things to me. Any time someone seemed like they didn't want to be around me, or didn't want their kids around me, I thought, 'It's because I'm a killer.' I was between jobs at the time, and I was sure that no one would hire me, or even let me live in their neighborhood."

"And moving out here . . . did that help?"

"I took anxiety meds for a while, and they helped. I sorted myself out, and then I moved here."

"Someday," Joe said, "maybe you can meet my brother. If you would rather not, that's okay, but . . . he served in Iraq and Afghanistan, and he had a lot of the same experiences you had. I know it's a different situation, but it's violence, and humans aren't wired for that kind of violence. And I know he needs someone to talk to about it, because he doesn't have people who understand." Joe leaned back, giving a brief wave of his hand. "But maybe that's not how it is. Sorry if I'm pressing you. If you would rather not revisit those things . . . ."

"No, I don't mind talking to people who have been through trauma. I think it helps."

"You still take the anxiety meds?"

"I weaned myself off of them," Mona said. "They made me feel better, but they made me lethargic. I'm fine without them now. People are my medicine. People, and animals. The kids at school, the other teachers who have reached out to me. The animals at the shelter. I need someone to care about, and I need someone to talk to, even when I don't feel like talking. I just need to know that there *is* someone. You know what I mean?"

Joe looked at her steadily, misty-eyed. "Yeah, I know." He paused, glancing around the room. "And I know what it's like to want to be haunted."

Days passed, then a week, and the house remained quiet, with hardly any sound but Mona's occasional putzing about and the blaring of the stereo. The kitchen phone, too, kept up a stubborn silence—and the longer it remained so, the more certain Mona was that she had driven Joe away with all of her pitiful babbling. *Who the hell says all that to a stranger? I'm traumatized, I'm lonely, and by the way, I killed people. Why did I say all that, when I didn't want anyone to know? Here he is paying his respects to his deceased wife, and some crazy lady is rambling about the horrors of her life. . . .*

Eventually, though, the phone uttered its shrill ring.

"I'm coming through with the kids tomorrow," Joe told her. "Marcela hasn't been out there in a long time. I want to make sure she gets a visit in."

Mona nearly missed their arrival. Their voices drifted in through the windows, and she hurried to the back door to find them already heading across the backyard. Marcela, clad in sandals and a black dress, spotted her first. Her brown eyes maintained that familiar look of caution as she met Mona's gaze. The others were dressed casually, though Sophie carried an elegant bouquet of red roses in her arms.

"Hey," Mona called, stepping outside. The rear deck was small and simple, just a wooden platform a foot or so above the ground; she crossed it quickly and hurried to join the group.

"Afternoon," Joe greeted her. "The yard's looking good. You've kept it up well."

Mona gazed out at the wide yard, admiring its border of oaks.

From their branches she could usually hear the staccato chirps of red-winged blackbirds and the sweet compositions of the sparrows; she had glimpsed the European starlings in their dazzling multi-color sheen of purples, blues, and greens before they started the transformation to their seasonal white-flecked brown and black. Now, though, she spotted only a plump mourning dove on one of the low branches. It turned its head, seeming to look back at her with one of its large black eyes, and uttered a sudden, soft call: *"Coo-OOH, coo, coo, coo."*

"Yeah, well, it's a nice yard," Mona said, returning her attention to Joe. "The only thing I want to change is the kennel frame. I'm not taking it down," she added quickly, "but I thought it would look nice if it was painted."

Sophie's eyes filled with indignation. "You said you wouldn't change anything!"

"I won't, if you don't want me to," Mona replied. "But wouldn't it look nice if we painted some pictures on it? Pictures of flowers, or . . . ."

"It already has real flowers."

"That was our dog's kennel," Tom said.

"What was your dog's name?"

"Eva."

"Well, maybe we could make it into a tribute to her," Mona suggested.

"She's still alive."

"That's even better. We can paint her name with some hearts, and . . . some things that she likes."

"She likes jumping on people and peeing on trees," Tom retorted. "How're you gonna paint that?"

Joe covered his mouth, trying to hide his laughter. "Oh, come on, kids," he said. "Mona's the boss here now, and I think it's a good idea. If she paints, I better not hear you whining about it."

"I think we should have a say," Sophie said, "since we built it."

"Maybe, but Mona isn't obligated to us. This house feels like ours because it's part of our memories, but it's also Mona's house now. She made a home out of it, and we have another home that we made in town. You got to respect that."

"But this is our *real* home," Sophie said. "I don't want anyone changing it."

Joe shrugged. "Well, I get that, but life is constant change. Refusal to change is the denial of life. It's the quick path to death. So, sometimes you just have to learn to choose life."

Tom rolled his eyes. He let his head fall back dramatically, as though the statement had felled him. "Do you always have to talk like a poet when you give advice?"

"Truth is poetry, son. Not always happy poetry, but it's poetry." Joe turned toward the road, squinting, as a musical tinkling sounded in the distance. "You hear that? Is that Gregson?"

Sophie gasped with excitement. "It is!" She broke into a run, shouting: "We have to catch it!"

"Ice cream truck," Joe explained, seeing Mona's confusion.
"Out here?"

"Yeah. Pam Gregson . . . ." His words trailed off as Mona bolted after Sophie. In a moment the rest were following behind, with Marcela straggling at the rear.

The little white truck had just passed the house. Its tires kicked up a fine cloud from the gravel road, leaving the runners to make futile attempts at waving the dust away as they pursued the truck down the street. Mona sprinted ahead of Sophie and flagged down the driver.

The truck slowed to a halt. Mona blinked the dust from her eyes as she tried to read the picture menu on the flank. "Darn," she said. "They only have generic stuff. I was hoping they had something fancy, like Cherry Garcia bars. Sophie, what are you getting?"

Sophie stood panting beside her. "Drumstick," she said breathlessly. "Tom always gets snow cones . . . but . . . they're just crushed ice with a little bit of syrup." She coughed and added: "You can make them at home for practically nothing."

Mona frowned, shoving her hands into her shorts pockets. "Oh . . . I don't have money on me."

"It's okay, my dad can get it." Sophie turned and called back to Joe: "Dad, you can get one for Ms. Koske, can't you?"

"Sure I can. What does Ms. Koske want?" Joe stopped and

waited for Marcela, offering her his handful of papers. "Hold these for a minute, will you?"

"Ice cream sandwich, thank you," Mona said as he approached.

"Sure thing." Joe gave the driver a friendly greeting, and then turned back to his oldest daughter. "Marcela, why're you standing way back there? Don't you want anything?"

"Ice cream sandwich," she said.

"Okay, wait. They got two different kinds. Which one you want? Vanilla or—"

"Chocolate chip," Marcela and Mona replied in unison. Marcela glanced at Mona—and, in a gesture that seemed rare and precious to Mona, she smiled.

On the walk back, Sophie gushed over her treat as she struggled to unwrap it. "Gregson drives everywhere else in town, but never comes to our neighborhood," she said. "And then we run into her way out here."

"She's going to her brother's house," Tom replied.

Sophie tried to rip the paper from her drumstick, but the roses fell from her grasp instead. She stopped too late, trampling them under her feet and gasping in horror. "Shit!" she exclaimed.

"Language, language," Joe said. "Find a different word."

"Don't worry." Mona stooped, scooping up the stray petals with her free hand. "They're still pretty. You can scatter the loose petals when you get there."

"I mean it, now, find a different word," Joe said. "What's it gonna be?"

Sophie sighed. "Crap, dad. I meant 'crap.'"

Mona finished gathering the petals and stood up. Her ice cream sandwich broke from its base, landing with a thump in the gravel. "Shit," Mona said, and then covered her mouth. She glanced at Sophie with a guilty expression. "Pardon my language."

"What the . . . my teacher just said a swear word! You hear that, Dad?"

"So did you," he replied.

"Yeah, but you scolded me and gave me the 'find a different word' lecture. Are you gonna scold her, too?"

"I'll leave that to you," Joe replied. "Scold Ms. Koske if you want, but you might sound like a hypocrite."

Sophie gave him a scathing look. Then she turned to Mona, saying: "You should come with us to the cemetery. We have a surprise for you."

"In the cemetery?"

"Uh-huh."

"We let Dad set that tombstone back up," Tom told her. "You know . . . the bad one. For luck."

"For new beginnings," Joe said.

They continued their chatter as they crossed the yard, past the burgeoning hostas and flower-laden wooden frame, and down the wooded path to the solemn graves, where together they laid petals and poems.

Acknowledgements

Many thanks to members of Minneapolis Writers' Workshop and my other beta readers who gave feedback on these stories, especially to those bibliophiles who didn't even know me but gave the stories a chance for the simple love of storytelling.

Also, thanks to my dad for providing the inspiration for the story *Something Undone*, and for the countless people who provided resources and insights that helped me develop the lives of my characters. This work couldn't have been done without you.

Also, thanks to my dad for providing the inspiration for the story *Something Undone*, and for the countless people who provided resources and insights that helped me develop the lives of my characters. This work couldn't have been done without you.